Necromancer's Fall

Book Three
of the Flesh & Bone Trilogy

A J Dalton

authorHOUSE®

AuthorHouse™ UK Ltd.
500 Avebury Boulevard
Central Milton Keynes, MK9 2BE
www.authorhouse.co.uk
Phone: 08001974150

First published by AuthorHouse   7/29/2010

ISBN: 978-1-4520-4510-8 (sc)

This book is printed on acid-free paper.

To Siouxsie, Mum, Dad, Chris, David, Galen,
Caspar, Lachlan and Katarina with love.

Beware all demons, real and imaginary,
for they are friendlier and more fun than any other being.

With a salute to my vigilant reading group, who left no typo unturned:
Paul Leeming (stalwart), Kate (and Rebecca) Alcock, David Wood
(without as 's'), eagle-eyed Mike Ranson and Daniel Darlington.

With thanks to Matt White, Nick White, Tom Martin
and Kasia Martin, for their unstinting support.

And a hearty hail to my long-suffering cover artist: Oliver Flude!

Chapter One: Dread

The wisp suddenly sensed danger and began to zigzag. Vidius snatched it up, crammed it into his mouth and swallowed. It would hopefully sustain him until he could reach the first barrier. He tried to snag another but it stayed well out of reach. None would come near him now – unless he visibly began to fail, in which case they might swarm to try and overcome him. They would not tolerate a predator amongst them any longer than they had to.

The first sphere of the demon realm was as insubstantial and ethereal as its inhabitants, so much so that the weight of his mortal body caused him to sink up to his knees in the fogginess of the ground. He moved as if he were wading, which made the going slow and difficult.

It wasn't just his weight that this sphere of existence was loath to support. It was his very physicality. His skin was a barrier that separated him from his surroundings. Where the wisps were entirely porous to the thin substance of this sphere, he disrupted its fragile continuum. He caused a hole in the sphere's essential fabric just as a blade shears silk.

It tried to pass uninterrupted around him, but there was too much friction and he tore more and more of it with each step he took. His flesh burned as if being eaten away. He began to tear his face from his skull to give himself but a moment's relief – but then reminded himself he would need this body if he were to see his way past the other spheres. He gritted his teeth, clenched his hands into fists and put each of them under the opposite armpit.

Trying to ignore his agony, he pushed on, causing more and more damage to the sphere. The wisps occasionally flared with light, trying to tempt him from his path with a show of life force. He drooled at the thought of consuming their power, but knew they sought to lead him into one of the inky pools of nothingness concealed in the mists to either side of him. When wisps had drifted into the mortal realm from this sphere, they'd been known to do much the same with travellers in swamps, deep forests or other remote

1

places. Like any other denizen of the demon realm, they always hoped to find some opportunity to steal the body or life force of a being from a higher plane of existence, and such opportunities more commonly presented themselves at the precise moment of the being's death.

It was ironic, but perhaps inevitable, that it was the least powerful of all demonkind – the wisps – who inhabited the sphere closest to the mortal realm. They had easier access than any others to the mortal realm, but the least innate ability with which to manipulate the mortals. They were privileged to see at first hand what life could be, but at the same time were tortured by what they could not have. It was just one of the paradoxes upon which the magic that sustained the demon realm was built.

When demonkind had been consigned to this realm, they'd been in disarray. The infighting had started immediately, as sustenance had been scarce. Larger demons had devoured smaller ones, the smaller ones hunted those even smaller in turn or occasionally came together in packs to overthrow a larger one. They'd been close to consuming themselves entirely when the six Princes had emerged, one from each of the demon Houses. To save their species, they'd created the seven spheres, one inside the other, each separated from the other by a barrier. The wisps had been assigned to the outer sphere, as they were the only ones who could really exist there, and each subsequent sphere had been assigned to the next most powerful sub-species and so on. The innermost sphere belonged to the Princes, of course, yet they did not possess the absolute centre.

At the core was the Relic, the artefact of power that sustained the entire demon realm. Before the coming together of the Princes, the Houses had warred back and forth for possession of the Relic, each seeking to have sway over the others in order to ensure its survival. Yet each time one House captured the Relic, the others would unite against it and the struggle would start again. Finally, the Princes had sealed the Relic within an adamantine sphere at the core, so that none had it while the realm stayed intact.

With the creation of the spheres, the rate at which demonkind devoured itself had no longer outstripped the rate at which it multiplied. A balance of sorts had been established. Some might even have described it as a life, limited though it might be. Yet it was only the spheres closest to the Relic that had the gravity and density of power required for anything like full physicality. The majority of demonkind still hungered for more, wanted to *be* more.

No, Vidius had seen what true life was like when in the mortal realm, and the demon realm was nothing but a pale shadow by comparison, a mockery.

He'd seen the life he'd wanted, even experienced much of it, but he'd not yet managed to experience it in full. He'd always been forced to hide from some enemy or other, or bow to another's authority, even when he'd been a general in the army of some mortal despot. Then there was also the terror of the gods of the mortal realm. He'd been forever looking over his shoulder to see who might be creeping up on him. It wasn't enough! He would only know life in full if it was he who ruled, and rule he would, even if he had to destroy the demon realm to do it.

In many ways, the Princes had done him a favour when they'd banished him and the others. Once the Princes had established the new order, they'd carried out the Purge and exiled those considered to have too much power and a philosophy that was not commensurate with the new way of the things. The Banished had been put out of the demon realm, to perish or survive as best they could in the terrible cosmos. Vidius and a few others had fought hard and managed to win for themselves positions as slaves to the gods in the mortal realm. Now, however, he was home. Now, he would return the favour done to him by this realm so long ago.

He ploughed on, ripping through the gossamer of the first sphere. He dared not linger, not just because he would begin to weaken if he took too long, but also because time in the mortal realm passed so quickly compared to here. The demon who would open the door into the realm for him at the same time every year – 'Jack' – might already have opened the door once. Who knew how many years Jack would be able to access the site they'd agreed for the door? Who knew how long Jack could remain free of the meddlesome gods and their servants?

He glimpsed the first barrier through the clouds swirling around him. He'd arrived, and not a moment too soon, for the wisps were beginning to congregate and buzz angrily about how he'd harrowed their home. Light oscillated and cycled through them faster and faster. They began to vibrate – it would not be long before either lightning sparked and arced amongst them or the air was ignited.

Mercifully, he reached firmer ground as he got to the barrier, so could cover more ground with his long strides and put some distance between himself and the agitated, bobbing wisps.

The barrier manifested itself as a high ironstone wall down which water dripped and trickled. The warning to keep away was clear, for no demon was fond of either iron or running water. The thing was unscalable, of course, and even if he'd had wings, the scudding sky high above him told him that he would have been thrown back, if not cast down, by unforgiving winds.

He followed the wall round to the left and eventually came to the small gate set back into it. The demon gatekeeper slept with one eye open while curled up in the small recess. It was an insubstantial catlike creature, but Vidius knew better than to judge it by appearances. All the gatekeepers were more than well equipped to deal with any that might try to force entry to another sphere. In addition, the gate would be keyed to this demon alone, so none could pass through without the demon's co-operation. Even if a supremely powerful being were to force the demon to open the gate, the demon could still magically close it while the being was stepping across the threshold, thereby slicing the being in two. Vidius knew he would need some other approach if he was to win his way into the next sphere.

He watched as the cat-demon stirred, stretched slowly and then rose onto its hind feet. It leaned an elbow between two prongs of its trident, rested its head in its paw and regarded him.

'I wish to pass through the gate,' Vidius announced.

The cat-demon scratched behind one of its twitching, pointed ears. 'So?'

'Open the gate to me, demon.'

'Why?'

'Why open the gate, or why do I wish to pass through?'

'Yes.'

'To get to the other side.'

'Hmm,' the demon frowned, clearly not sure if Vidius had provided an adequate answer. Then the demon brightened and asked smugly: 'Who are you?'

'I am no one.'

'Aha! Well, I may let no one pass!' the cat declared, obviously having repeated this statement and ruse for half of the eternity during which it had guarded the gate. It suddenly looked crestfallen. 'D-Did you say you were no one?' it asked in confusion.

'That's right. You may let me pass. Open the gate. Quickly!'

'Wait, wait!' begged the simple creature. 'I asked you who you were, isn't that right? And you said -'

'Come now, demon!' Vidius said shaking his head. 'You know as well as I that something spoken cannot be unsaid. It is an offence against the old laws to pretend or attempt anything otherwise. It is the basis of the words of power that first breathed life into demonkind. I would hate to have to mention this to any of the archdemons.'

'N-No!' the cat-demon stammered. 'I will open the gate. Give me a moment while I remove the ward.'

The cat-demon waved his trident across the wicket gate and the air around it suddenly became more solid, more real. The cat-demon undid the latch of the gate, pushed it wide and then held it open for Vidius. Vidius stepped through and pushed the gate wider still, until it was all but flat against the far side of the wall.

The cat-demon almost overbalanced as the gate went beyond its reach. With catlike reactions, it twisted and pulled back just before it could tumble across the threshold.

'Master!' it yowled. 'Please close the gate behind you. I would be eternally grateful. It seems to have swung out too far. It is beyond my reach now.'

'I know!' Vidius smiled.

The cat-demon froze. 'But, master, if the gate is not closed, the denizens of the second sphere will enter into the first and begin to devour the wisps. I will be in so much trouble with the Princes, good and kind master! They will as surely destroy me as the elementals of the second sphere will destroy the first sphere. I did what you asked me by opening the gate. Will you not now show me some gratitude by closing it?'

'Demon, it does not suit my purposes to close this gate. However, I will show you the gratitude you crave next time I pass through. Instead of destroying you, I will allow you to join my retinue. In the meantime, you will not attempt to prevent any of the elementals who seek to pass into the first sphere. Do you understand? There is only one correct answer here, demon, for you will not have the favour of any of the Princes to call upon now that you have been so careless in seeing to your duties.'

The cat-demon looked thoroughly miserable. It was beaten, and knew it. 'Yes, master. Thank you, master!'

Vidius smiled. 'Good.' Then he turned his back on the dolt and hurried into the very different world of the second sphere. He had to shield his eyes from the six white suns moving across the sky. In fact, it was a good few minutes before he could see anything. The blazing orbs did not just blind him – they all but bleached out his vision. He wasn't sure if he even remembered what the colours red, green and blue looked like anymore. Some of his brain's memory centres were beginning to burn out.

He looked down at the six shadows he cast, and that allowed him to begin to make out a few things. The ground was hard and dusty here. As soon as a drop of sweat fell off his brow and onto the compacted surface, it evaporated so thoroughly that there was no sign it had ever existed. Everything around him shimmered with heat.

Flame flared into being not a dozen metres from him and he realised he must be in the part of the sphere that was home to the fire elementals.

He cursed, knowing his body was physically incapable of devouring such an elemental for the purposes of sustenance. What he wouldn't give for a nice, cool water elemental right about now!

Seeing a slash of blue off to his right, and conscious the flame was beginning to flicker towards him, he set off at a flat run. With the heat of six suns beating down on him, he was not sure how long he'd be able to survive in the furnace of this featureless desert, but he knew he didn't have time to sit down and work out the answer.

His skin had burned as if attacked by acid in the first sphere. Here, it was eaten by fire. It pained him so much that again he wanted to tear the flesh from his bones. Why was the mortal form so cursed weak and prone to agonies? Was it so that the gods could more easily control mortals? Probably. Would mortals become close to unstoppable, even able to challenge the gods, if they did not have such frailties? Probably. And did mortal life have so much more value, sweetness and need for preservation because of just how vulnerable it was? Undoubtedly, for was it not precisely those qualities and aspects of life that he so coveted? Was it not for such a full experience of life that he was prepared to sacrifice the entire demon realm? Of course it was. Perhaps he should look at things the other way round then. Perhaps he should wonder if he wasn't yet strong enough to bear carrying this mortal frame. Perhaps it was his spirit and resolve that were weak, not the body.

He began to understand that his running the gauntlet of the demon realm would be the true testing of him. He would be crucified in its crucible. He would then be tempered upon its anvil. If he won through without breaking, he would have become worthy of the full life and self-rule that he so desperately sought.

With renewed determination, he ran on. He now found that he could block his physical discomforts from his mind. Amazing. How could he have so underestimated existence for so long? It was even more glorious than he had thought. Of course, he'd never fully experienced it really, so could never have fully understood it. The fact that he could see it more clearly now meant that he must be coming closer to it. He was becoming more and more alive. He felt sure he would continue to grow with every sphere he passed through, until he ultimately became that higher being he'd always dreamed of becoming. His transformation would be complete by the time he returned to the mortal realm to claim what was his by right, to claim his new throne.

He arrived at the edge of a muddy waterhole. It was about six feet across and not much to look at. Could a water elemental really survive in that murk? Surely it couldn't be all that powerful if it lived in little more than a polluted puddle. It was probably safe to approach. Still, it had managed to survive all the way out here in this arid landscape. And he had no idea how deep the water went. Perhaps it was a sinkhole. If so, it might be home to a mighty elemental indeed, one that would drag him beneath the surface as soon as he dipped in a finger or toe. He spied a spindly stick of a tree on the other side of the waterhole. It had few leaves and only came up to his chest: he should be able to uproot it and use it to probe the water without much trouble.

Something fluttered. He stopped and watched the tree more closely. Then he dashed around the pool and grabbed the wood dryad from behind its narrow shelter by the neck. It screeched and he snapped it in half. He tore its bark-like skin open, ripping a nail in the process, and gnawed on its soft heartwood. It wasn't the most palatable meal he'd ever had – in fact, a nice glass of a full-bodied red would have improved it significantly – but it returned some strength to his limbs. He just hoped it would be enough to see him to the next barrier.

The mud around his feet began to stir and he leapt back onto the desert surface. A golem of clay and silt began to rise and take shape. It slid towards him. He turned and began to run again. He was sure he could out-distance the earth elemental for a while but it would prove tireless, whereas he would eventually begin to flag. Also, the elemental would begin to pick up speed once it had overcome its initial inertia and begun to find some momentum.

Wondering how on earth he was going to lose this elemental, he put his head down and tried to concentrate on maintaining a high pace and not losing his footing. Now he thought about it, how exactly would the elemental be able to track him? Of course, as long as he trod upon the earth, it would feel his vibration. He realised he needed to find a river or wood, anything that would allow him to leave the ground.

One of the suns dimmed slightly, and he felt the slightest bit cooled, or was that his imagination? No, there was definitely a shadow... He ducked as he tried to avoid the swooping wind elemental, but it snatched him up and drove up into the sky with him. Talons pierced his shoulders and immobilised him. By the humourless nature of Lacrimos, how it hurt!

Finally managing a laboured breath, he looked up at the creature that held him. It was not as big as he'd first thought, albeit that it was plenty strong enough to carry him and its serrated beak looked like it would be able to tear him to pieces in a trice. He looked down between his feet at the ground far below. It twinkled and sparkled as if they flew over a sea of diamonds.

Vidius began to swing his body forwards and backwards, wincing and then crying out every time the talons sank deeper into him. The wind-demon's flight became erratic as it pitched about in the air. It cried raucously and stabbed at him with its beak. There was an echoing cry and another wind-demon came arrowing down out of the sky towards them.

Then he was falling, feet first and then head down. What was the best way to fall or land? Hadn't he heard somewhere that it was better to be relaxed when you lan… argghhh!

Vidius was sure he had got the demon to drop him over water. But perhaps not, for it felt like he'd smashed into rock. Surely the water hadn't been a mirage, had it? Or too shallow?

His consciousness began to slip, to drift, to tumble and somersault, as if was falling all over again. He clung onto it like a lifeline and his mind righted itself. He was face down and apparently drowning. He pulled his head up and dragged a breath into him, although it felt like molten lead. He spluttered and coughed, snot running from his nose and blood from his ears. Gratefully, he let the tide tug him towards the beach.

After some minutes, his feet dragged against the bottom. Groaning, he got his legs under him and started using them despite their complaint. The water level obligingly lowered itself so that it was easier going. Hang on… He looked back and blanched in fear. Massive swells were building out on the open water and rushing towards him. He picked up his knees and began to half skip and half jump through the shallows.

There were roars behind him. By the time they reached him, they would be enormous. What chance did he have against a demon tsunami? The stones beneath his feet began to rush away as the sea demons pulled themselves up to their full height and prepared to descend on him.

Not knowing what else to do, Vidius curled himself into a ball, pulling his chin towards his chest and keeping his arms and elbows protectively to either side of his head. He was battered and pummelled into the sea bed, then kicked and thrown forwards, over and over, head over heels.

So disorientated was he, he was not exactly sure when the punishment stopped. He coughed up water and sand and it felt like his throat had been torn out by glass or sharp rocks. He shivered for a while and then vomited down his face and neck. In some ways, that turned out to be the best thing for him, because his body released adrenaline into his system at the same time and accordingly he had a few moments of lucidity.

The sea demons were summoning their strength to hit him again. He crawled higher up the beach and into some long grass and scrub. He lay there panting for a while, desperate for respite. How long did he have? How long before the elementals found him once more?

'I'm not going to let a bunch of miserable second level demons get the better of me!' he growled, and almost immediately regretted it as grains of sand left in his mouth ground painfully against the enamel of his teeth. He spat.

Vidius hauled himself upright and marched forwards purposefully. He could see the barrier now, for it was manifest as white marble and shone for all to see as it reflected the six suns.

Grunts and howls came to his ears as elementals called to one another. They were organising themselves to hunt him. How dare they! If they'd had any inkling as to his true nature, they would have immediately ended themselves rather than face his displeasure and judgement. But he dared not reveal himself yet. He could not afford for word to get to the Princes ahead of his arrival.

Besides, the snivelling denizens of this sphere were too late to stop him now, as he was into light woodland. Water elementals could not leave their parent pools to pursue him. Fire elementals were slowed by the green foliage hereabouts, and would no doubt be challenged by the local dryads. Wind-demons would lose much of their aerial advantage in attack once beneath the canopy. And the larger earth demons would remain bound and trapped below by the roots of the trees and plants.

Nonetheless, he didn't linger to take in the flora and fauna. Time lost here might put him at a disadvantage later on. The longer he took, the more chance there was that the Princes would divine there was something amiss in the demon realm. Their minds were so acute, cunning and twisted that they often seemed prescient. They understood the psychology and motivations of pretty much every being in the cosmos. His only hope was to strike before they realised the threat.

He hurried through the wood, ignoring the constant fluttering and twitching of dryads at the edges of his vision. The wood ended just short of the barrier and he paused to assess the hundred metres or so of empty ground he still needed to cover. Shrugging, he ran towards the gate.

Wind-demons launched themselves from the top of the barrier and flapped quickly towards him. Their ugly cries shouted to others that the quarry had been found. The ground began to churn and golems of mud and stone rose up around him. Cracks appeared in the earth, steam jetting forth from some and fire venting from others. Had he run into an ambush? Had they been waiting for him all along?

The gate appeared unguarded but, again, he knew better than to trust to appearances. He pulled up short and did not attempt to try the handle. Anything else would have been suicide.

9

'Gatekeeper, this traveller presents himself to you. If you will grant him passage to the next sphere, then your protection is also mine.'

The elementals rushing up behind Vidius were forced to come to a halt, and not a moment too soon. He could feel the heat from the fire-demons against his back. The demon host crackled, hooted, gurgled and rumbled in frustration, but they dared not come any closer.

Part of the barrier began to move and the chameleon gatekeeper allowed itself to be seen. It had the form of a lizard, stood on just two powerful legs and was well over eight feet tall. The end of its tongue protruded from its mouth and flickered as it tasted the air. Could it discern Vidius's true nature?

'Why?' croaked the gatekeeper, his reptilian eyes unblinking.

'In exchange for certain gifts. I have a gift for the inhabitants of this realm if they will let me pass. Similarly, I have gifts for you.'

'What need have we of gifts when we can take them from you by force?' the lizard rasped.

'You cannot take what has already been given.'

The lizard cocked its head for a second. 'That is so. What, then, is the gift you have given the demons here? And what is it you give me?'

Vidius smiled. 'Why, I have made a gift of the first sphere for these elementals. The door in the first barrier remains open. That sphere is now theirs to plunder.'

At this news, the elementals began to slip away, all wanting to be first to the prize. The gatekeeper shook its head, but did not speak. It awaited his offer.

'If you let me pass, then my first born child will be yours. The child is mortal.'

The lizard's tongue lashed with excitement but the gatekeeper otherwise remained unmoved. It was cannier than the cat-demon, that was for sure.

'My further gift to you, therefore, will be access to the mortal realm. How else could you claim the child?'

Now the lizard stirred. 'How am I to have this access?'

'Come, demon, I think you know. The door to the third sphere must be left open.'

'And all will be undone.'

'It is the only way.'

The lizard bowed. 'So be it… master.'

Vidius stepped into the third sphere and looked round warily for the imps and gremlins.

✳ ✳

'By the diseased groin of Lacrimos, are you trying to get us both killed, lad?' the Scourge shouted as he ducked Strap's wind-blown arrow.

'It keeps you on your toes, Old Hound!' the younger Guardian smiled as he pulled two more arrows from his quiver. He nocked one to his bow and held the other in his teeth so that he could fire it quickly after the first.

'Besides, I thought you never missed a target,' the Scourge grumbled as he straightened back up and shaded his eyes so that he could get a better look at the winged creature menacing them.

'I ngever miss wheng the wingd in ngatural!' Strap mumbled around the quarrel in his mouth and pulled back his bowstring.

He released one missile under the swell of the wind straight at the screeching target, and sent the other looping over the swell so that it would descend back down at the thing. There was a strange sequence of whistles and shrieks, the wings clapped together and the arrows were buffeted back towards the Scourge, who was forced to fling himself to the side and into one of the field's many muddy puddles in order to save himself.

'By the restless bowels of Wim, you're right! It has magic! It's no part of Shakri's creation, that's for damn sure. A demon, no doubt!' the grizzled, older warrior spat and pulled his long knives from their sheaths at his belt. He dexterously flipped the weapons in his hands so that he had them by the blades and ready to throw. 'Save your arrows, Strap.'

'Yet how is it able to control the wind?' Strap frowned. 'Surely it should have no power here in Shakri's realm.'

'We'll worry about that once we've got it skewered on one of my knives and over our camp fire. Look out! Here it comes!' the Scourge called as he braced himself to face the diving creature.

It fell straight towards the Scourge, sweeping its wings back to attain even greater speed. It extended its neck and long, serrated beak, becoming a living lance hurtling down from the heavens towards the mortal warrior.

'Holy…! It's even bigger than I realised!' Strap gasped. 'Err… Scourge, I think you'd better…'

'Oi! Get orf out orv it!' hollered a voice from not far away and a dog started to bark.

Strap looked up and saw the old farmer brandishing his stick and shuffling into the field. His mid-sized mongrel ran around its master, barking angrily at the sky.

'No, stay back!' the young Guardian cried and began to run towards him.

Spotting easier prey, the monstrosity began to level out its trajectory and fly straight for the elderly landowner.

'Come here!' the Scourge shouted and hurled his blades with all his might at the ugly bird-come-gargoyle.

One knife sank deep into the large creature, but it seemed unaffected, only a few drops of ichor falling from it. The other dirk narrowly missed as the abomination twisted along its length as a javelin will do in flight.

'I's not avin some oversized goose runnin amok on me land, ascarin the hands an taintin me crops!' the aged farmer yelled, and waved his stick even more wildly than before.

'Get down, you fool!' Strap cried in despair, pulling on his bowstring and releasing even though he knew it was already too late. The terror was well ahead of him, and his arrow would not be able to catch it in time.

It speared through the man's chest as meeting mere paper and carried his body twenty feet before letting him fall back into the mud. Strap's arrow punched a hole through one of its wings but its flight only wobbled slightly as a consequence. The dog had been brushed aside in the initial onslaught; now it yelped in distress over the battered corpse of the old man and tried to keep the aerial threat at bay. The monstrosity seemed to take delight in taunting the canine, swooping low and cackling or mimicking its barks.

'I hate demons!' the Scourge muttered and began to sprint. 'Strap!' he shouted. 'Brace!'

The young warrior's eyes went wide. He threw his bow aside, planted his feet, bent, placed his hands just above his knees and locked his arms straight. Then he ducked his head.

The Scourge snatched his lost knife out of the muck while on the run. *Concentrate*, he told himself. He watched his footing to be sure he wouldn't slip and lose his speed. Eyes flicked up to Strap, and then the demon, judging distance.

He leapt onto Strap's back and pushed off towards the flapping monster. He plunged his blade through the membrane on its wing and used his body weight to drag the metal down the entire length of its span.

As the Scourge splashed back down into the field, the demon screamed in pain and clawed at the sky. It could no longer stay aloft and crashed down a few metres away from the two Guardians. It was the size of a wagon! It would have no trouble crushing them if it decided to roll over right then. As it was, it shunted round awkwardly, all clumsy angles and levers here on the earth, in stark contrast to the grace it had displayed when arcing through the air and riding the wind.

It curled its powerful neck and jabbed with its vicious beak at the Scourge. The grizzled warrior leapt on top of the beak and wrapped his arms and legs around it to keep the mouth tied shut. The bird-demon swung its head back and forth and then started hitting its beak upon the ground in an effort to dislodge its assailant.

'Strap, get on with it! I can't hang on forever!'

'Alright, alright!' the younger Guardian yelled, getting a firm grip on his bow and nocking an arrow. He fired at close range but the arrow simply hit the demon's skull and flew away.

The demon flapped, coiled into an s-shape and then became a living whip. It smashed its beak down hard again and again. The Scourge's face could not hide his hurt although he made no sound.

'Hold on!' Strap shouted in panic and pulled out the short, heavy rod of iron he'd never had cause to use before. He fitted it quickly and released. The bolt buried itself deep into the demon's head and it crashed to the ground. After a last twitch, it stopped moving.

'Well help me then!' the Scourge wheezed.

Strap helped his commander up and sought to steady him. The Scourge pushed him away roughly and kicked the prone demon carcass, which already appeared to be collapsing in on itself.

'Stinking thing! Strap, see to the old man. You never know.'

Strap nudged the farmer's dog aside and bent down to examine the body. He sighed and shook his head.

The Scourge spat on the demon. 'Let's burn it. Then we'd better carry the old father back to his people.'

❋ ❦

The pretty young maid in the yard dropped the bucket of milk she'd been carrying as she saw the Scourge and Strap and ran towards them.

'Pappy, no! No! Is he… is he…? Noo! How could you let this happen?' she demanded of the Guardians, hot tears rolling down her cheeks. She slapped Strap on the shoulder and he shied from her, although he still had to keep a hold of the old farmer's legs.

'There was nothing we could do,' the Scourge said in a not unkind voice. 'He came into the field while we were fighting the winged demon that's been plaguing you hereabouts. He died bravely. The unholy harpy is no more. Let us take him inside, lass, so that those who loved him can show him the respect he's due.'

'If you'd just left the thing alone, none of this would ever have happened!' the maid accused him. 'It's never attacked anyone before. All it ate was field mice. Some thought it a gift from Shakri Herself. And you killed it! Take my grandfather and lay him out on our kitchen table. Then begone, before I tell the field-hands what you've done and they run you off our land... or worse!'

'Now just you listen here!' the Scourge began to remonstrate with her.

'Scourge!' Strap interrupted. 'Now is not the time. Leave it!'

The Scourge glowered at his young companion, but bit his tongue and gave a nod. The maid turned on her heel and walked stiff-backed towards the farmhouse. They struggled after her in silence, with the farmer's dead weight between them. The mongrel walked with them sadly, its ears down, eyes wide and shoulders hunched.

They laid the body on the table as gently as they could. The old man's wife was there and she started to moan and rock, her arms wrapped round herself. The young maid hugged her and started to sob into her shoulder. Strap stood awkwardly by, not sure where to put his eyes, let alone the rest of himself.

The Scourge cleared his throat clumsily. 'I need to know if a minstrel and musician have passed through these parts recently.'

The farmwife showed no sign she'd heard him and stared sightlessly ahead of her. The maid wiped her eyes and nose on a handkerchief and glared at him.

The Scourge wasn't sure if she'd heard him properly through her crying so tried again: 'This minstrel is a demon we're hunting. Have you heard tell of Jack O'Nine Blades and the musician accompanying him? I don't know if there's a connection between them and the demon in your field.'

'Get out!' she said softly. 'Haven't you done enough already? There's nothing for you here. Just leave us to our grief!'

Strap put a hand on the Scourge's upper arm and gently pulled him towards the door. The commander let himself be led away, anger and confusion warring across his face.

They made camp that night on the same wooded knoll as they'd used when travelling through the area in previous years. The small store of wood that Strap had left under a particular bush was still there, and he used it to get a fire started.

The young Guardian set a pan of water to heating over the flames and threw some herbs into it to make them some tea. He glanced sideways at the Scourge, who sat on a log nearby brooding. He'd been quiet since they'd left the farm that afternoon. Having travelled with the Scourge for many years, Strap knew better than to disturb him when he was like this. It was better to stay outside in the cold than enter into the cave and risk arousing the bear. It was better to think of himself as travelling alone for this part of his journey.

After a few minutes, Strap stirred the tea, and then took the pan off the fire with a cloth. He poured out two cups and went and balanced one on the log within reach of the Scourge's hand.

'How long have we been hunting this cursed minstrel?' the commander suddenly asked, catching Strap by surprise.

Strap squinted and looked up at the sky as he counted. 'Five years, give or take.'

'Five years!' the Scourge repeated and fell into a reverie once more. Some time later, he asked: 'Have I become so obsessed with him, Strap, that I'm now insensitive to the troubles and suffering of others? What use am I as a Guardian if that's true?'

Strap sighed. The old warrior was increasingly prone to bouts of melancholy or dark introspection. The last one had lasted over a month and Strap feared that one of these bouts would become permanent if whatever afflicted the commander's spirit wasn't dealt with soon. He resolved to talk to Saltar and Mordius about it the next time they passed through Corinus, but for now knew he could do little more than try and keep things as positive as possible. 'Old Hound, the girl was in shock. She did not know what she was saying. In her pain, she lashed out at whoever she could. The world probably seemed a very cruel and unfair place to her at that moment. It was interesting that you thought the demon in the field might have been related to Jack somehow. I've never seen its like before.'

'Me neither,' the Scourge said morosely. 'I don't even know for sure it was a demon. I think I'm starting to see them in every hedgerow and around every camp fire. I'll be scared of the dark next. We haven't even heard a report of Jack being in these parts, Strap. I'm just leaping to paranoid conclusions, I fear.'

'No, that's not true,' Strap hurried to say. 'We know that Jack and Lucius take almost the same route every year. They are due in this area round about now. As to whether it was a demon we faced, Mordius is sure to know. We'll ask him when next we see him. You are right: it was no part of Shakri's creation, no matter what superstition the simple folk round here may have. The question has to be what the creature betokens. How did it get here? Was it conjured, and if so by whom? Someone round here must know something. We simply have to find them. We'll stop in the hamlet of Windrun and ask some questions in a day or two.'

The Scourge nodded heavily and contemplated Strap's words. The younger man started to cut some beef jerky into smaller pieces. He added them into the remains of the herb tea, to help soften them. A couple of wild onions followed and then he set the pan back on the fire.

'Strap, tell me truthfully: should we stop pursuing the demon? It seems that he and Lucius haven't got up to anything criminal in all the time we've been on their trail. In fact, they seem to be lauded up and down the kingdom. Do you remember when we had them cornered in that inn in Stangeld and the locals actually helped them escape, even though we are meant to represent the law of this land? Have we simply wasted five years of our lives, Strap?'

Strap frowned. 'No, we have not wasted our time. We've settled no small number of local disputes while we've been on the road. And we've put an end to several magicians who were terrorising towns and villages. There were those bandits we despatched outside King's Landing, don't forget! How can that have been a waste of time?' He paused. 'But as to whether we should stop pursuing Jack and Lucius, well, I just don't know. It's not like they're doing anyone much harm, is it? Quite the opposite, in fact. I know that you'd want to put an end to Jack, but I haven't really got the heart to harm gentle Lucius. Besides, every Memnosian owes him a debt, the way Kate and Saltar tell it. They would not want to see him harmed, I'm sure. It could be that Lucius is also a positive effect on Jack. Perhaps we should leave them be.'

The Scourge massaged his temples and closed his eyes for a second. *He looks exhausted*, Strap decided. The commander of the Guardians then opened his eyes and said in a hollow voice: 'I see now that I truly have fixated on destroying this demon beyond all reason. I should not have been allowed to drag you up and down this kingdom on such a long and wild goose-chase. You are of an age, Strap, when you should be courting maids and setting down roots. You should not be forced to waste your youth and energy on playing wet-nurse to an old fool who should know better.'

'Now hold it right there!' Strap protested angrily and rose to his feet. 'I am my own man. I make my own decisions, thank you very much. I chose to accompany you because I believed it to be the right thing to do. We cannot generally afford to let demons remain at large, particularly when they are a threat to the population. I still believe that. We will find out what we can about the creature in the field, and whether Jack has been seen in the area. Damn you, Scourge! What's gotten into you?'

Strap had hoped the Scourge would react with anger of his own and show some of his old fire. Yet the commander seemed incapable of even looking up at the young Guardian. And he seemed smaller somehow, as if he had collapsed in on himself like the winged demon had. Emptily, the old warrior said, 'I will think on all your words. I will take the first watch, Strap. I doubt I would manage to sleep, anyway.'

With that, the Scourge moved away into the darkness, leaving Strap wondering and frightened.

Chapter Two: And Suffering

Saltar glared angrily at the old man sitting across the table from him. It wasn't the fact Trajan had claimed he was too infirm with age to make his way up to the palace and that Saltar must therefore come to him instead. Nor was it that when Saltar had arrived at Trajan's dark and dingy home and been offered refreshment, he'd then been given wine in a glass that looked suspiciously like it had been stolen from the palace. Of course, Saltar wasn't bothered that the vintage served was also remarkably similar to one of the rarer ones stocked in the royal cellars. Further still, he wasn't offended that Trajan's two lackeys – rat-boy and Sotto – openly wore weapons, where Saltar and his Chamberlain did not. No, what angered the Battle-leader was that Trajan had deliberately intoxicated him with his hospitality and cameraderie in order to get the upper hand in what was now turning out to be a business negotiation for the entire population of the Outdwellers of Corinus.

All knew that Trajan ruled the Outdwellers, those who scratched a living beyond the city walls, but the patriarch always refused to fill the role in any sort of formal or official capacity. The meaning of any discussion with Trajan was therefore invariably about what had *not* been said. It was all tacit understanding and oblique implication. Saltar thought he'd come for something of a social visit and a casual discussion about how the city guard or army might extend their patrols to take in the Outdweller farms beyond the city. Before he knew it, he'd been on the verge of handing over the keys to the entire kingdom.

For a second, the Battle-leader of Dur Memnos had been angry at himself – how could he have been so naive? Surely he should have known better. Yet he would not blame himself for relaxing and then being manipulated by someone else. He would not accept responsibility for the unprincipled behaviour of others. Beyond that, the Outdwellers had been gifted their farms by the palace, so they should show some gratitude rather than trying to trick yet more out of people.

Saltar scrubbed his face with his hands to try and rid himself of the muzziness besetting him. He wouldn't put it past Trajan to put something in the wine either!

He glared at the old man and said tightly: 'None of the discourse of the last hour has happened. We will start again. Anything I have agreed to thus far is now unagreed.'

'What?' Trajan choked in outrage.

Sotto surged to his feet in protest, his hand going to the blade at his waist. The Chamberlain hissed in warning at Trajan's lieutenant. Rat-boy crouched slightly, ready to leap.

'You know as well as any that an oath spoken cannot be unsaid!' Sotto breathed. 'There would be no order were it otherwise. No man would be able to know another. No man would even be able to know the gods. Life could not exist then. Even Shakri is bound by such a principle. When She commands a tree to grow, does it not grow? It cannot then ungrow! Would you be known as an oath-breaker then, Battle-leader? Rather than be known as the Builder, would you prefer to be known as the Betrayer of this realm?'

Saltar slapped down the berserker within him. 'Trajan, do you have any water? I find this wine somewhat heady.'

Trajan scowled at him, but signalled rat-boy to pour a beaker.

'Thank you. Now, if I recall, I have made no oath nor given any command in all the time I have been here. I am not some novice mage thinking to do the impossible and unsay a spell. I am merely a man talking through options and alternatives with friends. I am a man who has not yet heard anything to his liking. Friend Sotto, perhaps you also are finding the wine heady, even though you still have the wit to use your words like the blades of a master knifeman. Surely your skills are such that they give you as much advantage seated as standing? Yet is it not more comfortable to sit?'

Sotto glanced at Trajan for a lead. The old man spat into the poor and empty fireplace. 'May as well sit, Sotto, before you start looking as dumb as Dijin. Besides, I can't see us coming off well in any fight with these two, even if they are unarmed. They have a tendency to *cheat*.'

Both Saltar and the Chamberlain began to rise at the obvious insult, but Trajan cackled and they realised they were being embarrassed as much as Sotto. Saltar took his seat with the others and ground his teeth in irritation. He knew that he wouldn't be able to get the better of Trajan, but surely there were aims they both shared. Surely! After all, did they not both have the interests of the realm at heart?

Too tired to order his thoughts anymore, Saltar said, 'Chamberlain, perhaps you could help us here.'

The thin and long-limbed courtier blinked in surprise. He tilted his head strangely and regarded Saltar with unfathomable eyes. 'It would be my pleasure, hmm?' His head jerked back to Trajan. 'Old one, what is it you want of us? Speak plainly, hmm, or we will have to start this conversation again and again… or give it up, hmm?'

Trajan chewed on the insides of his cheeks, but they were too spare to last him long. 'The land given in payment to the Outdwellers for supporting your fight against the blood-mages is not enough to support my people. The soil is thin or little more than dust and rock. We cannot grow enough to feed those we have, let alone grow in numbers, and Shakri knows how important every child is to the kingdom. Those with cattle find little worthwhile grazing land hereabouts. Those who venture beyond the immediate environs of Corinus find themselves bedevilled by bandits or… or… ill luck.'

Saltar leaned forward to ask the obvious question, but Trajan held up his hand to forestall him.

'I do not know how else to describe it. Freak storms, wild animals trampling fields, strange crop blights, all have befallen those looking to settle further afield. We have enlisted the help and blessings of the priests of Gart, but they are as baffled and defeated as we are. Either we are given a share of the land or crops of the nobles who own the richest estates around Corinus or we need priests and the soldiery to provide us with protection far beyond the locale… or we starve. Is that plain enough for ye?'

The Chamberlain tutted as he considered the words of the Outdwellers' leader. 'It is curious that I have not heard complaints before concerning the land you were given over five years ago. Your people are still exempt from the taxes the throne collects from all other farms and estates, hmm? Neither do your people pay a tithe to the temples, hmm? In that respect, you are already subsidised by the nobles and in receipt of the charity of others, no? Yet you ask for more, hmm? If you have more people than you can feed, then why are the Outdwellers not swelling the numbers of the depleted Memnosian army? They would be housed, clothed and fed, and the palace would then have a sufficient number of soldiers to organise the patrols you ask for. It is hard to credit that you Outdwellers cannot feed or protect yourselves. Or are you too used to feeding off others, hmm? Are carrots and beef still unappetising to your palette? Perhaps you yet crave the flesh of your fellow man, hmm?'

Trajan's face turned red and then screwed up into a fist. Saltar had never seen such a reaction in the old man. Was it anger or embarrassment? Or both?

The Battle-leader wasn't sure but he suspected he'd just heard Trajan speak with as much honesty as he could manage. A glance at the miserable and flat Sotto confirmed his suspicion. These were proud men. They did not like to admit that they could not look after their people.

'Thank you,' Saltar said to the Chamberlain, pre-empting any retort from Trajan. 'Trajan, I have not forgotten the sacrifice made by the Outdwellers. I am sure that without them we would never have triumphed against our enemies. I am mortified to hear of your troubles, truly I am. If the Outdwellers suffer, then the whole kingdom suffers. Our population is precariously low and yet we still struggle to feed ourselves. I'd been hoping we'd be able to start taxing the Outdwellers, but clearly that won't be possible. The palace will have to continue using its reserves to feed the army. Chamberlain, would you talk to the Merchant's Guild and see how far we can increase duties on goods?'

The Chamberlain pulled his face into a rictus of distaste. 'The Guild will not receive me well, hmm? They have lost a number of their ships to unreasonable weather of late, no? I am not sure what the palace has left to offer the Guild that would persuade them to increase duties... but I will try.'

Saltar sighed. 'Offer them one of our warships if you must. We've not needed our navy in decades, have we? Perhaps the Merchant Guild would be prepared to grow a *merchant navy* of sorts.'

The Chamberlain's jaw hung. Then he gathered himself and bowed at the waist. 'Milord, you are indeed the Battle-leader of Dur Memnos. Your tactical instincts have saved us many a time, hmm? Just as we would not be here without the Outdwellers, we would not be here without you, no?'

Saltar found himself slightly embarrassed and decided he'd be best off ignoring the Chamberlain. 'Trajan, I will now speak plainly to you. The army is stretched as it is. Its numbers have not recovered since the battle with the Brethren. We have increased the level of training of the men we do have, and they are now man-for-man a match for any troops in all the kingdoms, but we do not have the spare numbers for all the patrols you require. Despite the way in which he presented it, there is some merit in the Chamberlain's suggestion. In exchange for some of your men, we will give you the patrols you need and prevail upon the temples to provide you with more of the gods' blessings. The Green Witch, my wife, has particular influence within the temple of Incarnus, as you no doubt know. What say you?'

The old man pulled his clay pipe from one of his pockets and stuck it in one of the gaps amongst his brown teeth. He chewed on it for a while and then raised an eyebrow slightly at Sotto.

Sotto rubbed his jaw as he considered. He finally nodded. 'It is a sensible proposition. We could spare some few men who have little else to do at present.'

Trajan worried at his pipe for a few moments longer and nodded slowly. 'We will provide you with a hundred men. I expect the patrols to start within a hand of days. Sotto will co-ordinate with whichever army officer you name to decide on the patrol routes.'

'Chamberlain?'

'Two hundred.'

'What do you mean?' Saltar frowned.

'We should see the number of men as a currency, hmm? If Trajan offers one hundred, then he can surely afford two, no?'

Saltar smiled. 'I may have good tactical instincts in times of war, Chamberlain, but no one can out-manoeuvre you in a negotiation, eh? Two hundred it is!'

Trajan growled and spat again, but this time it was into his palm and he held it out for the

Battle-leader to shake. Saltar mirrored him and the deal was done.

⚔ ⚔

Saltar stepped out of Trajan's mean, one-room house and blinked against the light of the late afternoon. They'd lost nearly the whole day. If he didn't hurry, then he'd be too late to watch any of his son's weapons practice. He'd missed the last few and didn't want it to become a habit, not only for his son's sake but because he feared incurring Kate's displeasure. His life wasn't worth living whenever she was angry – in fact, everyone in the palace knew to avoid her when the wrathful passions of Incarnus moved her.

The Chamberlain accompanied him back towards the palace. Saltar watched the man skittering back and forth on the uneven cobblestones. What a strange creature the Chamberlain was. He was all long limbs and twitchy movements. He often veered under the eaves of the houses to either side of the street as if he sought to stay out of the sun's direct light. Indeed, the man's black pupils were so large that they all but filled his eyes and meant he would be more comfortable in shadows and darkness. He seemed for all the world like some sort of humanoid spider, complete with pointed, fang-like teeth.

Most people certainly reacted towards him with the sort of phobia spiders and snakes elicited.

Even Saltar couldn't help having a negative reaction towards the Chamberlain's alien nature. Even though Saltar's rational mind reminded him that the gods had deliberately given the Chamberlain the sort of body and mind that would alienate other *irreducibles* from him, and thereby discourage the irreducibles from sharing their unique knowledge and skills with each other, Saltar's instincts still screamed at him to flee this monster or stamp his boot down on it. There wasn't any sort of humanity recognisable in the Chamberlain's face. If the tight, hollowed and waxy skin around his thin nostrils and mouth could be called a *face*. And Kate had said that the Chamberlain didn't even have blood in his veins – he had some thick, dark ichor instead. She claimed to have shot a crossbow bolt into each of the creature's legs and still seen it walk from the throne room to hunt its prey.

How could such a creature be predicted and therefore trusted? Saltar had always found it hard to lay aside his suspicions of the palace retainer who'd worked under the despot Voltar. The Chamberlain had schemed with the necromancer for centuries, and still ran the same network of spies and informants. For all the Chamberlain had helped them against the Brethren, Saltar suspected he'd done so out of necessity, out of a desire to ensure his own survival.

Saltar knew he'd be a fool to place his entire trust in this creature, but at the same time he knew he would have to overcome the urges and tendencies of his own nature in order to find a way to work with him. After all, they had something of a shared past from millennia before, if they could but piece it together between them to unlock its secrets. He knew that their future might depend on it, but whenever he tried the topic directly with the Chamberlain, their conversation would break down, one of them would become distracted, or something would be said or done to cause a destructive friction between them.

He had to overcome his own nature, but how could any man hope to accomplish that? It seemed a paradox. Was it a condition then of the magic upon which this realm was founded? Would he have to undo the magic and destroy this realm in order to overcome his nature? No, that was not an option, even if he could manage it. Then it came to him. They would simply have to die.

Having worked that out, he then wondered how on earth he was going to get the Chamberlain to commit suicide, for the Chamberlain distrusted Saltar about as much as Saltar did the Chamberlain. Perhaps he would just murder him and explain afterwards. It wasn't going to be easy either way, that was for sure.

'Chamberlain, make sure the Outdwellers are spread throughout the army once they've joined. We don't want to make it easy for them to organise an army within an army. And make sure one of the Outdwellers is made an officer. We don't want to make it too easy for the other troops to victimise them.'

'Yes, milord. Anything else, milord, hmm?'

Saltar hesitated. 'Yes, come and find me tonight. Our little chat with Trajan has made it clear that a reckoning between you and me is long overdue. We are running out of options, Chamberlain.'

The Chamberlain licked his lips. 'I look forward to it, milord.'

❀ ❀

In his own turn, the Chamberlain had surreptitiously been watching and examining Balthagar — why he now chose to call himself Saltar, the Chamberlain still wasn't sure — since they'd left Trajan's hovel. Balthagar had appeared confused and directionless for a while during the discussions with the Outdwellers, although he had ultimately asserted himself, much to the Chamberlain's relief. Was some sort of illness or weakness beginning to affect the Battle-leader? At first, the Chamberlain hoped not, for his own day-to-day survival very much depended on his irreducible brother. Without the protection Balthagar afforded him, the Chamberlain was sure the mortals of this realm, and perhaps even its sponsoring gods, would turn on him. He could sense the fear and hatred with which they all looked at him when they thought his attention was elsewhere. He was such an anathema to their kind that many wanted him destroyed despite the help he had rendered them against the mountain people. Of course, he'd been motivated by a selfish desire for survival, for he certainly had no love for the people of Shakri's realm, and he suspected they could read that about him and held him in contempt for it. Self-sacrifice had never been his strong suit. It wasn't really something he understood either, if he was to be honest with himself. And that was one of the big differences between himself and his brother, for Balthagar excelled when it came to self-sacrifice, and Shakri's people loved him for it. In fact, the Chamberlain thought it was little short of a miracle that his brother still survived, so many times had he put himself at risk. On a number of occasions, the patterns of fate, chance and history had made it look absolutely certain Balthagar would meet his doom; and yet each time the Battle-leader had managed to grasp or tease out a loose thread with which he could change the weave of the Pattern. It looked like unexpected or blind luck whenever he succeeded, but it had now happened so many times that the Chamberlain was sure there was something else going on. Did Balthagar have some sort of power or tool he kept secret and, if so, how could the Chamberlain wrest it from him? It was one of the reasons he kept his brother under such scrutiny. So far, he'd discovered nothing and it appeared that if his brother did have some power or tool to manipulate the Pattern directly, then he exercised it unwittingly or without any true understanding of it.

The Chamberlain simply wanted the power or means by which to guarantee his own survival. Was that really so much to ask? He desperately wanted to have complete control of the Pattern rather than have his life manipulated and decided for him by it. Was his desire so outrageous? Yes, of course it was, for it was not how this realm was constructed or operated. No individual was meant to have absolute power in this place, for that would be in direct opposition to the realm's definition. The closest thing to omnipotent this realm had was its pantheon of gods, but even they could not absolutely guarantee the realm's future existence, for there were terrible counter-forces beyond that were intent upon asserting themselves via the negation and destruction of other cosmic wills and forces, wills and forces that were seen as competing by the very fact of their existence.

The Chamberlain had tested the principles of this realm's construction and operation a number of times in the distant past. In previous millennia, he had himself been a king, and even an emperor. Yet each time he'd been about to seize absolute rule, he'd been thwarted or on the brink of destroying the very realm he wanted to control and own. In his desire to hold his living prize tight in his hand or embrace, he'd threatened to squeeze all the life from it so that he would be left with nothing. In the end, he'd realised a loose grip on it was the best he could ever hope for. After all, this realm had become his home and sanctuary, so he should do nothing that challenged its safety if he wished to survive.

In testing those principles, of course, he'd covered his hands in blood. Countless innocents had died to satisfy his selfish desire for power. He'd become known as the Prince of Blood or the Blood King in a number of nations. A deep ancestral memory of his crimes had grown in Shakri's people, and that was another reason why he would always be mistrusted and loathed by them, even if such feelings were more instinctive than conscious in current generations.

Now he thought about it, just as miraculous as Balthagar's survival was the fact that Shakri had allowed the Chamberlain to survive after all he'd done to Her people. Perhaps he'd been protected by Lacrimos's shadowy hand in the past, though, just as Balthagar protected him now. There was a certain pattern to it that made sense. Yet it was still a pattern that controlled him. Why couldn't he be the one who had the power to decide whether protection would be afforded him or not? Why should he forever have to fawn and tread gently around Balthagar for fear that protection would be withdrawn? It was offensive to his own will and identity. It constantly kept him limited and confined. He had been dispossessed of his rights of being. His will was kept unasserted and in abeyance. He was a prisoner who had no choice but to watch and wait, in hope that his gaoler would one day forget to lock his door and therefore let him have his freedom. Or would the terrible counter-forces beyond this realm finally manage to break into the gaol and set all its prisoners free? He hoped so. He prayed for it. If he could find a way to provide them with information that would help them to break in, then he would not hesitate to do so, no matter the cause of the counter-forces! If a few monsters were set free in the process, then so be it – he could always help round them up afterwards.

And so he watched and waited. He eyed his brother beadily, now understanding him as a gaoler more than a protector. He tried to read any illness or weakness that might be there. Balthagar did look slightly haggard, the Chamberlain decided, although most mortal frames usually looked much the same to him. There was stubble on Balthagar's chin and there were dark bags under his eyes. He wasn't looking after himself properly, it seemed. His eyes were dull one minute and overbright the next. Could he be faking it, trying to draw the Chamberlain out? He certainly had the tactical genius for such a ploy, but surely it was too duplicitous for Balthagar's nature.

The Chamberlain looked closer. Balthagar's hair was somewhat lank. The blood red tunic he wore was rumpled and had a stain or two on it. He walked with his chin a fraction lower than usual and his shoulders were slightly stooped. They were small details, but all consistent. Had he been such when they had come down to Trajan's place this morning? The Chamberlain couldn't remember clearly and cursed himself for a daydreamer. Maybe he too was becoming unduly distracted these days. Were they both ailing? Or was some subtle force working against them? The kingdom certainly seemed beset by a number of troubles. Was there a common cause?

By nature, the Chamberlain had always been suspicious – paranoid, some might say – but as a consequence he'd rarely been caught off guard by anyone or anything. He trusted in his untrusting nature. It was a paradox, of course, but probably just one that underpinned the magic that enabled him to read the Pattern so well. He would think upon his latest suspicions further, but Balthagar was talking at him again, buzzing like a mosquito.

'… for the other troops to victimise them.'

'Yes, milord,' the Chamberlain extemporised. 'Anything else, milord, hmm?'

Balthagar hesitated. 'Yes, come and find me tonight. Our little chat with Trajan has made it clear that a reckoning between you and me is long overdue. We are running out of options, Chamberlain.'

The Chamberlain licked his lips. What was this? 'I look forward to it, milord.' Could this be the moment when he finally wrested power and control from Balthagar? After so long? It might prove to be the best chance he'd ever had, but it was also bound to be one of the most dangerous moments he'd ever faced. He would come equipped with every weapon, tool and trick he knew. To be free at last!

'Until later, Chamberlain. I will go see Kate and Orastes at the temple of Incarnus now. There are no other matters that require my attention today, are there?'

'No, milord. Nothing I cannot deal with in your stead, hmm?' the Chamberlain bowed.

❈ ❈

Saltar watched the courtier pick his way back up into Corinus and then struck out on his own for the fortified temple of the god of hatred and vengeance. The priesthood had been massacred in the mountain valley of the Brethren, their god Incarnus all but unmade, but one priestess had survived and managed to build a new order of warrior-priests. Their martial skills were unrivalled and it was said that their priests would occasionally be commissioned as assassins by the richest of the nobles who wanted to guarantee the death of a rival but also maintain anonymity.

Saltar turned a blind eye to the killings as long as they weren't too frequent and didn't get out of control. His wife had always been a favourite of holy Incarnus, so the throne was unlikely ever to be troubled by the warrior-priests. Besides, in their own way, the priests of Incarnus were vital to the defence of Dur Memnos, what with the army still so small. Therefore, they needed to keep their skills honed and needed to be indulged somewhat. And, of course, the head of the temple, Sister Spike, personally oversaw the combat training of both his wife Kate and his son Orastes.

He presented himself at the red gates of the large temple and was allowed to enter by the two guards on duty – they knew him as a regular visitor. He passed through the thick outer wall – the temple was more of a fortress than the sort of quiet retreat most of the other priesthoods built for themselves – and emerged into a large courtyard that also served as a marshalling yard and practice area. He bowed respectfully to the giant statue of Incarnus on the far side of the courtyard. It was three times the height of a normal man and made of red basalt – red to symbolise how He bathed in the blood of His enemies. The god was classically depicted in a giant suit of armour with visor lowered. He held an enormous hammer in both hands and looked to be in the process of raising it in order to smite someone unfortunate enough to have got on wrong side of Him.

There was the ringing sound of blade against blade and Saltar looked to his right. He smiled as he saw his son Orastes menacing Sister Spike. The high priestess was still in her early twenties and had boyish looks and a slight frame. With Orastes so large for his age – something Mordius attributed to the fact the ancient being Nylchros had once possessed the body and forced it to mature far more quickly than was natural – the two combatants were almost matched in size and strength. Sister Spike had trained her entire life, however, and could probably teach Saltar himself a thing or two if she were of a mind, especially with the battle-magic Incarnus gifted His priesthood. Now, she simply sparred with Orastes, playing the part of a weaker opponent so that the boy's confidence might grow. Orastes was still such a shy boy.

Kate stood watching the contest intently, arms folded. There was sweat on her brow and her hair looked damp – clearly, she'd been practising as well. Yet she did not look tired, or was it that she could not bring herself to relax? She hadn't unbuckled her green leather armour to cool off, Saltar noticed. And the gaze with which she studied her son was unblinking. Not for the first time, Saltar wondered if she was pushing the boy too hard. He understood how desperately she loved Orastes and how terrified she was for his safety, especially after everything that had happened, but surely the boy should be out playing with other kids instead of slashing at enemies with various lethal weapons. Several times, he'd tried persuading Kate to delay Orastes's training until he was a teenager, but she'd screamed at him that the realm was completely unsafe and had refused to hear another word. Saltar couldn't really argue with her, as he knew it was only a matter of time before the kingdom faced yet another threat. He and Mordius had had numerous conversations about the various paradoxes and tensions that underpinned the magic upon which the realm was built – one of those paradoxes was that the magic survived by propagating itself through the living things of the realm, but that those living things also died. The magic tended to unravel as quickly as it was propagated. When in the past the speed of unravelling had become greater than the speed of propagation, the realm would have been undone entirely were it not for the actions of Saltar and his companions. Even then, it was impossible for Saltar to save the realm once and for all, of course. In taking even a partial control of life in the realm in order to preserve it, paradoxically Saltar had restricted its propagation. As a consequence, there were fewer and fewer people left each time he "saved" the realm, which meant the speed of unravelling only increased. It was an erosion that was as inevitable and unstoppable as the tide coming in. It was only a matter of time before the realm found itself threatened once more. Events put in motion and patterns created by enemies of the realm generations or millennia before would increasingly come to fruition sooner rather than later. Saltar considered it fortunate that it had been five years since the last threat. He'd had five years of peace and happiness watching his son grow. It had given him the sort of contentment and self-completion that he'd hardly dared dream of in times past. But how many more years did they have? It could not be many. He knew he had to make the most of these times with Kate and Orastes while he could.

Saltar took a step forward and Orastes became aware of him, for he looked up with a slight frown. Sister Spike's sword clanged down and Orastes dropped his sword.

'I've told you before to focus on the enemy in front of you no matter what else is going on around you!' Sister Spike said with a half smile.

'Either your grip was too tight or you weren't keeping your wrist strong!' Kate said sternly.

Orastes looked distressed. 'The sword's too heavy!'

Kate opened her mouth to retort, but Sister Spike was ahead of her. 'Besides, it's been a long day and we're all tired. Enough for today!'

'Father!' Orastes said in order to displace the attention of his teacher and mother.

Kate turned, only now realising Saltar was there. She glared at him as she then realised that it was he who had distracted Orastes during his weapons practice.

'Milord Battle-leader!' Sister Spike nodded, insisting on the title as always since her temple apparently saw it as some sort of semi-religious rank.

Saltar smiled at the small group. 'Looks like I've arrived just in time to walk you home.' He kissed Kate on the cheek and mussed Orastes's hair.

'Father, don't!' the boy protested.

'Same time tomorrow then,' Kate asked the priestess, although there wasn't much of a question in the way she said it. 'With Mordius away travelling, Orastes doesn't have any of his usual book classes, so he has plenty of time for his weapons practice.'

Sister Spike nodded.

'Father, when *will* Uncle Mordius be home again?'

Saltar felt an unexpected twinge of jealousy at the question, but managed to avoid letting it touch his face. It was only natural that there should be a strong bond between the boy and the magician, for they spent more hours in an average day together than Saltar and his son did. And the relationship was undeniably good for the otherwise withdrawn Orastes, for it meant that he had more than just a teacher in Mordius – he also had a friend and confidant. Saltar searched his own heart and knew he was only jealous because his own relationship with his son had never been so strong – and he feared it never would be. He'd done everything he could, but Orastes was still somehow distant. Saltar sometimes noticed the boy giving him strange looks when he thought there was no one looking.

Mordius had said that Orastes had probably inherited memories from Nylchros of how Saltar had hurt him when his body was possessed, and might even remember Kate killing him! If that were true, then it was no wonder the boy still wet his bed at night and remained wary around his parents. Mordius had tried his best to coax Orastes into telling him about any bad dreams he had, but the boy was always adamant he could not remember them.

'Father?'

Saltar broadened his smile and put his hand gently on Orastes's shoulder. 'Don't worry, he'll be back soon. He's out collecting all sorts of wonderful stories to tell you when he gets back. You like Uncle Mordius's stories, don't you?'

'Oh, yes!' Orastes nodded with a rare show of enthusiasm. 'He has so many. They can't all be true, but they sound like they are. He never really finishes them, you know. He's so funny! He starts one, and then he'll have to explain something in it, which makes him start another story, and then he has to explain something else, so there's another story. Then he forgets where he started and it all ends up a mess, just like my bedroom!'

Saltar chuckled, and even Kate's lips twitched. 'That sounds like Mordius. Tell you what, Orastes, I'll tell you a story tonight when I come and kiss you good night, shall I?'

Orastes looked dubious. 'I guess so. What will the story be about?'

Saltar hesitated. 'It'll be a surprise!'

'I don't think I like surprises,' his son said with a serious little face.

'Ah, I see. Well, how about I tell you a story about the gods?'

'Really?' Orastes asked warily. 'Will it be about Incarnus beating all His enemies? I'm bored of those ones.'

Both women gave Saltar a warning look, one concerned that he might invent blasphemous stories about the god, and the other suspicious that he might encourage Orastes in resisting his combat practice. 'Err… what about a story about Shakri? I've met Her a few times, you know. And the Scourge was Her Consort. I can tell you one of his stories.'

Kate's face darkened.

'What's a consort, father?'

'Err, don't worry about that. Let's start walking and I'll practise the story in my head.'

'Can I run ahead?'

'Sure!' Saltar said indulgently.

Orastes started to run. 'Stay within sight, Orastes!' Kate yelled after him. Then she turned on her husband. 'I never let him run off like that. Corinus isn't safe! He's only seven, Saltar! Honestly, you can be so irresponsible sometimes.'

Saltar groaned inwardly. 'I'm sorry. There are guards everywhere… and he'll stay in sight like you told him. He's a sensible lad.'

'He's a child, Saltar! He can't make decisions for his own safety. We have to do that for him. It's called being a parent!'

Sister Spike cleared her throat awkwardly and excused herself.

Kate marched away after Orastes, leaving Saltar to catch up. As he hurried after his wife and child, he wondered what story he could safely tell Orastes that would not scare him or get Saltar in further trouble with Kate. Then he remembered he was due to meet the Chamberlain later that night. They had an extremely dangerous task to undertake. He just hoped that the bedtime story he told Orastes tonight would not turn out to be the last one he ever told him.

Saltar briefly pondered telling Kate about what he intended, and then decided against it. It seemed the less he said to her these days, the fewer arguments they ended up having.

Mordius cut his thumb and squeezed drops of blood into the bowl of fresh animal blood Larc had provided him. The necromancer then used the tip of his blade to stir the mixture. 'There you are. That's all you need. If you only used your own blood, you wouldn't have enough to practise magic more than a few times in a week. Just that small amount, combined with the magic-user's words of power and binding, will be enough to possess and animate the whole. Alright so far?'

Larc nodded, his brow creased. He'd always been a serious young man, but the nature of the task they currently undertook meant he was even more determined than usual not to miss a word Mordius said.

'Good,' Mordius continued. 'It's important to understand also that neither the designs the magic-user draws on the ground in blood, nor the words he speaks, nor even the blood itself, are intrinsically magical. They simply serve to channel the will and magic of the magic-user. And that magic is drawn from the life-force of the magic-user. That is why anyone casting a spell will be fatigued by it. Therefore, be cautious you do not attempt magic that it is too large for you and that you do not perform too much magic in too short a space of time. It will be the death of you, Larc. Take your time to discover your limits. Even then, continue to be cautious for magic can be intoxicating and seductive. Use it sparingly or before you know it you will be running mad and chanting your life away. Do you understand me?

'Yes, Mordius, I understand you,' Larc replied solemnly. 'From what you say, a practised magic-user will not even require patterns, words and blood to perform magic, is that correct?'

The necromancer smiled. 'Your instincts are good. Theoretically, that would be the case. Once a magic-user becomes truly adept, they should be able to shape their magic in particular ways by habit or as a matter of course. The likes of you and me still need to speak and draw out the patterns because the repetition helps us learn them by rote and gives us the guidance and boundaries we need to organise and construct our magic. Have you brought the book, Larc?'

The young man bobbed his head and pulled a slim volume from within his robes. He had recovered the book of forbidden knowledge five years ago from the very temple of Cognis in which they now stood when it had been desecrated by the blood-mages of the Brethren. Since then, he'd worked at Mordius's behest on deciphering its ancient and cryptic dialect. It had finally begun to give up its secrets to him and he'd written a letter to the necromancer. Mordius, realising the importance of Larc's discoveries, had wasted no time in travelling with Colonel Marr the long distance from Corinus to the small temple in the Needle Mountains. Now, they prepared themselves to try and gain mastery of a dark magic that was new to them.

Larc turned the pages of skin until he found the one that described the magic and provided the necessary diagrams for its completion. As ever, the words and images mazed before his eyes and an ache started in his temples. He ignored the pain and cast a small amount of will in order to see past the magical ward that protected the book. Even so, he was forced to squint at the spidery text on the page. He licked his lips nervously.

'Are we sure we want to do this, Mordius?'

Mordius sighed impatiently but then paused deliberately. It never did to rush at magic, even when it was familiar, let alone when it was uncharted territory. 'We will never be one hundred percent sure, Larc. We are fumbling around in the dark so how can we be sure? There are significant risks. But Saltar has asked us to build a cadre of magicians to help defend the realm in times of need. The names of those in the cadre are known only by Saltar and myself, so that those in the wider group will be protected should just one of our members be discovered by the temples...'

'... unless the temples capture you or Saltar, of course, and force you to give up the names.'

'They wouldn't dare. Besides, Saltar could not be held for long by or in this realm. But you're right. *I* am the weak link. Let's just hope my contacts amongst the temples will keep me safe for the foreseeable future. Very few even know the cadre exists, so we should be alright. You haven't told Sarla anything, have you?'

Larc shook his head. 'The less she knows, the safer she'll ultimately be.'

'Fine. Beyond forming the cadre, though, we must also increase our magical power as a group. Already we have made progress by my passing along what each of us knows, but we're now reaching a point at which we need to master the mortally-derived blood magicks of this realm. Saltar slaughtered all the Brethren blood-mages so there are none from whom we might learn. We have no choice but to search out old texts such as the one you have in your hands and attempt the instructions contained within. Larc, what other choice do we have?'

Larc pulled a face. 'But we're talking about demons here, Mordius. If something were to go wrong...'

'We will put wards in place as an extra precaution. I have faced at least three demons in my time, Larc. In taking on a form and shape in this realm, they are thereby bound by this realm and the magic of whoever conjures them forth. The biggest threat those of the demon realm pose is in the words they use. They have forked tongues and will seek to divide us. They will seek to shape our thoughts and minds, ultimately seek to control us. So we must trust nothing they say. Do not hesitate to do as I tell you, understand?'

Larc assented.

'Good. Larc, I do not undertake this lightly, believe me. But if we can learn to master demons and have them do our bidding, then this realm will be all the safer. Agreed? Then let us begin, before this blood becomes too thick to use.'

Larc looked back at the page where he held the book open and studied it for a second. 'Draw two concentric circles in blood on the floor.'

The small necromancer rolled up the long, wide sleeve of his robe and picked up the brush they'd brought into the small chamber beneath the temple for just this purpose. He frowned.

'How big?'

'Err... well, we'll be standing in the innermost circle of floor, so big enough for the two of us, I guess.'

Mordius worked in silence for several minutes, making sure he painted unbroken lines. Larc stood waiting, shifting his weight from foot to foot.

'What next?'

'Now these six glyphs have to be drawn between the two concentric lines.'

'I can't see them as clearly on the page as you. Can you do it? What are they? Runes?'

'Hmm. The book calls them *houses*. I'm not sure what that means,' Larc admitted as he took the brush, knelt and carefully began to transcribe the symbols.

When he was done, the two of them retreated to the innermost circle.

'Ready?' Mordius asked with only a slight catch in his voice.

'I'll raise wards around each circle,' Larc decided. 'The book says the demon will appear between the concentric lines, you see, so that'll help make sure it remains trapped. You can read the words of conjuration, right?'

'Not really,' Mordius confessed. 'I have to say them, though, because we used my blood for the diagram. You say the words and I'll just repeat after you.'

Larc's hands had become damp with sweat so he wiped them on the front of his robe before concentrating on the book once more. 'Okay, the words here seem to be in a different dialect to the rest of the section in the book, but I think I can make them out.'

He pronounced a few of the words, his syllables guttural and unpleasant to hear.

Mordius grimaced. 'It sounds like the demon-tongue. I've heard it used once or twice in my time. It's all but a physical and mental anathema to those of this realm. Alright, start again and I'll do my best to copy the sounds.'

Larc repeated the words and Mordius mimicked him, having to contort his face in ways that would have been comical on any other occasion. As they progressed, they had to steady each other, for they were both beginning to experience dizziness and nausea. Their eyes and their minds swam. The air became charged with energy and the hairs on their arms began to prickle.

Mordius felt like he was being pulled inside out and was about to call a halt when they were suddenly finished. They looked about but there was nothing to be seen. Everything felt normal and nothing moved.

It was Larc who ended the expectant hush. 'Looks like it didn't work,' he said and moved to step over the line of their circle.

Mordius hurriedly pulled him back. 'Larc, wait!' Then he addressed the air: 'If you are the demon I have conjured here, show yourself to us now!'

There was a snarl of disgust and a thin, grey being made itself visible right before them. Larc jumped and went pale, realising how close he had come to stepping into its clutches. The features of its face were long and pointed, and its slanted orange eyes were slightly feline. It had long, knotted limbs and its hands were large and gnarled. Its fingers ended in sharp, yellow nails which looked like they would have no trouble tearing through flesh. It had pointed teeth and a distended gut hanging over the loin-cloth it wore. The scrap of cloth might have been some sort of trophy rather than intended to hide its modesty, for the end of its member could clearly be seen hanging down below the edge of the material. Although the demon was slightly shorter than both Larc and Mordius, there was no doubt it would be fearsome and deadly in any sort of physical confrontation.

It crouched momentarily as it regarded them from little more than a few feet away, and then sprang screaming at Larc, claws extended and teeth bared. The young magician back-peddled. The demon was suddenly behind him, waiting with hungry anticipation for him to fall out of the circle. Again, it was only Mordius's quick action that saved him.

'Damn it, Larc! Get a grip, would you?'

'Y-Yes, Mordius. I'm sorry... it caught me by surprise.'

The demon tilted its head and narrowed its eyes as it listened to their words.

Mordius faced it. 'Demon, what is your name?'

The grey creature hissed and backed away. 'Do not want to tell!'

'You are bound by my blood and my words. Your must obey those words. Tell me your name!'

The demon wailed in frustration and pain. 'D'lax!'

'Then hear me well, D'lax, for I command you never to harm either myself or my companion. You will make no attempt to harm us. You will do nothing to cause some misadventure to befall us. You will aid no one else in harming us. Do you understand?'

D'lax howled and then sank its fangs into its own forearm. Blood spurted down its chin and it shook its head.

'Speak!'

'Yesss, snivelling mortal! Cursed wizard! Mordius is your name, yes? D'lax would like to eat your liver. Tender but rich, yes?'

'Be silent, D'lax!' Mordius shouted, but there was an edge of horror in his tone.

The demon growled but subsided. It hunkered down and watched them balefully.

'Tell it to close the door,' Larc whispered.

'What?'

'The book says that the door we opened to the demon realm should be closed as soon as one demon has come through, lest others follow it.'

'How do we close it?' Mordius asked in consternation.

'It doesn't say. Ask the demon to do it, maybe?'

'D'lax, close the door to your realm at once!'

The demon grumbled but nodded that it had been done. Then it changed its behaviour. Its eyes became doleful, it whined plaintively and it crouched as small as it could.

'What's wrong with it?' Larc asked with concern.

Mordius frowned. 'I'm really not sure. It seems afraid or in pain. D'lax, what ails you? Speak!'

'D'lax not like it here!' the demon whimpered. 'Trapped. Prisoner. D'lax will get nice things for masters if masters will let D'lax go. D'lax can get gold for the masters. Would the masters like gold, yes?'

'We do not want gold,' Mordius said sternly, not about to let this demon flatter or bribe him.

A cunning look came over D'lax's face and he whispered: 'Then the master Mordius might want a woman that loves him, yes? D'lax knows where to find such a woman. D'lax can bring her here. And Larc wants a child, yes? I can bring you a potion to help you have a child. But the masters must let D'lax go so D'lax can get these things for the masters.'

'Be silent, D'lax!' Mordius ordered the demon, his cheeks red with embarrassment.

'Do you think it could…'

'No!' Mordius said harshly to the younger man. 'Love and fertility are the domain of Shakri alone in this realm. The demon lies, Larc. I've already warned you about this. Close your ears to it or it will pour poison in.'

'But I have prayed to Shakri and nothing came from it.'

'Larc, enough!' Mordius snapped. A wave of tiredness swept over him and he was forced to close his eyes for a second or two. What was wrong with him? He'd expected some fatigue immediately after casting the spell but what he was experiencing now was something else. While the magic of his blood kept the demon captive, would it continue to drain him of life-force? If so, the longer they bandied words with the tricksy demon, the greater the risk they were running to themselves. Mordius looked more closely at Larc to see if he was suffering as a consequence of having to keep the wards in place. The youngster's eyes were unfocussed and his face was slack as he spoke.

'If D'lax can help then maybe we should let him do so. He has promised not to harm us, after all.'

Mordius grabbed Larc by the arms and shook him. Then he drew back his hand and slapped Larc smartly across the cheek. 'The demon is planting suggestions in your head. Ward your mind, Larc. Now! Come back to yourself.'

'D-Don't know how,' Larc mumbled.

One of Mordius's knees buckled and it was all he could do to hold on to Larc's robe to prevent himself falling across the boundary of the circle. His tongue thick in his mouth and his lips becoming numb, he looked towards the drooling demon. 'D'lax you will return to the demon realm at once and close the door behind you as soon as you arrive there.'

D'lax gnashed its teeth and howled its rage but was suddenly gone. One last thought came to them out of the air: 'D'lax will see you again soon, Mordius. We will have your liver before your very eyes. There are those hunting you in Shakri's realm. And you have eternal enemies in the demon realm. Watch for us, little wizard, for we will be coming. The demon realm is rising!'

Everything became still once more. Mordius collapsed where he was, uncaring that he smeared the lines on the floor. He panted for long minutes until he regained enough strength to raise his head and look round blearily.

Larc had sat down near the necromancer's feet. His head hung, his long hair curtaining his face. But the way he shook his head from time to time, and the way his shoulders were slumped, made it clear that is was also taking him some time to recover.

'That was *too* close,' Mordius observed.

Larc's head lolled up and down. 'Sneaky buggers those demons. Do you really think we could master one of them completely?'

'Well, we'd be better prepared next time. We'd have spent time planning the instructions we gave it. And I'd have taught you how to ward your mind in advance. I wonder if there's something in the book about the basic precautions a magic-user should take when conjuring a demon.'

'I'll keep studying it. What do you think…'

'Are you two in there?' came a shrill voice from outside the door.

'It's Sarla. She sounds worried,' Larc said immediately. He wasted no time getting to his feet and opening the door. 'Sarla, what's wrong?'

The high priestess of Cognis came breathlessly into the room. She wrung her hands. The bottoms of her white robes were muddy – she'd clearly hurried here rather than lifting the material and making her way carefully. Her bottom lip trembled. 'It's young Balkin. They found him lying broken at the bottom of Windhollow Cliff. They say he still breathes. You two are better at healing than me. But we must hurry.'

'Not Balkin!' Larc groaned but quickly pulled himself together. 'You two go on ahead. I have to get my bag of medicines. I'll catch you up. Go!'

They hurried from the room and up the stairs. Colonel Marr was waiting for them and joined Sarla and Mordius as Larc headed for his workroom. The group ran towards the stone path that led to the Brethren community. Dusk was falling but there were still a few rays of the sun to see by, and the moon was already up.

Unused to such exertion, and still weak from his confrontation with the demon, Mordius hardly had breath to ask, 'Who's Balkin?'

'He's one of the young men of the Brethren,' Sarla said over her shoulder. 'A hard-working and enthusiastic man who has done so much to help us rebuild. His loss will be devastating to the community. We must do whatever we can to save him, Mordius.'

'Did he fall, do you think?' the Colonel asked.

Sarla did not hesitate in her answer. 'I cannot believe it. The Brethren know every stone on this mountain and are more sure-footed than their goats. The Brethren children are climbing rocks before they can walk.'

'Then… then has he been unhappy of late?' Mordius wheezed. 'Rejected by a girl, perhaps?'

Sarla shook her head. 'Don't even suggest such a thing, Mordius. Balkin is full of life and has a constant appetite for it. He and Isa have been promised to each other since they were children. They love each other, anyone can see that. Word is that Balkin has started building a home for them and intends to ask her father for her hand once the house is complete.'

'There must be some other agency at work then.'

'It is a terrible thought, but I can see no other explanation,' Sarla agreed, her voice pained. 'And this is the third person lost in as many months.'

'Third!' the Colonel and Mordius exclaimed together.

Sarla nodded, massaging a stitch in her side. 'The first two looked like accidents. One was old Jess and the other was a young girl when the rocks were wet with rain. But I do not believe even holy Wim could cause Balkin to have an accident on the rocks. He would not have jumped, Mordius, believe me. And he enjoys this time of year so much, gathering in the mountain crops, looking forward to the visit from Lucius and Jack each year. We all look forward to that.'

'Hang on a minute!' Mordius said, bringing them all to a stop. 'Do you mean to tell me you've been getting visits from those two up here all along?'

'Come on!' Sarla said urgently and got them moving again. 'Of course we've had visits. Have none of us mentioned it before? It was never worth making an issue of, I suppose. Mordius, keep up, won't you?'

The necromancer's breath was becoming laboured. 'You two go on. I'll follow on as I can. Don't worry about me, I know the way. Go on!'

After a last hesitation, the high priestess and the army officer moved ahead of the flagging magician. Mordius leaned against a standing boulder for a moment or two to catch his breath and then started trudging forward again. Perhaps he should have insisted on riding his horse to the Brethren community – it would have meant taking a more roundabout route, rather than the direct one the locals used over sharp ridges and steep-sided canyons, but at least it would have guaranteed his arriving in some semblance of good order. The way he felt now, he wasn't sure he'd ever arrive.

The path took his upwards into the Needle Mountains and he slowed even further. It wasn't long before he was having to avoid looking at the dizzying drop off to his right. He'd quickly lost sight of Sarla and Colonel Marr, so had no one to distract him or give him reassurance. He schooled his thoughts though and pushed on. He had to remind himself he was no longer the timid man he'd once been.

The wind gusted around him, buffeting towards the edge. He pulled in tighter to the wall, even though that meant the path was less well trodden and less even underfoot. And then darkness descended around him. The air was suddenly so thick and murky that he could hardly see his own feet anymore. Where had the Shakri-cursed moon gone? He turned about, looking for it, but lost his orientation. His hand had lost touch with the wall and he stretched out in all directions but found nothing.

'Hello!' he called, trying to hear where the sound disappeared with the drop in one direction and echoed back with the wall in the other. Nothing. His voice was dead and flat in his ear, as if he was in the confined space of a coffin.

He slid his left foot along the ground one pace, but found no obvious change in the surface. Don't panic, Mordius!

A blue light bobbed into view off to the right and he sighed in relief and took a deep calming breath to try and slow his fluttering heart.

'Larc! The gods be praised.'

Mordius's immediate impulse was to walk straight for the light, but some other instinct made him resist the urge. You're not a moth, Mordius.

'Larc, is that you?'

The blue light swung back and forth, but came no closer.

'Answer me!'

The light moved up and down, as if he was being waved on.

'Either answer me or you come to me! I daren't move.'

The willow-wisp hesitated for a second, as if debating with itself, and then slowly zigzagged away, leaving Mordius all alone in the pall. He crouched down where he was, too scared to move and realising he would have to stay like this until morning. The phantom light had seemed some unnatural agency. All he could hear were D'lax's words: 'The demon realm is rising.'

Chapter Three: Weapons of the gods

Vidius's chest spasmed and he coughed flecks of blood into his hand. He tasted the unpleasant tang of metal in the back of his throat. It would be harder and harder to sustain this mortal body in the demon realm, yet he must seek to preserve it for as long as possible, to prevent his true self from being revealed and word getting to the Princes before he was ready. He would need to devour an imp or gremlin soon or his mortal frame would expire. Unfortunately, the denizens of the third sphere were almost impossible to catch unawares and moved as quickly as thought. Worse than that, there was nothing else here he could eat, as the tiresome sprites had burnt everything, from plant to peaty earth, during their nighttime revels.

He staggered over one strength-sapping ash dune after another. His progress was slow and he knew he wouldn't be able to make it to the barrier to the fourth sphere in his current state. As he topped a particularly high dune and began his descent, something clipped his heels and he went sprawling forwards. He landed on his hands and face. Clouds of powdery ash blinded him. He spat again and again to clear his mouth. He struggled back onto his feet and his trews fell down to his knees. Someone had loosened his belt without him noticing.

Swallowing his instinctive anger, he forced himself to smile. He faked a chuckle and then started to howl like a loon. He sat down holding his stomach as if it hurt because he was laughing so hard. He presented a man possessed and helpless with mirth. As he'd expected, it proved too much of a temptation for the local imps and they materialised around him and capered with glee.

A few rolled around in a parody of his own plight and it was those he watched more closely than the others because they occasionally came within his reach or had their backs to him. Most of the imps were around two feet tall and had thick black hides. They had lithe, agile bodies and unusually long fingers. Their eyes were red, green or orange – or a mismatched combination of those colours – and shone with an eager intelligence. One or two of them had more brightly coloured skin and short leathery wings which – even if they could not carry their entire weight for long – allowed them to leap and hop further than the others.

Seeing a chance, Vidius lunged for one of the imps. One of the others squeaked a warning and as a group all the creatures winked out. Vidius was left clutching nothing but air. There were hoots of derision and sniggers from the air around him. They'd clearly only appeared to him in order to taunt him. Still, their success was likely to mean they wouldn't be able to resist trying it again. And next time, he would have some tricks of his own up his sleeve.

He rose again and shuffled forwards on shaking legs. The body that transported him felt at one moment light, as it was so frail, and at the other heavy, because it was so tired. His head and thoughts were vague, his feet dragging and dense. He was stretched thin across the full spectrum of being, his mind a wayward wisp but his steps as final and doom-laden as the sounding of the bell at the end of time. The shallow troughs of his footprints were the words of judgement that would finally be passed upon his existence. Here it ended.

A wide, wide river blocked his path. It stretched to the far horizon both to the left and right. The ash-polluted, stygian waters flowed so quickly that he had no hope of being able to wade or swim across, especially in his weakened condition.

He looked around dully. The sky was a uniform slate grey and further drained any colour or shade from the landscape, meaning it was next to impossible to discern any depth to what he saw or any distinctive features within the geography. He hardly recognised what he saw, unable to distinguish object from shadow. There was simply no sharp relief. For that reason, he didn't see the wide hole in the ground until he'd slipped half way down it, twisting his knee in the process.

He'd fallen into the waiting mouth of an imp warren. He tried scrambling back up the sides of the hole, but the powder refused him purchase and he found himself further into the gullet of the devouring maw. He decided to have it swallow him whole, as that way he'd at least be in one piece and have a fighting chance once inside the belly of the beast. Vidius pushed off and shot straight down into darkness.

The deeper he went, the more compacted the ash became, until the cushion under him disappeared and he was eventually brought to a halt. The walls around him seemed made of a coal-like substance. The roof was propped up by the giant bones of creatures he did not recognise, and a thick substance dripped and oozed from cracks in the ceiling. Was it water seeping down from above? Hadn't the tunnel led off in the right direction to take him under the river? Although the huge bones were largely white, a fur of some sort – either algae or moss – seemed to be growing on them and phosphorescing just enough for him to see by. Everything had a sickly green tinge to it, as if even the rock could rot and putrefy in this place. Then the thought occurred to him that he might actually be in the gut of a leviathan. The walls might be its petrified flesh, and the trickling liquid its black blood. He dipped a finger in the ichor and found it burnt as if it were a stomach acid there to digest him. Could this colossus have been stranded on the riverbank or on a long island? Had the path of the river changed at some point so that now it flowed, like time, straight over the beast in its living grave? Was it the imps and gremlins who had snared the creature and dragged it out of its natural element?

His mind was definitely wandering. How had he decided some dirty water was blood and these walls were the fleshy sides of a massive, sea entity? How had he come to imagine these bones amongst which he walked were the ribs of an outsized, mouldering carcass? And what did it even matter if he was inside a dying leviathan that the imps and gremlins had captured?

He repeated that last question to himself. What did it even matter? There was a time when he would hardly have understood such a question. *How* could it matter? In the past, he would have shrugged and said the leviathan didn't deserve life if it was not fit enough to survive in this realm. So why did he dwell on such a question now? Had his time in the mortal realm made him so sentimental? Since when had he worried over the death or suffering of another creature? Such a moral dynamic was the quickest route to fear, capitulation and self-defeat, he knew. So why the preoccupation? Then he had it: he must be projecting his own mortal body's angst onto his surroundings. Yes, it was his own body that was dying, and so he saw everything else through such eyes.

Vidius sighed with relief. He had enough problems without having to deal with such self-diminishing doubt. It *didn't* matter if he was in a leviathan. His stomach growled, but he knew his body lacked the strength to rend or digest the material of the walls. And the water was poison to his system anyway.

Then the stone stomach in which he stood growled. It echoed all around him. Dozens of small hands with sharp claws pulled and grabbed at him. In a trice, his hands were bound together, as were his feet, and he was slung under a pole. The beam was carried between two large imps and they marched him further underground.

The acoustics of the place changed and he realised they'd moved into a wider space. There was a fire up ahead – he was carried over to it and then placed above it. They meant to roast him!

He looked around frantically. At the edge of the light and half in the darkness, imps and gremlins cavorted and licked their lips, pointing at him and then their mouths, finally rubbing their bellies. The largest of the imps and the gremlin boss came forward. They tore his clothes off him. Then they began to baste him with oil.

Vidius laughed nervously. 'You don't know what a relief this is for me. I was so worried that you'd all rush through into the second sphere once I'd left the door open. If that had happened, then I'd have had no one to come to an arrangement with for the protection of my gold.'

All the sprites suddenly hushed, then they began to whisper animatedly amongst themselves.

'You tell Ton about the door!' the large imp demanded.

'And tell Crag about the gold!' the gremlin boss grinned manically.

'If I die on this fire, it won't be so bad, I suppose,' Vidius conceded. 'At least I'll finally be free of the curse. And it amuses me that whoever eats me will take on the curse in turn.'

Crag's face fell. 'Get it off the fire, Ton, quick, at once! Before it is dead and crispy!'

'Where are you going?' Ton shouted as the imps and the gremlins around them began to slip away. 'Crag, what shall we do? They will get to the second sphere first and gobble up all the elementals. There will be nothing left for us.'

'Quiet, dullard imp! The secret of the gold will still be ours. Get it off the fire!'

Vidius could smell the hairs on his body singeing. His flesh was becoming painfully hot. Come on, you cretins!

'What if some have run to the Imp Queen to tell her of the gold, Crag? She will surely reward them.' Ton leered. 'Perhaps we should tell our beautiful Queen of the gold ourselves. She might let us take turns, and maybe watch.'

Vidius started to scream in agony.

'To-o-o-o-n! Get-it-off-the-fire-now-time-at-once-and-faster!'

'What? Oh, yes! It smells good, though,' Ton drooled.

Crag slapped Ton on the side of his head, but the heavy-skulled imp hardly seemed to notice. The gremlin boss shouldered him aside and hefted one end of the pole off its tripod. Vidius fell into the flames and glowing coals but was quickly rolled out by Crag. Cold water was sloshed down on him and he lay there gasping in relief, disbelief and shock.

Crag sighed. 'Alright, Ton, pick it up and drag it this way. Let's see if we can please or seduce the Queen.'

Suddenly focussed, Ton did exactly as Crag told him.

※ ▓

The Imp Queen was flame red in colour. Her long tail was wrapped twice around her middle, forming a girdle. Its tip was never still and constantly flicked at the nipples of the four pairs of breasts hanging down her front. Her tongue echoed the tip and flickered in and out of her mouth as she tasted the air.

She stretched languorously and her throne shifted around her. Vidius was amazed as he realised the seat was made of living imps who worked unceasingly to keep the Queen raised up.

The Queen smiled seductively at Vidius and then winked. Her tongue ran over her generous lips and small, sharp teeth. There was something horribly venal about her that fascinated Vidius, but he was a long way short of finding her attractive. The same could not be said of those who attended the Queen, for most of them stood slack-jawed as they gazed at her. A few whined, a few drooled and a few grabbed at their crotches.

Vidius looked sideways at Crag, who was the sharpest sprite he'd come across so far, but Crag's eyes were as wide and obsessed as those of all the others. Vidius considered it fortunate he was not affected by the Queen's magic, for no one could ever afford to lose their wits in the demon realm.

'You!' the Queen purred, pointing at Ton. 'Release the mortal.'

Ton whimpered with pleasure and almost tripped over himself in his haste to please her. In a matter of seconds, Vidius was torn free and standing on his unsteady feet.

'Thank you, Your Highness,' Vidius murmured as he bent into a bow and averted his eyes.

'Rise, dear mortal, and tell us why they have brought you here. My faithful servants currently find themselves at a loss, I'm afraid, so you will need to explain on their behalf. Tell me, how is it that a mortal comes to be in the demon realm?'

'I had heard of Your Majesty's great beauty and consequently knew my life an incomplete and ugly thing. What else could I do but set out on this holy quest?' Then he smiled ruefully. 'Plus, I was cursed and exiled by my own people. I managed to take much of my gold with me and bribe my way to your court. I would but beg to be presented to the gatekeeper of the next barrier so that I might attempt to win through to the fourth sphere and retrieve wonderful gifts for you, Your Majesty. I am ashamed that I have nothing to present now.'

She smiled knowingly at him. 'Your tongue is as quick and cunning as any I have come across, mortal. Mmm, come across indeed. Your sweet words tickled and flirted with my ear. You are eager to pleasure me, it seems. Perhaps you have something to gift and present to me right now despite your coy presentation. Here then is my decision: I will allow you to progress to the barrier once you have serviced me.'

Vidius almost choked on his tongue. This was most certainly not what he had expected.

'B-B-B...' he stuttered.

The Queen tittered. Her tail began to uncoil from around her. Its end beckoned him towards her.

'M-Majesty, you honour me more than I can say! I f-fear I will not have the strength to go to the lengths my mind and heart so desire. I have not eaten since entering this sphere.'

The Queen smiled indulgently. 'You!' she commanded of one of the smallest imps in the royal chamber. 'Rip yourself open and offer yourself to my paramour.'

The demon within Vidius was already salivating. He threw himself on the ecstatic victim and buried his face in its viscera. He lost all mortal sense of self and gulped down gobbets and strips of flesh. Hardly satiated, he glared around him.

'Mmm. I love a healthy appetite,' the Queen crooned. 'Come to me now,' she urged and pushed her hips forward.

There was nothing to be gained in denying her. He went to her, paying the onlookers no mind, and she sank her claws into his hair and scalp.

'That's it!' she hissed in pleasure. 'Give me your seed so that I may have offspring with a soul!' Her back arched and she shuddered in delight.

✄ ✄

With his back torn to shreds, a broken rib and what felt like two black eyes, Vidius had been dumped at the feet of the gatekeeper to the fourth sphere. The gryphon stared down at him quizzically and prodded him with its beak.

Vidius groaned and slowly got up. He could not stand straight because of his injuries. The gatekeeper squawked impatiently.

'Forgive me!' Vidius mumbled through swollen lips. 'I am a mortal and weak in this realm. However, I have something beyond value. A soul!'

The gryphon reared back its eyes wide and then intense and shining. It ducked its head, approximating a nod.

'Gatekeeper, allow me through the door, allow the door to be left open, allow those of the fourth sphere through and my soul will be yours upon my return.'

The gryphon's head tilted left, then right, as it considered him. It extended its wings and shook them.

Vidius refused to be cowed by its display of strength. 'Make your choice, gatekeeper! Remain fettered to this role for the rest of eternity, or let me pass and ultimately win physical and spiritual freedom for yourself. Would you not wish to ride the cosmic winds of both the inner and outer universes?'

The gryphon screeched its defiance of the Princes of the demon realm and pushed the heavy stone door to the fourth sphere open. Vidius stepped through and did not look back – he was too busy watching for the immediate dangers with which the sphere of gargoyles would confront him.

He'd emerged onto an exposed and dangerously steep slope. In fact, it was so steep and loose that he struggled to keep his footing. There was nowhere obvious that was level in the vicinity... except the bottom of the slope far below him. He was on the side of a needle-like peak, just one of the many he could see all around him. All the rock was dark grey or black. There was a watery sun that did little to lighten the depressed sky... so perhaps it was a moon instead. That might explain why even the thin grass and moss on some of the slopes also looked black and grey: he was seeing everything in a world of twilight rather than daylight. He noticed his skin was grey too, although he wasn't sure that was down to the current light conditions or his ill health.

To avoid sliding down to oblivion, he took a hold on some hardy tufts of grass and crouched low. He plucked some grass and moss and chewed on it experimentally – after all, who knew if he'd get the chance to eat anything else in this sphere? The stuff tasted of ash and charcoal. He forced it down but decided against having any more just yet. He didn't want to be throwing up the imp he'd had not so long ago.

He peered more closely at the spires around him. They were quiet and had an almost peaceful air, like a cathedral he'd seen in Accros once. Yes, it was as if he were amongst a host of cathedral spires. Then he spied a gargoyle sitting statue-like atop one of them. Despite the bestial cast to its features and the giant wings coming out of its powerful shoulders and back, it was largely humanoid in form.

Vidius knew very little of this race of demon, for the gargoyles had always kept themselves to themselves and, during the founding of the demon realm, somehow avoided warring with the other races. Their aggression had never been as overt nor their ambition as naked as that of the others. They might have had a *house* of their own if they'd but been wilful enough to force the issue or to create the opportunity. Still, in securing the fourth sphere for themselves, they hadn't fared that badly when all was said and done. They must have made shrewd alliances for themselves. Clearly, they were not stupid. He would need to exercise far more caution and cunning with the gargoyles than he had with the imps and gremlins.

He looked again and the gargoyle he'd seen before was gone. He hadn't seen or heard it leave. The hairs on the back of his neck rose – something that moved so stealthily would have no trouble sneaking up on him. It could be rushing up on him even now, gliding down on silent wings to snatch him up or throw him off the mountain. Is that how they tended to kill their prey – by hurling them down to the rocks below? The gargoyle would then be able to descend at its leisure to feast on the broken, tenderised body of its victim.

The wind moaned behind him and he instinctively ducked. His nerves jangling, he took a few hurried steps downslope, which became a slide of ten or so metres and saw him picking up speed rapidly. He only managed to save himself from a sudden drop by throwing his stomach onto a jagged outcropping of rock without any idea if it would hold his weight. His broken rib protested at the stunt and he found it now hurt him just to breathe. But at least he *was* still breathing.

He realised that if he didn't calm down and start thinking with a clearer head, then he'd end up doing the gargoyle's job for it. Is that what it had hoped for all along? Was it trying to intimidate him, trying to instil enough fear in him so that he would end up precipitating his own death? Why else would it have let him see it in the first place, for he was sure it would only be seen if it wanted to be seen? He imagined the gargoyle wouldn't know what sort of threat Vidius himself might pose, and therefore it might prefer a more subtle attack or test than a full on assault.

He started to make his way down the slope again, but this time he took more time and made sure each foot was properly planted before he put his full weight on it. From time to time, an unnatural movement of air came to him and told him that another living thing had just passed close by. He ignored it and stayed concentrated on making his way safely down. Then the leathery snap of wings sought to startle him, but he paid it no mind.

His lower back, knees and ankles aching, he finally descended onto the lower slopes. It was clear where the descent finished, because slopes and angles from all the different peaks were jumbled together. It was a weird analogy, but he felt like he was traversing a giant pack of cards that had been dropped from a great height.

He'd hoped he'd be able to find water once down from the heights, but the place was apparently dry. He'd step down into a promising v-shaped gully made by the meeting of two slanting planes, only to find that it ended in a sheer, vertical wall or a fall-away that was too difficult a drop for him to hazard. None of the features here showed evidence of having been formed by water, which begged the question how the grass and moss he'd found before had grown. Did it ever rain here? If so, where were the water channels that would have been formed by the run off? Perhaps there was enough water in the air instead to enable basic plant life, which meant there must be a large body of water somewhere that the wind travelled across in order to pick up the moisture.

He shrugged. All realities needed a logic of sorts. Who was to say the laws of life of the sphere of the gargoyles were the same as in the other spheres? Perhaps the grass and moss he'd eaten hadn't even been alive in the way he understood it. Perhaps life and death were inverted here. The grass and moss had certainly tasted like the petrified form of life long since gone. What did that say of the gargoyles then? He wasn't sure if this debate he was having with himself was of any significance or value whatsoever, or whether it gave him key insight into the nature of this sphere.

One thing he did know for sure was that he was lost. He could not even recognise which peak he'd come down. The twisted chaos of the terrain had him completely turned round. He had no way of being sure whether he was heading towards the barrier to the fifth sphere or back towards the third. He sighed, accepting that he'd eventually find out one way or another.

He followed his nose and then stopped. Crouched at the top of a slope ahead of him was a large, grey-skinned gargoyle glaring down at him with shining golden eyes. Its wings were folded behind it but towered so high they must have a span of at least two dozen feet.

Vidius hesitated. Should he flee or was it trying to intimidate him like the one before? Would he end up running over a hidden edge if he dashed back along the most obvious route behind him?

'Do you seek to prevent me progressing forward?' he shouted, his words echoing. 'I must pass through this sphere to the next.'

The gargoyle did not respond, did not move. Vidius did not know what to do, so chose to do nothing instead. He crouched where he was and waited.

Finally, the gargoyle rolled its head on its neck, rolled its mighty shoulders and flexed the muscles on its torso. It stood, turned and began to walk away. Vidius knew that it chose not to fly so that he would be able to keep up. Even so, the injuries of his mortal body meant he found the going extremely arduous. He wondered how much longer it would last.

Vidius followed the gargoyle into the wide, low entrance of a cave. The roof disappeared upwards almost immediately. The space was vast – a whole village or small town could have fit inside. Gargoyles festooned every spare piece of space – they roosted on ledges along the walls, by pools in the floor and atop old stalagmites. There should have been a terrible stench, what with so many bodies living in the same area, but there was nothing.

There was hardly any noise or movement either. They all watched him with their large, glowing eyes. It was more than uncanny: it was terrifying. He couldn't fathom these creatures at all.

The gargoyle he was following was the largest amongst them. They shuffled aside as he moved through the cave, Vidius in his wake. After ten minutes or so, they reached a point that was close to the centre. The gargoyle stopped and looked up at a small crag in front of them. Unlike the rest of the cave, this rock was free of gargoyles, all except one.

A small, wizened creature gazed down at Vidius, eyes red and rheumy with age. Its skin had lost whatever pigment it may once have had – it was now a translucent film that kept its innards in the right place. Disconcertingly, Vidius could see substances shifting within it and its heart clenching and unclenching. Its arms were so withered that it was probably only its clawed hands hooked into the rock that kept the limbs raised and the fragile body in place. The way its wings lay tattered and forlorn about it suggested it hadn't flown in a very long time. The way its cheeks and eyes were so sunken made its ears and nose look ridiculously large.

Vidius bowed deeply.

'What brings a mortal here?' came the wizened gargoyle's scratchy voice. 'And can you really be what you appear? No ordinary mortal would be able to come so far.'

Yes, the gargoyles were far shrewder than the imps. Mere blandishment and flattery would not suffice here. 'As you can see, great one, my journey has left me far from unscathed.'

The gargoyle did not answer. It waited for him to say more. Vidius cursed silently.

'Wise one, I seek access to the fifth sphere.'

Still they waited, the unblinking eyes of a gallery of thousands fixed on him. There was nowhere to run, nowhere to hide. It was hard to stay calm, hard to stay in control of himself. Once again, their predatory gaze threatened to be his undoing.

'I-I have… a message to carry there. I was sent b-by a demon called Jack O'Nine Blades. I am not to reveal this message to anyone else, but offer reward to all those who will help me.'

'You underestimate us.'

Vidius froze. Did the elder know him for a liar? Or were the elder's words a type of bluff and lie themselves? The large gargoyle behind him tightened one of his taloned hands into a fist and the sound of his knuckles cracking was the sound of rocks breaking.

Vidius's mind raced. Where were his own cunning and inventiveness all of a sudden? It was time to see if a few half-truths could save him. 'This humble creature could never truly appreciate one of such wisdom, great one. If I offend, then it is my nature that offends rather than my intent. Jack O'Nine Blades also commanded me to leave the doors to as many spheres as I could wide open, but why I do not know.'

That revelation did not gain Vidius as much reaction as he'd hoped, but at least it elicited a response from the elder. 'You are either extremely foolish or extremely dangerous. The fact that you have won your way through to the fourth sphere suggests you are dangerous. Tell me, mortal – if that is what you are – should we fear you?'

The old devil was not about to let Vidius off the hook. How could he answer such a question without revealing more than he wanted? 'I think, most perceptive one, I must have had extreme fortune. I met very few of the denizens of the previous spheres, and those that I did were eager to aid Jack O'Nine Blades, almost afraid of him.'

The gargoyle observed Vidius through slitted eyes. 'And the gatekeepers were eager to aid this demon too? What reward was offered them?'

Curse this wretch. It was going to force his hand. 'I offered them nothing specific. Most seemed to have heard of Jack O'Nine Blades. Just his name and promise of some unspecified reward seemed to be enough.'

The old homunculus grunted and then a stinking liquid sprayed down on Vidius. It was urinating on him! The gargoyles around him rose as one, their talons extending, wings flaring.

Vidius tensed, knowing he would only get one opportunity – yet there would certainly be an opportunity, for the gargoyles had arrayed themselves around the centre in an imperfect pattern. As much as they tried to behave in concert, as much as they studied form, movement and agency, the gargoyles tried too hard to mimic perfection. Rather than embracing their own imperfection and operating to the limits of their effectiveness, they attempted the impossible and guaranteed their own failure. They had forced this confrontation that doomed them to imperfection and a similar failure.

If they hadn't bothered attempting unity, and had instead simply sent three or four for him at once, they would have found him out. As it was, there were so many of them that they got in each other's way and collided with one another in their attempts to reach him.

Vidius crouched. Wait. Wait! A gargoyle about the size of Vidius was bumped so that it was half turned away from him. The demon beat strongly with its wings to pull itself free and Vidius leapt. He flung his arms around the demon's neck and it only just managed to get off the ground. It flapped frantically and they rose a few feet.

The largest of the gargoyles battered others aside in a bid to get to him. Vidius and the demon he hung from rose a few more feet. Come on! The large gargoyle slashed at them but Vidius kicked the lethal talons away. A few more feet. The giant reared back, gathered himself and then came forward with dreadful power.

Vidius threw himself at the small crag and cried out as his broken rib impacted with the rock. His fingers spasmed and for a second he thought he would fall. But at the last moment he managed to find a grip. Immediately he started to drag himself up through the agony.

Countless gargoyles dived for him. He could feel the breath of their rage and intent on the back of his neck. He landed his hand heavily on the shoulder and neck of the screeching elder, wrenched it from its seat and held it out for all to see.

'I will kill it!' Vidius shouted. 'Get back!'

The gargoyle host howled impotently, forced to hold itself in check. Those in the air pulled up sharply and then tumbled and spiralled to the floor as those rushing in behind injured them. Vidius shook the now mewling elder in their faces.

'Oh, be quiet! I bet you haven't seen this much excitement in eons. Anyone would think you're something other than demonkind, the way you carry on. I've told you the doors to the lower levels are open, so you should all be rushing to ravage those spheres rather than remaining here and making things unnecessarily difficult for me. What is it? Have you convinced yourselves you have some higher ideal or goal? Is that what unifies you and keeps you here for this pathetic scrap of flesh I hold in my hand? Do you not see that you will all end up like this broken creature if you follow its path and teachings.'

A number of the gargoyles towards the back of the host subsided and glanced uncertainly at each other. Those to the fore, those most loyal to the elder, still bristled with talons and fangs.

'So be it,' Vidius shrugged. 'You, Big Head, lead me to the gatekeeper. I will then give up the elder unharmed.'

The giant lieutenant snarled, gestured with one hand and turned away. Vidius made his way down and went after him. Against the far wall of the gargoyle cave was a stone sphinx.

The gatekeeper's eyes cracked open upon their approach. It yawned in exaggerated fashion and shook its mane. It had a bland, human face but the powerful body of a supine lion. Vidius waved the lieutenant away with an admonishing shake of the withered elder.

'None may pass until they have answered my riddle,' the creature intoned.

'I don't have time for this. The answer's *a man*. Now, open the door.'

The sphinx did not look happy. 'I had not asked, so you have answered nothing. I will have to think of another riddle. It may take some time.'

Vidius sighed. 'Look, I will give you this elder if you open the way and leave the door open for others to come through. When did you last eat?'

The gatekeeper licked its lips. 'I must admit, it was some time ago. The magic of the Princes means I do not need to, but I do miss it. It would be an indulgence, however. It is not enough for me to betray my role.'

'Then let me give you a reason to do so, sphinx. I have seen others of your kind.'

The sphinx's eyes widened. 'That is not possible. I saw them all destroyed when demonkind warred across the heavens. I am the last of the sphinkaes. I am content with my eternal role as gatekeeper.'

'Then perhaps you are unaware that the image of the sphinx is a common architectural and artistic device in the mortal realm. There is no doubt that some of your kind found their way there at some time. There is no reason why they would not still be alive. And there is a rumour, sphinx.'

The sphinx could not contain its curiosity. 'Tell me.'

'They say there are sphinkaes on the island of Jaffra and that they are worshipped. You could join them. The way to the first sphere is clear. When I return, my servants will open the door to the mortal realm. Think! The sphinkaes will be a force to be reckoned with once more. You can eat, procreate and rule! Or would you prefer to remain here as some living statue?'

'Give me the gargoyle then, mortal, for you have whetted my appetite and I must have my strength if I am to give up the protections of the Princes. Shall I spare you some morsel? You are looking weak yourself.'

'Thank you, yes.'

They began to devour the elder while it still lived. The gargoyles cried out in despair, but the gatekeeper's magic prevented them from approaching. Vidius picked a last shred of flesh from between his teeth and then prepared to enter the sphere of the demons proper.

⋈ ⋈

'They're here! The bump at the back of my head's itching.'

'Perhaps you've got fleas,' Strap supplied.

The Scourge ignored him and looked down the main street of the hamlet of Windrun. The way had been churned to mud by the passage of horses and wagons, but there was no one in evidence now. There wasn't even a dog to welcome them with a growl or bark. 'They're either all dead or they're all at the inn listening to the demon's music.'

'Perhaps they all saw us coming and are hiding until we go away and let them get on with their lives.' Strap watched the Scourge closely, wondering if he'd come too close to the bone with that last comment. Yet neither humour nor insult could elicit a significant reaction from the Old Hound. Strap was a storm howling outside a sound and tightly-shuttered fortress. Or a child ignored by a tired parent.

The Scourge rubbed at his long-unshaven chin. 'That's a good point. They might be waiting to ambush us. We shouldn't underestimate the demon's influence. Watch the windows carefully. These woodsmen know how to shoot an arrow or two. Perhaps we should circle round the town rather than ride through it, but if they're already in the woods around us, then at least the houses will afford us some cover.'

With that, the Scourge squeezed with his legs and his large, black destrier moved forwards with a snort. 'You may follow or not, as you choose.'

Strap sighed and rode forwards. He removed the cover from his bow and loosely nocked an arrow to it. With the Scourge in such a paradoxically remote but intent mood, there was bound to be some violence in the offing.

They passed the hamlet's trading house. Rich furs and fine skins were piled up outside, under the porch and on the well-maintained street boards.

The house was solidly built and even proudly bore some carvings of weights, balances, animals and grain, to show its purpose. Clearly, the house was a thriving business. In fact, despite the muddy street, the entire hamlet of Windrun looked to be well-maintained, proud and thriving. Strap couldn't help feeling he and the Scourge were about to bring chaos to harmony, pain where there had been happiness, death to the living. He hadn't become a Guardian for this. Surely they shouldn't be here, shouldn't be doing this.

But he couldn't abandon the Scourge. Not for the first time, he fought against his doubt. Sometimes, the physick could not save an apparently hale patient. Sometimes, the cure to an invisible illness was as fatal as a lack of cure. Sometimes, the smallest of cuts would become infected and kill the strongest man in the village. Perhaps Jack was the smallest of cuts that most would ignore, whereas the Scourge would not leave it untended.

Strap murdered the doubt within him and hoped that he had now managed to lay it to rest once and for all. Yet it was always resurrected whenever they came close to Jack. Did the demon have some sort of magic to raise it like an animee? Now he thought on it, the Scourge also took on his melancholic mood precisely when they came close to Jack. The creature must have some magic by which he could amplify the weaknesses and insecurities of any mortal's character. Amazed at the revelation, he was filled with renewed determination and commitment to the Scourge and his cause.

Strap pushed his horse into a faster gait and drew level with the Scourge. 'Old Hound, it's the damnedest thing! I suspect the demon is capable of manipulating our emotions. I should have seen it before, but perhaps that is also part of his magic.'

The Scourge's eyes widened as if he were waking from a dream. 'By the hairless scrotum of the child-god Istrakon, it's so obvious! That conniving, no-good stain on the sacred sheets of Shakri! He's been in our minds corrupting us, Strap! How can a man even trust himself with such a creature at large? It is the worst of blasphemies against Shakri's creation. No wonder we've struggled to take him when there is a crowd present – for he has them in his thrall. Strap, he must die... or be exorcised from this realm. His insidious influence will only grow otherwise. Perhaps Lucius remains with him because he emotionally cannot help himself. Yes, that's it. I'd never really understood why the musician would choose to accompany the demon before, but now I see Lucius is just another victim of Jack's evil wiles. The devil's calumny is without limit!'

'So how will we approach this?' Strap asked, giddy with relief to see the Scourge finally free of his dungeon.

'Differently to before,' the Scourge nodded, his eyes becoming distant as he envisioned new horrors he would inflict on his nemesis, 'but you might not like it.'

'Tell me.'

'I had intended to march into the inn as usual and confront the demon in front of the good people of Windrun. I now see that only holy Wim Himself would knowingly engage in such madness. Instead, we must skulk in the shadows and take them unawares, from behind if necessary. Or we sneak through the inn in the early hours and surprise them while they are asleep. It lacks honour, honesty and any sense of public trial, but we will never be able to visit any sort of justice on him if he sees us coming or if there are others around.'

Strap pursed his lips and nodded.

'There's more,' the Scourge said with a pained expression. 'In the past, we... or I... have fixated on bringing Jack to bay, leaving the innocent Lucius to escape as he could. Perhaps it was the demon's magic that kept us blind to it, but Lucius must also be a target for us.'

'What? Lucius a target? Surely not.'

'Strap, he is a victim who must be freed of the demon. More than that, though, he is a tool for the demon. The music Lucius plays helps the demon attract and command the crowd. The music may even enhance the persuasive nature of the demon's magic, for all know Lucius is a master and that his music can move even the heart of an animec. If we can separate Lucius from the demon, the demon will surely be diminished. Are we agreed?'

Strap nodded. 'We are. I take it, then, we now hole up somewhere and wait for it to become dark. Shame really, as I'd been hoping to free an ale or two from the local inn. It feels like a lifetime since I've had a decent brew.'

The Scourge looked sympathetic. 'I've still got a drop of devilberry liquor left.'

The young Guardian pulled a face. 'That stuff's good for cleaning horse brass and wounds, but I really don't appreciate how it cleans my insides too.'

'Requires a strong constitution, it's true.'

'There's nothing wrong with my constitution, thank you very much. And devilberry liquor is most certainly no fortifying spirit. You only still drink it as it's killed off the part of your brain that tells you you really shouldn't.'

'Who needs it, with you around to keep reminding me? Who needs a *wife* with you around? Look, if you don't want a real man's drink, then maybe some warm milk would suit you better.'

'Oh spare me the misogyny. You're the one who likes to bicker like you're part of an old married couple.'

'Miss who?'

'For the love of Shakri, you don't even know…!'

'And don't blaspheme, especially in Her name!'

'What?!' Strap squawked. 'You blaspheme more than anyone I know. Does a holy hairless scrotum ring in any bells?'

The Scourge shook his head. 'It's not the same.'

'And how do you work that out?'

'Simple. When I blaspheme, it is with feeling and purpose. I blaspheme meaningfully, whereas you are quite casual with your blasphemy. It's not right and you should stop it before one of the gods takes exception and you end up in real trouble.'

'I can't believe I'm hearing this! You thumb your nose at the gods and their priests at every opportunity you get. And now you're playing it holier than thou.'

'Well, I am holier than thou, lest you forget,' the Scourge replied matter-of-factly. 'I am the Divine Consort.'

'*Ex*-Divine Consort, lest *you* forget! Some would say a *failed* Divine Consort, one that is *not* holy *enough*.'

'You speak of things you do not understand, Young Strap,' the Scourge smiled indulgently. 'It is the priests of Shakri who have precedence in such matters, and they revere me as Consort. Or would you presume to argue with our learned fathers and mothers, in which case you would be guilty of an even greater blasphemy, and no doubt worthy of excommunication? Believe me, *no one* wants to be excommunicate from the favour of Shakri and Her temple, or the bounty of Her realm. Food would turn to ash in your mouth, your horse would not allow you to sit it, and no man would welcome you under his roof.'

Strap was silent for a moment. 'Do you know what? I preferred you when you were depressed.'

'So did I. You spoke less. You're about to give me a headache with your interminable yapping. And just look at all the trouble it gets you into. You always did talk too much, Strap. Now are you going to quit and drink some of this devilberry liquor or not?'

The Scourge held out a small silver flask and Strap snatched it ungraciously. They took it in turns to swig from it as they rode past the inn of the hamlet of Windrun, from which the strains of a greater lute, the singing voice of a demon-minstrel and the stomping feet of villagers caught up in the magic of the entertainment could be heard. They passed into the woods beyond and found a hiding place for themselves, from which they would emerge later to commit their bloody deeds.

✄ ✄

In the end, it hadn't gone at all well. Neither of them were practised night thieves, and Strap couldn't help remembering the Scourge's earlier blasphemy against the god of thieves, Istrakon. He decided against mentioning it now though, as recriminations would not help them. He was just surprised they hadn't succeeded in waking the entire hamlet, given their devilberry-fuddled state.

'The cursed demon probably sleeps with his eyes and ears open anyway,' the Scourge snarled. 'There! Through the trees. Strap, get the horses!'

'No, the trees are too crowded. We'll have to catch them on foot.'

The Guardians ran as fast as they could, turning and twisting around trees and bushes. There was no light to see by beneath the canopy of the woods, but the panting and footfall of those they pursued could be heard not far away.

'I see him!' the Scourge shouted. 'To the left! They've split up!'

Strap saw the Scourge throw a knife. There was a quavering cry ahead.

'Jack! Help me! I'm hurt!'

'I dare not, dearheart! Don't think badly of me!' came the fading reply.

'Jack! Arrgghh! Scourge, noo!'

The Scourge leapt on the limping Lucius. The musician swung his greater lute at the Guardian, but to little effect. The Scourge punched Lucius full in the face, breaking the man's nose and spraying blood everywhere. The one-eyed musician fell in a tangled mess of limbs. He could only move feebly after that.

'The demon has been controlling your mind. Snap out of it!' the Scourge demanded.

In a thick, choking voice, Lucius managed: 'Y-You maniac! Djack was rigdht to call you a mad dog.' He kicked out weakly at the Scourge's shins.

'You filthy demon-lover!' the Scourge sneered and kicked the musician in the stomach. Lucius had been unable to protect himself and suffered the full force of the blow. He threw up and gasped painfully, hardly able to breathe.

'Let's leave him and get after the other one,' the Scourge said.

'Are you insane?' Strap said with a shake of his head, but relieved the attack had ended without him having to intervene. 'We can't leave him like this! He won't stay conscious for more than a handful of seconds, and then if he doesn't choke to death on his own blood and vomit, he'll most certainly bleed to death. Look at his leg and nose. He needs help right away. I can make a tourniquet, but we'd best hope there's a physick or medicine woman back in the hamlet – otherwise, we'll be down one royal musician.'

'I can't afford to let the trail go cold,' said the Scourge. 'Suit yourself, but I'm going to get my horse from over there and finish this hunt once and for all.'

'Then we are forced to separate.'

'As you wish, Strap,' the Scourge said, turning on his heel and striding away without a backwards look.

Strap watched him go for a moment, shook his head and bent to tend to his rapidly failing friend.

✄ ✄

It was only when General Constantus's nose actually touched the paper of the report that he realised there really wasn't enough light to read by. He looked up and blinked his weary eyes. The candles had all burnt out and it was pitch black outside.

'As dark as Lacrimos's arsehole,' he smiled to himself, quoting his old friend the Scourge. What was the Guardian doing these days? Still hunting necromancers and their unholy minions, no doubt. He certainly wouldn't be cooped up in an office reading one soul-destroying report after another, that was for sure. The General was of half a mind to ban the writing of reports, except the kingdom of Accros only seemed to run because of them. He didn't fully understand how a trivial collection of words on a page could actually make trade between countries and taxation work, or how they could dictate the behaviours and employment of people in the farthest flung corners of the kingdom, but was assured by all his advisors that they nonetheless did and that his full understanding was not actually required. So he took it on faith, as if the written words were a prayer, blessing or magic spell. Certainly, the priests of Cognis always insisted there was a magic or power in written words, a power that only those chosen by the gods should be allowed.

He smiled wryly. He'd never been chosen by the gods, of course. That made him a magician who performed unsanctioned and blasphemous magic then. Indeed, many of the laws and dictates he'd put out over the years had been protested by the temples, particularly when his tax demands inevitably reduced the tithe people were prepared to pay the temples. Seen like that, he was precisely the sort of individual the Scourge hunted down. Where had it all gone wrong, for this was certainly not the life he'd foreseen or wanted for himself when he'd led the men of Accritania and unseated the despot Voltar. He spent almost all of his time in this office, as if it were a gaol cell. In some ways, it would be a relief if the Scourge were to find him and put an end to all this.

Perhaps he should give it all up and hand the rule of the kingdom over to the hungry nobles. Then he'd be able to spend more time with his beloved and long-suffering Hesta, who surely deserved better. He sighed. The nobles would tear the fragile kingdom of Accritania apart in a matter of months. Civil war would be inevitable. The kingdom would be unable to defend itself against any invader. All that he had worked so hard to build and safeguard would be lost. And if Accritania fell or collapsed, what would happen to the rest of the realm, a realm that was always balanced on the edge of the eternal precipice?

He'd lost track of time. He'd missed dinner again. Hopefully, Hesta would have left some cold cuts out for him. She usually did. He dreaded the day when she did not. At least he hadn't fallen asleep and spent the night here, which had happened a few times in the past.

Unthinkingly, he reached for his glass of Stangeld brandy and found it empty. He glanced at the bottle. That was empty too. Surely he hadn't drunk it all, had he? He decided it must have only been half full that morning.

He pushed himself up and found his legs reluctant to support him. Perhaps the bottle had been full after all. Or he was missing too many meals and not keeping his strength up. His uniform hung loosely on his frame, whereas at one time he'd more than filled it out. Perhaps he should have meals served in his office from now on, so that he would be sure to have them. He'd always resisted that option before so that hunger would force him out of the office every now and then. But it was a battle he was losing. He needed to do something very different, perhaps radical, or it would be lost entirely.

There was nothing else for it. He was going to have to let his adjutant take on the handling of certain types of report. Adjutant Spindar was a self-important prig whose buttons, boots and hair always gleamed more brightly than anyone else's. He was useless in the field, for he was always too busy checking his trews were not being splattered with mud to notice any enemy creeping up on him. But he had the sort of meticulous eye for detail that made him a near miracle-worker when it came to the logistics of running a kingdom. He also had a smooth and cultured manner that went down very well with the temples, an area of liaison with which the General always struggled himself.

Constantus was loath to hand over any decision-making to his underling, for the man's self-importance was already insufferable enough. Adjutant Spindar's nose was always slightly wrinkled as if it had a permanent bad smell under it. Constantus considered the close confines of the office, his sweat-stained uniform and the bottle of brandy – perhaps the man occasionally had good reason for his facial tic. Yet for all the Adjutant's groomed speech and efficient completion of tasks and orders, there was a subtle disrespect in his manner that verged on the insubordinate. The General's underfed gut told him that Adjutant Spindar was loyal only to Adjutant Spindar and could not ultimately be trusted. Such a man craved power for himself and would wield it in a petty and selfish manner.

Yet Constantus knew he had little other choice, for he did not want to pull one of his capable officers out of the field just to play fetch for his office. The army was small enough as it was: it was no exaggeration to say every man counted. And with the nobles always seeking to increase their number of armed retainers, the Accritanian army could not afford to be wrong-footed by the removal of one of its better officers from the frontline.

So the choice came down to tackling the nobles so that they would no longer be a threat, which would of course start the very civil war he wanted to avoid, or delegating more authority to Adjutant Spindar. The General told himself all would be well as long as his signature was required on every action the Adjutant decided upon. That way, he would be able to check that the Adjutant wasn't up to anything and that there wasn't too much power trickling away from himself to the man. Pleased at finally having made the decision, General Constantus made for the door and freedom. Perhaps, tonight, he would sleep well.

But as he opened the door, he was all but pushed back inside by an uncharacteristically agitated Adjutant.

'What is the meaning of this!'

Not only was the Adjutant sweating, but his top button was undone. 'They're rioting!' he said breathlessly.

'You're not making any sense man. Who's rioting?'

'The people, General, the people. They're out on the streets with torches!'

'B-But…' *Get a grip on yourself. You're no greenhorn.* 'How many? Have the troops engaged them yet? Are the guards ready to seal the palace?'

'Err… I… all I know is the streets are full of them. It looks like the whole of Accros has turned out. I was on my way to the barracks when I met them all coming this way. The troops are retreating in orderly fashion in front of them, as far as I can tell.'

Constantus didn't doubt it. His officers were all veterans and not prone to panic. His men were well-trained and disciplined. There should be no massacre of the citizenry.

'Who's behind it, Spindar? Lord Ristus? Are any of his men in evidence amongst the throng?'

'That's the strange thing, General, they were shouting a name I'd never heard before, something like *Cholerax*. It's not an Accritanian name, is it?'

The General frowned. 'What's going on, Spindar? We haven't passed a controversial law in years. It makes no sense. What's got them so riled?'

For once, the Adjutant was at a loss for an answer. He shook his head.

'Where's Colonel Vallus? In the palace?'

'I-I don't…'

'Well, we'd best find out, eh, Spindar? Get out there and find him. If you can't manage that, you'd better start organising the defence. Move, Spindar, move. On the double!'

The Adjutant began to turn away.

'Oh, and Spindar?'

'Yes, General?'

'Do your button up. I won't have you disgracing that uniform!'

Flustered, the Adjutant was unsure whether to salute, attempt the button, hurry away to carry out his orders, or attempt all three at once.

General Constantus swept his sword up out of the corner where it had leaned neglected for far too long. Then he roughly pushed his Adjutant out of the room, just as the man had pushed him inside before. He hadn't felt this alive in a long time. He was finally escaping his mausoleum.

Chapter Four: In the wrong hands

Saltar smiled as he thought back on having just told his son a few bedtime stories about the Scourge's exploits. He suspected he'd far from succeeded in making the boy sleepy, as his eyes had become wider and wider the more engrossed he'd become. In the end, Saltar had had to plead his own tiredness and that he wanted to save some stories for another night. He'd kissed Orastes dutifully on the forehead and left him staring at the ceiling, although the boy was no doubt actually looking out upon the planes of his imagination, across which armies warred, gods and magicians wielded their powers and bands of hardy warriors adventured. It was good for the boy to have such an escape.

Saltar climbed to the small room at the top of the tallest tower in the palace. It was said that the White Sorceress had once been incarcerated here by the usurper Voltar. In any event, he and the Chamberlain were unlikely to be disturbed here. His mood became far more serious as he pondered what lay ahead of them. He was unsure what the dangers would actually be, and he doubted there would be a guide conveniently to hand like there was last time. Ideally, he would have had Mordius on hand to assist him in the passage there and back, but the necromancer had become excited by a letter he'd received from Larc and rushed off in pursuit of the new and necessary magicks the realm required for its defence. Saltar had considered waiting for his friend's return, but decided things had become as urgent for himself as they had for Mordius.

He wondered where this sense of urgency had really come from. Was it sudden or had it been creeping up on him for quite some time? He reckoned it was like a clock. It had been ticking along quietly, the teeth on its cogs nibbling away at the world. But all the while the gears had been winding up; slowly, slowly increasing the tension in the spring, the spring that drew back the hammer. The long hand moved unnoticed round towards the twelve. The air... no, the very realm itself... groaned under the increasing pressure of the strike's imminence. It all pulled on his temples and made his scalp too tight. When the strike came, it would almost be a relief of sorts, as pent up forces were released, but it was inevitable that the peace would be shattered.

He dared not attempt to stop the hour hand or hammer now, for that risked breaking the clock's entire mechanism, but if he could be ready and close to the source of the impending concussion, then he might be able to muffle it so that it did not wake the sleeping monsters of eternity. For the clock was the clock of eternity. Time always progressed, sometimes quicker, sometimes slower, and always repeated the same times, events and strikes of the hammer. As he'd pondered with Mordius or the Chamberlain on occasions in the past, there was an inevitability then about the threats, challenges and crises Shakri's realm was faced with time and again. There was no escaping the mechanism of time it seemed. It bound life, death and the realm. And since the gods were tied to the realm, time even bound them.

There was no escaping it. No escaping? Was there no eternal plain one could access? He'd never heard tell of one. Was it not possible to become an actual part of the eternal clock? Who would know the answer to such a question? Cognis? He doubted it, for the god was limited by Shakri's realm and had been previously held in the Prison of All Eternity for some while. Still, it couldn't hurt to ask Him the next time Saltar came across Him.

Saltar looked up. He sensed the hazy signature of the Chamberlain's life-force ahead. It was not clear, but it was there. *Irreducible* in this realm he might be, but he was still framed by it and therefore possessing of a mortality of sorts. He could be killed in this realm, albeit not ended by it. He could not hide himself from the Battle-leader when they were in such close proximity to each other.

Saltar stepped into the largely bare tower room and faced the palace retainer. The Chamberlain glared at him. He *knew*, knew that Saltar intended to kill him. And it was clear he was not about to let it happen.

'How *dare* you!' the creature spat. 'You have *no right*, brother, hmm?'

'It must be done,' Saltar said mildly.

'It is an outrage! What are you, hmm? Just the same inflexible Balthagar you have always been. For all your posturing and posing as thisss SSSaltar, for all you play at the mortal preoccupations of family, you are that same Balthagar, no? You will *not* bend me to your will. I will not bend. You cannot bend me.'

Saltar hesitated. 'Chamberlain, I could ask you to trust me and you would tell me trust was irrelevant in this. I could remind you that we made a pact by which I vouchsafed your place in this realm. Were I to break that pact, I would threaten this realm. Yet still you would not find that a reason to submit to my will. So let me just ask you this question instead. Chamberlain, what is your name?'

'I have no need of a name,' the Chamberlain snarled.

'Yet I know my name where you do not know your own. How is that? How is it that you knew and understood Vidius was something called a nihil and I did not? How is it that I have some sentiment of being from another place and that a part of me is still there, lost to me? Do you have such knowledge? Well, do you?'

Dopily, the Chamberlain shook his head. 'No... I... what are you *doing* to me? I forbid it!'

'Chamberlain, I am taking you to a place where the gods of this realm do not prevent us from trusting each other, do not prevent us from sharing knowledge with each other, do not prevent us from arriving at answers as to our true selves. It is my belief we need such knowledge and power if we are to defend this realm against whichever threat it faces next. Just look how close Voltar and Nylchros came to undoing everything.'

'Fool...' the Chamberlain mumbled as the life-force drained from him. 'Can't you see? We're not meant to have such answers. They will threaten...'

❈ ❈

Saltar opened his eyes. He had the sort of headache that made it feel like there was a large spike through his head. The Chamberlain lay corpse-like not far away. Then the corpse opened its eyes. It struggled for a moment and then got stiffly to its feet. It lurched towards Saltar and stabbed at his face and hands with needles.

Saltar had been alert to the danger and skipped back out of range. 'Stop this! If we die here, then we could well be ended... or at least find ourselves in an inert state from which it is almost impossible to recover. Chamberlain, look around you, don't you want to know where we are? You are a smarter, more inquisitive being than this.'

The Chamberlain ignored him and came in quickly with his poisoned darts. A point flashed towards Saltar's thigh. He blocked the Chamberlain's forearm and, before the hand holding the needle could bend at the wrist and stab Saltar's blocking hand, twisted the Chamberlain's arm up and back so that the man-spider ended up stabbing himself in the side. The man-spider was apparently unaffected by his own poison, however. His other hand came spearing in and Saltar only avoided being pricked by pushing his chest back, bending at the waist and stuttering away on the tips of his toes. The needle kept coming. Saltar was forced to release the Chamberlain's first arm so he could pirouette out of the clinch.

The Battle-leader adopted the fighting form known as Air and put himself in continuous motion. The Chamberlain used his thumbnails to flick the cleverly weighted needles at Saltar, but Saltar was never to be found where he'd just been and his complex, swirling movements were not to be anticipated. The Chamberlain attacked with kicks this time, but Saltar buffeted them aside. Then he began to gust stronger, whipping himself up into a ferocious whirlwind. The Chamberlain was thrown hither and thither, spun around and then slammed into the floor on his front. Saltar leapt onto his back to keep him pinned there.

The Chamberlain suddenly had a needle between his teeth and sought to crane his neck round to reach any part of Saltar he could. A smack of his head against the floor soon disabused him of any notion that it might be a good idea to continue his assault.

'Now,' Saltar panted. 'This is the Prison of All Eternity. Each of the trapdoors that you see – there are some in the ceiling and some in the floor – is a route into a different realm. Some will be locked to us, some too small to fit through. *That* one is the way back to Shakri's realm. We must not lose track of it or we might be trapped here forever. I had to work quite hard during our fight to keep it in sight. I recommend we try and remember that strangely shaped crack in the ceiling above it.

The Chamberlain chuckled. It was a strange sound to hear in the deadened atmosphere of the vault, its stone pillars and torches apparently stretching to infinity in all directions. He kept laughing.

'What?'

'I always considered Shakri's realm a prison, hmm? Having escaped it, I now simply find myself in a larger prison. Prisons within prisons, yes, brother? I laugh, but I could as easily cry. You can climb off me now, hmm? And I'm sorry.'

'Sorry?'

'That I have poisoned you.'

'What! But none of your needles…'

'Your skin touched mine, did it not? I came here smeared in a rare and lethal tincture, brother. Well, it's lethal to all except me, actually. I have spent millennia becoming inured to it, hmm? Your joints will swell, your muscles will seize and then a permanent paralysis will set in. You will be naught but company and food for the rats in this eternal crypt, brother. Again, I am sorry.'

'Rats? That will be Samuel, one of the lower gods. He knows better than to attempt even a nibble,' Saltar replied absently as he searched for the toxin inside himself.

He found it and rearranged his physiognomy slightly to try and isolate it or render it harmless. He was partially successful, in that he managed to slow its onset significantly, but he could not remove it entirely as it had somehow infected or penetrated an essential part of himself.

'There must be an antidote.'

The Chamberlain shook his head sadly. 'There is no antidote to basilisk venom, hmm?'

'Basilisk! Surely that is naught but a fabled beast. Where would you get such?'

The Chamberlain shrugged. 'A long time ago, when I was wandering the length and breadth of Shakri's realm I came upon a witch's hovel in a swamp somewhere. She wanted to drink my blood, hmm, but I don't have blood in this body, no? I have some strange ichor. And the witch did not like the taste of it, no she did not. Yet she seemed lonely and wanting of company, hmm, so I stayed with her for some time and learnt from her. It was from her I borrowed the venom, yes?'

Saltar refused to panic. 'Well, we'll have to find Cognis as soon as we return to Shakri's realm. If He can't help, then no one can. So let us be quick here Chamberlain. Tell me what you know of our origins, how we came to Shakri's realm. I have already learnt a few things from the pantheon of gods of Shakri's realm – and these things I will share with you – but there must be things only you know. Why, for example, do you have ichor instead of blood? Why are you so *different* in appearance compared to the rest of us?'

The Chamberlain fingered his chin as he searched his most ancient memories. 'I believe I once had a form and nature so alien to Shakri's realm that it could not be framed in the typical way by the pantheon, hmm? Therefore, I must have always been an entity of a different manner and kind to you.'

Saltar absorbed this thoughtfully. 'And a different kind to Vidius then. You called him a nihil. Just what is that? It is meaningless to me.'

'It... is an entity of a particular... philosophy. It believes only in death and destruction, I think. The details are hazy, hmm? In killing, it somehow releases the energy or magic that once animated its victim. It either chooses to feast on the power released or lets it return to… to the cosmos, or some such, I am not sure.'

'A particular philosophy,' Saltar murmured. 'Do you know of other types of creature with differing philosophies?'

The Chamberlain closed his eyes. His brow creased so deeply that he looked to be in discomfort or pain trying to retrieve the information from his mind. 'They… do not want us to know such things.'

'Who are *they*?' Saltar asked quickly.

'It is kept from me,' the other said blindly. 'There are… *houses* of philosophy and existence. Vidius was of one house… owned it, perhaps. I was of another, and you were of another still. That's all!'

While the Chamberlain recovered himself, Saltar pondered what to ask next. What was the fear that had made him take the precipitous action of bringing the Chamberlain here? 'Chamberlain, hear me now, for this is important. You know it is only a matter of time before Shakri's realm is threatened again. Like all magic, the spell that sustains it constantly seeks to unravel. It is an aspect of the underlying and paradoxical nature of magic…'

'Allow me to qualify that, hmm? What you say is true of the magic in Shakri's realm, but I suspect there are other types, yes? For example, this place we are in has an aspect of eternity about it, does it not? That must be sustained differently, no? Surely eternity does not seek to unravel.'

'Interesting. Very well, let us think on that another time. Anyway, it is inevitable that another threat will emerge. It is my belief that, with sufficient knowledge, all the threats can be anticipated.'

The Chamberlain showed some surprise. 'An interesting notion. Say on, brother, hmm?'

Saltar flexed his stiffening fingers. Was this the first sign of the poison affecting him? 'The magic that allowed you, me and Vidius… and maybe some others… to harbour in Shakri's realm must, by its very nature, be unravelling. I know that to be true, for I am gradually coming to know more about myself, whereas the magic was designed to keep that knowledge from me. From what I can tell, we sought sanctuary and a hiding place in Shakri's realm. If the magic fails and we are no longer successfully hidden, then is it not inevitable our former enemies will find us?'

The Chamberlain looked troubled. 'And Vidius's disappearance from Shakri's realm is an ill omen. If he has found a way back to our place of origin, then he will only have helped speed the failure of the magic that conceals us, hmm? And from what I know of the nihil, he will seek to betray us to our enemies, seek to bring about the ultimate destruction of both us and Shakri's realm. And he will not stop there, for he will then seek to visit his philosophy on any other realm to which he can find access. He must certainly never be allowed to enter this part of the Prison of All Eternity! Ah, I see now that he is the Great Betrayer to which so many ancient cultures make oblique reference. We cannot be the first to anticipate this threat, hmm?'

'Precisely,' Saltar managed, his mind becoming slow. 'So... we need to... find out as much as we can about the place of origin... so that we can understand the threat and devise a defence... Cognis! Chamberlain, you understand? It is now the third time since we've been here that... I have thought we need to talk to Him! Chamberlain,' he mumbled, 'help me!'

The Chamberlain considered the Battle-leader for a while. Saltar had leaned heavily against a nearby pillar and then slipped down into a hunched seated position. It would be the easiest thing in the world to walk away and allow this troublesome entity to fade from all memory. He was sorely tempted, to repay Balthagar for all the difficulties and instances of humiliation that he'd suffered at his hands. Yes, it was his vanity at work, but he had no problem with being vain and disinterested – it was not contrary to the philosophy of his being. Then more practical issues entered into his deliberation. He sighed. 'Yes, brother, I will help you, hmm, for I still need you. Together, we will seek out Cognis and... what is that you say?'

'Something... coming.'

The Chamberlain's head snapped up and looked around. In the distance, a shadow raced towards them. The eternal torches on the pillars were extinguished one by one as the darkness came ever closer.

'What is this, hmm?' the Chamberlain wondered and readied some of his needles.

The shadow fragmented at its nearest edge and a tall, thin canine creature could be seen getting ahead of what was presumably a large pack behind it. It was slightly transparent, as if some sort of wraith.

The Chamberlain scurried forward as the lead creature bunched its hind-quarters and sprang at them. Swiftly, the man-spider pulled open a large trapdoor in the floor of the corridor and then threw himself backwards. The wraith at the head of the pack cleared the opening without much trouble, but its momentum took it a long way past the Chamberlain and Saltar.

White flames roared up out of the trapdoor and, in the blink of an eye, incinerated many of the wraiths coming on behind the leader. The rest howled in frustration and were forced backwards.

With unerring accuracy, the Chamberlain sent a needle into the leader, who was now turning towards them, but the weapon passed harmlessly through the smoky body. Cursing, the Chamberlain bent down and gathered Saltar up in his arms. He lifted him effortlessly.

'Back to Shakri's realm!' Saltar gasped.

'The way is blocked, brother, hmm?' the Chamberlain replied. 'For now, we must run and hide. Try not to move or talk, as it will only impede or distract me, not to mention speed the spread of the poison within you, yes? It is a long time since I was hunted. I must confess to a certain excitement.'

'I'm so happy for you,' Saltar said through gritted teeth.

❈ ❈

Orastes lay in the dark, his eyes wide open. Never had his father told him a bedtime story before. And what a story it had been. Uncle Mordius was usually the one to put him to bed with a tale, and on such occasions Orastes squeezed his eyes shut and imagined as hard as he could. But his father's story had been different to that. His words had created a whole landscape inside Orastes's head. It hadn't mattered if Orastes had closed his eyes or kept them open – the story had played out in front of his mind's eye regardless, exactly as Saltar described it.

Even though the lights in the room were dimmed, Orastes saw colours as bright as in the daytime. He saw the Scourge fighting evil magicians and their minions, saw him defeating Lacrimos, the god of death, saw him keeping the kingdom safe. He'd been scared during certain parts of the story, but had been powerless to stop it unfolding. It was like he was under a magic spell.

It was almost a relief when the story had finished. As soon as it had, however, he found he missed the wonder of the reality he'd been allowed to experience for a short while. He desperately wanted it to be real again, and he wasn't sure he could wait until the next time his father told him a bedtime story. Who knew if he'd have to wait another seven years?

He felt different too. The story had left a lasting impression on him. Had it changed him too? He now understood much more what his father wanted. He knew what would make him happy. And Orastes very much wanted to make his father happy; partly because Saltar was his father, partly because he was a bit afraid of Saltar and partly because Saltar sometimes looked so sad.

Orastes now knew Saltar wanted to make the kingdom safe. He didn't want monsters from outside attacking the kingdom, and he didn't want the people inside the kingdom attacking each other, which was what happened when the people became really scared of the monsters outside. But his father couldn't do it all on his own. He needed help from people like the Scourge and Uncle Mordius. He needed people watching out for the monsters and fighting the bad people. Orastes now knew it was the sort of thing he wanted to do too. It would make his father happy for once.

'I should go fighting!' he said out loud, just to see how it sounded. 'But mama will be cross. Mama doesn't like me going too far.'

'That's because she loves you,' came a gentle whisper from under the bed.

Orastes stilled in fright. He was too scared even to get under the blankets. His heart and lungs hurt, but he dared not breathe.

'Don't be scared, Orastes. It's me, Aa, remember? I'm like an invisible friend. I won't hurt you,' the kindly voice said.

Orastes's chest almost buckled as he gasped for air. 'Aa? But you're usually only in my dreams. I'm not dreaming now... am I?'

'No, but the story changed things, didn't it? You're glad I'm here with you, aren't you? I can help you. It'll be fun.'

'I-I guess so, but mama...'

'Oh, she just pretends to be angry sometimes to make you behave properly. I'm friends with your mother. I used to play with her and go on adventures with her when she was your age.'

'Really?' Orastes asked curiously. 'What adventures?'

'Oh, all sorts. We killed a monster once.'

'You did? Wow!'

'Yes. It was a monster pretending to be a normal man. And then we escaped the bad place together. I can help you escape this place if you like. Your mother won't mind if she knows I'm with you. I'll explain it to her before we leave if you want. I'll get her permission.'

Orastes was unsure what to do, confused. 'Only if my mother says it's okay.'

'Sure, that's the right thing to do. I'll go ask her now. You get your sword and armour from the other room and I'll be back in a minute.'

The room went quiet.

'Aa? Are you there?'

The room whistled with silence.

Orastes swung his legs across so that they dangled over the side of the bed. He cautiously stretched a foot towards the ground, ready to pull it back in an instant if the large, hairy hand of a monster came out from under the bed to try and grab his ankle. It would be terrible if a monster tried to attack him before he'd even got to his sword.

His toes touched the rug on the floor and then he threw himself off his bed and ran into the small side room where he kept his armour. His feet slapped twice on the cold flagstones of the new room, until he remembered the guard outside and went onto the tips of his toes.

He crept to the stand where his hard leather armour was kept and lifted down the torso, which was hinged on one side and buckled down the other. Sighing, he put it on the floor and went back to the bed chamber to retrieve his thickest shirt to wear under the armour to make it fit properly. He got into the torso and struggled with the stiff buckles for a while. His mother or Sister Spike usually helped him with this bit, but he finally managed it. Then he slipped on and buckled each of his arm guards.

He hesitated as he considered the cumbersome leather kilt they usually made him wear to protect his legs. He always felt so silly wearing it – it made him look like a girl. He wondered about just leaving it where it was. After all, he didn't want the monsters laughing at him as well. Still, he could kill them while they were too busy laughing to defend themselves. Decided, he hauled the kilt on. Besides, it was sometimes quite useful.

Finally, he took down his sword, which he called Monster-cutter, and looped his carry strap over one shoulder and diagonally across his body so that the hilt of Monster-cutter rested against his left hip. He was about to draw his weapon and investigate what was under his bed in the other room when a whisper came to him.

'Oh, my! You look like a hero I once knew!' admired Aa.

Orastes beamed at the comment. 'Aa, where are you? I still can't see you.'

'You'll see me later, once we're out of here, but for now I'll stay invisible so that we can trick the guard. Now, what we'll do with the one outside the door is…'

'Wait!' Orastes whispered as loudly as he dared. 'What did mama say?'

'Oh, she said it was fine. She only said we shouldn't be away more than a month, because then she'd start missing you too much. She said to be brave, and that if you brought back some monster's head, she'd stick it on a spike over the city gates so that everyone would know what a hero you are.'

'Wow! Really?'

'By my divine word as a god of the pantheon.'

'That's great, only…'

'What now?'

'Do you think we could take Sister Spike with us? She's nice. I like her. And she's very good at fighting.'

'But she's a girl! Orastes likes a girl! Orastes likes a girl!' Aa sang.

'Stop it! I do not!' the boy said a bit too loudly. 'If you don't shut up then I'm not coming.'

'Oh, don't sulk! Come on, I was only teasing. Alright, I won't say it anymore, I promise. Look, let's just you and me go kill some monsters – that way, no one will think it was Sister Spike who killed them all. Tell you what, we'll take her on the next hunt, okay?'

'I guess so,' Orastes answered dubiously.

'Right, now, I'm going to distract the guard outside the door. When he's left his post, you come out and run the other way down the corridor. Imagine that you were escaping from an evil monster's prison. This'll be good practice in case we ever have to do it for real. Ready?'

With residual images from the bedtime story he'd been told flickering in his mind and getting mixed up with what they were now attempting, Orastes nodded in tight excitement. What an adventure! His mother and father would be so proud. Mordius would cheer and slap him on the back. Sister Spike would smile and… and bow to him or something. The Scourge might even let him become a Guardian. 'Ready!'

'Wait a second. Okay, go! To the right. No, that's the left! The other way.'

Orastes kept his head down and ran as fast as his legs would carry him. The armour was heavy, though, and slowed him down. And his sword bumped awkwardly and unbalanced him slightly.

'It's okay, slow down. The next one's asleep. We need to be as quiet as we can. That's it.'

They made their way down through the palace and into the lower corridors.

'One more guard to go. I'll put out the torches in the corridor and you'll have to make your way past him in the dark. Stay close to the wall. We're nearly there. Let's go!'

'It's a good job you can do magic, Aa. I can't do any at all.'

There was a pause. Then: 'Everyone can do magic. It's just knowing how, and then practising a lot.'

Orastes shook his head, his small face serious. 'No. My magic's broken. It happened when I was young, I think. I can't remember. I can't do magic now, and magic doesn't work on me either. It's sad really, because I'd like to be a magician like Uncle Mordius.'

'Err… okay, I'll do the magic then. This is fun, huh?'

73

Orastes smiled. 'Oh, yes! Mama hardly ever let's me do anything like this or have any fun. It's okay, you can put the torches out now. I'm only a little bit afraid of the dark. And you'll be with me, won't you, Aa?'

'Oh, yes, my boy, have no fear of that. You won't just have to dream about me ever again.'

❋ ❋

The demon realm is rising. The demon realm is rising.

'Colonel, can't we go any faster?' Mordius called up to the man in front. 'We want to be at least to the next village before night falls.'

Clearly struggling with his self-control, Colonel Marr turned in his saddle and said through gritted teeth: 'For the hundredth time, Mordius, I'm going as fast as we should dare. We're already off the usual route because you wanted to take a short cut. If we miss the connecting side-trail to the main path in this gloom, then we could end up wandering lost for days. And there are so many awkward tree roots round here that we risk laming one of the horses if we hurry too much.'

'Sorry, sorry. It's just that I have this feeling we need to get a warning to Saltar as soon as possible. If we get separated, Colonel, or something should happen to me, then you have to find a way of warning Saltar that the demon realm is rising. He'll have to work out what to do without me. Tell him to consult the cadre as soon as he can. He'll know what that means. Do you understand, Colonel?'

'Of course I understand, Mordius. I'm not stupid, you know!'

'Of course, of course! It's just so important, you see,' the magician fretted. 'Perhaps we should start telling everyone we meet from hereon in. That way, there's a chance the news will travel on its own if something happens to both of us. The news might even travel ahead of us. That's if we ever meet anyone in these Shakri-forsaken woods, of course. And I keep getting bitten by something.'

'Don't speak too soon, Mordius. Look!' Colonel Marr said, bringing his horse to a stop.

On a low tree branch not far ahead of them was a small girl swinging her legs. The frown she gave them made her look impatient and as if she had been waiting for them. She had black hair, large blue eyes and the sort of fine dress on that would have been more suited to a city noble's daughter than a child living in untravelled and remote woods. She couldn't have been more than six years old.

74

Her appearance was so incongruous that Colonel Marr was forced to murmur, 'Do you think she's a goddess of some sort.'

Mordius pulled a face. 'You never know. She doesn't seem at all afraid of us. Better be polite just in case, Colonel.'

'Child, where are your parents?' Colonel Marr asked gruffly.

Mordius sighed inwardly. He should have remembered that the soldier's idea of being polite to someone was anything that did not involve insulting them, threatening them or physically harming their person. As it turned out, the girl was unperturbed by Colonel Marr's manner. After all, what exposure to courtly language and etiquette would she have had out here?'

'They're at home. They're trying to make me a brother or sister. I always have to wait outside when they do that.'

Mordius was surprised at how eloquent this child was. She seemed comfortable with language and ideas beyond her years. Still, maybe they had to grow up fast in these parts. Who knew what the age of adulthood was amongst the simple woods people of this region?

'So us finding you here is but chance?' the Colonel asked.

'No, I knew you were coming.'

That gave them pause. 'How is that, child?' Mordius asked gently. 'I am Mordius, by the way, and this is the Colonel. What is your name?'

'Father calls me *Girl*. You can call me that too if you like. I knew you were coming because the sounds of the woods changed. The birds went quiet, the small creatures stopped moving and the deer ran off deeper into the woods, away from you.'

The Colonel shook his head in wonder. 'You must have keen senses, Girl. I bet no one could creep up on you in these woods.'

'I suppose not,' she shrugged. 'But you *were* very loud. I don't think *you* could creep up on anyone.'

The Colonel's cheeks coloured slightly and Mordius had to hide a smirk. The soldier had always been quite proud of his woodcraft. 'Well, yes, anyway, what are you doing just sitting there? We're strangers. Don't you know we could be dangerous? What's your father thinking letting you come out here alone?'

The girl looked slightly scornful. 'You couldn't catch me anyway. You're too big and clumsy.'

Mordius couldn't hide his mirth this time.

'Father sent me to lead you to our home. We might be able to trade things with you. You are a very long way from anywhere else so will need somewhere to stay tonight. It will rain soon too.'

The Colonel looked horrified. 'But surely Twisthorn is only a few miles further on!'

'I think we'd better go with her, Colonel, don't you?' Mordius said with a slight smile.

The girl shook her head. 'No, that's the other way, at least a day's walk.'

'But we *can't* have missed the path…' the Colonel tailed off.

'It's alright, my friend, let's go with her tonight and then get an early start in the morning. We'll have only lost a few hours that way.'

Grumbling to himself, the Colonel pushed his horse forwards as the girl jumped down from her branch and led them away through the trees. They travelled for about twenty minutes, the small child showing no signs of fatigue and declining the Colonel's invitation to sit up on his horse. Mordius and the Colonel exchanged glances. Extremely hardy, these woodspeople.

They came to a relatively large log cabin with a veranda. It looked to be as solidly built and durable as the woodspeople themselves.

'I will see if mother and father have finished making me a sister or brother,' the girl told them and went inside the house, having stamped her feet on the wooden boards outside and rapped on the door.

She came out not long after, concentrating on carrying a beaker in each hand without spilling anything. She put the beakers on the floor and looked up.

'Father says to put the horses at the back. He is getting dressed. Mother told me to bring these drinks to you. Do you want them now or after you put the horses at the back?'

The Colonel chuckled. 'You are very kind, Girl. We'll see to our animals first and then be right back. I may have a handkerchief or ribbon in my saddle bag to go with that pretty yellow dress of yours.'

The Girl finally smiled at them. Her cheeks dimpled and she clapped her hands. 'Really?'

The burly soldier laughed and nodded. 'Come on, Mordius, it's not polite to keep a lady waiting.'

As the two men steered their horses round towards the stables at the back of the house, Mordius couldn't help asking: 'Colonel, what are you doing with a handkerchief and ribbon in your saddle bag, eh?'

'All the single soldiers carry such things… and some of the married ones too. Sometimes, they can help win a woman's favour.'

Mordius wasn't sure whether to be shocked or amused. In the end, he was neither. 'Do… do all women like such things?'

'Some, not all,' the Colonel replied uncomfortably. He finally met Mordius's gaze. 'Look, magician, I'm no expert in such matters!'

Mordius was silent for a second. Then he smiled. 'I doubt any man is, Colonel.'

That eased the awkwardness somewhat.

'Now, you tell me, magician. Have you ever cast a love spell?'

'I-I… why, no! I'd never contemplate doing such a thing. It's… it's…'

'It's a handy trick if you know it, I imagine. Trust me, it would simplify things a lot. I've heard that even the priests of Shakri are prepared to cast one for you if you offer them enough gold.'

'B-But that just doesn't seem right somehow.'

The Colonel sighed. 'I know what you mean. True love doesn't or shouldn't need tricks and the like. A bewitchment sullies it somehow. You might see it as a form of cheating.'

'Precisely!'

'Then again, the priests will tell you love is already a form of magic: Shakri's magic. It bewitches people and makes them act in ways that would seem contrary to their nature. They say the love spells they offer are nothing more than an enactment of Shakri's will, a will that will always override the normal inclinations of a mortal being.'

'Hmm. It still makes love sound like a cheap conjuring trick. I don't like to think of it that way.'

'But who are we to argue with Her priesthood?'

'Who indeed?' Mordius agreed. 'After all, neither of us are experts, eh?'

'In the meantime, I will stick to my handkerchief and ribbons. I think of them as my plumage. The brighter and showier my feathers are, the more likely I am to be seen by a potential mate.'

'Or predator.'

The Colonel laughed. They quickly rubbed down their horses and stabled them, making sure the tired animals had sufficient feed and water. Then they carried their saddle bags back round to the front of the cabin. The girl absently proffered them the beakers again, trying to see if the Colonel had anything in his hands for her.

'Once we're inside, Girl. Thank you for this. I was thirsty.'

'What is it?' Mordius asked as he sipped at his.

'A cordial mother makes from the yellow flowers that grow round here. She sweetens it with honey. It's my favourite!'

'It's good.'

'We can go inside now,' the girl said excitedly, her eyes shining at the Colonel. The soldier gestured for her to lead on and walked somewhat stiff-legged after her.

'Oo! I'm more saddle sore than I realised. I never felt it like this when I was young, you know.'

'I've never got used to riding horses,' Mordius complained. 'I'm feeling tired though.'

They followed the girl through the door, the Colonel ducking slightly to pass beneath the lintel, and entered the dim interior. As their eyes adjusted, they began to make out the clutter all around them. There was a table piled with plates, spoons, forks and curious metal implements. Herbs hung from the rafters in large drying bundles. Stacks of firewood and heaps of animal skins took up large sections of the floor. Hung along the length of one wall on wicked hooks were game birds waiting to be plucked, hares and rabbits waiting to be potted, and other carcasses waiting to be cured or eaten. In another corner was a large pile of bones, a set of saws and a cauldron, presumably for boiling stock or dye. There was a leather work bench, with wooden frames and templates scattered everywhere, and large shears, thick needles and sharp awls in evidence. In the centre of the room was a large fireplace within a wide, stone chimney. It blocked the view of some of what was beyond, but on one side there appeared to be row upon row of standing shelves stocked with sealed beakers and storage jars.

'And here are mother and father,' the girl grinned, waving them round the other side of the chimney.

The Colonel and Mordius shuffled round to the right to glimpse a large wood-framed bed.

'That's how they died. They were happy, so did not mind dying so much. They're still grinning, you see?'

On the bed were two bodies. The flesh on their bones had begun to decay and liquefy. The black liquor was pooled beneath them, and their faces were little more than skulls with damp patches of scalp and hair still clinging to the bone. Judging by the clothes still hanging loosely from them, one had been a man and the other a woman. He lay on top of her in a grotesque parody of what it was to be alive and loving another.

Mordius's tongue became a dead slug in his mouth. He wanted to spit or tear it out, then claw at his eyes and hide them in his pockets like precious jewels that he wanted no one else to see. His heart screamed.

'But, you, little magician, I cannot allow to die happily. For you and I are due a reckoning, eh? There is a great deal of suffering that I owe you, is there not? *A very great deal.*'

Choking, Mordius pleaded with the Colonel: 'The witch! She is the witch, Colonel! Draw your sword at once. Do not hesitate, I implore you! Kill her, quickly! Colonel!'

The soldier fumbled with the hilt of his sword, but he seemed to be lacking any strength with which to draw it from its scabbard. His eyes began to close.

'I'm afraid, little magician, he drank too muck of my cordial. He's done well to stay on his feet this long. A few more seconds and he will be oblivious to everything around him. Then you and I will be alone. And this time there will be no one to disturb us. Do not worry, you won't be oblivious to anything. I made your cordial a bit weaker than his. It will incapacitate you but won't render you unconscious. I wouldn't want you to miss a second of the suffering and torment that is about to be visited upon you. By the way, I wouldn't waste your time wishing for death, as I have no intention of permitting you any such relief or escape.'

Mordius tried to unstick his tongue from the floor of his mouth, desperate to appeal to the gods. He knew they could only take a direct hand once there had been a spoken appeal. But his body would not obey him and he slumped at the young girl's feet. He prayed fervently within his mind – the only thing that was left to him – but no one heard his prayers.

'Where are we going, Sotto? Are we going to get something to eat?' the giant Outdweller asked his small friend. 'I'm hungry.'

'You've only just eaten, Dijin. No, we're going on patrol, to check there's no trouble hereabouts.'

'What does on patrol mean?'

Sotto sighed and pulled the tight neck of his uniform away from his Adam's apple before answering. 'They explained that during the training we've just had. Weren't you listening?'

'Huh! I must have been thinking about something else.'

'Food, probably!' Sotto muttered. 'Anyway, it means we travel around and stop anyone stealing anything or killing anyone.'

Dijin scratched at his head as he pondered this explanation. Then he shrugged. 'Whatever you say, Sotto.'

'Come on then. We're going to patrol the Outdweller farms around Corinus. If you see anything, just shout.'

'But it's night-time, Sotto. We can't see much. And what sort of things should I shout about?'

'Look, the farmers have said most of the trouble happens at night – things get stolen, animal gates are opened, livestock are terrorised, meaning there're no milk or eggs the next day, and so on. If we're going to catch anyone, it's at night. And we can see better in the dark than most, Dijin, cos we grew up in the catacombs. We'll have the advantage.'

'I tend to smell things out in the dark rather than see them,' Dijin explained after a pause.

'Really?' Sotto asked with genuine interest. 'I'd never realised that. Okay, if you smell anything out of the ordinary, just let me know.'

'Hmm. Lots of strange animal smells outside Corinus. Confusing.'

'Well, do your best. Come on!'

Sotto led his large friend down the road out of Corinus. They'd both joined the Memnosian army three days ago, Sotto as a lieutenant and Dijin as a private. As an officer, Sotto had his own room in the officers' barracks, but he was ignored by all the others, who were from Indweller families. He dared not eat in the officers' mess, for he had never before eaten with a small knife and small trident like the others did. That and the fact that the pallet they'd put in his room was too soft meant he did all he could to avoid spending any time in the officers' barracks at all. Whenever he could, he found somewhere to bunk down amongst his own people in the privates' barracks.

As soon as the question of the new night patrols had been raised, Sotto had volunteered himself and Dijin. Anything to get out of the little four-wall cells and tunnels the Indwellers built for themselves and called buildings. He'd rather be in wide open space, even if he had to lose a few hours' sleep, than be trapped all night in a box with a group of army officers who really felt no fondness for him whatsoever. It wasn't that he believed the officers would come for him as a group when he wasn't expecting it, but given sufficient opportunity men forced to live in close proximity will find something to take exception to in each other. It was therefore better for all concerned that he was absent as much as possible. A falling out between officers, not to mention an accidental death, would cause divisions in the army and set the Indwellers and Outdwellers at each other's throats. And if the army, with all its discipline, couldn't keep itself together, then what hope the kingdom?

Sotto and Dijin made their way on foot. They had access to horses, of course, and would need to master them if they were ever to patrol the farms furthest out from Corinus, but neither of them had experience enough to want to use them unless absolutely necessary. Besides, the beasts always seemed skittish around Dijin, as if they knew he wanted to eat them, which he probably did. So, on this first patrol, during which they were more interested in getting to know the lie of the land than anything else, they had decided to walk.

They walked for an hour or so, easy in each other's company and neither feeling a need to make conversation. They met no one on the road as they travelled either. They passed a number of farms, all of them dark and quiet, nothing obvious amiss.

'Smell anything?'

Dijin snuffled the air deliberately and then shook his ponderous head. 'A fox, I think. Otherwise, less to smell than usual. Strange.'

'What do you mean *less to smell*?'

Dijin shrugged. 'Don't seem to be so many wild animals about. Usually, there are little warm creatures in the hedges around the fields, but not so many now.'

'You can smell creatures in the hedges?!' Sotto asked in amazement.

'It's the blood I tend to smell, Sotto. It's hard to pick out individual ones, but I can usually get an idea of whether there're lots or just a few. And not so many rabbits in the fields, either.'

Sotto wasn't sure what the lack of wild animals around Corinus signified, but it made him uneasy. There was something unnatural about it. It made the hairs stand up on the back of his neck. Surely Shakri and Her priests would be unhappy about the lack of life hereabouts. Was the realm under some sort of attack? 'There are some lights on the next farm. Let's ask some questions there.'

They made their way up to the farmhouse and knocked on the door.

'Who goes there?' came a man's startled voice.

'An army patrol, good farmer! We are Outdwellers newly joined up. I am Sotto.'

'Sotto, eh? I have heard of you. What is it you want here, eh? I have already sent Trajan what little I can spare. If you've come for more, then you must leave disappointed.'

'Nay, farmer, you misunderstand. We are a patrol sent to see that all is well with the Outdweller farms. We have heard there have been problems of late. Trajan himself has made a request to Saltar the Builder for help. Will you not open the door so that we may discuss such things without waking your household and neighbours?'

'Sotto, I can bash in the door if you like.'

'And who is that? Dijin?' the farmer yelped fearfully.

'Yes, it is Dijin,' Sotto replied on behalf of his friend.

'Dijin, I will feed you if you promise not to harm me or any of my family!'

Dijin looked at Sotto. 'He sounds like a good man, Sotto.'

'More than that, farmer, Dijin promises not to eat you out of house and home.'

Dijin looked disappointed, but did not gainsay his lieutenant.

There was the sound of a bolt being drawn back and the door slowly swung open. The farmer was silhouetted by a lamp behind him and held a pitchfork threateningly. Behind the light were a teenage boy, who gripped a knife and had a determined set to his young features, and the farmer's wife, who wielded what looked like a clothes-pole.

'Good farmer,' Sotto said in less of a shout than previously, 'no Outdweller trusts another unnecessarily. But, tell me, how necessary are things for you right now?'

'Indeed, they are passing necessary,' the man admitted. 'My vegetables are being pulled up each night and trampled underfoot. Who ever heard of such a thing, eh? Not eaten, mind – pulled up and trampled! No animal would do that – they've got too much sense to let good food go to waste. Can only be a crazed or jealous man or woman is my way of thinking. Yet we've kept a watchful eye most of the night, only to find the crop wasted when we wake an hour or so later. It's like they *know* when we're asleep, like they're watching us. We've searched the area, of course, but find no trace of 'em, not a footprint, not a hidey-hole. Now, I'm not a superstitious man like some hereabouts, but it's right queer and no mistaking. Farmer yonder says as it must be… ghosts.'

The farmer's son wiped one clammy hand and then the other on his shirt. The farmer's wife bent and touched the earthen floor, for the blessing of Gart.

'What ghosts?' Sotto asked quietly.

The farmer grimaced. 'Restless ghosts of the Outdwellers who died in the mountains fighting the blood-mages. Who knows what was done by those unholy mages to their poor spirits? The dead are right to be jealous of what we have. They died so that we could have these farms, after all. And they're right to be jealous that we still live.'

'I cannot believe they would begrudge you this,' Sotto replied. 'Securing these farms for the Outdwellers was their entire purpose.'

''Tis true,' the farmer nodded. 'And the priests have been out here and blessed everything until they've run out of blessings, and that includes the dark priestess of Lacrimos herself. So I cannot believe the gods are angry at us either, though some would have it elsewise. It can only be some crazed or jealous man or woman.'

'May we cross your threshold, good farmer, and see where they have been visiting? Who knows, there may be some sign by which we can fathom what is at the root of all this.'

The farmer stood his pitchfork on its end and moved aside for them. They entered, nodding respectfully to the farmer's wife and boy. They passed through the large and homely kitchen, which was decorated with all sorts of home-made wards, and went out to the yard beyond. By the light of the lamp the farmer brought with them, they considered the few woebegone root vegetables remaining in the neatly spaced furrows.

Sotto shook his head and looked up at Dijin, who dwarfed them all. 'What does your nose tell you, my friend?'

Dijin moved his head back and forth like an unhappy bear. 'Nothing,' he grunted. 'More nothing here than on the road.'

'You mean there's an even greater absence of life, right?'

Dijin shrugged.

'Where is the most nothing? Can you tell?'

Dijin looked about for a few seconds and then strode purposefully towards the far corner of the garden. The giant was so intent on tracking that he failed to realise his large feet were further damaging the furrows and struggling plants. Sotto looked apologetically at the farmer, but the farmer mimicked Dijin's shrug of a moment before and followed in his wake, his pitchfork at the ready.

There was a small irrigation ditch at the edge of the garden. Without hesitation, Dijin swept down and grabbed something. He dragged it wriggling and fighting out of the wet mud. It seemed to be about the size of a small dog.

'Hold the lamp up!'

There was a flash of white teeth and Dijin tutted and growled in annoyance. He held onto one of the creature's limbs and lashed its body against the ground. It made a gurgling noise and stopped moving.

'Well done, Dijin!' Sotto sang in praise. 'Hold it up so we can see it.'

'By the generous bosom of Shakri, what's this then, eh? Never seen the like.'

Sotto was at a loss. 'It's an ugly little runt, isn't it? Hmm. What should we do with it?'

'Kill it,' the farmer said without hesitation. 'We were beginning to go hungry because of that thing. Much longer and we could have starved to death because of it. It's only right we kill it in return.'

Dijin casually began to crush the small, man-like creature with his hand.

'Hold, Dijin!' Sotto said to him. 'Maybe it can answer our questions and tell us if there are others of its kind in the area. Farmer, do you have a sack?'

The farmer pulled a sour face but relented. 'Suppose I should be grateful you've rid me of the pest, eh? Very well, I won't insist on the blood-debt owed if you might find some advantage keeping it alive, although I hope it won't be for too long. It's clearly little more than an overgrown sort of vermin, eh? Got an old seed bag in the barn you can use over thisaways.'

With the creature deposited in a hessian bag and the opening securely tied with a scrap of leather, they took their leave of the farmer and his family and began the long trudge back to the city.

'Be sure to let us know if you or any others experience further trouble,' Sotto had said upon their departure. 'Oh, and make it clear to them there are no restless ghosts around. We don't want people refusing to farm the land we've been given because of some deluded belief that the dead forbid it. Tell 'em to start setting traps along the ditches and the like.'

Sotto blinked. Had he just nodded off while still walking? He'd heard of horses that did the same. To keep himself awake, and thereby reduce the risk of falling over and breaking his neck while asleep, he decided to attempt conversation with the massive shadow that was Dijin.

'No trouble from the little runt, then?'

'Err… no, Sotto.'

'Are you sure it's alive?'

'Err… no, Sotto.'

Sotto stopped. 'Dijin, what is it?'

'Err…' Then the big man said in a rush, 'Please don't be mad, Sotto, but it was in my head saying things, saying bad things, Sotto, *very* bad things. It told me to eat you, Sotto, said you had nice, plump legs that would taste good. I'm not as clever as you and couldn't work out how to stop it speaking in my head, except to…'

'Except to what? Come on, out with it, you big dope!'

'Well, the farmer didn't feed me like he promised. And the walk was very long and made me hungry. So I… so I…'

'So you ate it, right?'

'Yes, I ate it,' Dijin said miserably. 'It didn't even taste very good. I don't like imps, I've decided.'

'What did you say?'

'I'm sorry, Sotto. I ate it.'

'No, no. You called it – what was it – an imp? Is that what you said? How do you know that's what it was?'

'I... er... *I* don't know, Sotto. Maybe when it was talking in my head I learned it was an imp then. I'll try and catch you another one, I promise. You're not angry with me, are you, Sotto? I try to be as clever as I can, honest I do.'

Sotto sighed. 'Let's go home and get some sleep. No, I'm not angry with you. You're my friend. Do you know how I know that?'

'No, Sotto.'

'You didn't eat me. And friends don't eat each other, do they, Dijin?'

'No, Sotto,' the Outdweller replied, and the happiness could be heard in his voice.

Chapter Five: Become something else

The demons were nothing to be treated lightly. The right to exist was one that had to be earnt and defended every waking moment of the day. Those who had not learnt to sleep with at least one eye open were in need of the sorts of alliances that would see them guarded when it was their turn to rest. Even then, survival was not guaranteed. It made the need to be part of a powerful family, tribe or *house* absolute. None existed who were not the member of a house. Certain tribes existed across several houses, which made the relationships, alliances and politics of this sphere more complex than any others. Although there were individuals of greater power to be found in the sixth and seventh spheres, there was no sphere with more constant danger than the fifth.

Vidius was happy still to be alive, even though he'd only been in the sphere a hand of minutes or so. He'd been at his most vulnerable during those initial moments, like a child being born into a new world with no idea of where and to whom it had been born.

He'd emerged onto a bony, chalky plain beneath a roiling sky of red and grey cloud. A dark crag marked the distant horizon, where lightning spiked down every now and then. It gave him a target, so he began to walk across the hollowed landscape. A thin layer of messy turf covered much of the chalk except where there was a slight rise of some sort, when the skeleton usually shone through breaks in its dark skin.

He descended into a wide basin filled with milky water. Crouched at the edge was a demon that seemed to be doing nothing but watching the water and waiting. Vidius did not know if the demon was aware of his presence. Should he stalk him and seek to kill him? Vidius decided against it – the demon was much bigger than he was and was all wiry muscle and long limbs. Should he leave him undisturbed and carry on towards the black crag? He decided against that too – he was sure he would not be able to make it to the crag alone or unaided, but would the next demon he met even allow him to decide what sort of approach he made? For all he knew, a group waited to ambush him over the next rise, to tear him limb from limb before he could even speak.

He cautiously came down to the water's edge and crouched ten or so metres away from the yellow-skinned demon.

'I am a mortal called Vidius.'

Orange eyes flicked towards him briefly. 'I am Co-optis,' the demon managed to reply despite its long fangs and split tongue.

'What is it you do, Co-optis?'

'Wait for a fish to come near the surface.'

Vidius's stomach rumbled at the mention of food, causing Co-optis to glance at him again and smile knowingly.

Vidius looked at the water dubiously. 'How many fish have you caught here?'

'None, but that does not mean there are no fish in the pool.'

Vidius paused. 'Have you seen sign of any fish?'

'No. That is what I am waiting for.'

Another pause. 'How long have you waited?'

'How is such a thing measured? Until you came and asked such questions.'

Vidius decided the creature was either a bit simple or very wise. It didn't really matter which it was, however. 'Co-optis, what else is there to eat?'

Co-optis smiled knowingly again. Vidius felt like a fish that has realised too late it has drifted close to the surface and placed itself within reach of the predator waiting on the bank. 'In groups, Co-optis hunt the Hermis, who are solitary by nature. You have no choice but to join one of our groups, yes, Vidius? If you do not join us and do not operate under licence from the Fortress, then we must consider you Hermis. We will hunt you and your flesh will be divided between the Co-optis and the Fortress.'

Vidius now realised that he'd been mistaken in thinking Co-optis was the individual name of the demon he faced. Co-optis was actually the name of one of the demon *houses*, just as Hermis was another, and Nihil another. Yes, he remembered once having known that.

He chose his words carefully. 'Yes, I have no choice, Co-optis. I will join one of your groups. What would you have me do?'

The demon grinned more widely. 'You will join my group then. We are of the Xanthan tribe of Co-optis. We will hunt. You will show yourself to a Hermis as we direct. We will then do the rest.'

Bait! They needed him to act as bait, to lure a Hermis into some sort of trap. Unless the Co-optis were extreme cowards, a Hermis must be a dangerous demon indeed if it needed to be hunted in packs. Hanging oneself out as bait for a Hermis was probably a highly dangerous pastime. No doubt, there would usually be a lack of volunteers from amongst the Co-optis for such a role. They would therefore intimidate or threaten whoever else they could into playing the part. He saw now how the house of Co-optis survived and thrived – by ganging up and forcing someone who was weak or exposed into taking all the risk for them, scooping the prize and then using a share of the spoils to bribe the powerful houses of the Fortress into leaving them alone and guaranteeing that only the Co-optis would have a licence to hunt the planes.

Vidius bowed slightly. 'Co-optis, I would be honoured to join your group of Xanthan and do as you direct. We can start as soon as you wish.'

Co-optis rose smoothly. 'Follow then and meet my brothers.'

As they moved away, they heard a plop from the pool behind them as something disturbed its surface.

'Well, what do you know! Looks like there *were* fish in there after all,' Vidius commented.

The Co-optis glanced backwards, irritation plain on his face.

❈ ❈

He crept along the narrow bridge of land that spanned the wide, chalky lake. Bubbles fizzed up here and there, there were no signs of vegetation and there weren't even any lichens or mosses on the rocks at the water's edge. He surmised the milky liquid was more than a little acidic and that there wouldn't be any fish here.

At the end of the bridge, there was meant to be a low chalk cliff with a significant overhang. It was there that one of the Hermis was said to make its solitary home. The task the Co-optis had given Vidius was to confront the Hermis, provoke it and have it chase him back across the lake. The Co-optis had dug a deep pit at the end of the span and covered it over with a spindly, woven mesh of rushes and sticks. They seemed convinced that the Hermis would blunder into it once its ire had been raised and its significant bulk had picked up momentum and moved into a headlong rush. They then intended to stab down at the trapped demon with their long metal spears and tridents to finish it.

Vidius asked more than once how big the Hermis was and what sorts of speed it could get up to, but the Co-optis waved his questions away with laughter: 'Fear not, little mortal! The Hermis are heavy, ponderous beasts, all but witless too. Do not look so affrighted, little mortal! Look, it is in our interests that you outpace the Hermis, for how else would it be led all the way to the trap? We would not want it catching you before reaching the trap, as then it would pull up short, would it not? Come, be safe in that knowledge, although never complacent.'

Their logic reassured him, yet they were demons and not to be trusted. After all, they had not exactly given him a straight answer to his questions. Even so, he had little choice but to work with their house out here on the planes.

He came to the end of the land bridge and scuttled behind a thin, largely lifeless thorn bush. He spied ahead and saw the overhang. It was all but filled by the bulk of the Hermis, which was clearly enormous even at this distance. He trembled slightly at the sight of it. *What's the matter with you, Vidius? Get a grip! You are a Prince of the realm. None should unman you so.* He wondered if the Hermis had some sort of power to inspire awe and fear in all that laid eyes on it. If it was quite heavy and ponderous, as the Co-optis asserted, it would need such magic to freeze its prey with terror and be able to catch it... unless the Hermis was a herbivore, of course, and only used its magic to ward off predators. Looking at its fiercesome aspect, however, it seemed more likely an efficient hunter-killer than plant-lover.

The Hermis was at least eight feet tall and had a thick, bony exoskeleton. Its head, therefore, looked like nothing more than a massive skull with red eyes shining malignantly from its sockets. With its two horns and elongated snout, there was something almost bull-like about it, but the similarity ended at its powerful bone-crushing jaws. It had a wide chest protected by loosely articulated, bony plates, and then quite human forearms and hands. The forearms were sheathed in metal, as were its elbow, shoulder and knee joints. It stood on cloven hooves holding a spear longer than Vidius was tall. It seemed to be guarding a pile of metal armour which, based on its shape, probably also served as its bed, just as dragons were said to sleep on piles of gold. Had the Hermis really slain so many, and was metal really so valuable to the demons, or did the Hermis simply keep the armour as some sort of trophy of its kills? There were no bones of the dead in evidence... but then again the Hermis might have eaten those too.

Vidius licked his dry lips, summoning the courage to leave his hiding place, when the Hermis's head swung towards him and it looked straight at him. Damn! It must have scented him on the wind. Vidius stood and came out slowly from behind the thorn bush. The demonic minotaur snorted and made ready with its giant spear. It did not charge him however.

Vidius took tentative steps forward, and then a few more. The Hermis lowered its head and raked at the ground with one hoof. He stopped twenty paces short. His knees were shaking and his voice quavered as he called: 'I bring you warning, Hermis! The Co-optis have dug a pit on the other side of the lake. They have sent me to bait you, but instead I bring you warning.'

He prayed the beast understood him. It watched him carefully, its breath billowing out as if it was angry or there was a fire in its chest.

'I am Vidius, a mortal! I am a traveller here, but the Co-optis seek to use me.'

'I have no interest in you. Begone!' the Hermis boomed, and Vidius almost felt compelled by the magical resonance of its voice.

'I do not seek gratitude for the warning I have brought you. I want nothing of you, Hermis! I simply wish to pass through here and continue on my journey to the Fortress, just as I have journeyed through the other spheres, leaving the gates open as I have come. Do I have your leave to progress?'

The Hermis was silent for some moments. 'You would also leave the gate between the fifth and sixth spheres open perhaps. The archdemons will come through and wreak havoc. It is unlikely that this sphere and any of the others would survive,' the Hermis brayed like a war horn, its powerful voice echoing off the cliffs around him. 'I will accompany you, mortal!'

Vidius was wrong-footed. What could the demon hope to achieve by accompanying him? He could not fathom the logic by which the Hermis had come to such a decision. 'Err... Hermis, I would welcome your direction and protection. I was given to understand that those of your house are solitary in nature, however.'

Noise rumbled from the demon's mighty chest, but Vidius did not know whether to interpret it as anger, laughter or rumination.

'You have been speaking to Co-optis, no doubt. They are incapable of accuracy, mortal. It is true that a Hermis often enjoys its own company so that it may have the time needed for thinking, but the Hermis must breed like any other house. We find a mate for ourselves as and when necessary, and we care for our young in their first few days. Those of my tribe can physically move more quickly than some of the others, but we think more profoundly, and that takes time. We avoid those that are faster of thought, as they will invariably seek to exploit us or see to our demise. You, however, are naught but a mortal. You are slower than me in both movement and thought. Come!'

The towering demon turned its back on the bed of armour and began to stride along the base of the cliff towards the mouth of a ravine that looked as if it headed towards the Fortress. The Hermis looked ungainly on its cloven feet, but just one of its paces was the equivalent to four of most mortals.

Vidius hurried to keep up, his mind whirling. What did it signify that the Hermis was leaving behind the armour that it had been guarding not a moment before? Did it realise the metal would be valueless once the archdemons came rampaging through?

He missed a step and stumbled. He was struggling to stay on his feet, so weak was he. The previous spheres had taken their toll on this mortal body and he had not eaten since entering this sphere. And his thoughts swam like he was ill... or dying.

'Hermis!' he coughed. 'Hermis, as you say, I am slower in movement than you. Wait!'

The demon stalked back towards him and, without a word, scooped him up and slung him over his shoulder. The demon was helping him! Why? It made no sense. Generosity did not exist amongst demonkind. Did the Hermis want him to get to the Fortress and open the way to and from the next sphere for some reason? What could the Hermis hope to gain? There was nothing obvious, but this creature claimed to be a profound thinker. Surely it could not foresee Vidius's intent, could it? After all, it was a mere demon rather than an archdemon or Prince.

His head jolting and stomach churning, Vidius could make no further sense of it and his mind gave up and became all but thoughtless. His consciousness drifted away...

※ ※

He came back to awareness as rain pattered down from the sky and wetted his face and lips. He opened his mouth and let the water coat his tongue. He swallowed, then blinked his stinging eyes. They blurred and his throat burned where the liquid had touched it. His face tingled and he wiped at it with his hands. They came away bloody. His stomach began to cramp.

'Arrrgh!'

He rolled over onto all fours to hide the exposed parts of him. He tucked his burning palms under his armpits and leaned in his elbows.

'Acid!' he croaked to the Hermis sat nearby.

The demon did not respond – either by way of movement or word. Its back was straight and its shoulders were thrown back as if it were meditating – perhaps it was. It was no doubt engaged in some of its oh-so-profound thinking. Its pitted, bony plates seemed to provide it with all the protection it needed from the elements.

Vidius knew that if he didn't find cover quickly, then his mortal body would become damaged beyond saving. He'd experienced mortal death on several occasions and knew it to be highly unpleasant. He quite understood all the fuss mortals made about it, why the fear of death sometimes drove them to the most extreme acts. But his main concern was keeping the body alive to conceal his true nature from those of the demon realm. If he were to be exposed now, so far from the epicentre of the realm's power, then his chances of triumph would be very slim indeed.

He hesitated. What had he just decided he needed?

Think, Vidius, damn it! What's the matter with you? Cover! Yes, cover, he needed cover. He looked stupidly at the Hermis. No, that wasn't cover. He pondered prying a piece of its armour away from its body and hiding himself under the metal, but it all looked too securely attached for him to attempt. Cover elsewhere.

He peered at the walls of the ravine. Perhaps there would be a ledge he could hide beneath, a crack or a cave. He began to crawl away from the Hermis, his knee caps and elbows in agony against the fizzing, stony ground. The material of his shirt began to disintegrate. His scalp was on fire now and his hair began to come away from his head in clumps.

I'm going to die, I'm dying! Please! No! Not like this. Not after the thousands of years I've been working, watching and waiting.

His mind howled as if its raw and bloody mass were being dragged cruelly across the sharp rocks. The ancient being within him screamed at the bodily walls that were its fortress, prison and home. It clung to them as if it could hold them in place through force of will. The walls began to lean and slip.

Come on, he wept. Ankles, wrists and shins were twisted and torn as he wrenched his way down the ravine. His mind became clearer the further he got from the Hermis, and his customary poise replaced the panic that had been churning within him a moment before.

The Hermis had to have been feeding off his mind somehow, devouring his thoughts without his realising it... or rather, he hadn't realised it precisely because the Hermis had been devouring his thoughts. No wonder it had wanted to accompany him – it had not been looking to help him, but to keep him alive a while longer so that it had more of his thoughts to feed on. And that probably explained why the Hermis were fairly solitary creatures – they would pose a danger even to their own kind.

They were thought-leeches and mind-parasites. Who knew if he would ever have woken again without the rude awakening of the searing rain? He was lucky to be alive, but maybe he was now faced with a more grizzly death than the relatively peaceful one he would otherwise have had as prey to the Hermis.

An opening! He staggered into a small hollow and wormed his way deeper into the rock. He scraped himself down to the bone, or so it felt, but at least he was dry, although he could still fill the necrotising action of the acid on his skin. He would have got stuck in the small, tight tunnel, but his blood provided enough lubricant to keep him inching forward. At any moment, he expected one of his ribs to catch on a piece of rock or wedge him between the walls. The next moment and the next moment, like the beating of his heart.

He wriggled into a larger space, shafts of light and rain lancing through the otherwise dimly lit chamber. Noise thundered and echoed all around him. A river nearby? But what were those strange, clinking sounds? He tottered twenty yards or so and plunged into fast flowing water. He prayed it would clean and cool his suffering flesh rather than prove to be yet more acid. Bliss. He gulped down mouthfuls until his stomach hurt and his body's need for air became more desperate than his thirst.

He came gasping back to the surface and half pulled himself out of the flood. He looked back at the water. It was too much to hope there might be fish in there. Besides, he knew he should pay more attention to the large, shifting shadows at the other end of the chamber first, to see if they came from some sort of threat.

His breath caught as he realised that a number of cyclopaes were there working at one wall of the chamber. They hammered with metal picks and hard rocks – and one actually punched with his bare hands – at the softer rock of the wall. The chunks that came away were tested with tooth and tool and the bits that seemed tougher than the rest were thrown into a nearby box on wheels. The brute who mined with his fists actually seemed to be eating some of the rock that he occasionally put in his mouth. All the creatures were big and stripped to the waist, their muscled arms and backs glistening with sweat even though the air temperature was relatively cool in the chamber.

Vidius was about to thank Wim that they hadn't spotted him yet, when he remembered the god of the mortal realm was an irrelevance here. Luck and chance did not exist within the philosophy of demonkind. There was only superior knowledge, in which case all the aspects, convergences and possible outcomes of an event or series of events would be known, or there was ignorance, in which case vulnerability and death would eventually result. Mortals were mortals because of their inferior knowledge. They were contemptible and unworthy of their higher plane of existence in so many ways. It was for just that reason that Vidius could be sure the demons of all houses and spheres would follow him once he had the Relic and could show them an open door to the mortal realm.

No, it was not luck the cyclopaes had not spotted him. They were too absorbed in their work to pay him any mind. It must be part of their philosophy to be so, part of what made them demons of the third house of the sphere. What was it the house was called? Fortis, or something like that? He mentally shrugged. The name was of little consequence. The cyclopaes themselves were of little consequence to one such as himself... although they might be an inconvenience given the opportunity.

Vidius crept past them and down a small tunnel. His body still protested, but the cold water had numbed him to the worst of it. There was plenty of light to see by, for the roof had fallen in in places and the sky could be seen above. The resulting rubble had all been pushed to the sides of the tunnel, presumably so that the box on wheels could be manoeuvred through. There were wheel tracks, grooves almost, on the floor. He would be able to follow them all the way to the Fortress if he was lucky.

The tracks he followed soon joined other, deeper tracks. Presumably, this was the main thoroughfare and was used by the numerous boxes on wheels that went up and came down the tunnels branching off this route. He was actually in more of a wide corridor than a tunnel now, designed to take larger volumes of traffic. Something big trundled towards him. Vidius pressed himself against the wall and allowed a hulking cyclops to pass him. The worker-demon stared at him with its one red-veined, bulging eye, but made no move to attack.

Sighing with relief, Vidius hurried on. Unless he'd lost his sense of direction, he was pretty sure he was heading in the general direction of the Fortress. There was a din ahead of him – presumably from the work place to which the mined ore was taken.

The walls and roof disappeared and emerged into the open air once more. Mercifully, the rain had now stopped. He was much closer to the black crag known as the Fortress. The half mile between where he was and the foot of the crag was a jumble of fires, smithies and slag heaps. Demons toiled everywhere, either carting ore or newly made weapons and armour, building or stoking kilns and ovens, forging red-hot metal or building strange and alien energies.

There were a few cyclopaes here, but the majority were impossibly thin, spiderlike creatures. They invariably had more than six limbs and seemed to be able to do more than one thing at once. Their bodies – if they could be called that – were clusters of eyes on waving stalks. Their limbs seemed to be little more than wire that ended in spikes or little clutches of fangs. These things defied the eye and true description, yet they reminded Vidius of the intricate inside workings of a clock for some reason. They wielded hammers and delicate tools with equal ease. They picked at things, tinkered with things and sometimes smashed and discarded them. There was a high-pitched scratching and screeching noise in the air. Was that their speech? Then he detected a lower hum as well, and he realised these demons were more redolent of the Chamberlain than anything else he recognised. Could the Chamberlain actually once have been one of these things? The philosophy of this house seemed to involve designing and building arcane devices of power with which to change a realm or balance of power. Did they ultimately intend to design and build their own reality?

Curiosity got the better of him, and he stopped to watch a many-limbed creature using acid to etch alien runes into a weapon that was half sword and half scythe. The runes were more than the simple decoration they might have been in the mortal realm. In the demon realm, where there was no chance, every utterance and word had relevance, meaning and power. Runes more than *represented* a demon's will, they *were* the demon's will. They gave the weapon will, such that a weapon would seem alive when wielded.

Next, he came upon a demon pressing spring-mounted blades and objects into a metal box. The demon secured a plate over each set of projectiles as they were pushed back and then set a trigger. If an unsuspecting individual attempted to open the box in the future, they would be cut to pieces. Such a device would have been useful to him back in the mortal realm, Vidius reflected. He shuddered with a distant delight and the demon's eye-stalks swivelled towards him. It chittered something and a second later Vidius was seized from behind and lifted into the air. A cyclops began to stride with him towards the black crag.

'What are you doing?' Vidius yelled, struggling with the powerful hand all but encircling his waist. 'Tell me and I will not resist you.'

The cyclops did not break stride but rumbled in the demon tongue: 'The Arachis said you are dying.' It wrinkled its nose. 'Your flesh smells rotten. You are broken. You will be thrown in the pit and your substance reused.'

'What is this pit? I am a traveller! I bring news. I have gifts. I have opened the gates to the other realms. They are ripe for you to plunder. I have secrets I will tell you if you will but stop. I have powers and magicks I can share with you.'

'I have no interest in such things,' the cyclops said simply.

Vidius could not understand the creature. Its philosophy was so different to his own, that he could not fathom how to influence it. Apparently, it could not be bribed. It lacked greed and ambition, seemingly. But surely it had fundamental wants and needs! What could they be? It was a demon of the fifth sphere: it had to have an ego he could manipulate!

They were at the Fortress now. The cyclops passed through a pair of thirty-foot high gates sheathed in black metal. They stood open, but a pair of twelve-foot tall sentinels watched all who passed through. They were clad in twisted, rune-inscribed armour that hid all parts of them, including their faces.

'Help me!' Vidius screamed at them. 'This cyclops has run mad. I have been summoned by the demons of the next sphere, but this creature seeks to use me for its own purposes.'

The sentinels did not twitch.

'Cyclops, I have food I can give you.'

The cyclops did not answer.

They passed through the outer wall of the crag and into an area open to the sky. The crag had an empty core like a chimney or volcano. The inside walls were tiered and there were staircases and seating in evidence. Occasionally, a door or opening led into the wall. It had the feeling of an amphitheatre of sorts. Wooden bridges and walkways were strung across the open space at different heights, and every now and then there was a platform suspended in the air by rope and chains. But what drew the eye was not the wonder above them, but the horror below.

In place of an arena floor was a wide pit ahead of them. It stretched thirty metres across and was filled with a raw stew of the dead and dying up to a few metres below the edge. He had no idea how deep the soup of old blood and bodily juices went, but he knew anyone thrown into it would quickly be sucked down into the slurry, like in a bog. The surface seemed to *quiver* with the final gasps and moans of those discarded wretches no longer deemed more useful alive than dead. Despite himself, Vidius found his mouth watering. So much delicious pain and flesh!

A demon suddenly began to thrash about in the mire and made it to the wall of the pit. A cyclops standing above pushed it back under with a long, forked pole.

The air was thick with the smell of rotting bile and faeces, and clouds of flies drifted lazily from one place on the surface to another.

'Cyclops, hear me!' Vidius begged. 'I will willingly throw myself into the pit if you will but tell me what you want.'

'I simply do my work, nothing more,' the cyclops grunted. It held Vidius out over the pit with one hand and casually picked its nose with the other.

Rather than seek to remove himself of the hand as he'd done before, Vidius now held onto it with utter desperation. 'Work? Yes! We should all simply do our work. It defines the Fortis, yes? Cyclops, I have work too, mining ore like you. But I have found a substance that cannot be broken down and brought to the Arachis. I cannot do my work and that is why you found me with the Arachis. I needed their help. I needed their best worker. Are you the best worker, cyclops, or is this work you cannot do? This ore would defeat you, I think. It would prevent your work and make you meaningless.'

'There is no work the Fortis cannot do,' his captor growled. 'There is no substance in the cosmos we cannot break down given enough time. No such substance exists,' it said with certainty.

With that, it opened its hand to let Vidius drop.

Vidius clung to two of its fingers and the cyclops bent its elbow as it readied to shake him loose.

'You might be right, cyclops, but I dug deeper than I ever have before. I think I must have come close to the core and power of our realm, for there were signs of adamantium, which can only be used by magical means. But this other ore I speak of defied even magic. Imagine the work and labour it must represent. Perhaps such work would take you to a higher plane of existence, cyclops. Perhaps you could work on the very substance of the cosmos itself. Then your eye truly would be all-seeing. The divine work would be within your purview and challenge. Can you see it, cyclops? Do you see?'

The cyclops's eye had become unfocussed. It did indeed see the promise of a new, greater work. The vision bedazzled and transfixed it.

Vidius went hand over hand along the cyclops's forearm, past its elbow and then up its bicep. He slid down its torso and put blessedly solid ground beneath his feet. He skipped behind the demon and kicked it in the back of the knee that was carrying most of its weight. As its leg gave, Vidius drove his shoulder up under its behind and pitched it into the waiting pit.

The cyclops plunged roaring beneath the surface of the swamp but immediately surged back up again. Vidius ran for the nearest staircase. The cyclops with the pole moved to push its fellow back into the eternally hungry pit.

Vidius's heart trembled and he staggered. Not now! He took a step that seemed to take all eternity. Please, not now! Let the mortal body last just a bit longer. His left bicep began to hurt and then his heart spasmed.

He hauled himself upwards. The body had stopped breathing. The brain still sparked with energy, but it was too bright. It was burning itself out. In desperation, he joined his essential being to the vestiges of life-force in the mortal body and forced himself into its central nervous system and vital centres. It was the most disgusting feeling he'd ever experienced, like a slug crawling down his throat and leaving a thick coating of mucus and excrement on his palate, but it would serve to keep him within the all but dead body, and keep it animated even as it started to decay.

His steps were clumsy and he fell a number of times, but he managed to work his way upwards. He all but collapsed onto the first platform suspended above the pit. A sentinel stood before him. Its visored faced tilted so that it could look down at him. He could see nothing of what was concealed within the rune-inscribed armour. Its eye slots were black.

'Sentinel,' Vidius rasped. 'Are you Nihil? I am an emissary of your long-since banished Prince. He is returning. I need to get to the gate to the next sphere.'

The sentinel looked towards the heights of the crag – was that where the gate was to be found? – and then back to Vidius. Its voice was misty as it said: 'Our Prince would send an emissary strong enough to win his way to the door without aid. You are just a mortal. You cannot be the emissary.'

'I am! You must…'

'Silence. Your words are as empty as you are, mortal. You do not even understand what you say. Such a being should not even be here, unless it is to serve as entertainment for the greater houses of this realm.'

'Listen to me, sentinel! I can give you…'

'Nothing. There is nothing of value a being such as you can give me. We will use you as entertainment. You will fight the lowest warrior of our enemies, the Spartis.'

The Spartis? Now he remembered. The Spartis were the last of the six houses. More than that, they were Balthagar's house! They vied for greatness with the Nihil. But to avoid all out war and genocide, the two houses had agreed to organise themselves in ranks and periodically set individual champions against each other. A warrior's rank was marked by the level at which he or she lived in the crag; the greater the warrior, the higher up he or she lived. When the Nihil champion of the first rank fought the Spartis champion of the first rank, the winner of the contest would be permitted to join the second rank. The loser would be thrown down into the pit, where they would become food for all the houses. Champions of the second rank would then be set against each other, and so on.

The organisation of the society within the crag was therefore a highly formalised one, one in which every demon knew their place. And there was no place for the mortal he appeared to be, Vidius realised.

How was he to ascend the crag to the next sphere? Short of revealing his true self, it seemed impossible. But just as demonkind did not believe in chance, they did not believe in the impossible.

Vidius raised his shaking mortal body and managed a lopsided smile. 'Then I will be happy to be entertainment for the Nihil and Spartis. I know I am worthless. It would be more honour than I could hope to be watched by them.'

The sentinel nodded. 'That is good, and as it should be. Wait here. I will find the lowest of the Nihil and Spartis warriors and see if any is prepared to fight you. In many ways, it would be a dishonour for them to be pitted against a mere mortal.'

'I will wait here.'

The sentinel moved away. Vidius watched him leave the platform and enter a doorway into the interior of the crag's wall. Vidius immediately broke into an uncoordinated run. He left the far side of the platform and hurried across a bridge made of rope and wooden planks. He dashed up some external stairs carved into the crag's wall. He reached the second level. There were shouts but he ignored them. He scaled more stairs, the steps becoming larger the higher he got. He was surprised that he hadn't been forced to slow yet. But he no longer had to breathe, so there was no burning of the lungs, no heaviness of the limbs. In some ways, he had been relieved of a burden, but then he realised in horror that his body was now only making progress by drawing on his essential being. His power was being diminished with each passing moment. How much could he afford to lose if he was still to win past archdemons and triumph over Princes? Precious little. Damn it, he would need to absorb the life and power of many others if he was now to succeed.

The third level, fourth level. How many more? There were roars below him. He ignored them, ran forward, jumped, grabbed the edge of the next step and hauled himself up. The demons at these levels must be large and mighty indeed. One began to emerge from a wide crack in the wall. It was a heavy mass with protruding spikes. It grunted in surprise as Vidius skipped past.

He looked up. Just what manner of gatekeeper awaited him at the top? He shot past winged demons lazing in the sun, past clouds of darkness – surely disembodied Nihil – past one that feasted on unidentifiable matter, past demons practising battle moves.

All eyes in the crag began to turn towards him. There were squawks, calls, howls and hoots. The inhabitants at all levels began to stir.

Come on, come on! Surely there were only a few levels left, but they were now too wide and high to climb any further. A hand the size of a cart blocked out the sun and came crashing down. Vidius rolled to the side. Instinct made him keep low. Another fleshy boulder smashed into the walled step ahead of him. The rock shattered and crumbled. Seizing his chance, Vidius sprang up the broken wall and onto the next level.

A cobbled, sloping walkway spiralled up to the top of the crag. He lurched into a run. Where was the gate, where was the gate? The host of demons below shrieked in outrage and he felt something stir. It was more than a physical movement. The sphere itself shifted in response to the significance of his transgression. The air pounded at his temples and membranes and became too thick for him to breathe. If he hadn't already been dead, he would have died then. His movement slowed in the heavy atmosphere and the drain on his essential being only increased.

He forced his way onwards. He came to a long, narrow sliver of gold in the wall near the top of the crag. It blinked at him. He staggered back in horror and almost fell into the chasm so hard was it for him to take in where he was. He realised that he had not been climbing a cobbled path, but the scaled tail of a gargantuan grey dragon coiled around the top of the crag. He now looked it in the eye and knew himself unworthy of the fabulous beast's notice. He was torn between throwing himself on his front in order to grovel for its forgiveness and beg the chance to show it his adoration and throwing himself out into the void to end his paltry, flea-like existence.

Smoke curled from the dragon's stone snout and drifted into the eternal sky. Vidius wished he could hang onto it and drift away into the cosmos. It would be falling asleep forever, letting go of all his troubles and knowing only wondrous dreams for the rest of time. Just let go, Vidius. He wavered on the edge of the precipice. It was so easy. Just lean into the wind and let it cushion you. Relax. All will be well.

Dreamily, he let himself tilt forward. He would find his place in the cosmos again. He would be restored, as if the wars had never happened.

He frowned somnambulantly. The wars had been terrible. Demonkind had been consigned to this lifeless pimple at the arse-end of the universe.

Millions of their kind had been sacrificed to feed the few that now remained. Millennia of demon civilization lost in all but moments. No, he would not return to the cosmos until he was ready to defend his place there and perhaps exact some measure of revenge upon the enemies of demonkind. He would not return to the cosmos until he had the resources of Shakri's realm – its life-force and magicks – at his command. With such planes of existence as his weapons, he would surely triumph over the cosmic forces that had set themselves against demonkind. Then, demonkind would finally ascend to its natural and rightful position as rulers of the cosmos. And as Demon King, he, Vidius, would be the greatest of the rulers. None could stand against him. The cosmos would be his to use or destroy as his philosophy saw fit.

At the last moment, he pulled himself back from the edge and went to confront the dragon once more.

The dragon spoke in his mind: 'You smell like carrion and must therefore be more than you appear. You have come to this highest of levels in the fifth sphere and must by definition be more than one of the trivial beings below. You survived my glamour and must be an archdemon or Prince. The gate is open to you, highness.'

Vidius nodded. 'That is as it should be, gatekeeper. Show me the gate.'

'The gate is within me, highness. You must enter in through my mouth.'

The dragon began to open its mighty jaws. Smoke and fire billowed out between its teeth. Vidius stepped into the furnace and felt his mortal body melt away.

❈ ❈

Kate woke with a start and sat up in bed. Something was wrong. She glanced at the smooth sheets and tidy pillow next to her. Saltar had not come to bed during the night. There was nothing unusual in that – many a time he stayed up to work on matters of state. She missed her husband on such occasions, as any hot-blooded wife would, but never in the past had it caused her to wake with such foreboding.

She threw back the covers and went to the pitcher of water kept for her morning ablutions. She broke the surface ice and poured the pitcher's contents into a wider bathing bowl. She wetted her face and then used a fresh cloth to wipe herself down.

'Lacrimos's cankerous testes, that's cold!'

She went hurriedly to her green leather armour and shrugged into it. She secured a long knife to her hip and then strung her crossbow across her back. She left the room, her sense of unease increasing. She'd hoped she'd simply suffered a night terror that would begin to fade once she was up and moving about, but this appeared to be something else. Her instincts were rarely wrong. She was all but running by the time she reached Orastes's room.

'What is it, milady?' the sluggish guard asked as she brushed past him. 'It is early yet. I have heard no sound of your son stirring.'

'Orastes!' she shouted. 'Where are you?'

The young boy wasn't in his bed. No! She had flashbacks to the last time he'd been taken. A discarded rag doll. Blood. Limbs. The smell of death.

Panic all but choked her. 'Orastes! Answer me!' she called hoarsely.

She rushed into the side room – perhaps he was dressing for weapons practice already. His armour was gone! No! She would not let this happen again.

She pulled her knife and went for the guard. 'What have you done with him!' she hissed, her eyes blazing and the veins at her temples raised. 'Give him to me!'

The guard stumbled backwards, hands waving in denial, mouth opening and closing uselessly. No! She pursued him, knife held at waist height, ready to punch it forwards at a slight upward angle so that it passed between the man's ribs and into his heart or lungs.

The man backed up against the far wall of the corridor outside the room and fell sideways. 'Help! Milady, no!'

'What is the meaning of this?' called an approaching officer with a man in tow coming to relieve the night watch. 'Milady, what is amiss?'

Kate punched the officer full in the face, watched him go down and then went back for the first guard. She slashed at him; he raised his forearms defensively and yelped in pain as the wickedly keen edge cut through his uniform and into his flesh.

The remaining guard pulled his sword but dared not attack the Green Witch, beloved of Saltar the Builder. 'Milady, Jessop is a good man. Tell me what has happened. Where is your son? Please, leave off this man who would not even dare defend himself against you. Every man here is loyal to you. Where is Orastes?'

Mention of her son had her whirling for the new man. 'Where is my son?' she asked incredulously. 'Guards who are set to watch him have the nerve to ask me where he is! What use is your loyalty to me if it cannot safeguard my son? Your loyalty is meaningless, *you* are meaningless.'

The officer now struggled back to his feet. 'Milady,' he said thickly, his nose probably broken, 'allow us to raise the alarm. He may yet be found quickly.' He flicked his hand at the man he'd brought with him. The guard did not hesitate to turn tail and go raise the palace. The officer turned on his man Jessop: 'At attention, man! A few cuts and bruises are the least you deserve. Now, understand this well. If you value your skin, you'll answer my questions truthfully. Do you understand?'

The man nodded in wide-eyed terror. 'Y-Yes, sir!'

'Jessop, did you fall asleep at your post last night?'

The man shook his head furiously. 'N-No, sir! Honestly, sir!'

The officer was silent for a second. 'Very well. Did you leave your post at any point? To go find a piss-pot, perhaps?'

The guard trembled. 'S-Sir, there was a noise down the corridor there. I went to investigate. But I can't have been gone more than a few seconds, honestly, sir... milady!'

The officer nodded, apparently prepared to believe the man. 'Milady, there is no concealed passage into your son's rooms, I take it? If not, then Orastes must have slipped out unnoticed while the guard was distracted. It suggests that he wasn't taken; rather, that he left of his own volition.'

Kate ground her teeth and briefly considered punching the oaf again. No, it would only waste their time, and probably wouldn't make her feel any better than the last time she'd punched him. 'Orastes wouldn't just leave,' she said with certainty. 'He knows better than that. You will hold this man until the Chamberlain has had a chance to question him. We'll see if he has anything else to tell us then. And I want every guard who was on duty last night questioned and flogged.'

Jessop visibly paled and his knees buckled. 'Not the Chamberlain. Please!' he moaned.

'F-Flogged, milady?' the officer said aghast. 'W-We only lash a man for a serious crime like theft.'

Kate smiled. 'Their incompetence has effectively stolen my child from me. They may think themselves fortunate I have not ordered their deaths. Let me be clear with you, little man – if you cannot follow my orders without question, then I will find someone who can. I hear there are Outdwellers in the army now, and all know that they revere me. Would you rather I have you and your men replaced by their like? And you can take their former place in the catacombs, scrabbling around for whatever rotting piece of flesh or human bone marrow you can find for your survival. Well? Is that what you'd prefer?'

'Of course not, milady!' the officer rushed. 'I will see to their questioning and punishment immediately.'

'And make sure that you are also questioned and punished, little man, for are you not responsible for your men?'

The officer gulped. 'Yes, milady, of course, milady.'

'Now get out of my sight! And find me the Chamberlain and my husband! Go!'

The officer led Jessop away. Kate didn't bother to watch them go. She stalked back to her son's room and went through it again but more meticulously this time. Nothing. He wasn't there. Her hands shook and tears started in her eyes. What had happened to her beloved son? Who had done this? There was no way he could have got past all the guards on his own. There must have been someone else involved, someone no doubt with magical talent.

Rage and panic consumed her. It was so great that it could not articulate itself in any way except a primal, animalistic cry. Her torment echoed down the corridors – there were none that could not have heard it, not even those still sleeping. It was such an essential pain and sound that it disturbed the soul of the listener, tormented them, hurt the roots of the hairs on the head or made their hearts shudder in the same way as Kate now did as her body was racked with sobbing and lamentation. If anyone had not heard the guards' alarm, they were now in no doubt that there was something terribly wrong in the palace.

She savagely wiped the tears from her face, not caring that her nails tore deeply into her skin. Tears would do her no good. What was she? A scared child wetting herself while she waited for her mother to bring the bad man to her room? Or was she a girl who calmly pulled a spike of wood from the frame of her bed and waited for the chance to plunge it into the neck of the unsuspecting bad man? She knew which girl it was who had freed her from her prison and torment. She knew what sort of actions had saved her last time. It would be those that saved her again.

She stood and looked around the room one last time, this time with cold appraisal. Nothing. She did not know what was signified by the absence of his armour, so filed the item away for later examination.

Where the hell were the Chamberlain and her husband? They should have come running. Those arrogant bastards always put their own concerns before anyone else's. They were so convinced and full of their own importance for the safety of the realm. Well what use was a realm if it contained nothing of value anymore? If they couldn't look out for the safety of her son, then they were no use to her, whether as retainer or husband.

And they weren't the only ones who had something to answer for.

'Cognis! Show yourself! Where's my son?' She waited. There was no answer. 'Listen, you wouldn't even exist if we hadn't saved you. Where is he? Answer me, damn it!' There was distant shouting amongst her guards, but that was all. 'Don't give me your nonsense about certain knowledge being too dangerous to mortal kind and the balance. If you make me ask again, then I will make no effort to save you in the future. So, where – ?'

Her ultimatum to the god of knowledge was interrupted by a breathless guard bursting into the room unannounced.

'Apologies, milady! Come quickly. We have found the Battle-leader and the Chamberlain!'

'Why haven't you brought them here?'

The guard became distressed. 'You will see, milady. Quickly!' With that, he ran from the room, as if he were seeking to flee her.

'Where are you going? I haven't dismissed you yet! Come back here!'

Yet he wouldn't wait and she had no choice but to pursue him. By the divine compassion of Shakri, what was going on?

※ ※

She strode up the wide, spiral stairs to the room at the top of the tower. Guards pressed themselves hard against the wall to let her pass, but also as if they wanted to escape her. They had all refused to answer her questions – were they scared of how she would react to what they knew? Yes, she tended to have a short temper, but only her enemies and those who failed her through negligence had any reason to fear her. Had they all been negligent? Surely not – the men were well trained and disciplined. Yet a good number must have been lacking in vigilance for Orastes to be spirited away unobserved. Had they now failed in something else?

Kate ran up the final climb of stairs and into the round room. The captain of the palace guard, Silos Var, was already there. He was dour at the best of times – a scar down his cheek and across one corner of his mouth kept his face permanently downturned – but now he looked grimmer than she'd ever seen him. Saltar and the Chamberlain were stretched out in the middle of the stone floor. Saltar's eyes were closed and he looked for all the world as if he was asleep. The Chamberlain's eyes, however, stared vacantly at the roof above. His mouth was open in a frozen snarl of pain. There was no doubt he was dead.

'What is this?' she asked quietly.

'Milady…' Silos Var began.

'Saltar, get up! Haven't you heard our son is missing?'

'Milady…'

'Be silent! I am talking to my husband. Saltar, didn't you hear me?'

'He's dead, milady. I'm so sorry,' the captain whispered.

She rounded on the man and stared at him. He couldn't hold her gaze. She said lightly. 'Well it's not the first time he's been dead, you know. Hmm. You don't understand. Get every man who knows about this in here now, captain.'

'Milady?' he asked.

'Captain!' she growled.

'Yes, milady!'

The men filed in, some looking grief-stricken, some apprehensive and others stony-faced. Some stared openly at the bodies, some stole furtive glances at them and others kept their eyes averted.

'Pay attention!' she ordered them. They all stood a little straighter. 'My husband is not dead. He only appears to be that way.' She saw the doubt and pity on their faces. They thought she'd lost her mind to grief. She sighed. 'Listen to me! You will not breathe a word to anyone of what you have seen here, on pain of death! It will only damage the morale of our people and encourage our enemies. On pain of death, do you understand?'

'Yes, milady!' they said in clear-voiced chorus.

They believed her when she threatened death. It was well that they did, else she might have to act on her words. They thought her mad and therefore believed her, therefore obeyed her. Perhaps it would be best for all of them then if she gave herself over to Wim's divine madness of grief after all.

'Silos Var, the palace guard and army will turn out and scour every hamlet and town in the kingdom until they find my son. Inform the Guardians that they are to do the same – too long have they put their own interests ahead of those of the kingdom. Let it be known amongst the people that we shall reward any who help return my son. And have Sister Spike sent to me immediately. I will remain here with my husband until he awakes, or until Mordius returns.'

To his credit, the captain managed to keep any misgivings he had about the orders from showing on his face, and his hesitation in answering was hardly noticeable. 'At once, milady. Only those troops essential to the defence of Corinus will remain on its walls.'

'No, Silos Var. *Every* man will turn out. Corinus can defend itself as need be. We are not at war and the temples, nobles and merchants have enough men to deal with any other trouble that might arise.'

This time, the man's hesitation was more marked and his scar twitched. 'Milady, it is not my place to question the wisdom of any order you choose to give me, yet out of loyalty to you and the kingdom I feel I must. May I speak, milady?'

Kate smiled ambiguously. 'But of course. I am happy to stand here bandying words with you when every second that passes could see my son in greater and greater peril. So, please, say on, Silos Var.'

The soldier swallowed and then lifted his chin. 'Milady, the first loyalty of the temples, nobles and merchants is hardly to the throne. We cannot be sure they would have any interest in defending Corinus. In fact, it is the very fact that they have followers and retainers at their command that I am concerned about removing all troops from the city. I have heard it second-hand that there is talk amongst the people — talk no doubt started by the nobility — of restoring the monarchy of Dur Memnos. In the inns and drinking houses they discuss some fanciful notion of a lost golden age, an age of wise kings and queens and great prosperity for the people.'

What was this? His words genuinely shocked her. She'd heard nothing of such things from the Chamberlain, who was meant to have a network of spies throughout the city. Saltar would not have kept such a thing from her if he'd known, would he? Kate frowned. 'I see,' she said slowly. 'Of the existing nobles, whose blood line might give them claim?'

'Ah… er… I am not so certain, milady. The genealogy of the noble families is an area that…'

'Silos Var!' she snapped, tightening her fist until the leather of her green gloves creaked. 'I have indulged you thus far. Tell me who might make a claim! Which noble has enough men to give us pause? Speak up, man!'

'Milady, it is said Lord Selwyn is a man with strong opinions about how the kingdom should be ruled.'

'Thank you, captain. Please carry out your orders as I have asked. In the meantime, Sister Spike and I will pay our Lord Selwyn a small visit. Dismissed!'

Could it be this ambitious noble who had taken her son? She would take great delight in torturing the man whether he was responsible for Orastes's disappearance or not. The man clearly needed dissuading of any ambitions he might have towards the throne. How would she go about it? A blade? Coals? Hmm. Too prosaic. Maybe Sister Spike would have some ideas. In some ways, it was a shame the Chamberlain was dead, for he'd been a master of the art. Then again, she'd wished the spider dead a dozen times over the years, so perhaps it wasn't such a bad thing he was finally gone.

As for Saltar, as much as she loved him, he'd just have to wait till she'd seen to this Selwyn, as he might lead her to his son. Besides, Saltar was more than capable of looking after himself even when dead. That, of course, was one of the things she loved about him. And that useless necromancer should be back soon to start finally earning his keep.

※ ※

'They're inside the grounds!' came the panicked shouts of Accritanian soldiers from outside the palace.

'I don't understand,' Colonel Vallus said to his General. 'I saw to the sealing of the gates myself. They shouldn't have fallen so quickly.'

'It's Adjutant Spindar, sir!' shouted a man who dashed inside. 'He's gone mad. Killed some of the men and let in the mob.'

'What?' Constantus spluttered. *You old fool! You knew he was no good. Now you've got the death of those men on your conscience.*

'Orders, General!' Colonel Vallus urged.

'Get the men inside! Seal the palace doors! Move!' Constantus roared.

His men jumped to obey him, although he knew it was the drills Vallus put them through every day that saw them so disciplined. One of them guarding the doors called: 'There are still a dozen out there, sir. They will be cut down if they try to disengage the enemy. They will be overrun soon and then we might not be able to get the doors closed. Your orders, sir?'

Are you even still fit to lead these men, you old fool? No one will blame you if you have the door sealed… no one except yourself. 'You men with shields form up on me. We will charge with shields to the fore. Avoid killing civilians if you can, but do not treat them gently. We must batter them back and then retreat in orderly fashion. Are you ready? Are you Accritanians?'

'Yes, sir!' they shouted, chests proud.

'General, we cannot risk losing you,' Colonel Vallus protested. 'Let me do this!'

'Colonel, if you are my friend, then you will be silent. You men, for Accritania, charge!'

They ran out into the chaos of the night and slammed into the press of crazed citizens. A few elders tottered amongst them. Constantus saw one knocked to the ground and trampled underfoot by those coming on behind. Men and women, some in rags, some in rich garments, hissed and spat at the soldiers. Children screamed in high-pitched anger. They fought to get forwards and lay hands on the soldiers fighting a desperate retreat. A teenage boy hooked his hand into one of the old soldiers belt and sought to pull him down. The veteran slashed down with his short, heavy sword and lopped the boy's hand off. The boy didn't seem to notice the fount of blood now issuing from where his right hand had just been and tried to grapple with the soldier once more. The veteran booted the boy backwards with a foot to the middle of the chest and then turned to face the next raving citizen.

'They have no weapons but they do not fear us!' warbled a younger soldier on Constantus's flank.

Constantus punched the hilt of his sword into the drooling face of a man who seemed a carpenter by his apron and hollered: 'Yet they bleed like any other! Shields up! Form a wall! Fall back!'

One of his men slipped and fell to his knees. As he pushed himself up, a woman raked her claws across his face and drew blood. She grabbed the sides of his head and bit into his cheek. The trooper pushed his sword up under her rib cage, but then his hands fell away. His eyes glazed over and he slowly stood.

'Get over here, man!'

The soldier looked towards the General, no recognition on his face. Then he snarled and something else possessed him. A hate-filled intelligence glared from his eyes.

'Ah! Little General, there you are! Come fight me!'

'Who are you?' Constantus demanded.

'We are Cholerax,' the host brayed at him. 'Come, be one with your people, or do you need half a bottle of brandy before you can make any decision concerning the people?'

'What?' Constantus stammered. 'I-I...'

Adjutant Spindar strode out of the crowd towards him. The handsome young officer smiled smugly. 'Come on, you old sot, let's finish this once and for all. You've never been worthy of leading these people. In fact, you haven't really led them in years, for as we both know I've been the one running things. The people have had enough of you, you old fraud, and want you out.'

'Spindar,' Constantus growled, 'it will give me great pleasure to cut your waggling tongue out and force you to eat it!'

The General raised his sword and was about to rush forwards when strong arms hooked under each of his armpits, all but lifted him and ran him back towards the palace.

'Sorry, General!' Colonel Vallus said over his shoulder.

'Unhand me, you insubordinate dog!'

'Kill them!' Spindar yelled in a non-human, echoing voice.

But the General's men reformed their shield wall and retreated in disciplined order. The mob battered and clawed at them, but they stayed firm. The soldiers held the stairs up to the palace doors long enough to get their General inside and then backed in after him. They heaved the portal closed, crushing a frenzied, young woman in the process, and slammed home the heavy locking bar.

'What do you think you're doing?' Constantus shouted in Vallus's face.

'General, even if you had killed him, the mob would then have torn you apart. We could not afford to lose you.' Then Vallus added more quietly: 'A wise old soldier once told me that there was no such thing as glory and that they key to winning a war was staying alive.'

Constantus considered his man for a moment and then sighed. 'Then perhaps I'm not as wise as I once was, eh? Perhaps Spindar was right. Perhaps there are others better suited to leading than I.'

Vallus smiled gently. 'Forgive me, General, but I've followed you long enough to know that isn't true. You're just a bit... out of practice is all. The fire within you has become banked by your spending too many hours in that office of yours.'

'I've become a soft pen-pusher, you mean. There was a time when no two men would have been able to manhandle me like that.' He gestured at his loose uniform. 'You see, I am much diminished, half the man I used to be, eh? But to more pressing matters! Colonel, how many men are we?'

Colonel Vallus came to attention. 'Four hundred as near as I can tell, General. What are our orders, sir? To hole up here, defend the seat of government and wait for reinforcements? There's enough food in the kitchens to keep us supplied for weeks. Or to fight our way clear, General?'

Constantus shook his head. 'Neither. There's a tunnel out of here from beneath the old throne of King Orastes, Lacrimos preserve his departed spirit. Colonel, we are going to run away.'

Vallus hardly blinked. 'Very good, General.'

'I cannot ask our men to massacre the good people of Accros, Colonel, no matter what evil seems to have touched the citizens. I cannot ask our men to cut down their own kith and kin. And Accritania couldn't afford the loss. Our history is already so deep in blood that we are yet close to drowning in it. So we will run away, Colonel, and regroup. We will seek what friends we may. Let us only hope that the sickness or plague that is Cholerax does not reach them ahead of us. I must admit that I am at a loss as to how to fight this insanity. I just pray that we can find a priest or magician to help us, and that holy Shakri has not forsaken us.'

'As do we all, General. And what of your lady wife?' Vallus murmured.

Pain touched the General's face. 'My sweet Hesta! She knows to flee the city and not wait for me in such a situation. She will find her country relations, Vallus, I'm sure. And one last thing before we empty the kitchens and leave this cursed place, Vallus.'

'Yes, General?'

'Thank you for saving me, my friend.'

The Colonel nodded. 'You have saved my life often enough, General. Yet if you consider yourself in my debt, then I am sure you will soon have the chance to return the favour in this world-gone-mad.'

'Yes, my friend. And let us hope it will be a favour, eh? Otherwise, Lacrimos will have forsaken us too.'

Chapter Six: Become something worse

Ja'rahl, Eternal High Priest of the Living God Istris, resisted the urge to scratch at the face of the body within which he'd been trapped for millennia. It had died long ago, but for some reason his consciousness had survived and this body had remained animated. He wondered if it was Istris who had blessed or cursed him with such longevity, but the god had never mentioned it or shown any other real concern for its priesthood or people. In fact, Istris and the rest of the sphinkaes had entirely lost interest in the day-to-day life of Jaffra. Centuries before, they'd become listless and then stopped moving altogether. The last thing divine Istris had told Ja'rahl was that the sphinkaes would sleep until the time of *the return*. The god had not really explained what this return was, but had commanded Ja'rahl to watch the stars and the affairs of men closely for signs of the realms of god and man coming together. At such a time, it would be the priesthood's task to transport the divine sphinkaes to the place of the greatest power in the mortal realm. Then the god had fallen silent and the decades had passed. The flesh of the sphinkaes had hardened and taken on the colour of the desert dust that now all but permanently filled the air.

The sphinkaes had become little more than a collection of statues, and there were now no Jaffrans left alive – save for the eternal Ja'rahl – who had ever seen the sphinkaes otherwise. None had memories of the divine majesty of a sphinx when it moved. None knew the terror of when the sphinkaes announced a festival day and hunted their people for sport. None appreciated the devastating magicks that were the sphinkaes' to command, like the power to paralyse and power to read the minds of the people. The wonder of Istris had been denied the people – clearly, the people had been found lacking by the sphinkaes. Surely it was no coincidence that the island of Jaffra had fallen into decline since the sphinkaes had entered their long sleep. Where once the island had been an abundant garden of fruit and flowers, now the entire interior was a barren desert. Jaffra's power as a trading nation had similarly declined. Jaffra and its people were no longer sustained by its god, and that was why Ja'rahl suspected his own continued existence was down to something other than Istris.

Ja'rahl had come to realise that if he was not sustained by Istris, then he must be some sort of creature who was different to the people of Jaffra and had a different origin. But he lacked any clear memory of parents or a childhood. He remembered that he'd studied briefly to be a priest and then all but immediately been called on by Istris to serve as a high priest. The god had seemed to know something of Ja'rahl's past, but had always declined to make anything but indirect reference to it. Besides, the divine Istris had pointed out, compared to the honour of serving Istris, nothing else could have significant meaning, could it, so Ja'rahl should stop asking.

Ja'rahl had decided it ultimately did not matter where he'd come from. His god and position as high priest gave him purpose and all the direction he required for his continued existence. In addition to watching for the return, only he understood how lacking and unworthy the people of Jaffra were. Only he therefore understood what was required to make them worthy of the wonder of the sphinkaes once more. Only he understood how much awe and terror of the sphinkaes needed to be inspired in the people to keep them faithful, to keep them believing that the sphinkaes were just sleeping rather than a dusty collection of statues and stories. Only he understood how much blood had to be shed to keep them faithful and to sustain him as their eternal and puissant high priest.

When Ja'rahl had died, his flesh and become sunken. Then his skin had dried out and begun to flake away. He'd had the misfortune to get caught one time when the wind had suddenly changed direction: a scouring blast off the desert had all but stripped his face away. Terrified that all skin and sinew would be removed and leave nothing to keep his bones knit together and articulated, he'd tried all manner of things to keep his body protected.

First he'd tried bandages, but wind-carried grit would always find a way to get under the material, cause friction and abrade him. Veils and loose robes had provided even less protection. Then he'd realised damp material served to trap potentially damaging airborne particles, and so he'd experimented with different combinations of materials and liquids. Water-soaked wraps were no good, for the thirsty air dried them in seconds. Sitting in baths of water or milk only served to shrivel and rot his flesh – the black, putrefying flesh of his left foot was a permanent reminder of that.

He'd had more success with oils, for they'd both soaked into his flesh – apparently to give it more substance – and protected his skin. The only problem had been when the oil had become too full of dirt that it could do little to protect him anymore. His servants had gently tried to wipe him down – but the nature of the oil had meant that they only succeeded in moving dirt from one place on his body to another. Only quite firm strokes had succeeded in shifting the grinding dirt, but unfortunately that had resulted in black and red blooms of subcutaneous damage and bruising appearing all over him.

Perhaps unsurprisingly, the natural answer to protecting his body had been blood. And human blood had proven to be more effective than anything an animal could provide. He'd paint himself with fresh blood every few hours, and that would always keep his skin protected. Dust that got trapped in the glistening red paint stayed on the surface and never got to his skin. If the blood ever got too dry, it would begin to flake away long before his skin ever did.

Human blood seemed to make him stronger too. His command of magic had increased far beyond anything he'd known when he was alive. He could now sense the life-force within freshly drawn blood – that which came from the young was the most intoxicating.

In the early days, he'd had his priests sacrifice a dozen young criminals at a time – child-thieves and the like – to fill baths in which he could immerse his withered frame. They'd soon run out of young criminals and he'd moved onto young slaves, young worshippers who could be coerced by his priests and adults who had committed offences against the temple.

They'd been heady days, and perhaps he'd been drunk on power for a while, for Jaffra had reached a point where its population had begun to fall at an alarming rate. None had dared to challenge the priestly rulers of Jaffra, for the temple of Istris was all powerful and the will of its high priest was as law, but in his wisdom Ja'rahl had decided it was in the best interests of Jaffra that the people no longer sacrifice their lives – rather, they should bleed themselves as required by the temple and offer up their blood as a tithe. Besides, all knew that it was a sensible part of any health regime to bleed the body on a regular basis, to ensure its humours remained in balance.

The tithe offered up to the temple by the people of Jaffra usually sufficed, but very little of it was still fresh when it arrived, meaning that much of the life-force had dissipated from it. And the quantities supplied by the elderly were often meagre, thick or watery – only fit for use as manure on the temple's blood gardens. On one occasion, a sickly-looking worshipper had dared offer up pig's blood and pretended that it was his own. Ja'rahl had been forced to make an example of the man and drain him of every drop of his blasphemous blood in the middle of the capital city's main square. Did the infidel not understand that the blood required by the temple was used to keep the high priest both eternal and powerful so that he could work to keep the people worthy of Istris and the time of return? If in their selfishness any infidel refused to understand it, then they had no place amongst the people of Jaffra, and the life gifted to them by Istris was therefore forfeit. Furthermore, it was because of such problems that Ja'rahl was forced to maintain in the temple a group of young slaves who might be bled when he needed to perform a more complex piece of magic than usual.

That morning, he'd had all fifty of his slaves bled, for today would see him attempt a far greater working that he ever had before. Today, he would finally start to capture and destroy the false gods of the powerful infidel kingdom of Dur Memnos. Long had he watched this kingdom, for there was little doubt that it was the most powerful place in the mortal realm. He'd even sent spies into that foreign land and purchased commissions of Holter's Cross to help destabilise the rulers of Dur Memnos and keep them at war with the other great infidel kingdom, Accritania, but all to no avail. It seemed that this unholy Builder who had seized the Memnosian throne was not to be easily dislodged. Well, brooded Ja'rahl, it was time to see just how well the Builder fared without his false gods, who were surely nothing more than posturing mummers and magicians, to support him. Once they were removed, the way would be clear for the sphinkaes and the return. For the signs were unmistakable: the stars were close to a celestial alignment that had not been seen in millennia; his spies reported that the people of Dur Memnos and Accritania spoke on the streets of the sighting of numerous djin, the holy servants of the true god Istris; and the purges through which he'd put the people of Jaffra in the last few weeks had surely made them worthier than they'd been in centuries.

'Is all prepared?' Ja'rahl gurgled to one of his attendant priests.

The priest bowed. 'Yes, Eternal. The blood gardens have been fed until the plants can take no more and the blood will no longer soak into the ground.'

'Very good. And the god house has been built to my specification?'

'All as you commanded it, Eternal. The ground beneath was saturated. The mixes for the bricks and mortar of the double walls were rich in blood. No gaps or windows. Only a door that makes an air-tight seal on the cell, and the door is made of the flesh of the oldest tree from the blood gardens.'

'Then I will prepare myself and come to the gardens. Be sure all our priests are in position and ready for my arrival. Go now.'

'Yes, Eternal,' the priest said without hesitation and quickly departed.

'You, you may approach,' Ja'rahl directed one of his young body slaves. 'I must be painted afresh before I attempt this sacred undertaking. Come, gently remove my robes and cover me with the bloody emulsion here in this ewer.'

The pale boy shuffled forwards and began to unfasten Ja'rahl's priestly robes. The boy's eyes were dull – either because he was dim-witted or as a consequence of being bled that morning – but he trembled with excitement as he undertook the honour of serving the eternal high priest of Istris. Then again, maybe the boy had heard what had happened to the last body slave to remove Ja'rahl's robes too roughly, and was therefore quite rightly shaking in terror.

'Take the brush, boy. Make sure that you don't miss any area. No need to be coy.'

The slave was tentative at first.

'Work faster or the blood will begin to dry. Then I will need more fresh blood. Do you take my meaning, boy?'

The threat had the desired effect and the slave applied the blood much more quickly.

'Be particularly generous on the areas that chafe together – the inner thighs, the armpits, and so on. That's it. And where my robes rub – the knees, shoulders and elbows.'

Life-force suffused the red priest. He felt so strong, almost virile, though of course his dead body could produce no seed. He saw everything more sharply, he could tell where his priests were positioned out in the gardens by smell alone, on his tongue he could taste the onion eaten for breakfast by whoever had supplied the blood that now coated him, he felt his body slave blink by the mere movement of air, he could hear the heavens turn and he could sense the thoughts of the beings and gods who existed beyond mortal scrutiny. There was nothing he could not touch. Now he was ready to face the false gods who confused, misled and used mortal kingdoms for their own ends. In many ways, what he did now would be the saving of the entire mortal realm. He would become the eternal priest to all peoples, and the wonder of Istris would surely be returned to the people of Jaffra.

His robes were refastened and he carefully made his way out into the blood gardens. His priests lined the perimeter, each holding a bowl of fresh blood. In the centre of the garden was the newly constructed god house. Now was the moment. *Now began the return.* He was herald, prophet, priest and messiah. Just as Istris gave him meaning, Ja'rahl gave the people of Jaffra meaning. There was a divine and natural symmetry to it that meant his words and actions must be justified and self-fulfilling. The cosmos itself turned on what he did here: the stars, timing and patterning of events in the mortal realm, the working of his magic, the fall of the false gods and the beginning of the return all coming together in harmony and accord, just as it had been spoken, decided and pre-destined by divine Istris. Ah, wondrous Istris, all-knowing and all-powerful! How blessed was Ja'rahl! What enlightenment and epiphany were his when he acted by the will of Istris. What would he not do for his beloved god!

'Morphia!' Ja'rahl cried plaintively, and all his priests echoed him. 'Hear me, holy Morphia!' Again the priests repeated his words and those that followed: 'Hear us in our suffering, Morphia! Too long have we been lost. Too long have we turned away from you. Too long have we been in the thrall of the cruel and bloody god Istris. But some few of us have seen the beauty and truth of your divinity in our dreams, those holy visions with which you bless mortal kind. At great risk to ourselves, we have come together in secret to join our voices in prayer to you. Holy Seeress, hear us! We are blind without you and Jaffra will continue in darkness without you. We exhort you to light our way! We exhort you to appear to us here so that we might know you hear us. Bless us with a waking dream and come to us, holy Morphia! Morphia! Morphia!'

'Morphia! Morphia! Morphia!'

The priests chanted on and on.

The air between Ja'rahl and the god house began to sparkle and shimmer. The world seen through the light twisted and shifted slowly, like in a dream. Ja'rahl saw moments from his past and other scenes he did not recognise – were they his future? No, they were the lies of the false god, nothing more.

'Morphia! Morphia! Morphia!'

Eyes like the sky, like the sea, like void, looked out at them. She was beautiful and loving, ugly and terrifying, tantalising and confusing, wistful and forgetting.

'Morphia! Morphia! Morphia!'

The eyes moved behind a mask, then a veil, then the bandage of a seer. She approached.

'Morphia! Morphia! Morphia!'

And stepped into the blood gardens of the temple of Istris. The priests drifted in from the perimeter towards her, drizzling lines of blood as they came. Ja'rahl moved towards Her and threw his blood-coated corpse on the ground at Her feet.

'Sweet Morphia!' he moaned in a parody of religious ecstasy.

The priests drifted in further. Their trails of blood became connected, creating an unbroken cordon around the god house and the Memnosian god.

'Morphia, speak to us!' Ja'rahl pleaded.

'It is dark here,' She whispered. 'I do not understand why the future is dark here. All I see is black blood, a sea of black blood. Its meaning... its meaning is...'

Ja'rahl came quickly to his knees and moved for the blind goddess before She could divine what he was about. 'Now!' he screeched at his priests.

'... is more than simple death! It represents an end to the pantheon!'

Ja'rahl quickly poured blood around and under the feet of the goddess and splashed it up Her clothing and onto Her hands. His priests threw strings of blood over them, creating a shining cobweb over them.

'Shakri, help me! No!' Morphia screamed, Her usually peaceful face racked in nightmare. 'Mortal creatures, sleep! Morphia commands you sleep forever more! You are now subjects of the realm of sleep, where my word and will are absolute!'

As one, Ja'rahl's twenty priests collapsed to the ground, eyes rolled back in their heads, bowls and ewers of blood falling from their hands. Some fell badly and did not move again – their lives ended. Others twitched violently or drummed their heels as they were visited by the horrors of Morphia's realm.

Ja'rahl chuckled.

Morphia's head moved this way and that. 'Who's there?'

'Can't you see, dear Morphia? What worth is a seer who cannot see? You are rendered empty and false before the power of Istris and the eternal priest of Jaffra. I do not sleep, you see, so your parlour tricks will avail you naught. Are there no other magicks with which you might defend yourself? Is this all you have? And you call yourself a goddess for this? I have seen stablemen put horses to sleep, farmers down bulls, charmers bespell snakes and fakirs mesmerise their audiences, yet they do not set themselves up as gods and goddesses and demand worship from others. You are a blasphemy! Your life is forfeit to Istris'

Morphia backed away, mouthing words and making hand gestures to conjure a gateway back to Her own realm. Tears of panic trickled from beneath the bandage over Her eyes.

'By the words that summoned you, I bind you here,' Ja'rahl croaked happily. 'By the blood dedicated to Istris that describes this place and paints your body. I bind you here. By the words and actions of my will do I bind you. You are incapable of speech or movement except as an extension of my will.'

Morphia choked on Her words and Her hands curled into useless claws. She trod clumsily on the trailing edge of Her light, floating robe and it tore away from Her shoulders. Near naked, She fell to the ground and lay sprawled on the bloody grass.

Ja'rahl picked his way over to Her and slowly lowered his decayed body down to Her. She was beautiful, even he could recognise that. If his body had had any life in it, it might have responded more lasciviously to that beauty, but if it had had any life in it, he'd have been the one stretched out on the ground – like his priests – at Morphia's mercy. He would take his pleasure of Her in different ways. 'Now, sweet Morphia,' he murmured intimately. 'Let us see how a goddess bleeds. Do not resist and I will be gentle with you. I must insert my blade here. That's it! So delicate! See how it flows, as if eager to give itself up to me, as if desiring to surrender itself to its new master.'

He gathered Her shimmering blood in a deep bowl and then stemmed the flow. He did not want Her to die just yet. He would keep Her imprisoned in the god house and tap Her each day, for as long as he needed Her blood, or until it became so thinned that is was no longer of any use to him.

Shaking with anticipation, unable to wait for body slave and brush, he used his thin fingers to start daubing his black-crimson with the divine ichor from Morphia's veins. The substance was so powerful that he was instantly drunk on it. It was the life-force of a being of an entirely different nature to any he'd experienced before. It was like a pure and distilled form of magic itself. It was matter as power, power as matter. It was so intoxicating and addictive that he felt thirst for the first time in centuries. He guzzled it down his throat, not caring that he'd long since lost all of his soft internal tissue. He almost felt alive!

He desperately craved more. He looked down at the small cut in Morphia's arm and was tempted to suck at it with his desiccated lips. Imagine what it would be like to have all of Her inside him, to consume Her flesh, eyelashes, hair, lungs and nails. His imagining became a sight of sorts and he saw pieces of different futures as clearly as he saw the blood gardens in the sunshine before him.

Yes, he had Her visionary power. He saw the convergence happening throughout the mortal realm that would return Istris to them. He saw Morphia thrown into the god house, to service him as required. He saw him summoning the boy-god Istrakon next. Ah! How sweet, how delicious, the child's blood! He saw the war fleet Jaffra had secretly been building for decades finally launched against Dur Memnos. He saw the sphinkaes delivered to Corinus. He saw the fall of Shakri's pantheon of false gods. As much blood as he could ever want, seas of black blood!

❈ ❈

Jack knew that if he didn't stop soon, then he would collapse and perhaps never rise again. Yet he dared not stop. He looked anxiously back over his shoulder. The forest seemed quiet but he knew the Scourge was somewhere out there. He was always out there, always tracking, always hunting. Whether at night or during a storm, he kept coming.

Even with his demon magicks, Jack had only just managed to stay ahead of the seemingly indefatigable Guardian all these years. He simply had to be more than human! Since when had simple obsession ever given a human such stamina and endurance? And was the Scourge not beloved of Shakri? That certainly meant he was more than your average mortal. Could he be something else then? Just how long *had* the Scourge been alive? When had Jack first met him? He couldn't quite remember. It seemed like the Scourge had always been there, with the same wolfish features and black, glittering eyes. Yes, there was more white in the mortal's hair now, but he wore it like a winter coat that he would shrug off with the season. He was stronger and more savage than he'd even been, a true and daunting guardian of this realm.

And now Jack was without either his horse or Lucius. Could he really hope to stay ahead of the Scourge? He could almost feel the wolf's breath on the back of his neck. He was genuinely afraid. And he missed Lucius – the closest thing he'd ever had to a friend. Who'd have thought a mortal could have proved so... useful? Not only had he been educated and courtly enough to make them welcome in the most respectable of establishments, but he was also the most gifted musician Jack had come across, and capable of earning them great sums of money and any manner of hospitality they might require. Lucius's music combined with Jack's voice of persuasion so that they could induce the hardest of hearts to love again, compel the most stubborn of individuals to co-operate and move the most remorseless of criminals to tears. Together, there was no argument they could not win, no enemy they could not win over or sentiment they could not create or destroy. They'd been as powerful as the gods themselves. Yet the Scourge had found a way to undo them, and now they were nothing but fallen gods. Was not *godslayer* one of the Scourge's monikers anyway? Jack should think himself lucky he still survived then.

Worse, Jack was only as scared of the Scourge as he was frantic about getting to the Valley of the Brethren for the appointed day and time. Unhorsed as he was, he stood little chance of getting there in timely fashion. Normally, he could have lost the Scourge by laying elaborate false trails or travelling from tree to tree amongst the branches. Then he could have found a small hamlet and stolen a beast to carry him at his leisure. As it was, he would have to take a direct route and just hope that the wolf did not find him before Jack had come across a small home with a stable somewhere.

Every part of him was in pain. He wasn't as fit as he'd once been. The comparative luxury of life on the road with Lucius must have softened him. And his body wasn't as young as it had once been either. Perhaps he should have given it up a while back – and tricked some unsuspecting youngster out of their own sack of flesh – but somehow he'd grown attached to it. The skin was comfortable. It felt like his own. And the mortal women of this realm certainly seemed to find this visage and shape agreeable. There'd been a wonderful mother and daughter he'd met in Stangeld... but, no, now was not the time to be thinking of such things. If he was to carry on eluding the Scourge successfully, then it was probably time for a change. He resolved to pick up a new body for himself if he could at the same time he procured himself a horse.

He slowed from a run to a quick walk and then an even slower pace. He needed to recover somewhat, for he knew there was a deep and fast-flowing river not far distant, and he would need considerable strength to cross it at even the best crossing point. He dared not use magic to run on such water, for it might kill him given his weakened state.

He reached the top of the steep bank down to the river and followed it half a mile to the relatively narrow place Lucius and he used when they came through here each year. He held onto fragile ferns as he carefully made his way down the slippery slope. His feet went out from under him and he hit the ground hard with his shoulder. He couldn't halt his slide and was suddenly plunging beneath the surface of dark, rushing water.

Jack struggled back up, gasping. He cast out for the other bank, but one of his arms had gone dead because of how he'd landed on it and his clothes dragged at him like a millstone round his neck. He tried to gulp extra air, but he only succeeded in taking water into his lungs. He spluttered and came dangerously close to going under. Close to panic, he heaved himself up, grabbed half a breath and then speared down to the river's rocky bottom. With his legs, he pushed himself forwards and up and came back to the surface a metre further across the river than he had been before. He repeated the trick several times and felt giddy with joy – although it could have been the cold of the water making him light-headed – now he knew he would live.

He hauled himself out on the far side and lay panting and wheezing for long minutes. He knew he had to get moving to warm himself up but his muscles shook with fatigue. He shivered and his teeth chattered painfully.

'Up, you weakling!' he chided himself. 'Anyone would think you'd taken on mortal failings along with this body. Up! You wouldn't catch the Scourge lying about and sunning himself when he had enemies at large, now would you? Up!'

He rose on unsteady legs and surveyed the bank ahead of him. He sighed. He kicked at the muddy bank until he'd made a secure stepping point to place all his weight. He stepped up and began to kick the bank again, this time with his other foot. He was soon breathing hard again. This was going to take a long time.

Jack finally crawled over the top of the bank and rolled onto his back. His chest heaved and tears of exhaustion ran from his eyes.

'Ah, there you are, demon! I've been waiting so long I'd begun to fear you'd lost your way. But I've spent five years looking for you, so I'll forgive the few extra hours. There is much else that I cannot forgive you for, however. It is not for me to forgive you for crimes such as murder and body-theft, you see. Yet, as a Guardian, it *is* for me to punish you for such crimes. It's rare that I take much enjoyment from meting out punishment. But on this occasion, I feel I might. Let's see, shall we?'

So the wolf had found him. Jack raised his heavy head and saw the Scourge glaring down at him from a massive destrier not more than fifteen yards away. The Guardian had a long knife free of its scabbard already, and was unnecessarily testing its edge with his thumb.

Jack let his head bump back on the ground. He stared up at the grey, implacable sky. What hope did he have of resisting a realm driven by such forces? None, of course. So why bother? There'd been an inevitability of sorts in his finally meeting the Scourge like this. There was little point fighting it. Where once this realm had been one of freedom and chance, the steady rise of the demon realm meant that servitude and predestination would only increase and begin to dominate. All the colour and individuality of this place was draining away and leaving only the prospect of a grey and featureless eternity.

'Come, demon! Why so melancholic? Have your tricks and japes deserted you? Where are your banter and witty riposte? You see, demon, what I have come to realise is that you need an audience. That is why your chose the role of minstrel for yourself. You live off the energy of a mortal audience, do you not? You drain it from them and feed on it. You deliberately sow division and discord and you deliberately create mischief so that you can live off the strong emotions that are then released, do you not? You are some sort of psychic parasite, are you not? It is the source of your magic and power. You persuade people to misstep, you help exaggerate their paranoia, you stoke the fires of their anger and you give them false promises and dreams. You make fools of mortal kind so that you can master them. But without an audience, what are you? Look at you now. You are lifeless. You lie there in the mud like the filth you are. You are naught but an empty ghost or evil spirit who has stolen some unfortunate's body. You are unworthy and undeserving of that body. You are *less* than mortal, demon, certainly no master of this realm. And so, with the empty meaning of your life played out, with the sham at last revealed, here it ends.'

The irony of the moment could not be escaped either and Jack laughed bleakly.

The Scourge could not help himself. 'Why do you laugh, demon?'

'I think I said it to you once before, my love. You would make a fine demon. Indeed, you would, for seeing my exhaustion and melancholy, you worked to grow the self-doubt and self-hatred within me. You sought to persuade us both that what you are about to do is justified and righteous. Did you not feel indignant and stronger as a consequence? Did you not draw energy from it? Are you not that same sort of parasite of which you accused me? My love, do you not see? In obsessing about me for all these years, in studying me for so long, you have become my student. You have dreamed about me and tried to anticipate me. You have put yourself in my shoes and made me your role model. Come, sweet Guardian, do not be abashed, for it is only you and I here. As you yourself pointed out, there is no audience to embarrass us. Come, do not fear, do not be coy! You have admitted your love for me with your pretty speech. Declare your love for me! I will not reject you. I will smother you with kisses and hold you close! I will be the woman if that is your wish.'

'Foul twister of words and meaning!' the Scourge raged. 'I should have known better than to allow your forked tongue even one word. Now I shall silence you forever!'

The Scourge dug his heels into the sides of his destrier. Jack O'Nine Blades arched his back, put his hands on the ground and flipped himself up onto his feet. The destrier had not even completed its first step. Quick as a flash, he had blades juggling in the air around him, ready to throw. He used the last of his strength and stepped up into the air. He ran at a rising angle directly for the horse and then veered to the Scourge's off-side, where the Guardian would find it difficult to get his blade across. Jack knew he might never recover from this last act of madcap defiance, but better to know this one moment of bright colour, jester glory and elfin heroics than to live in darkness forever. His blades of light made a halo for him and bedazzled the destrier. Now was the time to strike. Time to chase the snarling wolf away with its tail between its legs.

A whip of iron came snaking out of nowhere and wrapped itself twice around Jack's neck. He was pulled violently out of the air and slammed into the ground. The world made no sense. What had happened? He was choking. The lupine links of a chain bit deep into his neck. Holding the other end of the chain, standing over him now, was the Scourge.

The grizzled warrior gave Jack a wintry smile. 'Did you think you'd be able to tweak me by the nose and then show me a clean pair of heels? Or did you think to take advantage of me as you have so many other innocents? Even now you fail to understand that I see you for what you are. I saw you coming and prepared well for this moment. No longer will I let you act the fool or treat others as fools. No more, demon, no more.'

The Scourge deliberately placed the point of his blade above Jack's heart and pushed down hard.

Noo! The chain cut off any cry Jack might have made. He twitched once and died in the next blink. The Scourge splashed water from the temple of Shakri onto the minstrel's corpse and Jack's spirit was driven out. It rose screaming and immediately began to dissipate. Without a tether, Jack was at the mercy of the wind, snatched up and thrown high, hither and thither. He became just another wailing voice of despair lost in the winds of the mortal realm.

❋ ❋

Mordius's eyes snapped open in panic and he tried to move. As hard as he strained, he couldn't move his head or limbs more than a fraction of an inch. His jaw ached and he realised his mouth was stretched open by something across it.

He couldn't feel his tongue! He prayed the insane hag hadn't cut it out and devoured it. Tears of panic came to his eyes but they did him no good.

I don't want to be awake. I don't want to be alive. I can't do this.

He couldn't turn his head at all. A metal band seemed to be strapped around his forehead. He tried to look down. It looked as if metal bars held his mouth open. Was his tongue held in some sort of clamp? He faintly felt the tip of it, he thought, but didn't know if his mind was playing tricks on him.

There was a creaking above him and he turned a few degrees to the left. Was he suspended by a chain? He was in a body-shaped cage of straps and bars suspended from a chain?

His eyes slowly adjusted. Yes, he was still in the jumbled horror chamber that had once been the home of a woodsman and his wife. They were decayed corpses on a bed across the wide space from him. And he hung a few feet from the floor.

Colonel Marr's body lay on the floor where Mordius had seen him fall before they'd both lost consciousness. The magician made a whine in his throat to try and wake his friend, but there was no response from the soldier.

Come on, Marr, get up! Quickly, before the witch gets back!

As if in answer to his thought, a young girl's singing filled the room. Where was the hate-possessed child?

'My blood is blessing
My blood is joy
It's sweet as a girl
And sour for a boy!
My love is a curse
My love is a shame
So come no closer
For death is its name!'

She was suddenly at his feet, swinging his cage gently. 'Ah, there you are, little magician. It's rude to keep a lady waiting, you know. What's the matter? Cat got your tongue?' she laughed throatily.

Then the girl-witch pouted in mock sadness. 'I'm sorry, little magician, but I have had to still your tongue and body so that you won't be making any sound or gesture to exert your will. I doubt you'd have sufficient power to cause me any real trouble, but it's probably best not to underestimate you, don't you think? You were, after all, very naughty the last time we met, weren't you? And after you'd told me you loved me too! You literally broke my heart. Shame on you, little magician, to treat a maiden so! So you must be punished. Then you'll learn not to be so cruel to others. You'll learn to do as you're told. First, I'm going to bleed that presumptuous soldier who thought to have his way with me for the price of a few ribbons.'

The six-year-old girl started to hum to herself – it sounded like the same cantrip she'd been singing before – and skipped away across the kitchen. She sorted through the assortment of strange metal instruments on the table and plucked up a pointed hollow tube that was about a foot long. She stepped carefully over to Marr and crouched down next to him. Her small fingers struggled with the stiff buttons of his tunic until she finally had them undone. She opened his uniform, exposed an area next to one of his armpits and then punched the hollow tube in deep. Almost instantly, blood gouted out of the end of the tube. It made a big arc at first and the girl directed it into her mouth. She swallowed and swallowed and then smacked her lips wetly. She looked muzzily up at Mordius and mumbled: 'Don't worry, it doesn't hurt them. They make no noise or anything, so I doubt they even feel it. Oo! Strong blood in this one!' Her hand went to her head as if she'd become light-headed. She rubbed her swollen tummy. Then she burped and giggled.

The witch, her lips crimson like the painted women of Stangeld, crawled over to a stack of bowls and dragged one over to Marr. The blood came sluggishly from the tube now, as Marr's heart pumped the last of its life into the wooden collecting bowl.

'I don't actually need the blood in order to stay alive like I used to,' the girl slurred happily. 'But I miss the taste of it, you know? Still, mustn't be greedy. We need the rest for our magic, don't we, little magician? Oh, dear. I think he's dead already. Oh, well. Your turn, now, little magician!'

She pulled the tube out of Marr's body and, with the bowl in her other hand, wove her way a little drunkenly over to Mordius.

Noo! You mad bitch! Marr! Shakri, save me! Ye gods, ye gods! No, no, no!

He didn't hear what she said to him. All his panicked attention was on the point of the tube weaving back and forth in front of him.

The witch moved round behind him.

Argggh! Not like this! Where's she going to stab me? Saltar! Lebrus! Pleeease!

The spike thumped into the back of his right thigh and he almost fainted in terror. So shocked was he, his rational mind was unable to face what was happening to him. No sane narrative could describe it. Mercifully, all he caught now were fragmented images and sounds.

Horrible pain in his leg, and then a numbness seemed to spread to his very mind. The sound of blood spattering into the bowl and onto the floor. Her accursed humming. The intermingling and drinking of blood. Strange words he didn't understand. A red circle. A movement in the air around him. His cage swinging violently. Guttural chanting.

Stop it! Stop it!

He felt strange. His body didn't feel like his own. He realised he'd allowed something in. He tried to batter it back, but it had too firm a hold already.

'Just as you allowed Lacrimos to possess my body, little magician, so now will you be invaded and your being raped. Now you will be possessed by another. You will have to watch impotently as your body is abused by another, as your life is trodden underfoot. And then you will bear witness to the dismantling of this realm; as the pantheon is torn down and all mortals are enslaved to the greater powers of the cosmos. Finally, I will be free! It is not about revenge on those pitiable fools who call themselves the gods of this realm for me anymore; but my escape will still be a revenge in and of itself in many ways.'

Mordius, is that you?

W-Who's there? Get out of my body! You have no right!

Calm, Mordius! The only reason your consciousness continues to exist is because I allow it. Mordius, it's me!

J-Jack?! What are you doing here? How did - ?

Shh! Listen, I was lost and you were my last chance. But now we can help each other. If you give me this safe harbour for a while, then I will play our part with this delightful girl sorceress.

She's a witch. Don't trust her.

Come, dearheart, I'd already worked that out. But she needs to believe she now communes with a demon proper. Let go. Let me do this. It's the only way. That's it.

Jack took his place and glared menacingly through Mordius's eyes at the witch.

'Oo! You're here!' the little girl clapped gleefully. She unwound the chain from where it was attached to the wall and the cage was lowered to the floor. 'Now listen well, demon. By the words, blood and deeds that summoned you, so do I bind you to my will. You will think, say and do nothing that might lead to my being harmed in any way. You will think, say and do nothing that might challenge my will. Are you so bound? Speak!' Then she removed the bars from Mordius's mouth.

'Yes, I am so bound, ridiculous mortal!' Jack creaked through Mordius's unfamiliar voicebox. 'Yet I am similarly bound by my *house* and the philosophy of its rulers, for they make and bind my essence. If your will conflicts with my *house*, witless breeder, then you will have no joy of me.'

'You will spare me your insults, ignorant demon, or I will dispatch you back to your realm and find another to take your place. Do you not see what deal we can make? I have given you a mortal body so that you can remain in this realm without gradual dissipation. Search the memories of that body and you will see that mortal blood-magicks are now yours to command. You will use some of this blood and your magicks to raise that dead soldier and bind him to our will. That animee will be the first amongst the undead army that we will build. Our army, combined with those of the demon realm, will give us absolute sway over the realms of both Shakri and Lacrimos. Without command of the dead, you demons will be unable to take full command of the living.'

'Ah, we see! You will be a Queen of the Dead. You will then be consort to the Demon King. Together, King and Queen will rule. Is that the deal to which you agree, fair mortal? Of course, come its fruition, this deal will see you become more than mortal, will it not?'

Naked ambition and a lust for power distorted the innocent face of the child in ways nature had never intended. 'Oh, yes, sweet demon, it is the deal to which I agree. Are demonkind so agreed?'

'We are!' Jack pronounced solemnly and then howled triumphantly.

The witch cavorted wildly to the mad song of the demon's cry. The consciousness that had once been Mordius wept unendingly in the infinite void of nowhere. He had lost them everything. Everything!

❧ ❧

The Chamberlain sighed. Balthagar had been insane to bring them here. How could such a risk ever be justified?

He had no idea how long he'd had to run, nor how many trapdoors he'd had to haul open, before he'd finally managed to lose the grim hounds of the Prison of All Eternity. Did time even have a meaning in this place? Several times he'd stopped to put Balthagar's dead weight down and rest, only to feel the hairs on the back of his neck rise, sense that a hunter was close and have to start a staggering run once more.

The Chamberlain thought he had a fairly good idea of where the trapdoor to Shakri's realm was, but the grim hounds – or Grim, as he'd started to think of them – seemed to be working to shepherd him further and further away from it. Were they steering him towards a trap of some sort or did they hope to make him completely disorientated so that he would eventually stumble back into their clutches? Whichever it was, he began to realise there was little chance of their allowing him either the chance to try and navigate back to the trapdoor or the chance to lose them completely.

He who'd read the Pattern so well and been a master strategist amongst the mortals of Shakri's realm was all but at his wits' end. He couldn't outdistance the Grim. In fact, he was rapidly tiring, so he would not be able to remain free of them for much longer. He couldn't fight them either. He was running out of options.

The Chamberlain had considered escaping through one of the trapdoors with Balthagar but he had no way of knowing where they'd end up or, more importantly, whether they'd ever be able to get back. He was slightly surprised that he was so keen to return to Shakri's realm: after all, it hadn't been so long ago that he'd considered that realm little more than a prison and had been prepared to do almost anything to win free of it. Now, he thought of that realm as a... a home of sorts. Yes, most mortals there feared and hated him, but he had a place and role in which he was accepted, in which he had relative freedom to do what he chose. Yes, it was all relative really. The Prison of All Eternity had completely changed his perspective, changed *him* even, for he would not think and behave in the same way should he ever be fortunate enough to return to Corinus.

Fortune? whispered a voice in his head. Did fortune exist in the Prison? Or did all beings and patterns here play out to an inevitable, and therefore entirely predictable, conclusion? *Where is your prediction, hmm, where is it?* The Prison was infinite, which made things difficult. But what was finite or fixed? The position of the trapdoor was fixed. The number of Grim was finite. Ah! The further he went from the trapdoor, the more widely they'd be spread in seeking to maintain a cordon around the trapdoor, and the more widely they were spread the more chance he should have of slipping through the cordon.

Rather than continually trying to angle back towards the trapdoor, therefore, the Chamberlain carried Saltar in the opposite direction. Questing howls rang out behind him. He struggled on. Now there were howls flanking him. He'd stayed still too long and they'd begun to converge on him!

It was now or never and forever. He snarled, spun on the ball of his foot and zig-zagged round pillars and half-walls. Far away down one of the alleys, a Grim spotted him and bayed excitedly. It raced towards him.

To the left, past several pillars, back, right, forwards! Faster, faster. Aiee! Another Grim. He was beginning to lose his internal compass. Was he surrounded? Mustn't panic, hmm, mustn't panic?

'Chamberlain!' Saltar wheezed through his constricted throat and lips.

'Sweet brother!' the Chamberlain exclaimed. 'If you can help us, now would be the moment, hmm? Quickly!' He bent his small ear close.

'Follow... rat!' came the gentlest of sighs.

'Rat? Rat?' the Chamberlain panted. He looked around. Incredibly, thirty or so yards away, a brown, furry rodent scampered through the light and shadows cast by the fiery torches in their sconces fixed to every other pillar.

Hadn't Balthagar mentioned a rat before? What had he called it? A lesser god? *Samuel,* whatever that was. Species or name, he cared not. He wasted not a second getting after it; and a tangled, stop-start chase it turned out to be. Samuel ran behind one pillar, waited some seconds, ran to another pillar, halted, ran back to where it had been before, then back again. The rat's movement seemed random, but they weren't spotted by the Grim again as far as the Chamberlain could tell. They came far closer to the spectral hounds than the Chamberlain would have dared on his own, however. On one occasion, they ran across a corridor directly behind a Grim facing the other way – if the Chamberlain had but reached out his hand, he might have touched it. They came round pillars just as Grim were disappearing round others not far away. They turned onto paths just as Grim turned off them. How was Samuel doing it? Was it pure instinct or some magical ability to read unseen patterns, just as the Chamberlain read the course of events in Shakri's realm?

The risks they took became greater and greater. They were deep amongst the Grim. How had they not yet been discovered? Grim sniffed the air and whined in confusion.

Suddenly, Samuel squeaked and raced ahead, his little legs a blur.

'Wait!' The Chamberlain lengthened his stride but even so struggled to keep up, burdened as he was with Saltar's awkward and uncoordinated weight.

There was a bark of excitement and triumph not far away. They'd been seen! He heard large claws scrabbling for momentum against the stone floor and then the drumming of heavy paws.

Samuel ran straight for a distant trapdoor, squealing in such a high pitch that it was painful to hear. The Chamberlain leapt and spidered for all he was worth. He threw Saltar's body unceremoniously to the floor and yanked the trapdoor open. He pushed the Battle-leader into the void and then threw himself after him, the sound of jaws snapping on empty air where he'd been a second before. It was only as he spun away through the darkness, watching the square of light that was the trapdoor rapidly recede, that he realised the particular crack in the ceiling marking the way back to Shakri's realm hadn't been there above the trapdoor to which Samuel had led them. To which hell had they been consigned by this vermin of a lesser god?

❦ ❦

The sun blazed down on Corinus and its surrounding lands. Water vapour began to rise as grateful trees began to dry out. Wild flowers dared raise and turn their heads. Forest creatures peeked out from where they'd been sheltering and cautiously emerged. The world began to stir.

'Such fair weather at the start of our heroic quest can only be a good omen!' Aa declared to his young companion. The god of adventure removed his long, tailored jacket and slung it casually over his shoulder. His loose shirt billowed out and exaggerated the size of his swagger. He tilted back the wide, feathered hat on his head, twirled one end of his moustache, jumped into the air and clicked the heels of his knee-length leather boots together. ''Tis a fine day to be alive, to be sure. Brigands and monsters beware! Aa and his young companion Orastes are abroad in the land to protect the innocent, all pretty maids from the mundane chores imposed upon them, and punish the wicked.' He pulled his rapier, swished it and then pinned an imaginary foe with a disdainful laugh.

Struggling though he was under the weight of his armour, Orastes couldn't help being caught up in the excitement of his first real adventure. 'Ha, ha! We will make all monsters sorry for being monsters! Aa, what's an omen?'

Aa smiled. 'An omen, my young companion? Why, it is a sign from the gods to which the wise pay close attention. It is a message seen in nature by which we know whether what we do has the approval of the gods or not.'

Orastes looked around with a frown. They were walking through a copse at the edge of some noble's estates, but he didn't see any messages. The birds were singing, but he couldn't interpret any of the sounds. 'What do these omens look like? I can't see anything.'

Aa winked and tapped the side of his long nose. 'Trust me, lad, the will of the gods is there to be read, if we but choose to see it. Do you see that cloud? Does that not look like a woman with a large bosom beckoning us towards her? See that thorn tree? Is it not a fanged and sharp-clawed spindle-shanks who has been turned to wood by the holy magic of the gods? Is not that rock placed there so that an honest warrior who is hot and tired from carrying his weapons so far in the midday sun might take his rest? Please, milord, your throne awaits. And does that stream not run close so that he may cool his brow and slake his thirst? See, young Orastes, all these things are gifted by the gods to the worthy, faithful and pure of heart.'

Orastes thought about what Aa had said and shrugged. 'But the rock and stream would be there for warriors who weren't pure of heart, wouldn't they? And they could always take the road instead, which is far easier than going cross country. Why aren't we taking the road, Aa?'

Aa ruffled his hair playfully, which Orastes didn't like, but decided against mentioning lest it encouraged the playful god. 'Because monsters don't live on the road, now do they? No, they live in secret places, in dens and caves where they can gnaw on the bones of their victims at leisure. Sometimes they will watch the road so they can snatch an unsuspecting traveller, but there's no way of knowing which stretch of road it is and when they will strike. And if they were to see two heroes like ourselves on the road, they'd run and hide and then we'd never catch them. No, young companion, it is in the countryside that we will find them, in the dark places of the forest, amongst foetid swamps and bogs, by stagnant pools, and in the corrupted, scabrous parts of the earth which are hot with disease or cold with death. We will visit the more remote and vulnerable villages between here and King's Landing, to be sure the people are safe, yes?'

Orastes nodded slowly and scooped up water from the stream.

'As to the rock and stream, young companion, who is to say they would ever be found by those who weren't pure of heart? Such warriors are an offence to Shakri's realm – why would the realm then offer up its bounty easily? Once a man has stepped onto the path where he rapes, pillages and plunders, he will find the going harder and harder. More dreadful will his deeds become as he seeks to keep what he has stolen and he has to work harder to ensure his own survival against the ever increasing number of enemies he wins for himself. Desperate do such beings become. They become so steeped in blood and their tally of unholy deeds becomes so high that the only creatures who will give them succour are demons and monsters. And these creatures demand a heinous price – a warrior's very soul. And so the warrior becomes one more demon or monster, all because of that very first step taken onto the wrong path. On such a path, there are no conveniently sized rocks on which to perch and rest, no sweet-tasting stream from which to drink. Oh, they pass near to such things, but the realm will always contrive to distract or deceive them at the very moment that would otherwise mean some wondrous discovery. They will forever seek the ease that others know, hunt it in a rabid, crazed frenzy even. But they will have forever denied themselves any ease in this realm. With the gods' faces turned from them, they will find the realm completely different to the one they'd known before. They will find it a realm devoid of any of the pantheon's gifts; they will find it a cruel and twisted place. That, young companion, is how a rock and stream may be there and may not be there at the same time. That is how different realities and magicks can share the same realm and cosmos. That is why there is always something new to discover, always some new adventure to be had and begun. In many ways, you are fortunate that it was I from amongst the entire pantheon of the gods who chose to take you in hand. You would have had a frightfully dull time studying at the feet of Cognis or been led a pointless chase by that loon Wim, trust me.'

'Oh, I see,' Orastes replied, as that seemed to be the sort of thing adults said at such moments. Actually, he didn't really see what Aa was going on about at all. The god had used some words and said some things that he didn't really understand. And the one or two things he had understood sounded just plain silly. A rock couldn't be there and not there at the same time. Rocks weren't like that. They were always there, solid and reliable. But Orastes knew better than to argue with an adult – it wasn't allowed, because it was *rude*. Besides, people did sometimes seem to miss things that Orastes never did. Perhaps Aa was right when it was about most people, because most people were affected by magic, just as most people could do magic. But his own magic was broken and other people's magic never affected him. Maybe that was why he always saw everything. Maybe that was why he knew there were monsters when others didn't. He brightened at that because surely it meant he would be better at hunting monsters than other people. Maybe he could be the best monster-hunter in the world one day!

So Orastes decided not to argue with Aa and instead mentioned something far more important. 'Aa, I'm hungry. When are we going to have something to eat?'

The god looked slightly put out, but reached up to a tree and pulled an apple out of nowhere. 'Yes, I forget that mortals need to eat every five minutes or so. Here you are.'

Orastes looked at the apple. 'Aa, you gave me an apple for breakfast. Isn't there anything else?'

The god sighed impatiently. 'Maybe you'd like to return to the palace, my young companion, where it's comfortable and you can have whatever you want to eat. Maybe the life of a hero is too much for you. Is that it?'

Aa began to withdraw the apple, but Orastes snatched it back before it could be entirely taken away. He bit into the fruit's juicy flesh and mumbled: 'This is good for now. Mmm! Maybe we can hunt something later or catch a fish.'

Aa smiled indulgently. 'Of course, my young companion. It will all be part of the adventure to snare our supper. And it will be good hunting practice too. I tell you what, you make sure you keep your eyes and ears open and we might flush something out as we go. What do you say to that, eh?'

The boy nodded vigorously. He'd never been allowed to go hunting before. His mother had always said the forest animals were too dangerous, and that staying in the saddle when the chase was on was too much of a challenge for a young boy, even one as good at riding as Orastes. 'Maybe we can catch a wild boar, or… or… a pheasant or a dragon even!' Then he asked uncertainly. 'Does a dragon taste nice? Is it poisonous?'

The god gave a melodious laugh. 'Do you know what? I have no idea. I've never even seen a dragon. I must ask Shakri the next time we meet.'

'Oh. Well, maybe the boy who's following us knows.'

The god stopped. 'What?'

'The boy following us. Maybe he knows what dragons taste like.'

The god stared at the trees, a little nervously Orastes thought. 'Heh, heh! There's no boy. You're just trying to trick me! You can't trick the god of adventures, you know. Argggh!'

Aa jumped back as a dark-haired, sallow-skinned teenager stepped out from behind a tree. 'Demon!' The god drew his rapier with a flourish. 'Fear not, young companion, I will send this unholy creature back from whence it came.'

'I'm not a demon,' the newcomer replied with a glare. 'I am called rat-boy. Trajan said I was always to keep an eye on the Builder's son. And I promised the Green Witch I would too. Where are you taking him?'

'How dare you!' Aa said in outrage. 'You young rapscallion! Don't you know who I am?'

'Some noble ninny or other,' the teenager said, showing small pointed teeth.

Orastes stifled his giggle, as it was *rude* to laugh at others.

'I am Aa, god of adventure, derring-do, bravery and risk, god of beginnings and enterprise. I am the alpha, the holy ictus. Without me, there would be no – '

'Orastes, where's he taking you?' rat-boy asked the younger boy.

'We're on an adventure!' Orastes said enthusiastically. 'Mother said it was alright. We're going to hunt monsters and visit King's Landing. Would you like to come too? It'll be fun! Aa, can he come with us? Please!'

'Well, I'm not sure,' the god demurred, his dislike and disapproval of rat-boy evident. 'He's not very respectful. And I'm not sure how well he could follow orders. It's important to have good discipline from the start if we're to build an army, you know. What say you, rat-boy? Can you follow orders, eh?'

'Aa, I think he's one of those good omens you were talking about,' Orastes bubbled. 'And he's very good at moving quietly through the forest, isn't he? He'd be a good hunter, don't you think?'

Orastes decided not to point out that rat-boy had caught Aa completely unawares and was probably a better hunter than the god Himself, as he didn't want to be told he was rude.

Aa had not taken his eyes off rat-boy. 'Well, can you follow orders?'

'Of course, holy one,' rat-boy replied cautiously.

Aa smiled. 'Then we are three! We will make for a merry and fearless band, eh?' He clapped rat-boy on the shoulder. 'What say you, rat-boy? Will you be our stout and resolute comrade-in-arms? Will you guard our backs as we guard yours? Shall we cut our palms and swear blood oaths to each other? Are we friends forever? Are we brothers?'

Rat-boy gave a nervous sort of smile in response. 'I-I've never had a brother before.'

'Me neither!' Orastes yelped. 'Now you have two! Let's cut our palms and swear! Can we, Aa, can we?'

The god beamed. 'Of course, my good fellows, of course!'

Chapter Seven: The end of worlds

Finally released from his mortal body, the towering being that was Vidius glided through the spectral halls of the dragon demon. He entered amongst the archdemons of the Nihil, who were as disembodied as him and all fire, smoke and dark clouds. They recognised him as their Prince and cheered his return, bruited his fame, bowed in respect, shouted their loyalty and cowered in recognition of his might and authority. He beckoned the largest of them closer and absorbed it into his being. It tried to resist but did not have the necessary words of power to gainsay its Prince's will.

Vidius shuddered with pleasure as he was replenished by the essence of the hapless archdemon. 'You! Come to me! Do not fear, for I no longer hunger. Come to me or you will know my anger.'

Another archdemon drew close. This one was all horned white flame, flares of light and crackling pleas. Vidius absorbed it in the same way he had the other.

The remaining archdemons of the Nihil fled in a howling panic. He decided not to waste time and energy chasing them down. They'd served their purpose, so there was little more to be gained from them, save for a moment or two of excitement and diversion.

He moved into the archdemon chambers of the Co-optis and was immediately assailed by whispered enticements and promises of pleasure. Then came threats and visions of horror, then a host of questions to create self-doubt and dethrone his self-rule. He kept his mind closed to them, but decided to take on a weak physical appearance that might persuade them to approach rather than remain in the shadows. Whether it was habit, nostalgia or genuine preference he was unsure, but he chose to create a simulacrum of the mortal body he had inhabited before entering the sphere. Ah! It was good to indulge in such physicality again. Simplistic it may be, but it gave everything he experienced a more concentrated sense of significance, gave consequences a greater feeling of immediacy, and made meaning more concrete and real. Physical form and action made the ego more manifest but also more exposed. There was a thrilling exhibitionism to it that was quite intoxicating. It reinvigorated his desire to have the mortal realm as his own.

And his exhibitionism attracted the Co-optis, drawing them out of the darkness. How could they resist such temptation? Here was a higher life form that possessed a soul and was weak and ripe for the plucking. One or two hung back, intellect or instinct warning them that no mortal could enter this sphere, that they were being deceived, and that they should exercise extreme caution. But the majority were overcome by their own desire and appetite. They even adopted a physical form by which to apprehend him, similar bodies to those that he'd seen Co-optis wear in the fifth sphere, albeit larger. They dwarfed him, of course, slavered greedily and clutched at their sexual organs in excitement.

The first one to reach him had sickly puce skin pulled tight over large bones and a painfully swollen gut. Its saucerous eyes stared in an attempt to mesmerise him. Its forked tongue flickered around and through oversized fangs. It lurched at him and brought a massive, splayed hand down from on high in an attempt to crush him. The hand span was larger that Vidius's shoulder width.

Unperturbed, Vidius caught a club-sized finger in each hand and effortlessly held the archdemon away from him. Then Vidius made one of his own hands incredibly dense and pushed it through the skin of the demon's wrist. He cruelly parted tendons and detached ligaments, until his hand had passed straight through the archdemon's arm.

The archdemon shrieked in horror and raised its arm to try and shake Vidius loose. The other archdemons hooted in derision and amusement as they watched their fellow struggle. Vidius waited until he was properly above the giant and then dropped down onto one of its shoulders. He thrust his flat hand into the soft dip at the base of the demon's throat. Blood sprayed all around and the other demons moved to catch the jets in their mouths. One gargled in its throat with the blood and that had the others rolling around in laughter. They collapsed with the hilarity of it all. Snot flew from the nose of an off-white demon, so hard did it laugh, and then hot wax from its ears, which set them all off even more.

His own appetite roused at the sight of the blood, Vidius sank his teeth into a soft part of the archdemon's neck and began to eat its flesh before it was completely dead. That cued a feeding frenzy, and those archdemons not helpless with mirth threw themselves on the failing Co-optis. Vidius was thrown clear as the demon's body hit the floor. He jumped up, ready to wade back in amongst the giant Co-optis, but his mortal frame checked him with warning that he was all but full. He couldn't eat much more, and if he did it would only make him ill.

He shook his head and got his bloodlust under control. He checked all the Co-optis were properly distracted and passed beyond their chamber. Immediately, things became colder, so cold in fact that he struggled to breathe. This was the cold of absolute emptiness, a place where all energy had been drained away or exhausted. Frost already forming on his eyelashes, he peered through the fragmented air. He was in a vast, dim chamber that disappeared into darkness above him. He made out an enormous, pale figure seated in a similarly pale throne. He wasn't sure how far away it was but he guessed it to be several hundred metres away. As he tottered closer, he realised that just one of its sandaled feet was as high as he was tall. Craning his neck, he made out the chiselled chest of the colossus, but its shoulders and head were lost in shadow. It was unmoving.

By the time he reached the base of the figure, Vidius was shivering uncontrollably. He reached out a hand and touched the white-rimed surface. It was as hard and cold as stone. A statue? No, it was the solitary archdemon of the Hermis. It sat parasitically feeding on the energies of this sphere and contemplating eternity. No wonder its flesh had petrified like this.

Vidius tried to pull his hand back but found it had frozen in place and his fingers were already turning blue. He felt tired too. Maybe he should rest here. He should place his forehead against the statue and close his eyes for a few seconds.

His shivering began to subside and he didn't even feel the cold so much anymore. He let go of his mortal form…

… and became a being of light, fire, smoke and darkness once more. His life force burned fitfully, but now he was free of the Hermis. The frigid stone of the statue cracked explosively across one ankle. A groan passed up and down the colossus. Marshalling himself, Vidius threw flames of his life force against it. Yes, he would deplete himself dangerously in doing so, but he had no choice if he hoped to survive. Even in the previous sphere, the Hermis had come close to defeating him.

Cracks spidered all over the statue. Steam billowed all around them and the Hermis roared. Slowly, it began to move. It rose ponderously from its throne of millennia, stone grinding torturously as it placed weight on its ankle. It leaned slightly and then began to topple, slowly at first, and then faster and faster, until it hit the floor… and shattered into a million pieces.

The last of his essence flickering weakly, Vidius drifted through the deathly vault of the Hermis and limped into the halls of the untiring Fortis. Taking on his small, mortal form again, he crouched and prayed that none would notice him. *Who do you pray to, Vidius, eh? Demonkind know no gods. Are you so fallen that you seek comfort in the empty beliefs and paltry magicks of mortal magicians and priests now? Your will is not broken. The pattern exists. The words of power that bind, define and give form to this realm cannot be unsaid. They must and can only repeat in this realm. You are a Prince who believes he is more. This is your test, Vidius. If Shakri's realm has made you more, then you will seize and hold the Relic. It will allow you to translate the words of power of this realm to other realms, and you will become a king of realms, and assume a higher plane of existence. But if you have not become more than a Prince, if your wanting deludes you, then you will not be able to hold the Relic. You will know defeat and another will rise from amongst the Nihil to replace you.*

Do you know fear, little demon Prince? Then perhaps you have become more mortal than you realise. Perhaps you are more after all... or less. But it is too late to go back, little demon Prince. There's nowhere else to go except forward, either to a pretender's doom or a king's glory. All beings are tested in their time, little demon Prince, and it is always a test brought on themselves. It is existence or non-existence, your life or death, your renewed beginning or final ending. It comes to all – mortals, demonkind, gods or other beings of existence. Come, let's find your worth, little demon Prince! There's no use hiding there in the corner – the Fortis are untiring, remember, and will find you out sooner or later. And time is short, yes, time is short. Eternity doesn't wait on individuals, you know. It tests you even now. Stay where you are and all is lost, little demon Prince, all is lost.

Vidius yelped and scurried out into the large, arched hall. His bones and back teeth ached. He realised the entire place was reverberating. It thrummed just beneath hearing level. He felt pounded, as if on an anvil beneath a titan's hammer. The temples at the side of his head felt such pressure that it near blinded him.

There was a rumbling behind him. He turned and found an indistinct giant was pushing a heavy truck straight at him. Vidius hurried to the side but wasn't quick enough to avoid being bumped by the heavy, wheeled container. He sprawled and the back wheel crunched down and through his ankle. His foot was entirely removed from his leg and then smeared beneath the foot of the worker-giant.

Vidius blacked out for a second. Blood haemorrhaged from the stump of his leg. He concentrated as best he could – struggling through the whine and buzz of industry that impinged on every membrane, cell wall and part of his being – and mentally stemmed the flow of blood. Making extreme effort, and wasting much of the muscle on his frame, he made another foot for himself. If he lost the ability to walk, then he would be stranded here forever, at the mercy of every passing truck and giant.

The Fortis had ignored him and moved off into the distance, intent upon its task. Vidius shuffled after it.

There was more rumbling in the gloom around him. He knew he might be run down at any moment! He jumped left and right, forward and back, desperate to keep any rumbling at a safe distance. Soon, he was forced into a staggering run to keep ahead of it. He wept with terror and exhaustion. He expended more and more of his body just to stay ahead of it. He could no longer maintain the illusion of hair. He no longer had enough substance to maintain defined facial features. The energy he spent to continue forging through these halls and remain free of the jaws of the Fortis machine meant he would be reduced to all but nothing upon entering the hall of the Arachis. Surely there was no hope now of winning through.

He was now little bigger than a mortal child. Although less energy was now required to keep his smaller size moving forward, his length of stride had reduced and the archdemons of the Fortis gained rapidly on him. The size of a dog. Then a rat, a mouse, a flea...

A giant passed close by and he threw himself onto its leg. He was swept through the hall at impossible speeds. The contents of the truck – rocks, bones, flesh and all manner of matter – was dumped onto a vast pile. Other Fortis came, selected items and began to pound them with adamantine hammers on anvils of a similarly unyielding element. Legions of archdemons worked, the halls ringing, clanging, cracking and thundering with their awful and relentless labour.

They pulverised everything to dust, and then atomised it further, till it was infinitesimal. Vidius drifted through the air with a tumult of invisible particles. He moved into a river, then an avalanche, then through constellations and heavens. The further he travelled, the larger the archdemons became, until they were so large he could not fit them within his vision. The scale of hammer and destructive power they wielded was impossible, large enough to challenge the cosmos, but increasingly undetectable, beyond his tiny and immediate experience. They were an unknowable universe to him, vast beyond imagining. If he were an ordinary mortal, he might think of them as gods and wonder if they really existed.

What was it they did? What did they think to achieve with their hammers? What did they search for? He realised that the destruction they wrought actually created whole galaxies, albeit of a radically different scale. Destruction was no more absolute than creation was able to achieve universality. Their hammering released motes of substance that could become infinitely smaller but that never disappeared completely. They had to be seeking the secret of substance and existence. They sought the original matter, matter which would give them omniscience and omnipotence.

But in undertaking such an endeavour, the Fortis had become so immense that relative aeons would pass for one of his size before the apocalypse of the Fortis blows finally arrived. They'd all but disappeared and effectively become irrelevant to everything. In pursuing their philosophy, they were nothing of immediate meaning or concern.

Vidius drifted through space gazing at the glowing motes and stars around him. They began to form chains, then webs, which trapped more and more matter. He thought about trying to land on one, but suddenly spied dark things scuttling back and forth across the mesh. They plucked the brighter specks of matter and devoured them. They were many-limbed but were so dark little more could be seen of them except when a flaring speck reflected in row upon row of obsidian eyes. Foul Arachis! There was no doubt.

Perversely, Vidius was glad that his life force no longer burned strongly – otherwise, the Arachis would have been on him in a trice. He was sure he would not survive being consumed by one – although, by all rights, a Prince should not be able to fall to a lower level demon in this realm. It could only be a sign that he was moving closer to success if the natural order of the realm was collapsing. After all, he'd left the gates between the spheres wide open, so the realm should be in complete chaos and disarray by now. It was yet one more reason not to dally: the longer he took, the fewer inhabitants of the realm were likely to be left alive, and the smaller his army of invasion would be.

He pushed himself off a nearby particle and steered away from the snare of the web, away from the spidering Arachis. The further he went, the more the web was a solid plane, the less there was in the air. He passed over an Arachis city of gossamer towers, arches and spans. Clusters of eggs pulsed and shifted in large, transparent sacks. Near the centre of the city was a black, beating heart. Its limbs couldn't support its bloated mass, but it turned a thousand eyes towards him and screeched commands to its children. Arachis came swarming from their city and lairs and turned the plane black with the foment of their twisting, scratching forms. They climbed and tumbled over each other, the swell of their numbers lifting them above the plane and providing a platform for a number to cast themselves onto the wind. They spun threads behind them and then wove skeins ahead of him.

Rather than seek to avoid the Arachis closest to him, Vidius targeted it, rising slightly as he met it, so that he avoided its jaws and then trod on its eyes. It squealed with pain and turned about in the air, getting caught in its own trailing thread. Vidius spread himself on top of the Arachis and held on tight. The demon began to fall, and in desperation shot more thread out. Vidius had used his weight and momentum to make sure the Arachis was facing away from the city, so they were now suddenly pulled straight towards the skeins guarding the limits of Arachis territory. Vidius and the Arachis rushed through the air at such giddying speeds that if the body of the Arachis hadn't been barbed and sticky Vidius would have been torn loose.

The heavy mass of the demon punched through the web, its legs getting tangled and tied as they spun towards the ground far below. Vidius clung on with the last of his strength and prayed the Arachis would land the right way up. They impacted hard on the waiting surface and the demon's soft body splattered wide. It had cushioned Vidius's fall and allowed him to survive. Vivid green and orange fluids dripped from the wreckage of body parts. He wondered which colour was poisonous, and decided they probably both were.

He picked up a twitching leg that had been separated from the demon's body and pulled a hairy strip of tissue off one of the large tendons with his teeth. He chewed on it methodically. It was tough, but had a meaty taste that wasn't entirely unpleasant – though it would never be his meal of choice. He hungrily bit off another piece. He felt better and a little stronger now.

He ventured over to the ruined abdomen of the Arachis and felt deep inside one of the splits. His hand came out clutching a pale, convulsing egg. He popped it into his mouth and bit down. Sweet juice and a brief wriggling sensation were his reward. He swallowed and almost instantly felt energy spreading out along his limbs.

He looked up quickly to check the other Arachis hadn't come storming out past the edges of their territory and then greedily helped himself to a few more eggs. They were so... potent! It was tempting to stay here until they were all gone, and then sneak back towards the Arachis city to catch another demon unawares, but time was short. He could not afford to linger any longer than was absolutely necessary. Besides, he was now into the halls of his most hated and dangerous enemy: the unrelenting Spartis. It was time to be on his guard and start moving, for there was nothing easier for a predator than a stationary target.

The Spartis followed a militant philosophy of order, obedience and rank. Their discipline was anathema to Vidius, for it left no room for the chaos of dreams and inspiration. It made them quite undemonlike really. It made them the most hated of the houses, but also the most feared. It was notoriously difficult to bribe a Spartis, so inflexible was their philosophy, and woe betide the demon who made an enemy of a Spartis, for that demon would then have an enemy for life. A Spartis never forgot its enmity, gave no quarter and was annoyingly diligent and dedicated in its weapons and combat practice.

Of course, the impractical philosophy of the Spartis would have long since seen their house wiped out or triumphing over the other houses were it not for the strange and archaic concept of *honour* that the Spartis also observed. It was a concept that was all but meaningless to the other houses and irrelevant to the nature of the demon realm, making the actions of the Spartis seem bizarre and unpredictable indeed. Just when absolute victory looked to be theirs, they would withdraw; just when defeat looked assured, a number of them would perform a near-suicidal manoeuvre to allow others from their house to withdraw to a safe distance, regroup and try another tactic, sometimes immediately, to save their companions, and sometimes not on another occasion. They were perverse. In fact, many of the demons of the other houses considered the Spartis insane or brainwashed. But all knew to fear them too. After all, who did not fear the insane? They needed to be plotted against lest the disease of their insanity spread too far and undo the entire demon realm.

Vidius peered through the murk ahead of him. He thought he saw something glint within it. There it was again. Something was coming towards him. Surely their magicks hadn't found him already, had they? He looked off to his right. There was movement from that way too. And the left. They were converging on him!

He knew that tactically he should attack one of them immediately so he wouldn't face all three at once, but who was to say only one came from each direction? He might be better off fleeing back into the territory of the Arachis. Could he hope to persuade the Arachis to follow him and then march through the halls of the Spartis at the head of an army? Of course not. Better, then, to take a more defensive than aggressive stance.

Out of the murk came three armoured beings. The first came on four legs and was encased in iridescent dragon scale. Fire-gem eyes glittered high up on the helmeted head, and smoke curled from the nostrils of the visor. The next came shambling forwards on two legs, dressed in the thick hide of a bear. And the last slithered forwards on its stomach, wearing the tough, red skin of a snake. Its head reared up and wove backwards and forwards as if to mesmerise him. Vidius knew he faced three very different types of fighting style here, and it would be very touch and go as to whether he would be able to defeat them. Even if he did and then by some miracle won through to the sphere of the Princes, he was likely to be so depleted that he would have nothing with which to face his true rivals.

'What is it you do here?' the dragon breathed.

'You must be a Prince to come so far,' growled the bear.

'And therefore one of the Banished,' hissed the snake.

'I have come for an audience with my fellow Princes,' Vidius informed them cautiously.

'Not to fight us then?' snorted the dragon.

'To ask us to stand aside or to provide you with aid, perhaps?' whined the bear.

'Or with a desire to lead us?' grinned the snake.

Vidius hesitated. 'Yes.'

The three Spartis were silent for a while, perhaps communing with each other through some magical means. Finally, the dragon nodded and said, 'Then follow us, Prince, and we will escort you to the Princes' gate.'

Amazed, Vidius followed the archdemons of the Spartis. They apparently had no quarrel with him, nor wanted anything of him. Truly, they were insane. Or were they just more subtle than the other houses? Had they fathomed his true ambition and decided they would ultimately gain from it? He decided to test them.

'Spartis, know this: I have left the gates between all the spheres open.'

The Spartis stopped to listen to him, almost as if to be... polite, like a mortal! When he didn't speak further, the dragon asked: 'Shall we continue on towards the gate, Prince?'

Slightly stupefied by the lack of reaction, Vidius stammered: 'Er... of course!'

Was that it? No other reaction than to ask his permission to proceed? Did they have no ambition to rampage through the spheres, indulging themselves gluttonously in order to establish themselves as new powers of the demon realm? No, of course not. That would be too self-indulgent and ill-disciplined for the Spartis. Just what was the ultimate goal of the philosophy of the Spartis, then? He'd never really given it much thought before, but now he found himself unnerved. Did they play a far larger game than he actually appreciated? Was he playing into their hands even now?

He deliberately fell back a step behind them so that they would not be able to read the misgivings that were no doubt flickering across his face or showing through his eyes. Who knew how they'd react to any perceived indecision or weakness in a Prince? They'd probably be intolerant of it as they were of so many other things.

Then again, maybe paranoia was getting the better of him. In seeking to assert his own will as dominant and defining in the demon realm, perhaps it was inevitable he would consider all other assertions and philosophies as a personal threat. It might well be all in his mind. After all, how credible was it that mere archdemons could out-think and out-manoeuvre a Prince and future Demon King?

Satisfied that he'd suitably second guessed them, Vidius matched his step to the movement of the dragon, bear and snake once more. The Spartis were all discipline and conformity. In many ways, it was from such unity and compliance that their strength came. It probably didn't even occur to them to challenge a Prince of the demon realm. They would make for reliable generals in his army, he decided.

They brought him through the murk and stopped. A massive, obsidian dome towered above them. No doubt, there was a matching, inverted hemisphere beneath the misty plane on which they stood, forming a complete sphere. They stood before the Core of the demon realm, where the most dreadful and devastating demon magicks were to be found, and where the Relic was housed.

There was a door into the dome, but before it lay a giant three-headed dog. The central head rested on its front paws and had its eyes shut. The head to the left watched them carefully with glowing orange eyes, and the head to the right sniffed the air.

Vidius stepped forward, leaving the Spartis behind him. The black-furred head on the left growled menacingly in its throat, and the blonde one on the right howled mournfully. The brown-furred head in the middle rose up and barked ferociously. The teeth and three mouths of the Cerberus were large enough that they would dispose of Vidius in a bite or two.

He took another step forward. The middle head whined, the one on the left panted heavily and the one to the right yipped excitedly. It's tail wagged! It recognised him! After all this time, its master was home at last.

Vidius ducked the watch dog's boisterous attempt to lick him, patted its chest and passed under its belly. He pushed the door open and went inside.

Opulent red carpets, painted frescos on plaster and glass chandeliers all reminded him of the sort of state rooms he'd only ever really seen within the Guild of Holter's Cross. Vidius moved silently down the corridor and came to a pair of carved, white, wooden doors with brass handles. He'd forgotten that the Princes liked to indulge themselves with the trappings of civilization, whether that civilization had ever been theirs or not. It prepared them for a higher plane of existence, he had once claimed along with the others. Now, though, he understood it as nothing more than vanity, a thin veneer to disguise the ravages of time and millennia of abuse.

He hesitated at the doors, half inclined to knock before entering. *Idiot! That will give warning to your enemies within. This is no time to be adopting meaningless mortal manners.* He grasped the handles firmly, turned them and pushed the doors open. Summoning his magic and raising all the power that remained to him, he strode into a high-ceilinged audience room.

A small goblinesque creature looked up from where it sat behind a heavy wooden desk at the far end of the room. It grinned. 'Ah, there you are, at last! Took your sweet time getting here, didn't you? Still, at least you made it, despite your best efforts to fail in doing so, what? And me oh my! Just what were you about with that cyclops? I really thought you were going to end up in the soup on that one, what?'

Wrong-footed, Vidius gazed round the room, trying to regain his balance and restore his orientation. Behind the goblin were shelves of books and scrolls that reached all the way up to the ceiling. A tall ladder on wheels was attached to the stack so that texts could be more easily retrieved. The walls of the room were decorated with moulded panels, and within each panel was a mirror. But the glass did not reflect the contents of the room; rather, it showed moving scenes from the different spheres of the demon realm.

'You've been watching me all along then,' Vidius said slowly.

'But of course, dear chap! My, you really have forgotten a lot, haven't you? Ah, I see! You thought you might be able to pass through the spheres undetected. That's why you insisted on adopting that disgustingly inadequate human form and made such heavy weather of it all. You should have realised we would be aware of your presence as soon as the first gate was left open. And the gatekeeper of that sphere really does not have sufficient wit to keep anything secret, no matter what bargain you struck with it.'

If they'd known he was coming all along, then they'd have had ample time to prepare against him. There was no point lashing out with his power now then, as he had probably just walked straight into a magical prison or some other sort of trap. He decided to keep himself in check for a while longer. 'Where are the others?'

'The others?' the goblin asked with a frown and self-consciously patted its thin, greasy hair to be sure it was still in place. 'You are the first.'

'I don't understand. Where are the other Princes?'

'Hmm. Incredible! Who would have thought you could lose so much but still manage to return? Quite remarkable really. Still, that's what we designed the Banishment for, brother, what?'

The goblin's elliptical statements were starting to frustrate Vidius. 'Speak plainly!' he growled.

'Of course, brother, of course,' the goblin replied unctuously, putting down the quill he'd been writing with and beginning to rub one hand over the other. 'When we were exiled here by our cosmic enemies, we began to fight amongst ourselves. It became clear that none of the houses would allow any of the others to hold the Relic long enough to be able to wield it effectively. We quickly began to destroy ourselves. Is this ringing any bells, brother? No? Very well. So, we Princes came together in conclave and agreed the organisation of the spheres. We also agreed that one Prince would remain here as caretaker, while the other five would be Banished and thrown upon the mercy of the dangerous and restless winds of the cosmos. Those winds would either see to the undoing of the Princes, in which case all would be lost, or remake the Princes so that they might represent something different in some new part of the cosmos, an eventuality that would see the Princes implicitly changed so that they would not know themselves. It was extremely risky, of course, but we'd run out of options and had nothing left to lose, brother. And the prize would be our ultimate freedom. Now I rejoice, brother, for one of the Banished has returned and our deliverance is finally at hand! After aeons of suffering this cruel incarceration, we will at last reclaim our place in the cosmos.'

Something didn't feel right to Vidius. Despite his claim, the goblin didn't really look like he was rejoicing that much. There was something the wretch wasn't telling Vidius. 'How did we know the Banished might be able to win freedom for demonkind?'

'A compulsion was laid upon the five Princes so that they would eventually seek to return to the demon realm, even if they no longer knew who they truly were. In finding a way to return, of course, the Banished might also establish a way in which demonkind could escape from this prison. The magicks of demonkind were bound by this prison, yet we hoped the cosmic winds would remake and change the Princes so that they might discover new magicks that were not limited by this realm and that might be used to break this realm open. And that is precisely what you have done, brother, is it not? You have forced a return, thrown all the gates wide and opened the way to the mortal realm for all demonkind.'

'And what of the Relic?'

There was the slightest of hesitations. 'It was agreed that the Prince who returned first and managed to win through to this sphere would be permitted to claim the Relic without contest.'

'You are Prince of the Co-optis, are you not? How is it you were chosen to stay behind? You have effectively ruled demonkind alone for millennia. Are you really willing to let me assume the rulership of demonkind without contest? And why did you never claim the Relic for yourself?'

The goblin shook its head and smoothly said: 'Had we Co-optis claimed the Relic, we would only have been able to wield it within the demon realm. But to what end if we already ruled?' The goblin shrugged. 'None. And if we had attempted to wield it, the other houses would have risen up against us, even in the absence of the five Princes. No, we are content to have ruled, even as caretakers, and now we are further rewarded with the prospect of freedom for all demonkind.'

'Yes, and as Co-optis, you are content if you are but close to the centre of power and able to influence it. You do not always seek to hold power directly yourselves. In fact, you often prefer to manipulate things from the shadows rather than occupy a place of glory, as that way you do not take risk or make sacrifice yourselves. You prefer the role of administrator or regent over that of rebel or leader. You prefer to hide behind this desk covered in papers than walk the field of battle covered in the bodies of enemies. Of all the Princes, then, it was only you who could be relied on to play the role of caretaker and then step aside once one of the Banished returned.'

The goblin half-bowed in his seated position. 'Such is the philosophy and nature of the Co-optis.'

Vidius smiled knowingly. 'Which brings us to the question of how things will stand once I assume rule of this realm.'

The smile of the Co-optis froze. 'What do you mean, brother?'

'Well, you step aside now so that I may take risk and make sacrifice on your behalf, do you not? We have already agreed that is your philosophy and nature. So, tell me, Co-optis, precisely what risk and sacrifice you foresee for me. Come, play the role of counsellor, as is your wont. Explain to me what challenges I will face, for I cannot believe that it will be as simple as demonkind having its freedom, my having the crown and all of us living happily ever after.'

Now the goblin looked slightly nervous. 'Brother, there is nothing to fear. The Relic will be yours and you will be able to wield it beyond this realm, since you became more than demonkind during your Banishment. The fact that you won through all the spheres is proof you are more. You are the Demon King, my brother!'

'Yes, I will wield it beyond this realm, Co-optis. But I asked you of the risk and sacrifice you expect me to take on your behalf. Why else would you so happily step aside for me, Co-optis, eh? I know it does not come easily for one such as yourself, but I advise you to speak plainly. Otherwise, things might not go so well for you and I will be forced to find another counsellor for myself.'

Vidius watched the Co-optis carefully. He knew better than to judge by the harmless and diminutive form it chose to assume here. It was a being whose power had long been unrivalled in this realm. If it suddenly chose to turn on him, it was far from certain Vidius would triumph. After all, he had not claimed the Relic yet. And even demons of lesser spheres had already come worryingly close to devouring or murdering him.

Tension scowled from the goblin's face. It deliberately took a calming breath. 'Brother, I would advise you not to make threat against me. I will allow it, however, as you are still somewhat ignorant of our realm and you have been severely taxed by your passage through the spheres, so your better judgement is inevitably impaired. But do not err again, I beg you, for the sake of all demonkind.'

Ah, how cunning were the words of the Co-optis. In the space of a few simple sentences, it had completely reversed the power dynamic between them. He must not apologise or concede any point to such a creature. 'Will you make me ask a third time, brother?' Vidius queried in the mildest of tones.

The goblin audibly ground its teeth and a snarl of distaste flashed across its face. Then it was in control of its emotions once more. It smiled ingratiatingly. 'My brother is wise. All existence knows limitation and challenge, does it not, even for the Demon King? Risk and sacrifice are givens, brother, but you are right that some might be anticipated. To demonstrate the support and loyalty of the Co-optis to you as Demon King, therefore, I will tell you all I can. As ever, it is the letter of the word of the agreement that should be scrutinised. If you recall, my phrasing was that the Prince who returned first and managed to win through to this sphere would be permitted to *claim* the Relic without contest.'

Ah, so there it was. 'I will not be allowed to wield it uncontested perhaps. Yes, I can see that the Princes of the other houses would baulk at being ruled by the Nihil and their philosophy for the rest of eternity. So, they will fight me at some point in the future then. And with challenge from other enemies in the cosmos, the Demon King will be hard-pressed. Let me guess, however: none of demonkind will seek war with me until I have won us freedom of this realm and established dominion for demonkind in another realm. I imagine that my efforts on behalf of demonkind will take their toll on me and I will inevitably be vulnerable to usurpation. I see, I see. Thank you, Co-optis.'

Damn it! He hadn't even claimed the Relic yet and already he felt undermined. It was ever thus with demonkind. But he had an advantage over the other Princes, for he had foreseen their betrayal of the Demon King, while they were probably still ignorant of their true natures. He should continue to anticipate them. There was no doubt in his mind that the skulking Chamberlain of Dur Memnos was Prince of the Arachis, and that the tiresome Saltar was Prince of the Spartis. But who were the other two? He had no idea. It would be too much to hope that they'd been torn apart by the cosmic winds or carried to the other ends of the cosmos. It was more likely that they had also found refuge in Shakri's realm. It was simple then: he would have to slaughter every individual of any sort of prowess or puissance in Shakri's realm when he claimed it for his own. No one could be spared, no one of apparent innocence, no one of soul-wrenching beauty, male or female, no one of apparent value or meaning. After all, how else would the philosophy of the Nihil be made manifest? There was a convergence and patterning to it. And so it would be.

The wart-faced Co-optis was speaking again. '… you won't be alone, brother. The Co-optis will stand with the Demon King against all enemies. We have already demonstrated our support and loyalty.'

Vidius was not about to be cozened, but was wise enough not to show it either. 'I thank you again, brother. Very well, I will take the risk and consider some self-sacrifice, but we must watch the other houses carefully the whole while. Now, where is the Relic, for the cosmos will not wait on us forever and we must not allow our enemies too long to plot, plan and prepare?'

The goblin was all relaxed smiles again. 'It is there on the top book shelf, brother, the black sphere of adamantium. Would you like me to get it for you?'

'I have journeyed this far, brother. I will complete this last and shortest part of the journey. It would be strange not to.'

'As you say, brother, as you say. It is a strange coronation, but I think one day we will have another and you will be anointed with the blood of our enemies.'

Vidius gave a perfunctory smile of his own and scaled the ladder to the top shelf. As he touched the top sphere, it fell open and a plain, horned helmet was revealed. The horns were slightly twisted and came from a creature unknown to him. Was this it? Millennia of pain and effort and this was his reward? Some trinket that wouldn't even keep the rain off? It was hardly a bejewelled, dazzling crown, was it?

He lifted it out of the sphere and jammed it on his head. It was a tight fit. He held his breath… nothing happened.

Vidius looked down at the goblin and shrugged, at a loss. Then pain like two sharp blades punched through his temples and into his mind. There was no Vidius anymore, no demon Prince, no *he*. There was just something so vast it barely had character or name. But it was an intelligence. Vidius realised it was an intelligence not his own, an intelligence that had been trapped in the helmet for aeons. And it had knowledge he could use. The wearer of the helmet had access to unimagined secrets of power! Ah, yes! Of course. It was so obvious, so childishly simple. How had he not understood such things before?

He realised he was stealing the wisdom and memories of another's mind, but that did not make him uncomfortable. Why should it? The Hermis did something very similar in order to survive, did they not? As Demon King, the ways of all demonkind were his to aggregate, master and value. Indeed, to survive as Demon King, he would need to master the ways and magicks of each philosophy, and then be more than each.

'Are you well, brother?' the goblin called up to him.

Brother? The pathetic creature dared call him brother?

Vidius began to fold the demon realm on top of the Prince of the Co-optis.

'Ack! Brother… sire, what are you doing? We are loyal! Do not turn on your allies so soon, sire!'

Allies. The creature was too inadequate to understand that the Demon King was not interested in allies. The Demon King would rule all houses absolutely, and would not tolerate anything less. The Demon King was the will of demonkind, it was as simple as that. Houses that resisted would be destroyed, as was the way with the Nihil. Even if he had to destroy most of demonkind to exert his will cosmically, he would not hesitate, for the proliferation of demonkind was of no interest to him except when it represented the wider propagation of his will. Only the Demon King was of any consequence. He owned demonkind – it was his to use as he saw fit.

The goblin was an annoyance. It had the temerity to seek to bargain with him, to threaten him even! For such treason, it must be ended.

'Sire! I die!'

'Then hurry up and do so and stop bothering me. There are higher things I must contemplate.'

'The Co-optis can help you, si-i-i-re!'

'The Co-optis *will* help me, Prince who is little more than a wisp. All demonkind will be my army. But you forget I am Nihil. Now begone.'

Space closed in on the goblin, crushed it and extinguished its spark of life. There was no sign that it had ever existed.

Vidius strode forth from the core of the demon realm to raise his army. First the stepping stone of Shakri's realm, then the other planes and realms of existence would be his.

⚔ ⚔

A lifetime ago, the Harbour Mistress of King's Landing had been a young girl called Lystra whose father had been lost during a storm and had left a pregnant wife and four children without means of a living. The nine-year-old Lystra had had no choice but to take out their leaky rowing boat each day to cast the few nets left to the family upon the treacherous waters beyond the harbour. Well, there had been another choice, providing "comfort" to lonely sailors far from home, but she'd never been as pretty or slim as the other girls of King's Landing so would always have struggled to feed all the mouths at home pursuing that course. Mean though the sea god Maris could be – and she would never forgive Him for taking pa from them – He at least allowed all comers an equal chance. He did not judge her by her looks, her large shoulders or jutting jaw. He did not care if she was male or female. He was only interested in testing the mettle and character of those who sought His bounty, and ensuring that he received proper respect. In that way, Maris was a bit like pa, for her pa had never said her face was precisely the sort that made men put to sea in the first place. And he hadn't minded that she was more thickset than many of the boys of her age. In fact, he'd often proudly said that Lystra was as much son as any man could want! She missed him terribly now that he was gone, and felt very alone.

Yes, there was something about Maris that reminded her of pa, and she'd got them slightly confused in her young, grieving mind. She fancied that her pa might be a member of the sea god's court and be called on for advice every now and then. Maybe the sea god actually felt... sorry for having taken her pa. The sea had certainly been kind to her in the early days, when on fair weather days she'd ventured beyond the harbour walls and cast her nets wide but brought them up empty, for then irresistible currents had dragged her boat along the coast and dangerously close to the rocks, but also to where the fish had been hiding. She'd filled her boat until it had been over-flowing and then been taken home safely by other currents. There'd been days when she'd been the only one in King's Landing to land a catch, and she'd won nods of approval from even the eldest of the fisherpeople. And she'd managed to sell her extra fish for a good few coin, which she gave her mother so that the family could obtain other foodstuffs like milk and vegetables.

It was as if her pa had been watching over her and teaching her the patterns of the currents, weather and movement of fish. And she'd been so grateful to learn, for it had allowed her to be close to her pa again and have something of him to carry with her always. She soon began to feel more comfortable at sea than on land, and on one or two occasions had slept in the bottom of her boat out on the water when she had seen that all the patterns would not take her too far. The people in town began to whisper that she was beloved of Maris.

The first time one of the fisherpeople had come to her mother's home to solicit Lystra's advice, Lystra had been more than shy about giving it. Who was she as a mere teenager to tell her elders what to do? Besides, she preferred to be out on the sea talking with pa than speaking to people. But her mother had urged her on and then happily taken a coin from the visitor. More and more of the inhabitants of King's Landing came to hear the words of Lystra, beloved of Maris. Not all of them asked about the sea. Some talked of the things that happened between a man and a woman and turned Lystra's cheeks scarlet. These she sent away disappointed despite her mother's protestations.

Then came the winter storms and the people came asking if Lystra would agree to pilot the ships that came into the harbour, as none understood the waters and weather as well as she. The town offered her both a new boat and regular payment. Her mother hadn't hesitated to accept on Lystra's behalf, and the family had moved into more expensive accommodation near the docks.

King's Landing prospered greatly as the fame of the beloved of Maris spread. Trading ships began to favour King's Landing over harbours further along the coast like Soldis and the Spit of Tyr at certain times of year. And because of Lystra, King's Landing could remain open to ships when other harbours were forced to close for the season.

When the old Harbour Master Danus died one winter – unexpectedly, for it had never occurred to anyone that the tough old sea salt wouldn't last forever – many of the people had immediately called for Lystra to be made the next Harbour Master. The oldest of the town councillors had pointed out, however, that Lystra was female and therefore not eligible for the position. It was irrelevant that the town councillor's nephew was also interested in the position, for all knew that councillors only had the best interests of King's Landing at heart. And it was generally accepted that elders were wise with experience and should not be questioned.

Lystra would therefore have continued happily with her life as fisherwoman and seasonal pilot had her mother not then let it be known the length and breadth of King's Landing that the harbour town of Soldis had asked the beloved of Maris to be their Harbour Master instead. An emergency meeting of the King's Landing town council had taken place and, in their wisdom, the councillors had created an entirely *new* position for Lystra: that of Harbour Mistress!

There had been celebrations in every inn in King's Landing that night and toast made to the wisdom of their elders. Lystra hadn't wanted to ruin everyone's happiness or embarrass the councillors by pointing out that no one had actually asked if she wished to be Harbour Mistress or not. And her mother wouldn't have let Lystra decline the position anyway, so Lystra had just allowed everyone to start addressing her as Harbour Mistress if they wanted to. Besides, there was the odd benefit to the position that thrilled Lystra, principal among them that she was allowed to take on the small dockside cottage of old Danus, who had died without kin as far as anyone knew. Lystra's mother had assumed that the cottage would simply serve as Lystra's place of work – only realising too late that Lystra intended to live there alone, closer to the sea and away from her family. Her mother had been furious, shouting that Lystra was a heartless ingrate to abandon her family in such a manner, and that it was unseemly for an unmarried woman to live alone, but Lystra had remained as stubborn as a barnacle and let it all wash over her. She'd deposited a tall stack of coins on the family's kitchen table, which continually distracted her mother and interrupted her arguments, packed the few items that belonged to her and moved into her new home.

The cottage was small but cosy, and she didn't miss having to share the bed with three younger sisters and two younger brothers. She didn't lack for company either, for now she was close enough to the sea to hear it speaking to her during the night. Both her father and Maris were there, speaking of the wonders and dangers of the world, singing songs of glory and tragedy, or simply breathing deeply with the swell. They warned her of bad weather ahead, told her of the ships of man tossed back and forth by their whim and laughed and cried over the trials and tribulations experienced by all that lived in the sea.

Lystra didn't particularly enjoy the job of Harbour Mistress, for there was too much dealing with people, and too little to do with the sea – too much of the mistressin' and too little of the harbourin', as she liked to think of it. She was even expected to see that the peace was kept in the inns of the waterfront, although it was rare that a sailor or fisherperson would be foolish enough to bring Lystra from her bed and provoke her displeasure – after all, what living could be made upon the waves by anyone frowned upon by the beloved of Maris? On one occasion, a town rowdy named Goiter had caused a fight with a Jaffran sailor and refused to back down upon Lystra's request. She'd called him a cursed, squid-brained bottom-feeder, or some such, word had spread and from that day forward every boat captain in King's Landing had refused to hire Goiter for work or even let him on board. Boat captains were a suspicious lot at the best of times, so when they heard Goiter was cursed by the beloved of Maris, it ensured he never worked again in King's Landing. The last she'd heard, he'd gone inland and started up a successful farm. She'd been glad of that, else she might have felt a little guilty.

Not enjoying her job too much, Lystra sought to get the day's business over and done with as quickly – and with as little fuss – as possible. She worked in an efficient and no-nonsense manner, expediting the collection of harbour fees and passing them onto the council as soon as her cash-box was full. The town treasurer's eyes bulged at the amount of gold she handed over to him – apparently, old Danus had not collected nearly so much. And strangely the ship captains seemed happy to pay her, saying that harbour taxes had been higher in the old days. A few captains intimated that they would be prepared to compensate her for her trouble if she would allow them to moor before other ships and give them a good position on the quay. But such goings-on would only introduce complication and slow down her day's work, so she disdained such offers. King's Landing developed a reputation for honest trading, and that only increased the number of ships coming to dock there.

When her day of work was done, she would hurry to her boat and go out on the waters beyond the harbour no matter the weather. The trivial concerns of her job as Harbour Mistress would be forgotten and she would find true release and contentment for a few hours. Sometimes she would fish for her supper, unless the fish had started leaping into her boat of their own accord, and sometimes she would simply let herself drift where the current took her, gazing up at the stars on a clear night or watching the clouds race overhead when the weather was not so good.

Despite her job as Harbour Mistress, she was happy with her lot and would have been content to live out her days in this way. The lack of a life-mate never bothered her, as her relationship with the sea was all she needed. Over the years, a number of men came to her door with proposals of marriage, but they loved her position and wealth and not her, so she politely sent them all away. Her life had meaning and value, if value were needed; she cared for her family and the people of King's Landing, and they cared for her in their way; and then there were the spirits of her pa and Maris, whom she hoped to join in the fullness of time. What did she need with a husband who would be jealous of the time she spent at sea or would expect her to be home for the children he forced on her? Nothing. She helped make life good for the people of King's Landing, which ensured they showed Maris proper thanks for His bounty and awe for His majesty, and in return she was allowed a safe and prosperous existence of her own.

All had been safe. All had been prosperous. And then something changed. It wasn't clear what it was, but the size of the fish catches began to dwindle and the fisherpeople reported seeing strange creatures in the waters beyond the harbour walls. No one paid these things much mind at first, since the size of catch varied with the season and weather, and many a drunk sailor had claimed sight of giant squid, singing mermaids and sea dragons before. Then the boat of one of the more experienced fisherpeople hadn't come home at the end of a day's fishing. They hadn't returned the next either. All knew that meant Captain Blossholes and his crew of four would never be returning. The loss of the boat caused considerable disquiet in King's Landing for, although losses were not unknown during the stormy season and although Blossholes liked to fish the deeper waters, the really bad weather wasn't due for at least another month. So just what had befallen the boat of the fisher captain?

The size of catch of the fisherpeople did not improve. It began to be whispered around town that King's Landing must have lost the favour of Maris. People on the street still nodded to Lystra, but they did not smile. Then, mysteriously, there was a decline in the number of trading ships putting into dock at the harbour of King's Landing. The crews of the ships that did come in shrugged or shook their heads when asked why there weren't as many as usual. Suddenly, there wasn't enough work for the dockers, the inns became quiet and the mood in the town turned sour. When people passed Lystra on the street now, they avoided her eyes and hurried away. Pairs or small groups of people who stood talking on street corners would fall silent and go about their business when they saw her coming.

Lystra, Harbour Mistress of King's Landing, now stood at the far end of the spit that made up one side of the harbour. Night was falling, but she strained her eyes to try and read the weather and the water. Another of the fisherpeople's boats had failed to return that day. The wind smelt wrong and the water was chopped up in way she didn't understand. It didn't seem… natural. What did it mean? *Pa? Holy Maris? I can't hear you. What's happening?* She feared that fisherpeople were drowning while she wasted the time that could save them trying to divine whether they were dead or alive.

Cursing, she ran round the harbour to where her boat was moored and leapt aboard. The wind rose at that moment, whether to help her on her way or as the beginnings of a tempest; both seemed possible. Without hesitation, she took the boat through the harbour. The movement of the water was strange, but she could have taken the boat out of King's Landing with her eyes closed. Beyond the harbour walls, it was far more difficult. There were strange spiralling eddies everywhere. She knew that if they all combined, then a whirlpool larger than she'd ever seen would form. Then, no one would be able to navigate these waters safely, not even Lystra. Things did not look good, and time was clearly short.

The spiralling eddies told her that the water was disturbed even at the bottom of the sea, a place all believed to be the domain of Maris and His court alone. Either the sea god *was* displeased with King's Landing, or Maris's realm was under some sort of attack. But who would dare, even if they had the power, to challenge Maris? Was it the strange creatures Lystra had heard tell of, or had the creatures simply been drawn up from the depths towards the surface by the eddies?

There were neither stars nor moon to be seen. The sky was thick with low, black cloud that flared with first red and then white lighting. The wind whipped the waves up so they were the white teeth of a dark, slavering maw. The air felt heavy. Doom-laden.

For one of the first times in her life, Lystra felt afraid while at sea. She was surrounded by forces that she no longer understood, forces which felt foreign and malevolent. She wanted to turn back, run to her cottage and hide behind a thick door and tightly secured shutters. She wanted to shut the horror out, stoke her fire high to hold the darkness at bay. She wanted to stop her ears so that she couldn't hear it whisper and shriek for her to come out to face those things of which she refused, feared and hated to think.

She wanted to return to safety, to her safe harbour and safe home. But something prevented her. It held her as surely as the sun, moon and tides rose and fell. It held her as surely as a parent holds its child. It held her as surely as Maris held the sea in His hands. She wasn't sure exactly how it should be named, but it was everything she was part of. She knew she must sail farther, sail until whatever forced her on was satisfied.

She set off on the sort of bearing the fleet of the fisherpeople tended to take each morning, but her progress was painfully slow. She had to travel faster, but could not read the water as she usually did.

'Holy Maris! Pa! Which way should I go? I am lost!' Lystra shouted, but the wind tore some of her words away and drowned the others. Could anyone hear her?

The boat suddenly bucked and she would have been thrown overboard but for the strength of her grip. Her shoulder jarred and she felt muscle fibres tear. The wood beneath her bucked again, like a fish refusing to be landed, and she lost her footing. She caught a rope and cried out in fear and agony. Sobbing, she looped the rope twice around her waist and wrestled the boat's tiller back under control.

She oriented the boat by instinct and the last direction she had seen the water running. She couldn't see the shore through the murk, not even the great torch that burned at the top of the town hall every night. It was as if she sailed through the very void itself.

Then the sea beneath the boat lit up. Schools of glowing fish streamed around her and formed a path ahead of the boat. Lystra followed them and moved into a faster current. She was soon flying towards the unseen horizon.

The rising sun found her still holding the tiller grimly. She suspected that her cold fingers had become locked and that she would struggle to let go even if she tried. It had been a harrowing night. The light made her squint, her eyes tired and aching. How much farther? There were no more fish to light her way, so she prayed she would find what she was meant to find soon.

There. What was that? A black speck bobbed on the horizon, and her gut told her she had finally found her goal. She closed on it and it grew in size. She gasped as she realised what it was. She began to ease her fingers on the tiller and turn the boat slightly so that it slowed and so that she would be able to draw up next to the two barrels. They were lashed together and a storm-soaked man was tied across the top of them.

'Ahoy, there!' Lystra shouted. He didn't move.

She pulled her gutting knife, cut the man free and hauled him aboard. His dead weight would have defeated most people, but she'd been pulling up bulging nets of fish all her life.

Despite his youth, he had the ragged beard and well-weathered features of one of the fisherpeople of King's Landing. She thought she might recognise him. He was probably from the boat that had not returned yesterday. She quickly scanned the open water, but there was nothing else to be seen.

She pushed him onto his front. Water trickled from his mouth – not a good sign. She smacked him on the back, and again. The man spasmed and vomited water everywhere. Maris was merciful this day! He gasped like a fish out of water. She sat and waited for him to recover – there was little more she could do.

He spluttered and seemed too weak to pull his face out of the water swilling around the bottom of the boat. She went to her water-tight locker, removed a flask of rum, rolled him onto his back again and carefully poured a trickle into his mouth.

He gasped worse than before, which she adjudged a good sign.

'You'll be fine,' she decided.

'J-Jaffrans!'

'What?'

'Fleet of warships!'

Her blood went cold.

'What? You're delirious!'

'Ships fitted with rams. Ballista. Banks of oars pulled by slaves.'

She could hardly fathom what he was saying. There'd been no attack from any fleet, Jaffran or otherwise, in centuries, if not longer than that. Dur Memnos and Jaffra weren't even at war. Maybe the fishing boat had been caught up in some dispute between Jaffra and another island by accident. Or maybe the fisher captain had been fishing without licence in Jaffran waters and the Jaffrans had finally had enough of such thievery – maybe this youngster was spinning her a tale to save face and have the Harbour Mistress call for the lost crew to be revenged. Yet the fisherpeople were known for their straight talking and honesty. And the young man's watery eyes were easy for someone like Lystra to read. There was a war fleet not far away.

'How is it you are ahead of this fleet, man? Are they not heading for King's Landing then? Where are they heading? Only speak the truth, for Maris listens!'

The man trembled. 'Mistress, I do not know. They sank our boat with their first shot. When it was plain we were going down, the captain himself...

my grandfather!… tied me to the barrels. He wouldn't listen to any argument. And the barrels were carried ahead of the fleet – it wasn't natural. On my oath, and before holy Maris, 'tis the truth, I swear it, Mistress!'

'Their bearing, man, their bearing!'

'Mistress, I could not be sure. But they looked to be heading for King's Landing. Twenty or so large ships trimmed with red sails, sails as red of blood, and the wind refused to fill 'em so evil were they.'

In a panic, Lystra pushed the flask of brandy into the youngster's hands. She leapt for the tiller and wrenched it around. She began to pray out loud to her pa and holy Maris, so that they might speed her home. Dur Memnos had but a single warship, and it patrolled the coast all the way up to Soldis. King's Landing wouldn't have a chance, even if the Merchant's Guild were to commit every boat. If any were to survive, she must get home and begin the evacuation without delay.

Chapter Eight: The madness and stupidity of innocence

'So Selwyn has taken Orastes in the hope that you will turn the army out of Corinus to search for your son? Selwyn's men will then march on Corinus to seize the throne?' Sister Spike asked dubiously as she rode beside Kate.

'Selwyn or his sympathisers, yes,' Kate confirmed. 'What do you know of this Lord Selwyn? Has your temple had dealings with him?'

Sister Spike remained silent.

'I'll take that as a yes.'

Sister Spike sighed. 'I have sworn as High Priestess of Incarnus not to talk of such things. If the temple cannot keep the confidence of its clients, then the temple will quickly find it has no clients.'

Kate glared at her companion.

The priestess sighed again. 'I know, I know! I love Orastes as if he were my own son, but I'm not sure that I can put him before my duty to the god I serve.'

'I am beloved of Incarnus,' Kate replied icily.

'You need not remind me. And I suppose I would risk eternal damnation for Orastes. Very well, I dare tell you that I know Lord Selwyn to be a very ambitious man.'

Kate glared even harder.

'Yes, and if you bear me any friendship at all, then do not ask more of me. I must say this kidnapping does not feel like his work, though. It is too bold, too lacking in subtlety. There are no false trails laid. And it is too clumsy an approach if it is designed to seize the throne. He is not to know if you will leave a minimum number of men in Corinus to defend it or not. And he cannot think the temples would sit idly by while he ousts the Battle-leader who has safeguarded them so well on any number of occasions. It just doesn't feel right, Kate.' She put her hands up to forestall her friend. 'I am more than prepared to accompany you to Lord Selwyn's estate in order to put him to the question, for he is far from being my favourite person, but I think it would be wise also to consider other possibilities. What does Saltar say about this?'

Kate looked away, as if to study something in the fields to the side. 'Oh, you know Saltar. He's pursuing things in his own way. But he can't attend to everything on his own.' Her head came back. 'Look! This Selwyn has been agitating amongst the people and nobles of Corinus with talk of restoring the monarchy, with himself on the throne! And if he's had dealings with your temple, then he's ruthless enough to remove anyone who might stand in his way, by whatever means necessary. Where exactly is the subtlety in that, eh? He's clearly one of those nobles who likes to have other people do his dirty work for him. I bet he is all soft words, manners and hands. I've known men like him before. They see themselves as apart from the rest of us, as better and superior. By way of an unspoken threat to Orastes's life, he will expect to be able to negotiate himself into the position of power he ultimately thinks is his as a matter of right. He will expect us to stand aside, to leave Corinus, so that he can assume the throne without breaking a sweat or barely lifting a finger. Such a manner of ascension will be proof of everyone's recognition of his natural superiority and therefore right to rule. The last thing he will be expecting, Sister Spike, is the two of us marching into his front room to deal with him in a most uncourtly manner. Now, are you with me or not?'

She's not listening to me. Still, that's not so surprising given the circumstances. 'Kate, of course I'm with you. As Incarnus is my witness, I will not rest until Orastes is returned and holy vengeance has been visited upon those responsible. Tell me this, though, Kate – if Selwyn is holding Orastes somewhere, are we not putting the boy's life at risk with our uncourtly approach?'

Kate smiled wolfishly. 'If I'd brought Silos Varr and his men with me, our Lord Selwyn would quickly have raised up his drawbridge, posted archers atop his battlements and started issuing threats against Orastes's person. Instead, we will present him with two weak and unprotected women who have come to petition him for his help. You can be sure he will welcome us in.'

Sister Spike nodded. 'I can see that, although the Green Witch and the High Priestess of Incarnus could hardly be considered weak and unprotected.'

'At the same time, we are a distraught mother and female confidante, Sister. If I have judged Lord Selwyn correctly, he is the typical sort of male and will underestimate us. Beyond that, as an ambitious noble, he will not be able to resist the opportunity of playing Royal Protector or Queen's Champion. It will bring him one step closer to the throne he covets, you see. Be in no doubt,

Sister, he will be eager to entertain us, exclaim his outrage at the kidnapping and pledge all his resources to bringing the treasonous culprits to justice. He will insist that no reward is necessary.'

'Yes, his ambition will get the better of him, from what I know of him,' the high priestess agreed, her misgivings somewhat allayed. She was just glad Kate was not her enemy.

❈ ❈

Constantus breathed hard as he marched with his four hundred men towards the Needle Mountains. He was far from fit and it had been many years since he'd had to carry the weight of armour any distance. Beyond that, he'd always been a cavalry man rather than an infantry man. Colonel Vallus came up to his shoulder.

'Any sign of pursuit?' panted the General.

'No, sir! Perhaps Cholerax simply means to hold Accros for the time being to consolidate his position. I doubt he has troops or people equipped for a long march.'

'Hmm. The oblivious state of the people who besieged the palace makes me think he would not worry too much about equipping or resourcing them. At the instruction of Cholerax, they would march through the night or until they dropped dead. And they have horses, don't forget, if the horses can be used in the same way as our people.'

Vallus pondered his senior's words. 'Then I am surprised they haven't already caught up to us. Perhaps we are no threat or interest to this Cholerax and he therefore chooses not to waste any time on us. It begs the question what his ultimate goal might be, General.'

Constantus frowned. 'Colonel, what you mean is that the men are grumbling we're not doing anything to upset whatever the plans of this Cholerax might be, is that it? It cannot sit well with them that we are apparently abandoning our people to this creature, eh? It must stick in the throats of these fighting men that we are so quick to retreat, no? Well, man? Spit it out. And that's an order!'

The Colonel marched taller, as if coming to attention. 'Yes, sir. The General is correct, sir!'

Constantus relented somewhat, realising that his fatigue was making him more than a little irritable. 'At ease, Colonel, at ease. Please, as my second-in-command, and as my friend, speak more directly from hereon in. It helps none of us if I am not fully appraised of how things stand, for otherwise I might end up making poor and ill-informed decisions. I have not become so soft that you will hurt my feelings in talking plainly, Colonel. Give me some credit, man. Have we not known each other long enough that we need not stand on such ceremony?' He laughed. 'Besides, as I recall it, you dealt with me quite unceremoniously in the fight in front of the palace, did you not, and I thanked you for that?'

The Colonel half smiled. 'That you did, General.'

'Then I'll thank you to continue in such a vein. Starting tonight, when we have stopped marching for the day, you and I will engage in two hours of one-to-one weapons practice. If I am not bloodied and sore at the end of those two hours, then I will know you have been standing too much on ceremony and I will have you flogged. Do you understand me, Colonel?'

The Colonel looked at Constantus. 'Yes, General. It will be my pleasure.'

Constantus laughed loudly. 'I imagine it will, I imagine it will. Now, I suppose I should discuss plans with you, eh? We can decide what we will tell the men for the sake of their morale.'

'I think that might be wise, General.'

'Well, I'm glad it meets with your approval, Colonel.'

Vallus coloured slightly.

'Forgive me, Colonel, that was an attempt at humour. You're probably right — now is not the time.' *Stop behaving like a pompous, blustering ass and start acting like a soldier!* 'Colonel, I imagine you know whose lands we are now approaching?'

Vallus pulled a face. 'The lands of Lord Ristus, General. Will we be looking to be skirt around them, General?'

Lord Ristus had long been an opponent of General Constantus's caretaker rule. To be sure, a good many Accritanian nobles were dissenters, but Lord Ristus was chief amongst them and claimed his blood-line gave him greater title to the throne than any other. Matters had come to a head a year or so before at the temple of Shakri in Accros, when Lord Ristus had married the daughter of old Lord Lavere, thereby joining together the two oldest noble families in the kingdom and significantly increasing his own eligibility for the crown. A group of young nobles had over-indulged during the wedding banquet and started shouting for the restoration of the monarchy and the coronation of King Ristus the First. They'd taken up swords and gone out on the streets to raise the support of the people. Fortunately, it had been quite late in the day, so there were not many people around to get caught up in the "uprising". A few hundred people had noisily made their way to the palace, but easily been held back by the veteran troops, who had heard the mob coming a mile off.

The young nobles had been apprehended and had their hot blood cooled by a night or two in a draughty cell. Constantus had encouraged the gaoler to mention to each of the rebels that the crime for treason was punishable by death, and that only a speedy confession and a suitable display of contrition might provide some stay of the headsman's axe. Of course, Constantus had never had any intention of executing the noble sons of just about every noble family in Accritania, as that would have guaranteed a civil war, but he sure as hell intended to be certain that they never thought of causing trouble of this nature ever again.

Over the coming days, Constantus was visited by one noble-but-mortified parent after another. Each was forced to plead with Constantus that it was a common occurrence for poor company and youthful exuberance to lead good sense astray. Constantus asked for surety that the young rebels would be taken in hand, that they would find better companions for themselves from now on and that they would never reoffend. Out of a concern for the noble sons of Accritania, and for their own protection, Constantus had suggested that the noble sons be confined to family country estates for a period of no less than a year. Every parent had agreed and thanked Constantus for his understanding, but before he'd let them go to collect their sons, he'd forced one further pledge from them.

Unsurprisingly, not one of the rebels had been prepared to testify that Lord Ristus had incited them to march on the palace, but Constantus knew the lord was now a problem he could no longer afford to ignore. If he didn't take immediate action, then it wouldn't be long before another rebellion – this one no doubt more organised – sprang up. Yet that action would need to be well judged or Constantus would simply end up looking like a tyrant persecuting his political rivals. He'd gathered a thousand men together and marched them through the streets of Accros to the town house of Lord Ristus. Constantus had then informed the noble that the men had been assembled as an honour guard for the lord and his new lady wife. Further, the bride and groom would be leaving the capital immediately, and the honour guard escorting them to the Ristus country estates, where the married couple would honeymoon and spend at least a year getting to know each other. Lord Ristus had protested that there really was no need to go to so much trouble, but Constantus had insisted.

'By the wits of holy Wim and the patience of holy Lacrimos, man, no. We will not be skirting around those lands. Instead, we will be going to see our old friend Lord Ristus. He may have few virtues, Colonel, but one he does have is patriotism. His home is well fortified, I imagine, and I have heard he has added a small number of mercenaries to his retinue over the last year.'

Even the usually taciturn Colonel Vallus could not help expressing some shock at this revelation. 'Why, that treacherous dog! We should be going there to hang him if you'll forgive me for speaking freely, General.'

'Colonel, the ambitions of Lord Ristus are of no concern in the current circumstances, now are they? I'm sure Lord Ristus will also see sense in putting them aside until this greater threat to Accritania has been dealt with.' Then, General Constantus dropped his voice so that there would be no chance of any of his other words being carried by the wind to the men marching behind them. 'Besides, I am merely a caretaker for the throne. I must give serious thought to whom it will be passed. Lord Ristus would be a strong and astute ruler. The people would follow him. The kingdom would know stability under him.'

Vallus almost choked in outrage. 'General, you cannot trust this man! I would not trust him to defend your back in a fight. In fact, he's not someone to whom I would ever show my back. Is this the sort of man you would allow to rule over our fair kingdom?'

'Colonel, there is no other candidate who could keep this kingdom together. Yes, he is ambitious and has been known to put his own immediate interests before those of the kingdom, but in many quarters ambition is considered a virtue and a necessary trait in great men. Think of it like this, if you will: Lord Ristus not only sees himself as deprived of his birthright, but also a prisoner of our military rule. He sees himself as trapped and outnumbered. We all know how the hunted behave when cornered, we all know they are at their most dangerous at such times. Even the normally shy and docile stag is a terror to its enemies when threatened at close quarters. I believe Lord Ristus will prove far more majestic when given the space and opportunity required.'

Vallus shook his head. 'The man is more snake or wolf than stag. It is when a man is under pressure that he shows his true colours, not when he is shown indulgence.'

Constantus considered his man for a moment. Finally, he said, 'It could be that you're right, Colonel. After all, I've been wrong about men before, and just look at what havoc that has allowed Adjutant Spindar to wreak. However, we do not have many other options if we are to have enough men to face this threat. If we can convince Lord Ristus to join us, then surely the other nobles will join as well. And if he has horses, then we can send gold to Holter's Cross and a message to Corinus to secure aid from elsewhere. I pray you are wrong about Lord Ristus, Colonel, but would ask you to watch him and watch my back either way.'

'You do not need to ask, General.'

'I am sure we will find out just what sort of man Lord Ristus is during the coming days. Now, go inform the men we go to join Lord Ristus and begin to build the force that will set Accritania free.'

'Very good, General,' Colonel Vallus replied, his misgivings still evident.

I know, Vallus, I know, I don't like this any more than you do, Constantus sighed to himself.

⚔ ⚔

Big men in chainmail marched to either side of Kate and Sister Spike as they were led into the depths of Lord Selwyn's great keep. None had dared demand the Green Witch's crossbow from her, nor the holy blades from the High Priestess of Incarnus, but all the men watched them carefully and kept hands close to the hilts of their swords. In addition, Kate had noticed several bowmen with arrows loosely nocked joining the end of their procession.

Lord Selwyn's men were certainly intimidating, and moved with the sort of ease and balance only seen in practised fighters. The lord's keep had also surprised her, for if it were any reflection of the owner's character, then she may have seriously misjudged him. The stonework of the heavy fortifications was well maintained and there was no ornamentation or decoration in any of the internal corridors. All was no-nonsense efficiency, clear lines of sight and a preference for the practical over the comfortable. This felt far more like a place preparing for war than it was a family home.

Where had these men come from? They all wore Lord Selwyn's coat of arms on tabards over their chainmail, but the lord had not been able to put such a force into the field under Voltar's reign or in the army Kate had led against the Brethren. Yet these were experienced fighting men by the look of them, for many bore scars on their faces, so just where had their experience come from? A few of them had swarthy skin, which suggested they were not from around these parts.

There appeared to be a goodly number of them as well, for a patrol had found Kate and Sister Spike at least a mile before they had reached the keep, there had been at least a dozen men keeping watch atop the battlements, there'd been guards on every gate and now there was this escort. More than fifty, therefore. It appeared Lord Selwyn was *very* serious about his claim to the throne. And she'd just placed herself directly into his hands.

Kate didn't get the chance to ponder any further on how big a mistake she'd made, for doors opened before them and they were led into an ostentatious audience room. A vast, roaring fireplace occupied most of the back wall. A vaulted stone ceiling arched above them, supported by delicate, twisting columns. Rich, piled rugs covered much of the floor and light shone in through stained-glass windows containing depictions of Lord and Lady Selwyns from the past. This was more like the sort of vain display she'd been expecting.

The current Lord Selwyn was far from the finest specimen in his line, Kate reflected, very far. He was short and fat and occupied an oversized chair-come-throne in front of the fire. A similarly well fed woman and pair of children sat in chairs set slightly behind him. As they moved closer, Kate saw he wore a powdered wig of sorts and decided he must be balding. His face was also powdered, so it was hard to say exactly how old he was. His rouged lips pouted petulantly as if he were a sulky youth, but there was an old bitterness from years of imagined slights and failed dreams in his eyes that could not be hidden. A vain man Lord Selwyn might be, but he was still a dangerous one.

Armed men lined the walls and a boulder of a man, who was apparently the guard captain, stood near the lord's chair. Closer to a hundred men in total. There was no way any lord could afford to maintain this many men on a permanent basis. Kate's suspicions were therefore pretty much confirmed: they had to be mercenaries contracted for a specific job, that job no doubt the kidnap of her son.

Lord Selwyn did not come to his feet as Kate and Sister Spike were stopped twelve feet short of him. He would have struggled anyway, Kate decided. The mercenary captain gave her a perfunctory nod and said, 'Milady, High Priestess, welcome to the home of Lord and Lady Selwyn.'

Kate ignored the soldier and stared at Lord Selwyn. 'Where is my son?'

Lord Selwyn blinked and frowned slightly. 'You have misplaced your son, milady? How unfortunate!' His voice was high-pitched, but steady, and he did not flinch from meeting her gaze. 'We are honoured by your visit, milady. May I offer you a seat and refreshments? I have a pudding cook who makes wonderful little pastries, eh, children?'

The boy and girl who sat behind Lord Selwyn nodded eagerly.

'Where is my son?'

Lord Selwyn's frown deepened. 'Milady, you must be overwrought by your son's disappearance and by your journey from the capital. I must confess to being a little mystified as to why you have come to my door, however.' He made an expansive gesture with his hands. 'As you can see, we have not had adequate time to make preparation for your visit. You find us somewhat indisposed and have us at your advantage, milady.'

Kate turned her head to the side and said to Sister Spike in a not unquiet voice: 'Shall we prick this bag of wind?'

Lady Selwyn squealed and put a hand to her mouth. The armed men tensed.

'Milady,' the mercenary captain rumbled, 'that would be a very serious mistake.'

Kate eyed him evilly. 'And do the mercenaries of Holter's Cross now presume to concern themselves with the internal affairs of Corinus?'

Silence yawned around them like a chasm. Sweat trickled from a guard's brow, but he dared not wipe it away. All that could be heard was Lord Selwyn's heavy breathing. His face turned purple.

'How dare you!' he finally exploded, spittle flying from his mouth. 'How dare you come into my house and insult me like this! How dare you question my honour! And then you threaten me? It is an outrage! It cannot and will not be borne! I will defend myself and my rights, nay the rights of my family and family line. We have an illustrious heritage and done far more for this kingdom than your or this upstart Battle-leader of yours. And what are you? You are not even highborn. You are his lowborn *whore*! The lowborn whore of a brutal tyrant who knows nothing but the waging of war, nothing of art, nothing of manners, nothing of breeding! He may have ended the Accritanian war, but he has condemned this kingdom to a life of servitude and living in the mud amongst the pigs!'

Sister Spike shrugged. 'I think so,' she said in reply to Kate's previous suggestion. 'None of them has any intention of allowing us to leave this keep alive. And he's starting to give me a headache.'

'So, Lord Selwyn,' Kate said with a smile, 'it appears the question of your honour *will be decided by the gods.*'

On hearing the pre-agreed cue, Sister Spike slid into motion. Her movement was a barely caught whisper. As the divine instrument of Incarnus, there was no gap between will and action, intent and realisation. There was no time in which the mercenaries, seasoned though they were, could respond.

A spike plunged into the captain's throat, propelled him backwards and nailed him to the wood panelling of the wall. Smaller blades found the eyes and hands of other guards with unerring accuracy, incapacitating at least half a dozen of them.

'Kill them!' Lord Selwyn demanded, thumping his fists on the arms of his chair like a glutton who has been kept waiting too long. His son clapped in delight and his daughter began to cry. Lady Selwyn fainted in dramatic fashion, but managed to stay in her chair rather than falling to the floor and cracking her head open.

Kate heard the tell-tale creak of a bow-string being pulled and dropped low by doing the splits. Air and death whooshed over her head. She hadn't felt this alive in months! She slotted a bolt into her crossbow and cranked it. Instinct made her roll, even though her legs were still splayed. Metal sheered through the leather armour at her waist. The burning sensation told her it had parted flesh, but how deep she couldn't tell. She just prayed the arrowhead hadn't been poisoned.

She now had her crossbow up. She swivelled at the waist, wincing as her wound was torn wider, and fired. Her powerful bolt punched into the nose-guard of the offending archer's helmet and into his face. He fell back screaming. He would be unable to breathe through the mess of his nose, and once the blood started pouring down his throat, he would choke. He was no longer a threat... unlike the other archer, now drawing a bead on her, and the dozen men converging on them with blades drawn, one of them with a huge, two-headed axe.

Sister Spike bared her teeth at them. 'I hope you're on good terms with holy Lacrimos, for you will soon be meeting Him!' Needles glinted between her fingers and she cast them at their attackers with a casual flick of her wrists.

Yet these men had not been daunted by the fall of their captain or by the prospect of facing the High Priestess of Incarnus. They were not about to be phased by her threats and unorthodox weaponry. They lowered heads and hid their hands so that not one needle found its mark. Then the men were upon the two women.

Kate was still on the floor. One kicked at her midriff while another stamped on the inside of her right calf. She screamed in joy and stabbed the crossbow bolt she was holding into the stamper's inner thigh. The links of his chainmail parted and she hit one of his main arteries. Blood sprayed and then gushed everywhere, making the floor slippery. The kicker slipped to one knee and Kate smashed the heel of her hand up under his chin. His teeth crunched and splintered together and he reeled backwards.

'As much gold as you can carry for the man who parts the witch's head from her shoulders!' screeched Lord Selwyn in a castrato voice.

The sneering and broad-chested axeman swung his weapon in a flat arc to part Sister Spike's legs from her torso. She knew its weight and speed represented a momentum far too great for her to stop or even redirect. Like a partner in a formal dance, she stepped back from him, beyond his arc, and then stepped in close after the axe had gone past. Her chest brushed against the back of the shoulder he had nearest to her. He looked up into her eyes. His grey eyes widened in surprise to see her still alive. He was unshaven and stank of sweat and the onions he'd had for lunch, but now the sneer had fallen from his face he wasn't entirely unattractive, she decided. What a shame. She kicked the side of his knee on which he was carrying all his weight. As he went down, she grabbed each side of his head and twisted it, instantly breaking his neck.

There was no time to mourn the man who may have been the love of her life in other circumstances, for there were others eager to press their suit and have the next dance. She was without weapons now, except for the body given her by Shakri and the skills and secrets learnt in the service of Incarnus. She was forged and armed by the gods themselves. What hope could there be for these dull mercenaries? Imagine attacking the High Priestess of Incarnus and not realising retribution would be exacted even before they could land a blow. They deserved death for this stupidity, faithlessness and blasphemy. They probably deserved a worse death than was currently being meted out to them. Perhaps she should start striking to cripple and maim rather than kill.

A guard carried his sword an inch too low. She raised her foot and trod down so that the blade slapped onto the floor. She jumped with the foot she'd just planted and kicked the soldier in the chest with her other foot. He flew backwards onto the sword of the man behind him and screamed horribly as he died.

The high priestess swayed and twisted to avoid the slashing edges and stabbing points of at least six swords. Seeing her weaponless, the men crowded her eagerly, knowing that she could not survive long once they reduced the space in which she had to move. Now, she was forced to jump and duck, block and deflect. The men worked to get round the back of her. She would soon be surrounded.

Sister Spike caught the flat of a blade between her palms, pulled it towards her and out of the hands of the mercenary holding it. Then she spun the blade through one hundred and eighty degrees and stabbed it hard into the gut of the man who'd just been trying to kill her with it. He groaned and dragged the sword down to the floor with him.

Quick as thought, she used a foot to flick the sword she'd trodden on earlier up into the air. She grabbed it just in time to block a weapon cutting towards her face.

'Ha! Now you all die!' she promised them.

Something loomed behind her. Too late, she spun to find the mercenary captain descending on her. Amazingly, the spike that had nailed him to the wall hadn't killed him and he'd managed to tear himself free. One of his giant hands was clamped hard around his ruined throat. He hammered the other hard into her face, breaking her nose and splitting her cheek wide. Her eyes lost all focus. He hit her again.

Kate concentrated every bit of herself on the archer about to release his quarrel straight at her. She shut everything else out, becoming oblivious to the men harrying Sister Spike not far away. She would only get one chance. She trusted the gods would not let her down now – to think otherwise would be a sort of faithlessness that would be sure to doom her.

Death flew at her. At the precise moment, she swatted her hand and forearm sideways, knocking the arrow off course and into the leg of one of the soldiers harrying Sister Spike. The archer cursed and reached for another arrow. Several mercenaries then stepped between him and Kate, meaning that he would struggle to get a clear line of sight on her again. Snarling, he put his bow aside, pulled his sword and ran to join his comrades.

Kate finally got the chance to come to her feet just as Sister Spike was clubbed to the ground by the mercenary captain. The brute was still alive! But Kate knew better than to waste precious time worrying about her friend. Life, victory and survival were all about precise moments, precise moments like the one she'd just faced with the archer. If she hadn't moved her arm at that precise moment, all would have been lost. If she'd moved her arm the moment before or after, she would have been dead and found herself standing before a smug Lacrimos, who had been waiting a long time to pass judgement on the daughter of Shakri.

This was the precise moment to crank her crossbow and fit a bolt to it, before the captain and his remaining six men began to turn their heads towards her. This was the moment to step back and to the right. This was the moment to turn away from her friend, even as the captain kicked Sister Spike cruelly in the stomach. This was the moment to level her crossbow at Lord Selwyn's head.

'Enough!' Kate yelled. 'Leave her or I execute this gut-bucket sooner than I'd like.'

The mercenaries stilled, unwilling to make any sort of move that might lose them their client.

'Touch a hair on my head and your s-son dies!' Lord Selwyn gibbered.

'Oh, you can be sure that I will execute you, Lord Selwyn. You are guilty of the attempted murder of a Guardian and a high priestess of Dur Memnos, not to mention treason. But first of all, you will be answering my questions. If there's any suggestion that Orastes has been hurt or that you are lying to me, then your wife and children will die in front of you. Do you understand, Lord Selwyn?'

'No!' Lord Selwyn's son screamed, his face screwed up in rage. With small fists raised, he ran at the terrible woman who had come into his home, threatened his father and scared his sister.

Kate backhanded the boy and sent him sprawling. The tip of her crossbow did not waver for a second. The boy looked up at her from the floor with hate and tears in his eyes. His terrified sister ran to their mother, hid her face in Lady Selwyn's frocks and began to shake and tremble.

'Stupid child!' Kate sneered. 'Still, there's hope for you, as you're a sight braver than your self-indulgent father. He's only worried about his own skin, you know. Back to your chair, boy.' She jabbed the point of her crossbow bolt against Lord Selwyn's temple, drawing blood. 'Tell him!'

'Back to your seat, son!' the lord warbled.

'You mercenaries, get out! Move!' Kate ordered.

The captain glared impotently at her. His injury meant he was incapable of speech, but his eyes spoke volumes. Things were not finished between them. He had no choice but to do as she told him for now, however. He signalled his men to gather up the fallen who still lived and then they all backed out of the room.

'Sister Spike!' Kate shouted.

The priestess did not move.

'Sister Spike!'

This time, she groaned and began to stir. She got onto her hands and knees.

'Seal the doors! Then we will visit our retribution on this lord.'

The priestess began to crawl towards the doors, leaving a trail of blood across the flagstones and rugs. Reaching the doors, she dragged herself up into a standing position and tipped a heavy bar across the portal. Then she tottered back towards Kate. She held her ribs and winced. 'A few broken,' she mumbled. 'How do I look?'

Kate smiled. 'You don't want to know. Here, hold the crossbow.'

The two women swapped positions and Kate wasted no time dragging a large table into the centre of the room and gathering up some of Sister Spike's throwing knives. 'You!' she said to Lord Selwyn. 'On the table, now! Don't be shy. It looks well made and as if it'll take your weight. That's it. On your back! Put your arms out, palms face upwards. Do it!'

The lord began to tremble. Kate slammed a spike through one of his hands, nailing it to the wood. He screamed piteously, snot running from his nose. A dark stain began to spread across his britches.

'And the other hand!'

'Have mercy!' he shrieked.

'You ask me for mercy?' Kate asked derisively. 'Mercy from a lowborn whore? Surely there's nothing you'd ever want from a *whore*, is there, milord? Surely it would be beneath you. So why even ask? For, as you said, I am without manners or breeding. How could you even expect me to understand your request? If I live in the mud like a pig, then how could I be expected to show anything as noble as mercy? Therefore, put your hand out, or I will cut it from your arm!'

In anguish, Lord Selwyn extended his hand. She nailed it as she had the other.

'Oh, be quiet! Take it like a man, if man you are. What sort of example are you to your son, eh? Look, Sister Spike has suffered far more than you, and you don't see her crying, now do you? There, that's better. Now, my Lord Selwyn, for the third time of asking, where is my son? It would have been so much easier for both of us if you'd given me a civil answer the first time I'd asked. WHERE IS MY SON?!'

'I-I don't knooowww!' Lord Selwyn wailed.

'How unfortunate!' Kate said, mimicking the lord's high-pitched tones. She tested the edge of a blade with her finger. 'Yes, this will do. Answer me now or I will make you a eunuch. You will never father children again.'

The lord's eyes bulged. 'I-I'm begging you! I haven't touched your wretched brat!'

'Well, you had your chance!' Kate shrugged and began to cut the buttons at the front of the lord's britches.

'Kate!' Sister Spike warned in a low voice. 'I can read the ways of intention. He speaks the truth.'

Kate hesitated, annoyed. 'Then we have no other use for this traitor and he is mine to do with as I will. Incarnus Himself would urge me to take vengeance on this creature.'

'Kate,' Sister Spike said slowly through her swollen lips. 'You need not tell me of the Holy Avenger's will. Yes, you have a right to vengeance, but not to indulge yourself in gratuitous torture. I can foresee that if you commit any act of depravity in front of these children, then they will spend the rest of their lives seeking to revenge themselves on you and yours. That feud will create a civil war and ultimately destroy the kingdom. Kate, hear me! You do *not* have the right to punish these children, for they have done you no wrong.'

Kate hesitated again. 'What if I kill the children as well?' She sighed. 'No, we would not be justified in that. Damn it! We'll have to take this slug with us then and execute him elsewhere.'

Sister Spike nodded. 'We will need him as hostage if we are to win past the mercenaries in any event.'

'Don't worry about that. I'm sure a man like Lord Selwyn has a secret way out of this room. We'll just make him show us.'

'Something else occurs, Kate. Lord Selwyn may not know where Orastes is, but he may know who does.'

Kate smiled. 'You need not worry about that either, sister, for I know exactly who's got him. The same people who refused to take up arms against Voltar until Saltar gave them a bloody nose. The same people who tried to have me assassinated when we marched against the Brethren. And the same people who have been using Lord Selwyn here as their puppet. Don't you see? It's been them all along. It's always been them. The Guild of Holter's Cross!'

'Yes, it is possible. They have been responsible for many a dark deed in the history of this kingdom. That old crow Guildmaster Thaeon is quite capable of ordering the kidnapping. We cannot let him get away with this!'

'And indeed we will not. Their scheming ways have never served this kingdom well, but this time they have gone too far. They have sealed their doom. I will raze Holter's Cross to the ground, crucify every last Guild Brother and expunge every written reference to them.'

'Just allow the temple of Incarnus to be in the vanguard, Kate, I beg of you. I thirst for revenge, but if there is any chance Orastes might be saved, then it is the priests of my temple, with their various talents, who will have the best chance of saving him. The old crow will seek to negotiate with you, of course, and therefore will not be too quick to harm Orastes. There is our chance.'

'He may seek to negotiate, but he'll get nothing from me save the ugliest and most painful of deaths – and he should think himself lucky to get away with just that. If I had my way, Lacrimos would then slow-roast him on a spit for the rest of eternity. Maybe the god of death will oblige me in this. I must remember to speak to His high priestess when we're back in Corinus.'

Sister Spike shuddered. Not for the first time that day, she thanked Incarnus that Kate was not her enemy.

≍ ≍

Sotto led his two hundred Outdwellers south of Corinus. They'd been sent out to search the surrounding countryside for Kate's missing son. Sotto thought it highly unlikely that Orastes would have gone south on his own, as there was no significant town or other destination in such a direction. Similarly, if the boy had been kidnapped, there were none down here who were organised enough or would have motive to be involved in such an enterprise. No, all they were likely to find in the south, apart from the occasional hamlet, were difficult swamps, biting flies, bog-trotters and the ghosts of wayward travellers.

Yet orders were orders, and Sotto knew he would be shown little tolerance if he challenged them. The Outdwellers had still not managed to integrate into the army properly; and he got the impression that if the commanders were given just half an excuse, then they would seek to drum the Outdwellers out of the service completely. So, if Sotto's commanders wanted him and his men out of the way and out of trouble, then he would be happy to oblige them.

Or at least he would have been if it were not for the fact all the Outdwellers felt a particular loyalty to Kate and wanted to do all they could to retrieve Orastes. There was a strong sense of community amongst the Outdwellers and they considered Kate to be one of their own. Looking out for each other was the only way the Outdwellers had survived under Voltar and his Wardens, and probably since then. Sotto feared it was the only way Orastes might survive now.

And so, the further south they went, the more Sotto fretted they were getting further and further away from the boy. 'Anything?' he redundantly asked the latest group of men to catch back up to him after investigating a local farm.

'I got meself a couple of eggs,' Crazy Chella crowed.

'I hope you paid the farmer!' Sotto sighed.

Crazy Chella scratched his head and his companions looked confused. 'Pay, Sotto? But we hen't got no money, has we?'

'The army provides you with food, Chella, so that you don't have to steal it from everyone you come across. If every soldier stole from that farmer, he'd never have any eggs for his family or to exchange at the market. And call me sir when you speak to me!'

'Sure, Sotto... Sir Sotto, sure! Every soldier cen't steal from that farmer, though, cos there was only these two eggs. Then't enough for every soldier, Sir Sotto, you see. And I hen't got me army food cos I lost it at dicing to Slow Shento. And I cen't steal it back from Slow Shento cos he's eaten it already. So what am I to do but take a couple of eggs when no one's watching them? Or is this one of them new army rules no one's explained proper to me, Sir Sotto? Is it? Hope you en't mad then, Sir Sotto. Trying my best, I am.'

Crazy Chella's companions nodded in support of their fellow. They were all trying their best.

Sotto gritted his teeth. 'Did you at least search properly for the boy? And ask the farm folks if they've seen a boy travelling this way?'

'Sure, Sir Sotto, sure, just like you said we should. No sign. Teeler here has seen the Builder and Green Witch's boy a few times and would know if he saw him.'

'Alright, well done, Chella. Go enjoy your eggs. Where's Dijin?'

'His group's over there, Sir Sotto. Think he knows you want him, like he always knows. He's coming over. Don't mention me eggs to him, will you, Sir Sotto, or Dijin will take them off me? Always hungry, he is!'

Sotto smiled. 'Better move quick then, Chella, as I'm sure Dijin will have smelt them already. You know what his nose is like.'

Crazy Chella yelped and scuttled off.

Sotto greeted his big friend, who looked distractedly after Crazy Chella. 'Hello, Dijin. Any luck?'

Dijin's head swung back to Sotto. 'Luck, Sotto? With what?'

'You looked for Orastes with those others, yes? Did you find him?'

Dijin creased his huge brow and thought for a good few seconds. 'No, Sotto.'

'No trace of him, then. And no one else found anything?'

Another pause. 'No.'

'I see.'

Something was bothering the large Outdweller. Sotto waited for him to speak.

'Sotto?'

'Yes, Dijin?'

'How can anyone find the boy if he's not here?'

Sotto had learnt to be patient with his friend long ago. 'We're seeing if the boy was here before, even if he's not here now. We're seeing if we can find a way to follow him.'

'The boy wasn't here before,' Dijin said with conviction.

'Really? How do you know that?'

'The boy has never been here. No smell of him, Sotto.'

'No smell? Do you mean to tell me that nose of yours can tell if someone's ever been to a place?'

'Of course, Sotto. How else would I know what the past is? It's where a person has been before.'

Sotto blinked, unable to imagine quite how Dijin experienced the world. 'Oookay. But you're sure Orastes has never been this way? Absolutely sure?'

'I've forgotten what absolutely means, Sotto.'

'You're *very* sure, yes, Dijin?'

'Yes, Sotto. I told you the truth. I always try to tell the truth. You told me it was good to…'

'Yes, good, good. Now, I don't suppose your nose has any idea where the boy might be now, does it?'

Dijin breathed deeply and then raised one of his thick arms. 'That way… but not near, Sotto.'

East. The Outdwellers wouldn't be able to take a straight line from here as the terrain was too difficult. They would have to return to Corinus and then strike out once more. Sotto decided there would be less fuss all round if he didn't inform his commanders of his change of direction. What they didn't know couldn't upset them. Besides, no one had told him he should go south and just stay there until he was ordered to do otherwise, had they? And the overall mission was to find the boy, wasn't it, so as long as he did that then everything would be fine, wouldn't it? Of course, if he didn't, then he would probably be court-marshalled and executed, or some such. He was gambling both his own and the boy's life on the power of one man's nose.

'Are you sure it's that way, Dijin?'

'Abso…lutely, Sotto!' Dijin beamed.

'Right, that settles it. Everyone up! Back to Corinus, at the double!'

His orders caused general consternation. 'Sir, we won't reach the city till it's dark.'

'Precisely. And we will continue through the night until we are well past the city. I don't want our passing heard or detected by anyone, so move like your are back in the catacombs, you body-thieves and scavengers! Do you all get me?'

'Yes, Sir Sotto!' two hundred Outdwellers shouted, remembering where they came from and who they were once again.

'Has anyone got anything to eat?' Dijin rumbled, eyeing Crazy Chella.

><

Vallus advanced alone carrying a white flag.

'Stop right there!' one of Lord Ristus's men shouted from the top of the long rise up to the fortified hall. 'Take one more step, soldier, and you will be drilled with quarrels. You will be so feathered you will be mistaken for a dancing girl.'

'I carry the white flag of parley!' Vallus shouted back. 'Has the honour of Lord Ristus's house fallen so far that one of his men would ignore the universal principles of battle?'

'And what would the criminals who make up the Accritanian army know of honour? Should a farmer treat a crow with honour when it is stealing his corn? Should he treat the rats in his barn with kindness? Or should he treat them according to their nature?'

Vallus had never been very good at pretty speeches and witty retorts. That was why he'd become a soldier rather than some town speaker, councillor or actor. He was good at soldiering, damn it! He spoke via his actions, with the cut and thrust of his sword and the strength of his arm. But as much as he soldiered, it never seemed to be enough. No matter how many battles you won, or enemies you killed, it counted for nothing if you did not have the final say, the last word. Would the world need to see the final battle through before a man's actions would have as much meaning as – or *more* meaning than – his empty words? It certainly appeared so.

Vallus had begged General Constantus not to choose him as bearer of the flag of parley, but the General had insisted no one would be able to observe and assess the strength of Lord Ristus's position better than his loyal Colonel. So Vallus had been sent to bandy words that stuck in his throat, choked him and made him queasy in his gut. He responded to the challenge as any soldier would: with aggression.

'If that is how you wish us to treat you, then so be it, lordling! I am a straight-talking soldier. I will kill you if that is what you wish. From your vantage, you can see we are four hundred, at least four times your number, if I do not miss my guess. And know this, youth, for that is what you are, we are four hundred battle-hardened veterans. We were killing Memnosians before your mother had even spread her legs to conceive you. It saddens me that this is how fellow countrymen must now treat each other, but I will not hesitate to cut down those who will not allow me peace when I sue for it. It saddens me that a man with your cultured tones and apparent education does not know better than to hasten his own death, but neither does it surprise me. Now, are we done talking, for I am eager to return to my General and confirm that there is no one worth sparing here?'

For some while, only the wind answered the words of Colonel Vallus. He watched carefully for movement, so that he would bravely look death in the eye when it came for him. Finally, though, a tall, lion-haired man in a red surcoat came to the edge of the slope.

'Constantus himself has come? With so few men? When he escorted me to the edge of my lands before, it was with a thousand. Does he no longer fear the support I have amongst the other nobles, for we here more than match your number and have the advantage of the higher ground.'

Vallus suspected the lord was bluffing, but it mattered neither way. 'We have not come with any such concern, Lord Ristus. We have not come to bring you to justice, but the General wishes to explain to you himself how things now stand in the kingdom.'

Another pause. 'What do you mean *how things stand in the kingdom*?' Then eagerness entered the lord's voice. 'Have my people thrown off the shackles of his rule at last? Has he been ousted from Accros?'

'Nay!' Vallus shouted back. 'Believe me, I even wish it was such that had brought us here, for it would be a far lesser evil than that which has now befallen our beloved Accritania.'

'What do you mean, man? Explain yourself!'

'Milord, will you have parley with General Constantus?'

A final hesitation. 'Very well, tell him to bring some few men forward and I will meet him at the bottom of the slope.'

❊ ❊

With his fine features, clear, blue gaze, halo of hair and blonde moustache, Lord Ristus looked every inch the wise and noble king of fairytale, particularly when standing opposite the battered and gaunt General Constantus. The old soldier still had a full head of flame-red hair, but it looked out of place next to his sallow skin, as if he wore the wig of a clown, actor or painted lady. The General had once been known as the Red Dragon, but there seemed precious little fire in him when he was compared to the rising sun that was Ristus.

Several young nobles attended on their lord, presumably the sons of ambitious families who wanted to be well placed in the court of a future king. However, none of the lordlings wore a coat of arms by which they might be identified, and Lord Ristus declined to introduce them by name to the General or Colonel Vallus. Vallus inspected them for a few moments and then decided to pay them no more mind – the only person who might consider them a threat in a confrontation was an unchaperoned maid looking to keep her virtue, and even then Vallus would have been tempted to put money on the maid coming away the victor.

'Who is this Cholerax?' Lord Ristus was asking in neutral tones. 'I have not heard the name before. It sounds foreign to my ear.'

'A demon, we think,' General Constantus said carefully.

Lord Ristus raised one of his eyebrows. 'A demon? What makes you think so? The fact that so many people were of one voice and called for you to be removed? The fact they valued their freedom over their lives, braving the eager swords of your men with their own bodies, sacrificing themselves so that their children could grow up to be something other than slaves?'

Vallus couldn't stand to hear his General mocked by this preening, arrogant...

'No, Vallus. Hold! We speak under the white flag. Remember yourself, man!' Constantus said before the Colonel had even touched his sword.

One of the young nobles smirked and Lord Ristus gave the youth a reprimanding glare.

Constantus took a calming breath and shrugged his shoulders to keep himself relaxed. He deliberately looked his opponent in the eye. 'I know how it sounds. Indeed, I would ask you to consider the fact that it would be easier to invent a more credible story if our purpose were to deceive you somehow. With my own eyes, I have seen a soldier scratched till he bled by one of the mob and turned against the comrades with whom he has fought side-be-side all his life. I have seen people tread friends and family underfoot without a flicker of emotion. I have seen people forget themselves entirely and become nothing more than rabid animals. There is a dark and unholy magic at work in the kingdom. I swear on it as a soldier of Accritania. I swear it before holy Shakri, Lacrimos and the entire pantheon.'

Lord Ristus considered General Constantus, his eyes calculating. Then he made a decision. 'Follow me,' he said, and turned to lead them up the slope.

Constantus and Colonel Vallus exchanged glances, and Vallus shook his head.

'Lord Ristus...!' Constantus began.

The lord hesitated briefly, saying over his shoulder, 'You will not be harmed. You have my word,' and carried on walking.

'Hah!' Vallus spat.

Constantus motioned the two soldiers he'd brought with him as a precaution to follow after Ristus. Then he began to climb the slope himself. The grumbling Colonel Vallus had no choice but to follow suit.

❄ ❄

'One of my workers came out of the fields with his eyes burning. He laughed like a lunatic and foamed at the mouth,' Lord Ristus explained as they went. 'We thought he had worked in the sun too long or eaten some poisonous plant, or some such, and my people went to help him. He attacked them and the madness took them in turn.'

Armed men in the colours of Lord Ristus watched them all the way. A number of them were little older than children, their armour ill-fitting or made up of odds and ends. A few appeared too old to carry a weapon anymore, although their keenness of eye made it clear they did not lack for experience. Several dozen were middle-aged men dressed in the colours of the young nobles attending on Lord Ristus – but looked soft and indulged to Constantus's eye. And the rest, four dozen or so, were dressed in a neutral-coloured livery that marked them for mercenaries.

A hundred of them, just as Vallus predicted, Constantus realised. *They have long bows and some few horses. Perhaps they would have given us some trouble, but not too much.* Yet it was significant Lord Ristus had given up on his bluff and was now allowing Constantus to see their numbers at first hand.

'I see,' Constantus replied. 'The same as we experienced at the palace in Accros. How did you contain the outbreak?'

Lord Ristus gave him a pained look. 'We had no choice but to defend ourselves.'

Constantus nodded.

'We lost good people that day, General, good people. Some, we managed to bind and imprison, in the hope that they would come back to themselves, but... well, you will see.'

They reached the top of the climb, and Constantus found himself slightly winded. The rest of his breath was taken away by sight of the ancient seat of the Ristus family. The late afternoon sun gilded the mighty, silver-wooded hall in burnished gold and made it look the most sacred temple in Shakri's realm. The giant pillars that gave the building its strength were carved in the form of noble-featured, armoured warriors. They bore shields marked with the Ristus coat of arms – the flame-tongued lion beset by hounds. Constantus had heard countless descriptions of the hall, but never had he imagined it would make him want to fall to his knees.

'Vanity, nothing more!' Vallus grumbled quietly. 'Bet his ancestors were a bunch of crippled and mean-spirited dwarves.'

'Even if they were,' Constantus murmured back, 'is it not right that they sought to inspire mortalkind's spirit? Do we not need to remember our better selves more now than ever before? What else will encourage us to raise our heads and pick ourselves up when we have been beaten down?'

Vallus grunted. 'I will not judge a man by his appearance, General, and if it please the gods you will never have me do so. Do you judge a woman by the jewellery she wears?'

Constantus sighed. 'Peace, good Vallus. The moment has passed. Look, Lord Ristus leads us further.'

They moved to the rear of the hall and a little down the far slope, where they found a locked metal gate in the rock. Filthy men and women ran to the bars and reached for the soldiers, who cautiously hung back. The prisoners were wild-eyed and incoherent. They screeched, spat and hissed. One man pulled his member from his trews and urinated at them.

'Gah!' Vallus uttered in disgust and stepped back from the steaming rivulets of piss.

'Poor wretches!' Constantus said with a mix of pity and horror. 'Are the people they once were completely gone? Have you tried appealing to them?'

Lord Ristus nodded sadly. 'Do you see the young woman with matted, black hair, the one who has torn bits of her scalp away? May I introduce you, General, to the daughter of Lord Lavere, the Lady Jessmine, my dear, beloved wife.'

❋ ❋

'How are you feeling?' Strap asked Lucius, who was finally beginning to stir.

'So bad that the priests of Malastra would probably give up on me,' the musician gasped, his voice resonating strangely because of his broken and still swollen nose. 'Any water?'

Strap laughed. 'You know very well the old woman said you were to drink as much of this tea as I could get down you.'

'I'm sick of drinking her bathwater!' Lucius grumbled. 'She's completely batty. Whoever heard of drinking tea for a knife wound? I'm sure it's her evil brew making me feel so bad.'

Strap shook his head. 'I've never seen a wound heal so cleanly or quickly though. A miracle if you ask me. And for all your claims to the contrary, there's plenty of life in you when it comes to complaining about nearly everything.'

'No thanks to the Scourge!'

'If you ask me, Lucius, you got off lightly. When the Scourge's ire is raised, even the gods look for cover these days. It is proof of how much he thinks of you that you still breathe.'

The one-eyed musician made a dismissive noise and waved Strap's words away.

Strap became intent. 'Listen to me. The Scourge compromised his principles for you. He allowed me to neglect my duty as a Guardian so that I might look after you. Do you not understand what that means for someone like the commander? His principles and his duty are everything to him, everything! It is the self-sacrifice of people like him that keeps this realm safe, Lucius. So quit feeling sorry for yourself and…'

Colour had come into Lucius's face now. His one eye blazed at the Guardian. 'Have you forgotten who I am, *Young* Strap?! You talk to me of sacrifice? Me, who had to haul corpses into Voltar's crypts everyday! Me, who was tortured by the usurper and had his eye put out! Me, a mere musician, who did more than a little to bring the evil necromancer down when the gods had failed! Me, who continued to follow Saltar into the mountains when the likes of the Scourge had fallen by the wayside! Who single-handedly prevented Nylchros's victory! Who has spent his entire life pleasing, entertaining, serving or obeying others! You talk to *me* of sacrifice? And then the one time in my life I try to live my own life, to be free, I'm hunted down like I'm some sort of criminal. Just what have I done to deserve this, Strap, tell me that! What have I done to warrant being stabbed and having my face broken? Have I killed someone, Strap? Stolen a holy object? Brutalised a woman? Tell me, Strap, tell me. Oh, I know what it is. I spent time in the company of Jack O'Nine Blades, a being personally thanked and set free by Shakri Herself. For that, the Scourge stabs me, cripples me and leaves me for dead. Strap, he is a maniac! *He* is the one who kills, steals Shakri's holy spark and brutalises people! *He* is the criminal!'

Lucius's voice became weaker as he spoke. By the end, he had started to choke and was now racked by a spasming cough that would not end. Strap held a cup of cold tea out to him, waited while Lucius groped for it, sipped, spluttered and eventually managed to swallow. His chest heaving, the musician lay back and waited for the attack to subside fully. He had become exhausted once more. His body trembled and shook.

Strap paced back and forth in the small back room they had claimed for themselves in the inn in Windrun. When he could wait no more, Strap stopped and faced Lucius again. 'Have you finished? Good. You will hear me now, musician. Understand this, then – you are guilty, Lucius. Yes, guilty! You knowingly consort with a demon and aid it in all it does. You aid an unholy creature that stole its body from some unwitting mortal. You have helped it influence large numbers of people the length and breadth of this kingdom. Do not pretend to me you do not know the power of your music, Lucius, for it was that self-same music that helped bring down Voltar and Nylchros, and of which you still proudly boast. The Scourge and I have come to realise just how invidious this Jack O'Nine Blades is and how you have sown the seeds of chaos wherever you have gone. No, do not deny it, for we have seen it first hand. Between you, you and the demon have turned whole crowds, nay towns even, against the Scourge and me, making usually good, law-abiding citizens capable of murder. You have corrupted them! And we have seen the division, despair and damage your passing has caused.'

'It cannot be!' Lucius whispered in frightened and desperate denial. 'My music brought people joy.'

'Lucius,' Strap pursued, 'the Scourge and I now realise that the demon has been feeding on the emotions of the people it tempts with its entertainment. It encourages strong emotion, be it revelry, lust or anger. It encourages people to indulge their appetites wantonly so that there is more energy to feed on, energy that ultimately feeds its magic and makes it stronger.'

'No, stop! Do not say such things. I am too weak.'

'Think, Lucius,' Strap pressed. 'Where is it all leading? Why does the demon wish to grow its own magic? Why does it set mortal against mortal? Why does it travel the kingdom spreading its influence and dissension? Why does every temple condemn demonkind? Tell me, Lucius, why?!'

The lute-player shook his head in a mute agony of horror.

Strap began to speak slowly now, horrified himself as, out loud, he thought through all the implications. 'It will destroy the love and harmony that exists between and within people. It will undermine Shakri's love and will, undermine Her holy magic that created this realm. It will undo Shakri's realm and remake it in its own image. This will become a realm of demonkind! Ye gods, Lucius, what have you done? You may have destroyed us all.'

'I didn't know,' Lucius squeaked. 'What can we do?'

'I-I do not know. I do not think even the Scourge has understood the threat fully.' Then Strap gasped.

'What is it?'

'The Scourge and I fought some unholy winged creature not so long ago. I am sure it was a demon. And we have heard stories of similar things while we have travelled during the last year. Shakri preserve us, Lucius, they must be everywhere! If they all rise against us at once, mortalkind will surely be overwhelmed, few as we are.'

'What have I done?' Lucius moaned. 'Tell me what we must do, Strap!'

'Let me think, let me think! What would the Scourge do? We must stop Jack at all costs, before it is too late.'

'We must pursue them then?'

Strap nodded firmly. 'Yes, but I will also hire whatever messengers I can as we do to hurry word to Saltar, Kate and Mordius. Every Guardian must be warned so that they can help towns prepare whatever defences they may. And we must send messages to every major temple. We mortals must beseech our gods for aid more now than ever before in our existence. I've never really prayed much, but I think now might be a good time to start.'

'Sweet Shakri preserve us!'

'For nothing else will.'

'Help me up. Give me that tea, and tell the old woman to prepare me some jars of her bathwater to travel with!'

'Need we alert Constantus in Accritania?'

Lucius looked miserable. 'I fear so, for Jack and I have toured there every year during the winter months. Gods, forgive me, but we played to packed houses!'

'Ah! That explains why we always lost your trail during those months. Lucius, I think it would have been better for all of us if we'd caught you immediately and you'd never been allowed even a moment of freedom or your own life. To think I ever doubted the Scourge! Like you, there were times I questioned his instincts and his sanity even!'

Lucius looked terribly sick. 'I fear it would have been better if the Scourge had caught me immediately, ignored instinct towards mercy and killed me there and then.'

Strap couldn't find the words with which to argue.

⚒ ⚑

'So what do you propose?' Lord Ristus asked as he poured Constantus a Stangeld brandy.

They sat in the lord's hall around a monolithic table, the wood of which was black-old and metal-hard. The General sipped the amber-coloured liquid and sighed. It had been days since he'd had a drink. Remembering himself, he said: 'If any of us is to have any chance against this unholy threat, then we must unite against it. We must warn the other nobles and have them rally here. We will request aid from our friends in Dur Memnos also. Then, we will strike at Cholerax from this fortress. If we can discover the centre of his power, I am sure together we can defeat our common enemy. Apart from the nobles, though, our principal allies must be the temples, for they represent our best chance of combating the spread of this plague that robs people of their self-possession. I am sure that, if we can find a priest, they will be able to help your good lady wife, Lord Ristus. What say you?'

Lord Ristus was silent for a second, swirling his brandy in the bottom of his glass. 'And who do you propose leads us, General?'

'The General will!' Vallus said without hesitation.

'Vallus –' Constantus began.

'The General has the most experience in the field. He knows more of the art of war than any other Accritanian alive. The men will follow no other!'

'Vallus, that is enough!'

Lord Ristus looked briefly amused. 'Yet the General apparently struggles to maintain discipline in his second-in-command. Is it you who gives the orders and dictates terms, Colonel? No, Colonel, allow me to apologise before you respond. I spoke half in jest and half in rebuke, but now realise that will only provoke your passion further, so peace, good Colonel, peace. Remember your white flag and allow me to address your General again. General Constantus, I am prepared to allow you to lead in this, content to place my own men under your command, but there is a price. Once we have defeated Cholerax and restored peace to the kingdom, you will relinquish your rule in my favour.'

There was silence throughout the hall, as servants, guards and young nobles froze so that they might hear the words of General Constantus. The future of the kingdom, and perhaps the lives of everyone in the room, depended on what would be said now.

Constantus licked his lips and smiled. 'Lord Ristus, I am prepared to agree such terms but will only do so with the consent of good Colonel Vallus.'

All eyes turned to Vallus.

'Well, my friend, what do you say? Will you finally let me retire one day, so that I may spend some real time with my beloved Hesta? Will you let me hang up my stirrups, place my sword over a fireplace and enjoy as much brandy as my joints require to forget their aches and pains? Will you allow me to rest finally?'

Vallus swallowed and quickly looked down at the table. He scratched at something invisible with a cracked fingernail for a second. Then he sighed and looked up at Lord Ristus. 'If we all live through this, then milord Ristus will have proven himself several times over, I am sure. I will support whatever decision my General makes.'

Cheers suddenly went up around the hall. Word spread outside and there was more cheering and happy shouting.

Constantus put a grateful hand on Vallus's shoulder. 'Thank you.' The General then stood and shook hands with Lord Ristus. They clinked their glasses together and drank.

Everyone began to drift outside to share the news, when an urgent shout of 'A horse comes! A horse comes!' rose up.

They hurried outside and watched a distant rider galloping away from the four hundred men camped below the hall and making for the slope.

'It is one of the mounted men sent to trail along behind us, to watch for trouble,' Colonel Vallus informed the General and the lord. 'One of the few horses we managed to bring from Accros with us.'

The horse rushed up the slope and was pulled up just short of Constantus. The rider, a small, wiry soldier, jumped off and saluted. 'Sir! They are coming! They are largely on foot but are no more than a few hours behind us.'

His mouth dry, Constantus asked: 'How many?'

'Thousands and thousands, sir! Maybe tens of thousands.'

Constantus turned to the suddenly nervous-looking Lord Ristus. 'We cannot hold against so many. We have no choice but to retreat towards the Needle Mountains. Tell your people we are leaving.'

Lord Ristus gulped. 'W-We have some horses.'

'Good. If you have any children or old people, they should probably be allowed the mounts, but make sure there are a dozen mounts left for my best cavalrymen. We leave in five minutes.'

'B-But there are family heirlooms that I simply cannot...'

'Ristus, if you hope to live long enough to rule this kingdom one day, then you'd better work out precisely what is more valuable – the lives of people, including your own skin, or some dusty, old keepsakes. Vallus, see to the horses and get these people moving!'

'Yes, sir!' Colonel Vallus saluted and hurried away.

'And Ristus?' Constantus said more gently.

'Y-Yes?'

'I am sorry but you will have to make a decision about Jessmine. You can either leave her here or she will be bound and gagged everyday she is with us from hereon in.'

Chapter Nine: And the laughter of misery

The Scourge's destrier wandered off the path and started to eat some of the late autumn shrubs that still covered the forest floor between the trees. The commander realised his attention had also wandered, and dragged his mount back onto the main route.

'Come on, another hour of daylight yet. I'll give you a nice brushing and some oats when we stop, how about that?'

The horse harrumphed and defecated.

'Well, I thought it was a good offer. Suit yourself then,' the Scourge shrugged and took a swig of devilberry liquor from his flask.

Since killing the demon, they'd travelled without direction for a number of days. The Scourge had been of half a mind to head back for Corinus, but had realised there wasn't really much for him there, so had decided to see where the path took him. It was only fair to see if his horse had a particular desire to go anywhere for once, given that it had faithfully carried him wherever he demanded for the last decade or so. Alternatively, Wim could decide their course as He saw fit.

'So, we're engaged in an act of faith, eh, boy? And it's right that we throw ourselves on Wim's mercy and show Him this respect, for we've just killed one of His most avid followers in the shape of Jack O'Nine Blades. So this is in some small way an act of repentance, eh? See, who says I never do my duty by the gods?'

The horse sighed in a long-suffering manner.

'Well, it made sense to me!' He raised the flask to his lips again and paused. 'Or as much sense as anything about the Holy Gambler makes.' Then his mood darkened. 'By the putrid infections of Malastra, I'm even beginning to sound like that stinking demon. Even dead he still plagues me! Gah! I bet he or some other has cursed me. If I find out that holy cow has anything to do with this, then I'll... I'll... hmmm.' He laughed bleakly. 'Well, I won't be that surprised, will I?'

The thing was, there probably wasn't much for him anywhere in this realm now that he'd finally laid the demon to rest. The knowledge that he'd implicitly promised Shakri he'd return to Her once he'd completed his task kept nagging in the back of his head, and couldn't be quietened, no matter how much devilberry liquor he drank. That didn't mean he wouldn't continue to try, however. Perhaps he hadn't tried the right kind of alcohol yet. Now, a good bottle of Stangeld brandy, or failing that some fermented Herbfruit from Marsby, might just do the trick. Besides, a promise wasn't the same as a vow... was it? Oh, yes, a promise to a goddess – and the Mother of All Creation at that – probably counted for more than a promise made to just any old person, but he hadn't sworn on anything, had he? So, She couldn't expect him to give up everything just like that, could She? The Scourge clenched his jaw in exasperation. Unfortunately, She was just plain unreasonable and wouldn't see it like that. He knew he'd have to come up with something much better, and soon, if he wasn't to end up as Her plaything for the rest of eternity. He shuddered and wondered if it wasn't too late to build some bridges with the Keeper of the Dead. Unfortunately, on the last two occasions they'd met, the Scourge had murdered Lacrimos in the most humiliating of fashions. In fact, Lacrimos probably despised the Scourge more than any other being in the entire cosmos. Still, the Scourge reflected, things could only get better from here, couldn't they?

The sound made by the horse's hooves suddenly changed as the ground became more compacted. They'd moved onto a better travelled route now.

'Eh? Where are we then? Are those mountains?'

The path they were on was wide and chalky. It followed the edge of a long, curving riverbank. Did he recognise this place? As he rounded a large stand of trees, he found a line of cottages along each bank and saw the familiar outline of the Needle Mountains in the distance.

'Well, I'll be. I didn't realise we'd come so far. We're in Swallowdale! We came through here on our way to the Brethren community five years ago, do you remember, boy? Oh dear, this is the place...' and his voice trailed off.

The Brethren magickers had visited this place and killed every single inhabitant. Many of the bodies had been piled up and burnt, but some had been left where they'd been killed in the middle of some harmless, small-town activity. The scene of slaughter here had shocked the Scourge in a way none of the countless battles he'd witnessed in his lifetime had. During a war, people largely chose to pick up weapons and risk their lives, but in Swallowdale innocent people, including children, had been murdered for no good reason. One moment they'd been fishing, shading their eyes from the sun, chatting happily to neighbours or exchanging words of affection with their loved ones, and the next they'd had their throats cut and life-blood spilt across the ground. He became irrationally afraid of entering the town now. What horror awaited him this time? Ghosts of the restless dead?'

He had no idea if the town had been left abandoned for the last five years, whether because it was seen as cursed or because it was considered a graveyard or memorial of sorts. The town was in too important a location to be simply left to rot, wasn't it? Then he saw smoke. His heart began to pound. A pyre of the dead?

The sound of young laughter drifted to him. He managed to calm himself and realised the smoke had been coming from the chimney of one of the cottages. He forced his mind to adjust, and finally understood he was seeing something more idyllic, more peaceful.

'You're so used to seeing horror and suffering that you don't recognise anything else anymore, you relic. Maybe your time in this realm has passed after all. Life certainly seems to be passing you by.'

The horse snorted and stamped impatiently.

'Alright, alright. You can smell the clean straw and dried oats of the local inn's stable, yes? Come on then.'

He pushed his horse forward and moved into Swallowdale. The place was relatively quiet given that the sun still hadn't fully set, but there were signs of life. A woman picked up her young boy from where he played on the doorstep and gave the Scourge a small smile. A grandfather sat on a tree stump, where he smoked his pipe and nodded. A dog sniffed the air and watched with its tongue lolling out.

The Scourge came to a building larger than most, which appeared to have a stable. Room for both traveller and horse to sleep. The door was wide open in welcome.

'Hello, the inn!'

A fat man in an apron came bustling out and looked the Scourge up and down. The innkeeper took in the quality of the stranger's horse and weapons and then put on his best smile. The Scourge returned the scrutiny and noted the fellow's bare and muscled forearms. Not shy of heavy work, so probably honest, or as honest as innkeepers ever were.

'Good day, sir traveller. We can tend to your horse if you care to stable him. Four coppers the night, but that includes good feed, currying, any shoeing you need and fixing of your tack.'

The Scourge nodded. 'And how much to stable me, good innkeep? You will recognise me as a Guardian by the sigils on the handles of my blades and my saddle.'

'A Guardian!' the innkeeper said with what seemed relief. 'No charge, no charge. Boy, where are you, you lazy tyke! Come see to this good man's horse. Come in, sir, come in! Please, make yourself comfortable.'

Slightly bemused by the innkeeper's effusive manner, the Scourge entered the inn's large and currently empty main room. The place was light and airy and the rushes on the floor were relatively fresh. There were three tables with benches and chairs near the well-built, central fireplace. The Scourge was a bit surprised that there was no fire lit, for it appeared from the hooks and spits in evidence that the hearth was usually used for cooking. Surely this inn, which was on one of the major routes into the mountains, saw enough passing trade to have a pot of something always bubbling away.

'Sit, sit! You look weary. You travel the length and breadth or the kingdom searching for perpetrators of unholy magicks, yes?'

'Before we get into that,' the Scourge said a little gruffly, 'what do you have to drink?'

The innkeeper's face fell. 'Ah! Err... well, the brandy's still good.'

The Scourge brightened at that. 'That's good. Any local ale?'

Now the man looked desperate. 'Good sir, we usually produce the best ale this side of the mountains, but now... now, it's all gone rancid. There doesn't seem to be anything we can do to keep it fresh. We even got some barrels of Accritanian Black in, but that went off within a day of opening. We are cursed!'

The Scourge had heard such excuses before. The innkeeper probably didn't look after his vats properly. Mice were no doubt getting into his vats and barrels and drowning in the ale. He would then accuse some local competitor or neighbour he'd fallen out with of cursing his establishment and expect the Guardian to go and rough them up or imprison them.

'Well, we'll start with something to eat then. Don't want to have too much brandy on an empty stomach.'

'Sir!' the innkeeper all but pleaded. 'We cannot even get a fire lit. When we try, sudden gusts of wind come down the chimney to blow out the flames or fan them so wide that they threaten to burn us down. Or the chimney will become mysteriously blocked and fill the place with smoke, but when we search the stack later there is nothing to be found. And then it will rain down the chimney even when there is sunshine outside. Sir, I am a god-fearing man who...'

... who has been at the brandy too much, the Scourge thought to himself. 'Very well, bring me some bread and strong cheese instead.'

The innkeeper looked close to tears. 'The milk in the town is mostly sour now. We have not been able to make cheese in months. And the bread starts to moulder before it has barely cooled from the oven. People in the town are close to starving. Shakri save us, but we are truly cursed!'

'Well, you don't look like you go without...' the Scourge started to observe when the hairs on the back of his neck prickled and he felt another pair of eyes on him.

He turned quickly in his seat to find a large, black cat watching him with interest from where it sat a dozen paces away.

'What creature is that?'

'Why, that is just Black. He belongs to the inn, good Guardian. An excellent mouser. You will find all our rooms vermin free.'

'Why does it stare at me so? It has green eyes!' the Scourge growled.

'Err... that is what cats do. Black is the curious sort. He's very friendly. No harm.'

'Male, is it? Well, I don't like cats. I don't trust them at all. Just move him along, innkeeper.'

The innkeeper frowned at the same time as trying to smile, which made him look very strange indeed. 'Of course. Will you not help us, though, Guardian? Is that not why we pay our taxes?'

The Scourge really didn't like the man's tone. Worse than that, the man probably had a point. It made the Scourge angry at not just the cat and the innkeeper, but also himself. And that depressed him, which in turn made him thirsty.

'Look,' he said in a flat tone, 'bring me your mouldy bread, rancid ale and bottle of brandy and I'll think about it. How about that?'

The innkeeper stared at him, clearly deliberating how far he wanted to take this argument with his only customer, a customer who was armed and no doubt dangerous. With a huff, the innkeeper finally turned on his heel and stomped away.

'And get rid of that cat!'

The Scourge released a long, tired sigh and tried to settle comfortably into his wide, squat chair. He wondered what direction he should head in next. He realised he needed some sort of purpose to help him decide that. Maybe he should head back to Corinus after all, to see if Saltar, Kate or Mordius needed him for something. The innkeeper had been right when he mentioned that it was the taxes paid to the palace that indirectly financed the Guardians. It was for the palace, therefore, to direct him. Then again, he already knew the palace's expectation of the Guardians and their commander:

to travel the kingdom looking for trouble, usually an ungodly sort, in order to put a stop to that trouble.

He realised that if he couldn't find trouble, he didn't really have much purpose. And he really wasn't very good at dealing with peace and harmony, precisely because it meant he was without purpose. Therefore, he was usually morose and unhappy precisely when others were content and fulfilled. What sort of messed up and backward existence was that? It was perverse. He was cursed in a sense. And those responsible were the bloody gods who had fashioned such an existence for him. He was right to despise them.

The Scourge knew he only ever had a meaningful role, his life and principles only had value and expression, when the world was going to rack and ruin and he was in the thick of the action. It was bizarre really, because it was almost in his own selfish interests to see the world taken to the brink of destruction, so that he could then show his value in trying to save it. It was a dangerous game to play. A single misjudgement and it could all be over for everyone. And he ran this risk with the entire realm just so that one man's ego and need for meaning could be satisfied? He was as bad as Voltar!

As bad as Voltar. In that case, the realm would be better off and far safer without him, he brooded. His mind turned to Lacrimos and the realm of the dead once more. Was the nether realm really so bad a place? There were many who worshipped the Keeper of the Dead and looked forward to joining Him. Many called it a release or final freedom from their mortal woes, worries and weariness. Would Shakri give him leave to go? If She loved him, She would; and She was the goddess of love, after all.

The innkeeper thumped a greenish heal of bread, a tankard of anaemic-looking ale and a bottle of brandy down on the table. Without a word, he then left.

The Scourge eyed the bread. He tried some and shrugged. He'd eaten worse. Then he sniffed and sipped the ale. His stomach turned over and he almost lost the morsel he'd just consumed.

'By the poisonous piss of Lacrimos, that's bad! Not even holy Aa would attempt that a second time! Ye gods, who'd have imagined mortalkind could even create such?'

The Scourge felt a change in the movement of the air through the room and looked up to see a tall man in a brown, hooded cloak stoop and enter. He wore his hood up, so the Guardian couldn't see his features clearly at first. But the Scourge was on guard, for the visitor moved noiselessly. There was no telltale bulk or stiff line about the cloak that suggested any weapon of length. A master thief or assassin then? Yet there was something uncanny, almost unnatural, about how quietly he moved. The Scourge's suspicions were confirmed when the newcomer slid into a seat opposite the Guardian and allowed himself to be seen properly. Vainly violet and impossibly knowing eyes gazed at the Scourge.

'What the hell do you want?' the Scourge spat.

'I haven't come here to fight,' the visitor rumbled placatingly.

'Whether it be verbal or physical, you only seek to manipulate the living. It defines you.'

'Yes... and no. Our definition has changed, perhaps lessened, in recent years. Besides, it was the direction of your thoughts that allowed me to come here. You tire of this realm, Scourge. I have come to tell you that there is a place of honour for you in mine.'

'My thoughts allowed you to come here? Since when have mere thoughts been enough to allow a member of the pantheon to become manifest in this realm? There are usually spoken words and the mumbo-jumbo of your priests required. And what of the balance? It is damaged by your coming here. It gives Shakri an advantage over you, does it not?'

Lacrimos, the Divine Assassin, sighed. 'Again, yes... and no. Do you have a flask of water blessed by a priest of Shakri with you?'

The Scourge's eyes narrowed. 'Ye-e-s. Why?'

'Put a drop into that ale and try it.'

The Guardian fumbled briefly with his tunic and did as he was bid. The ale tasted wonderful. He downed half of it without thinking. Then he offered the god some, but Lacrimos shook His head.

The Scourge frowned. 'If Shakri's blessing has cleansed the ale, then there is indeed dark magic at work in this town. It is the work of imps and demons, yes?'

Lacrimos nodded.

'But where are they all coming from all of a sudden? Is there some warlock or sorcerer at work?'

'Although they are but lesser demons, there are now so many of them that no mortal conjurors would have sufficient power to be responsible. It seems they are leaking through from the demon realm because the divide between the two realms has become so thin or been compromised somehow. Some agency from the demon realm must have effected it in some way.'

The Scourge looked worried. 'Jack O'Nine Blades? I have at last laid that troublesome sprite to rest. Did I take too long?'

Lacrimos chewed on the issue for a moment or two, and then decided He did fancy some ale after all. 'Ah! That's good. Jack will no doubt have been partially responsible, but there must be more to it. There must be other powerful beings at work against us. Guardian, hear me. Certain members of the pantheon have recently disappeared and cannot be located.'

'What?!' the Scourge replied slightly too loudly.

The innkeeper looked up from where he was wiping down his tankards and frowned. He hadn't noticed the person sitting opposite the Guardian arrive. He shook his head and muttered, deciding he didn't want to know what was afoot between the two warriors.

Lacrimos nodded heavily. 'Morphia, Istrakon, Aa, Tebula, and then some you will not have heard of though the damage done by their loss is no less significant. The realm is already showing signs that it is fragmenting, becoming thinner, whatever metaphor you prefer. The dynamic of the balance is becoming weaker, and that is why I am able to come to you so directly now. The realm is struggling to sustain itself. If the strength of my magic is failing, then so must my sister's. The spell that created our realms is unravelling.'

'B-But can't you do something?'

Lacrimos rolled His eyes. 'You mortals can be so dense sometimes. What do you think I'm doing here talking to you? The gods can't just do everything for you, you know, for we are caught up and sustained by the same magic as that which anchors this realm. If the rise of the demon realm is harming gods and mortals alike, then mortals will have a vital role in throwing them back, will they not?'

'So you want me to... to do what precisely?' the Scourge asked, still not entirely inclined to trust the god who was sometimes described as the Divine Deceiver.

Lacrimos looked exasperated. 'That's part of the problem, you see. I'm not sure. Cognis and I have never... well, we don't quite see... look, we just don't talk to each other, alright? I can't have every mortal knowing the mysteries of death, now can I?'

The Scourge shook his head in disbelief. 'You're telling me you don't get on? And you want me to talk to Him for you? Is there anyone you do get on with, Lacrimos?'

'Don't push your luck, Scourge! I am prepared to offer you a place of honour in my realm one day in return for your help now, but I can always find another if need be.'

The Scourge wasn't fooled. 'I doubt that. Given how much bad blood there is between us, most of it yours, it must really grate to have to ask me for help. That's a lot of pride you're swallowing there: I'm surprised it doesn't stick in your throat. There has to be some hell of a reason for it. What is it?'

The god of death glowered at the Scourge. 'I will not answer to a mere mortal. Will you accept my offer or not?'

The Scourge was tempted to tell the arrogant god to stick his offer up his holy arse, but instead he said, 'It was very careless of the pantheon to mislay some of its gods. And it seems those who remain just can't seem to get along. Look at the mess you've made. Maybe we mortals would be better off without you. Maybe you gods have had your day.'

'I will not tolerate such blasphemy from the lips of…'

'Yes, yes, *a mere mortal*, I know. I may be dense, but you are dull and predictable, you know that? And it is because you are so predictable that I know there will be some catch to the deal you offer. There will be no deal between us, Lacrimos, but I *will* visit the temple of Cognis near here and see what His priestess can tell me. I will not do it for you, but for the mortals of this realm, who have suffered so long and so much for its gods. Now, it was time you were leaving, for I intend to have a decent drink and don't want you making it an unpleasant experience.'

Lacrimos leaned forwards. 'Time is short, mortal.'

'When isn't it? Good day, holy one!'

The god pushed His chair back with a sneer of contempt on His face. His eyes locked with the Scourge's as He said with soft menace: 'You will be a long time dead, mortal, but I suspect it will seem a lot longer for you than any of my other subjects. I have a special place waiting for you.'

'I think you'd better pray I never make it to your realm, you whining boy-actor, since I will spend the rest of eternity punishing you there as I have punished you in this realm. Be gone!'

Lacrimos spat at the Scourge's feet and then stalked from the inn without a look back.

The Scourge harrumphed, 'Hardly behaviour becoming of a god,' and reached for the brandy. He took a mouthful and allowed himself a moment. 'I suspect things are going to get pretty ugly from hereon in. A man needs to make the most of good brandy when he can, particularly when time is short. I should have been more careful what I wished for, I suppose.'

Sighing deeply, he got to his feet and dropped a gold coin on the table. The innkeeper's trained ears heard it ring from the other side of the inn and came hurrying over.

'That'll more than cover it, I'm sure. I'll take the rest of the bottle with me. Please have your boy ready my horse, good innkeeper. I'll be leaving right away.'

The innkeeper's jaw dropped.

'And if I were you, I'd see about getting a priest of Shakri from the nearest temple to come visit Swallowdale, for you are plagued by imps and so forth. Tell the priest that the Divine Consort of Shakri demands they become more active in sanctifying the homes and people of this realm. Well, don't just stand there, man! Don't you know the whole realm's going to rack and ruin? And keep that cat out of my way or I won't be answerable for what happens to it.'

⚕ ⚕

The trio of adventurers had been all boisterous enthusiasm for their first few days travelling through the Memnosian countryside. They often played a game whereby Aa would disappear from the path ahead of Orastes and rat-boy – when the boys were daydreaming, talking to each other or the god was first around a blind bend – and then leap out from the trees to attack them. Rat-boy tended to have an instinct for when Aa was about to launch Himself at them, but Orastes was caught out almost every time. Other times, Orastes and rat-boy would seek to outflank and ambush Aa with sticks for swords, but the god seemed to have eyes in the back of His head and the ability to be in two places at once. They'd been unable to lay a stick on Him, except for one time when Orastes had got in a lucky jab, which had caused the god great consternation and the boys' great hilarity. And then other times they'd stepped along singing marching songs or listening to one of Aa's new and funny rhymes.

Yet as they got further and further from the environs of Corinus, the going became much tougher and none of them had the spare energy or breath for more than pushing aside tree branches and warning each other about treacherous footing. They'd left all sign of managed fields and estates far behind them now and in some places the path disappeared altogether amongst the undergrowth of the briar woods through which they fought.

Not for the first time that day, Orastes begged for a halt so that he could put down the weight of his leather armour and rest. He asked their leader, Aa, if He had anything they could eat other than apples. The god threw a stone and a wood pigeon dropped out of the sky, He thrust His hand into a stream and pulled out a fat trout, and then He twisted a wire for an obliging rabbit to jump into without delay.

'There you are!' the god said a little testily. 'That should help you keep your strength up and stop your nagging. Make a fire, someone.'

Rat-boy devoured his piece of fish hungrily and then carefully licked each of his fingers. He watched the others to judge if either of them were unlikely to be able to finish their own portions. To rat-boy's disappointment, Aa had finished His already and was now plucking the bird. Orastes was clearly weary, but had a determined look on his face as he chewed and swallowed.

'Orastes, why don't you just leave the armour here?' rat-boy asked. 'It isn't really much good for anything except the thick of battle, when everything's so crowded that you're sure to be hit by a weapon or two. Out in the open, it's just a hindrance. If you're worried about it being valuable, you parents are rich and can always get you some more, can't they?'

Orastes frowned at this information. 'Mother and Sister Spike said I should always wear armour when I'm using my weapon. What does *a hindrance* mean?'

'It means you don't need it. It gets in the way. I suppose when you're training, it's a good idea to wear armour, but it would just slow me down, I think.'

Orastes looked to Aa. 'Is that true?'

Aa shrugged. 'I haven't given it much thought really. I don't wear it myself, as it lacks a certain elegance. As to the practical considerations, I never get hit, do I, so it's not an issue for me?'

'But I got you with a stick earlier.'

The god looked put out. 'Yes, that really shouldn't have been possible. It must be something to do with what you say about magic not working very well around you. An aberration, nothing more! I tell you what, I think the best way to test things is for the two of you to have a fight of sorts, to see who wins. You can both use sticks, of course, but Orastes you should use your armour too.'

The boys thought it was a splendid idea and soon squared off against each other, Orastes with a medium-length, heavy branch and rat-boy with two short sticks.

'Take no prisoners! To the death!' Aa shouted.

'You smell like a dog!' Orastes taunted.

'What?' rat-boy demanded.

'You Outdwellers never wash!' the younger boy laughed.

'You take that back!'

'Make me, stinkweed!'

Shouting with rage, rat-boy threw himself recklessly at Orastes.

Aa cocked an ear towards the woods. 'Wait! What was that?'

Rat-boy slashed high with one stick and jabbed low with the other. Orastes blocked the top stick with his branch and slid his wood towards rat-boy's knuckles; at the same time the youngster twisted his middle so the lower stick slid off his armour. Rat-boy jumped back in a blink and Orastes tried to move after him, although his armour made him too slow to close the gap.

As if cutting in for a dance, the libertine god stepped in between the two combatants just as Orastes began an extravagant swing of his branch.

'Owwwww!' screamed the Divine Adventurer.

'Oops! Sorry, Aa! I didn't see you there.'

Rat-boy giggled. 'That's twice he's hit you now.'

'Yes, and he shouldn't be able to, so just stop it, will you!' the god said heatedly, rubbing His side.

'I didn't mean to. It was an accident!'

'You should be more careful when two people are fighting, you know, Aa,' rat-boy said helpfully.

'But...! What you don't understand is... Oh, what's the use! You're too young and *too mortal* to understand!' the god said, tossing His sacred head of oiled ringlets and stroking out both sides of His holy moustache.

His two followers smiled at each other.

'Now, if you two young ruffians would pay attention to the world going on around you for a second, you'd realise there are screams for help coming from yonder grove. No doubt it is some damsel in distress who needs rescuing from marauding monsters and terrible fiends. Do either of you know of any brave and noble heroes round here who might rescue her virtue?'

'Come on, let's go!' Orastes shouted excitedly, picking up his sword Monster-cutter and brandishing it.

'Last one there finishes plucking the pigeon!' Aa shouted and bounded off through the trees, rat-boy hot on his heels.

'Wait for me!' Orastes called.

'Hurry up!' rat-boy teased. 'Or there'll be none left by the time you get there.'

'Save one of the monsters for me!'

The three companions burst into the glade to find a tall man in a white robe being defended by a youth in grey vestments against dozens of slavering forest wights, fire imps and goblin-like creatures.

'Shakri help your faithful servant!' the tall man screamed as he hugged the trunk of the tree atop the small rise where he and his retainer made their stand. 'Boy, if you know your duty or bear any love for me, then you will help me up this tree!'

'Sorry, master!' the thickset youth grunted as he flailed his improvised club at their nearest aggressor. 'I will attend you as soon as I may. At you, you creatures of corruption!'

The besetting mob hooted gleefully and taunted the tall man and youth with mimicry. A goblin darted forward, made a grab for the youth's arm and was rewarded with a hefty thwack to the head. The goblin yelled in pain, much to the amusement of the rest of its kind.

'At them, lads!' Aa shouted and leapt forward with his poniard extended. He skewered a large goblin through the back of the neck, kicked two others and then jumped up high so that He stood on the broad shoulders of a surprised forest wight. As the wight began to collapse, the god jumped to another, and then another, until He was running over and upon the heads of the host, stabbing and kicking as he went. All the while, He sang in praise of His own prowess. 'He is a wonder to behold, that god so brave, so glad and bold! So bow your heads, you simple crowd, for Aa is here to make us proud!'

Orastes and rat-boy stood agog at the divine display, until they realised the horde was now turning back towards them.

'Come on!' rat-boy urged his new friend. 'Bet I can kill more than you!'

'Death to the monsters!' Orastes shouted by way of a battle cry and hurried forward to start the slaughter. He chopped and hacked with the sort of close-quarter efficiency of which Sister Spike would have been proud. Then he changed his strokes to slashes and stabs so that none would think to predict his rhythm in order to find an opening. Monster-cutter was soon covered in bright green ichor.

'Death to the monsters!' rat-boy echoed, and nipped forward and back to cut sinews, pierce lungs and cut throats with his two short knives. He was so quick that none could lay a hand on him, and the longer he fought the quicker he seemed to get. He even became quicker than Aa, his movements starting to blur and his eyes beginning to shine with a magical light.

Dismayed by the surprise attack from behind, the demons formed two big groups and attacked en masse those they considered the weaker of their foes: Orastes and the grey-robed youth.

'Incarnus, I pray!' Orastes bellowed as per Sister Spike's instruction for times of difficulty. He felt his arm become stronger and he decapitated two wights with a single mighty blow. 'I am the divine engine of destruction!' came a deep voice from the boy's lips, although he had not knowingly spoken. He swatted a fire imp so hard that its being was extinguished in the instant.

'Brother!' Aa sang. 'It is good that you join us, but the glory is mine this day!'

'Glory is of no interest to me!' Orastes rumbled. 'Only vengeance on those who would challenge the pantheon of this realm. I will smite them all!'

'Shakri be praised!' the tall man wept.

'Ungrateful mortal!' Aa shouted. 'It is the god Aa who is your salvation.'

'You are but Her instrument! As Her priest, I know this!' Then the tall man yelped in fear as his young acolyte was caught up in some invisible spell and thrown roughly to the ground. 'Holy Aa, save me, I beg you!'

More unseen magic swept up the rise and pole-axed the priest. Aa whipped His head round, a sudden look of concern on His face. 'A demon magic-user! Rat-boy, it's the tall, pasty one! You must kill it. Throw one of your knives if necessary. Quickly, before –'

Rat-boy didn't hesitate and threw with his right hand. His aim was true, but the demons had read the threat and bunched up at a bark from their spell-weaver, meaning a drooling wight took the blade in the throat instead of its leader. A whirlwind of magic then spun out from the pasty demon, froze rat-boy where he stood and then swirled around the adventurer god until His movement slowed to almost nothing.

'Cannot be!' Aa managed before His jaw locked.

Only Orastes remained fully animated. He continued hacking at any demon within reach, but there were now dozens mocking him with cat-calls and whistles. The spell-weaver gurgled in amusement and then directed the eddies of its spell at the lone boy.

Orastes soldiered on, the spirit within him undaunted. Long arms reached for him and he lopped them short, leaving the owner bemused and then to howl in pain. The magic buffeted Orastes and he lowered his head into it. It suddenly dissipated and the spell-weaver was thrown from its feet by a backlash.

All the demons suddenly stopped their cackling and turned their heads to regard their fallen leader. It twitched a few times and then its body structure completely collapsed. In less than a few seconds, there was nothing but a white, powdery residue left on the forest floor and a lingering, unpleasant smell that could not quite be placed, although it conjured images of bodily effluence, decaying fruit and rotten eggs.

Rat-boy and Aa were suddenly released from their immobility, as were the priest and his acolyte. The god immediately looked to thrust with His blade, but was stupefied to discover that the twenty or so demons had thrown themselves to the ground in attitudes of worship and submission to the young son of Saltar and Kate.

'This is a blasphemy!' He fumed. 'Have you forgotten who the god is round here?'

'S-Sorry, Aa, I didn't ask them to bow like this, honest! And I wouldn't dream of demanding anyone bow down either, Aa. It's only gods who do that.'

Rat-boy sniggered and Aa glared daggers at him.

The priest sat up with a scream. 'Kill them, holy lord, I beseech you, before they turn on us! Such devils cannot be trusted. They befoul Shakri's realm with their presence. Boy! Help me up! Boy, you hear me? Worthless layabout! Up, I say!'

Orastes stared at the strange, white-robed priest. He had little hair to speak of, wet-looking skin, a pronounced Adam's apple and strangely plump limps for such a thin face. *Like a fish*, he thought to himself and had to work hard not to giggle. *His eyes bulge like a fish's too!*

Aa waved His hand in a bored fashion. 'The priest is probably right, Orastes. If we come across a demon as powerful as the one that so carelessly destroyed itself, then this lot will defect in the blink of an eye. Have done with them!'

Orastes exchanged an uncomfortable glance with rat-boy. Although the creatures before them were monsters, they weren't behaving like monsters anymore. It therefore didn't feel quite right to kill them anymore either.

A small fire imp looked up at Orastes timorously and crawled forwards with an imploring look on its jagged face. 'Pleaggge! We want live, mahgter! We not betray mahgter!' it managed. 'We want live!'

'Err… maybe they could be of some use to us,' Orastes tentatively suggested.

The thickset acolyte, who was about the same age as rat-boy, had finally managed to get beneath his sprawling master in order to lever him up. As he pushed, he panted: 'Yes, please consider it, good masters, for we were passed by a terrible number of these creatures heading for one of the villages my master and I tend. I fear for the innocent souls there, for they have naught but a crude palisade around their homes and I saw a devil as big as a tree.'

'You speak out of turn, boy!' the priest snapped. 'What are you thinking to speak on behalf of these devils? Have they corrupted your mind, simple as it is, or tempted the sin that already exists within you?'

But the promise of further adventure had already made Aa impatient. 'There is no time to kill them, lads! Let's be away, for there are innocents to be saved, battles to be fought and fame to be won. Onwards, brave sons!'

'You!' Orastes said to the fire imp. 'Do you promise not to betray us? Will you fight with us against your own kind?'

The imp hesitated and then said with evident reluctance: 'Yeg, mahgter. We bound by thege wordgg.'

'What is your name?'

The imp tilted its head in confusion. 'No name, mahgter.'

'Hmm. I have to call you something. How about Pug or something? I always wanted a dog to call it Pug, but mother wouldn't let me have one... although she said it would be fine if I could find an invisible one. So, I will call you Pug.'

The demon moved its head back and forth as it tried to follow the strange mortal's words. When it grasped it had been named, it crackled with joy. 'Thank you, mahgter. Pug! It a name of power! Me Pug!'

Orastes wasn't sure if it was his eyes deceiving him, but the imp seemed to grow by at least a hand of inches as it spoke its gratitude. 'Well then, Pug, bring the others and we will go fighting monsters. Aa, rat-boy, wait for us!'

'Wait! Doesn't anyone wish to know my name?' the priest of Shakri shouted. 'What of good manners and formal introductions? Surely such civilized behaviour is more important now than ever before, with the world being dragged down by devils, sinners, bestial fornicators and the like. I am Ninevus, a good priest of Shakri. Boy, where are you going? Return, I say! You cannot leave me alone here, with all manner of evil abroad. I must be protected, for I am the instrument of Shakri's will in this world. Do not leave me! Attend, I am coming now I have recovered from my recent trials. Good masters, slow down for a moment so that I might join you!'

❦ ❧

'What's your name?' Orastes asked the dark-haired acolyte as they hurried through the woods in Aa's divine wake. The twenty or so demons that Orastes now seemed to command had gone out wide on their flanks and become invisible amongst the trees.

'Distrus,' the youth panted. 'I have served Master Ninevus for nearly a year now. It is hard work but he is not unkind.'

'But you didn't say he was kind either,' rat-boy observed.

Distrus scowled at rat-boy but did not say anything immediately. Instead, he turned his head away and addressed Orastes only. 'Your armour looks awkward. Would you like me to carry your sword for you?'

Surprised – for none of the others had ever made such an offer – Orastes gratefully passed over his sheathed blade and its strap.

'Wouldn't catch me handing over my weapons to a complete stranger,' rat-boy muttered.

'Boy! There you are! What do you mean by abandoning your master in such a fashion? I am sure Shakri would take a very dim view of such behaviour. Have you learnt nothing under my tutelage? Are you still so easily led astray?'

'Sorry, master!' Distrus mumbled, although Ninevus was already talking again and not interested in hearing his apprentice's contrition.

'Perhaps I erred in allowing you to come on this trip. And because of your clumsiness, we have lost our mule and supplies. It's only by the grace of Shakri that we still have our lives. We are fortunate not to have ended up in the cook-pot of the forest wights. Well, what do you have to say, eh, and speak up so that Shakri can hear of your failure!'

'I-I'm sorry, master,' Distrus said in red-faced distress. 'But the demons scared me and I had to defend –'

'Neither Shakri nor I are interested in your excuses! When will you start taking responsibility for your own actions, boy? When you seek to blame the world around you, you blame the holy goddess's creation, and that is the most wicked of blasphemies. Do not think I enjoy haranguing you like this either, for it is but my holy duty to care and worry for the sanctity of your soul. What's more –'

'Cease your carping, priest, or I will cut your vocal chords!' rat-boy suddenly snarled, brandishing his knives.

Ninevus's eyes went wide in outrage, his nostrils flared and he drew himself up to his full six and a half feet. 'How dare you, you young ruffian! I will not be silenced by the likes of you, you who openly consorts with demons. *Demon-friend* I name and condemn you! Boy, are you going to allow –'

'And you can leave him alone too!' rat-boy spat and placed himself between acolyte and master, bringing their progress through the forest to a halt. He took a threatening step towards Ninevus and the priest stumbled backwards.

'Stay here until the fighting is over,' rat-boy advised him, 'for we would not want to see you injured, now would we? Priest, it is my great belief that were you to say another word or take one more step after us until given leave, then you would suffer dreadfully. Distrus, Orastes, you will come with me. Let's go!'

The three boys turned their backs on the dumbstruck priest and began to move away. The first time Distrus looked back at his master, it was with helpless guilt on his face. The second was with a more mixed set of emotions. Then he caught up to his two companions and did not look back again. Perhaps his master would be safer here anyway.

Orastes was aghast at how rat-boy had dared talk to Ninevus, who was not only an adult but also a priest. Should Orastes be more scared of rat-boy then he was of the priest then? No, rat-boy was his brother – they'd cut their palms and sworn blood oaths together – so he should trust him rather than be scared of him. And Orastes should support his brother. Maybe rat-boy had been *right* to threaten the priest then. Orastes looked across at Distrus. The acolyte looked confused – so at least he wasn't distressed anymore. Yes, rat-boy had been right. And monsters were tricky. They came in all shapes and forms. For all Distrus knew, a shape-shifter had taken the place of his master when Distrus wasn't looking. Rat-boy was right! Orastes could not let himself be scared of anyone anymore, in case they were a monster. The seven-year-old smiled, feeling more powerful than he had before. It was like growing a hand of inches, just as Pug had.

He whooped in excitement as he heard the roar of battle from amongst the trees ahead. Aa's challenge rang out and the three boys shouted in answer as they ran forward.

'Death to the monsters!' Orastes screamed at the top of his lungs.

'Death to the monsters!' rat-boy and Distrus yelled.

᪽ ᪾

Orastes was completely engulfed by the shadow cast by the cyclops. How could he stand against such a giant? It raised a boulder bigger than Orastes above its head and prepared to bring it crashing down on top of the boy.

'Ahh! Help!' Orastes squeaked.

'Fear not!' Aa called, throwing His cape over the head of the demon He faced and ducking past it. He sprang forward and stuck the cyclops in the back of the thigh.

Rat-boy hurled one of his knives from fully twenty feet away and saw it thud home in the towering demon's side. Then Pug flared up and threw fire in the cyclops's face.

Roaring in pain and confusion, the cyclops tried to shield its face with its arms and ended up dropping the boulder on its own head. There was a sickening crack and it fell to its knees and then onto its back. Orastes leapt on top of it and plunged his blade deep into its heart. Black blood gouted up and covered him from head to foot.

The skirmishes amongst the demons and with the villagers gradually ceased. The entire demon host then prostrated themselves on the ground to Orastes.

'No, no, no! This is not right!' Aa insisted, jumping up and down in frustration.

Over a hundred demons raised their heads and glared at the god, who suddenly decided it might be more politic to save His opinions for another time.

'Pug, thank you very much,' Orastes whispered to the fire imp. 'You were as true as your word and helped me a great deal, almost as if we were friends.'

'Friendgg?' the imp puzzled and shrugged. 'But mahgter ig powerful,' it crooned. 'Will mahgter grant ug boon?'

'Err... of course. What boon?'

'Let ug eat enemiegg before they digappear.'

Slightly appalled, Orastes looked at the others. Most shrugged, while Aa chuckled to Himself.

'Well, Pug, I suppose you must all be hungry, yes? You mustn't ever eat a mortal, even if they are dead, you know that, yes? I suppose it's all right to eat these demons...'

Pug leapt on the cyclops and began tearing lumps of flesh free and hastily devouring them. The demon flesh was seared by the touch of the fire imp and a strangely foul but mouth-watering aroma drifted across the village. The other demons scrambled to feed upon the giant carcass and in less than a minute there was no sign that it had ever existed. Pug rubbed his swollen belly happily and grew another hand of inches. He was now close to Orastes in size and dwarfed most of the others of his kind.

With a nauseous look on his face, Distrus turned his head away and asked rat-boy if he could now be permitted to fetch Master Ninevus.

'If you must,' rat-boy sighed.

'And may we join your party, holy one?' Distrus asked Aa. 'As you have seen, the woods are dangerous and we are otherwise without protection, oh bravest of the gods. And we will seek to be of good service and value to you, oh wondrous adventurer!'

Aa could not help preening at the flattering words. He struck a suitably heroic pose and replied magnanimously: 'I don't see why not. You Shakrists are quite handy at gathering food, yes, and calling the animals to you? You see, I think my lads have had about as many of my apples as they can stomach, and we need someone who is good at plucking birds and skinning game. Handy cook, are you?'

'Oh, yes, most beneficent master. I will be more than happy to tend the cook-pot if there is one who is prepared to kill any animals Shakri sees fit to provide us.'

Rat-boy flourished his knives, one of which he'd just retrieved from where the cyclops had lain. 'Don't you worry about that. I'm more than happy to skin anything that tempts me too much.'

Distrus nodded his understanding and went to get his master. He prayed – for all their sakes – that Ninevus would accede to the bargain their situation had now forced on them. Otherwise, if Ninevus didn't end up in the demons' cook-pot then he would certainly end up in rat-boy's. How had Shakri's realm come to such a pass? How was it that mortalkind had fallen so far? Surely any state of grace would now be beyond them forever. *Shakri, where are you? Have you forsaken your children? Have we failed you? What has happened to your guardians and followers? I try my best, but it does not seem enough. I am scared, sweet Shakri! Who will help us, goddess? Where are your Consort, Builder and Witch? I pray for them, holy mother. I pray that you will protect them with your divine love.*

❧ ❧

The Chamberlain opened his eyes and looked up at the vault of a blue sky. A bird flapped lazily far above him. Other large, black birds began to fill his vision. A murder of crows. The scent of death assailed his keen nostrils.

He sprang up, alert for any predators in the vicinity. Nothing. Apart from Balthagar's body lying nearby, he was alone. They were near a road, which was lined with gibbets, large wooden crosses and spiked poles. They were decorated with a range of rotten and freshly immolated bodies. He'd never been troubled by the sight of mortal suffering, for the body was just a vessel. Death was a departure of the spirit that turned the body left behind into meaningless garbage. So why was he experiencing a feeling of… a feeling of *familiarity* now? It couldn't be that he felt any sort of maudlin identification with the detritus surrounding him, so what was it? Then he realised he knew this place.

He frowned and eyed the lines of the hills and trees around him. He suddenly felt sure that if he followed the road over the next rise then he would see Corinus! But how could that be? He hadn't seen bodies staked out like this since the time Voltar had been on the throne. Surely Kate wouldn't have done such a thing, even though Balthagar hadn't been around to keep her more homicidal impulses in check. No, some of the bodies looked to have been hung there mouldering for far too long – and the Chamberlain and Balthagar hadn't been away that long... had they?

'Curious, hmm?'

The Chamberlain scampered to the top of the rise and stared across a dark plane towards the capital city of Dur Memnos. The dead lined all the roads to the city and smoke smudged the sky. Small units of men patrolled the wide expanse, harassing refugees, Outdwellers and merchants here and there. The men in uniform seemed unnaturally large and smelt wrong.

His suspicions were finally confirmed when he spied four ogrish Wardens heading in his general direction. This *was* the Dur Memnos of Voltar's reign! The trapdoor from the Prison of All Eternity had brought them back to the most terrible age the realm had known! Things just went from bad to worse. Whichever god or other cosmic being was responsible, they must be laughing pretty hard right now.

There was a shout and one of the Wardens pointed towards the Chamberlain. The dull creatures had finally noticed him. They began to lumber towards him, their powerful legs carrying them over the ground with surprising speed.

Tall though the Chamberlain was, the creatures towered over him. Voltar had used his dark magicks to grow ordinary men to their full physical potential, thereby creating a force with which to cow his own population and prevent the Accritanians ever overthrowing him. The smallest of the Wardens – and therefore the one with the least swollen and damaged brain – began to pull up as it realised the Chamberlain was unconcerned by their approach and happy to stand his ground. The others followed the smaller one's lead.

The Warden wrinkled its snout and snuffed the air. 'You Chamberlain?'

The Chamberlain showed his fangs as he grinned. 'Yes. I've been waiting for you. It is mid-morning, hmm? I cannot tell, for my eyes are generally sensitive to light, yes?'

The Warden grunted in the affirmative. 'Milord!' it then remembered to add.

'Good, then we will have time. You! Pick up that body there. You will all accompany me south, hmm? We will be travelling as fast as we may, yes?'

The small Warden frowned. 'But Chief Warden Brax sent us to find him fresh food. If we not back soon, he will be angry, milord. Then he will eat us! Brax always angry when he hungry.'

All the Wardens nodded fearfully.

'I speak with King Voltar's voice, hmm? If you do not do as I tell you, then the King will be angry and *he* will eat all of us, including Brax, yes? But do not fear! We will be quick. If you do as I tell you, then the King will not let Brax eat you. And we will find food for Brax as we travel south, hmm? Now, you, pick up the body.'

At a nod from the small Warden, one of the others lifted Saltar's body and sniffed it. 'Dead. Good eat?' it asked hopefully.

'Its flesh is poisonous, hmm? It will kill you, yes, even a small bit? It sleeps, hmm? Do not try to eat it or you will wake it. Then its angry poison will be awake too and it will chase you and kill you.'

The Warden looked slightly panicked and made to drop the body.

'No! It wishes you to take it south, hmm? If you do not, you will make it angry and it will wake, yes? You will all take it in turns to carry it. Come, follow me!'

⚔ ⚔

The Chamberlain and the four Wardens pushed south along the moss-covered and creeper-strewn road. The further they went, the more boggy the ground to either side became, and the more unstable or rotten the trees became. Ancient oak giants stood petrified or toppled and broken. Giant woodlice and centipedes crept out and sensed the air as they passed. They dared not linger anywhere, even when short of breath. The air buzzed and clicked silently – the pitch of it above their hearing range – yet still impacting upon their membranes and causing them to itch, twitch and imagine movement all around. The phantoms of the Old Place haunted them and kept them constantly on edge. They all felt watched by a vast and malevolent intelligence, or expected to be tapped on the shoulder at any moment.

Bog turned to swamp and the air became foetid and stagnant. They sweated and rotted in the heat. As the sun passed its highest point in the sky, the Warden carrying Balthagar collapsed and lay shivering and shaking, his skin a grey pallor.

'You, you will now carry the body, hmm? We will allow this one to rest a while and recover, yes? Then, he may return to Corinus. We others will continue on without delay, however, hmm?'

The Wardens accepted the Chamberlain's logic and command without question. In fact, they moved somnambulantly, their eyes glazed. The insidious magic of the Old Place naturally worked more quickly on those who were weak of will. It didn't matter, for the Chamberlain could not afford to have any of the Wardens make it back to Corinus alive anyway, lest they alert Brax, Voltar or the Chamberlain's other self as to this expedition into the south. If the basilisk poison contaminating Balthagar's body didn't finish off each Warden tasked with carrying him, then the paralysing, leeching and carnivorous nature of this place most certainly would.

'Quick, quick!' the Chamberlain urged, driving the remaining three Wardens forward.

❈ ❈

By the time the Chamberlain reached the ruined cottage that marked the edge of Marsby, another two Wardens had fallen by the wayside. Only the small one remained, carrying Balthagar's body over one of its broad shoulders. There was a distant howl, which caused the Warden to growl deeply in its throat and scent the air.

The Chamberlain reassured him: 'Fear not. The Elders are night-stalkers and we have at least an hour of daylight yet, if I do not miss my mark, hmm? The town of Marsby is not far now. But let us lengthen our stride so as not to risk any confrontation with them, hmm?'

As they reached the edge of the woods, a large silhouette stepped onto the path and blocked their way. In one of his paws, the newcomer carried a longbow with an arrow nocked against the string. He was not as tall as the Warden, but if anything seemed broader. He was a bear of a man.

'Lebrus, that is who you are, yes?' the Chamberlain crooned.

'I do not recognise you, stranger. I do not care how you know my name either, for his kind are not welcome here,' Lebrus replied, gesturing with his bow towards the Warden.

The Chamberlain turned to his Warden. 'Put the body there.'

The ogre complied, and as it straightened back up the Chamberlain sank a pin into the back of its neck. The Warden frowned and then blinked its eyes heavily before keeling over, never to rise again.

'There, Keeper. My gift to the Elders, hmm? I have paid the blood-price, so may I now pass? I have come to see *her*.'

Lebrus reared back. 'How is it you know of such things? What manner of being are you? No mortal knows of the Covenant. Yet you cannot be a god of this realm, else you would not need my permission to pass. Speak! What are you and what do you want of *her*? No being, even one divine, would have a reason to seek her out that would be in the interests of this realm.'

Eerie howls came to them out of the woods, howls that sounded worryingly close.

The Chamberlain flashed the bear a quirky smile. 'I am indeed a selfish being, hmm, as every other being is, at their core, at the place of their definition. Lebrus, are you with Astraal because you love her or because your ego requires the reassurance and comfort of her love and companionship, hmm? No, do not think a response is required, for both things are true when combined, but neither is the absolute truth when taken in isolation, yes? Perhaps I wander, however. My thoughts too often spider through patterns, Keeper, so forgive me. So, to speak more plainly, then I tell you now that upon this occasion my selfish interests coincide with the wider interests of the realm. Those interests require me to save the Builder from basilisk venom, which I can only do with the swamp witch's help, yes? Without the Builder in attendance, I fear this realm will fail, hmm?'

Lebrus shifted slightly and a final, flaring beam of the dying sun lit his face. 'I have never heard of this Builder. What is significant about him that the realm should rest on his survival? And how can I trust a creature such as yourself?'

The Chamberlain shrugged delicately. 'Indeed, what is the significance of any being? Why is it that any mortal, demon or god is of any value, hmm? There have been times when the Builder has been a nexus in the Pattern, there have been times when he was all but absent from the Pattern. He has been just a man, a King's hero, an animee and then something altogether more irreducible, yes? What is the significance of just a man? Keeper, you may know more of that answer than I, as I may as well ask you what the significance of a Keeper is, hmm?

'Keeper, you ask how you can trust me. Yet I do not know if I can trust you, hmm? Most would not consider me trustworthy, however. I am a spider that spies from a dark corner and spins webs to trap and devour the largest prey I may. It is my nature and philosophy, hmm? So I tell you you cannot trust me. Yet can you trust what I have just said, hmm?

'Keeper, you are looking for me to give you an answer that will reassure and comfort you, like Astraal's love, hmm? You are waiting for me to say something that will convince you not to release your quarrel, are you not, else you would have already released it, hmm? Keeper, I will not seek to manipulate you. I do not have such answers.

'You must make a decision nonetheless, hmm, for I hear the Elders drawing close and time is short. Time has ever been short for this realm. The lives of the mortals within it are short, yes? Even the existence of the gods of this realm has been relatively short in the context of the cosmos, I suspect, hmm? And I tell you now that the future of this realm will also be short if you cannot see beyond the likes of me.

'The body of this Warden will delay the Elders but a few moments as they sate their initial blood lust, hmm? Now is the moment that your instincts must decide, Keeper, else we will be forced to confront the terrible ancestors of mortalkind, yes?'

'Curse you, spider!' growled the bear, swiftly raising his bow and firing.

Marr, Jack in Mordius's body and the child witch wound their way down into the flat-bottomed valley of the Brethren. At Jack's urging, they had made the trip from the witch's home in the woods to the Needle Mountains and not met a single soul. Jack and the girl had travelled on horseback, while the animee Marr had run untiringly beside them, no mount willing to take his unnatural corpse.

Jack had been extremely wary of speaking too much to this creature who wished to become the Demon-King's bride, for he did not wish to give much away about himself. If he displayed even a modicum of understanding of the things she said or any knowledge of Shakri's realm, then she would become suspicious that he might not have been summoned directly from the demon realm as she thought. Then she would suspect he was not bound by her will in the way she assumed and that he might not have had any authority whatsoever to make a bargain on behalf of the Demon-King. He had already taken a considerable risk persuading her that his knowledge of a black pyramid of power that could help them open a way to the demon realm had come from the memories of Mordius rather than from a previous visit he'd made to the pyramid himself. At the same time, he needed to find out more about her, and could only do that through sly conversation. Were her interests really aligned with demonkind or would she ultimately become a threat to them, just as she had to mortalkind and presumably to the gods of this realm too? How far could demonkind usefully use her, and how far did her knowledge and power really extend?

Jack had mixed feelings about what she had done to his erstwhile companions, Mordius and Marr. He could not condemn her actions entirely, for they had ultimately saved him from being irreversibly dissipated by the wind. Yet he also felt some disappointment that those who had once been his steadfast comrades had been forced to become mere vehicles of the will of others. He remembered with a certain fondness his time on the road with Marr standing shoulder-to-shoulder against Nylchros and the blood-mages who'd been responsible for devastating the travelling temple of Wim and its followers. They'd then worked together to bury the bodies of the unfortunate. It had been the first time in his existence Jack had shared a journey and cause with another being. It had felt strange, although not unpleasant. He felt its loss now, that was for sure. What the witch had done to Mordius and Marr created a sense of loss and absence in him, and that he did not like.

And it was passing strange to Jack that just when he'd most needed saving, he'd been drawn to two of his old comrades. It couldn't be coincidence, could it? Although Jack had once proclaimed himself a follower of Wim, delighting that luck and chance operated in the realm of mortalkind and apparently bestowed a freedom of sorts on all events and beings, demonkind did not actually recognise or believe in such randomness. The demon he'd once been therefore couldn't help speculating that it had not been coincidence that had brought him to Mordius and Marr. No, it was more likely a necessary nexus in the Pattern, or the results of the manipulations of a powerful being. And if the power of Wim were now in some sort of decline in this realm, then surely it could only mean and be because of the fact that the demon realm was at last rising. Yes, it was not coincidence that he had been brought to the prospective bride of the Demon-King and that he was now leading her to the black pyramid. Five times he'd made his annual trip to the black pyramid and opened the way to the demon realm, and five times he'd been disappointed (he wouldn't dare feel relief). This time, though, this time, there could be no doubt that the legions of demonkind would march through into Shakri's realm and claim it for themselves. It was as inevitable as a world without luck and chance.

Vague intimations from Mordius's mind also told Jack that the Pattern that had ultimately brought them here had been established long, long ago. Yes, Mordius had known the witch before. She'd been killed but Mordius had been forced to agree to her being reborn in return for vital knowledge about the nature and intent of Nylchros. And the witch had that knowledge from the ancient time when the realm had been formed! The gods had been forced to agree to the witch's living in return for... ah! but it was lost in the haze and confusion of the mortal's dull thoughts. The witch's return had been inevitable, just as perhaps Nylchros's had been, and just as it seemed the Demon-King's now was. There were so many echoes and similarities. He was close to the moment of an understanding of a far larger scheme of things than he had known before; something he would grasp if he could but extend himself a little further; a revelation that was perhaps the door to a higher plane of being and existence; the recognition of the Pattern Eternal! Just as there were gods, there was the Ungod, so perhaps just as there was a Demon-King...

'Stupid, demon!' the child spat violently, scaring Jack's horse and making it dance and saw sideways. 'Pay attention! You all but forced my mount over the edge!'

Jack blinked and fought his beast back under control. He smiled at the witch, to hide his newly formed fear of her. 'Your pardon, Your Majesty. I was distracted with thoughts of how best I should announce you to His Majesty. And then I was visited by visions of your resplendent wedding day. Forgive this poor creature for presuming so much!'

His words pleased her, for she blushed and nodded magnanimously. 'Very well, demon, for I know you are a simple creature incapable of any thought, word or deed against me. Tell me of your King. Is he fair of face, gently spoken and firm of hand?'

Jack knew a moment's panic. He knew nothing of this King, or did he? Time to test her. 'Your Majesty, I dare hope he will please you. His Majesty is familiar with the ways of this realm, you see. He was known as Vidius for many generations, they say, something called a King's hero. Did you hear tell of such a hero?'

The witch hesitated. 'Why, of course,' she replied lightly. 'Vidius's fame precedes him. How is it then he returned to the demon realm from here? Is he so powerful?'

'As to that, Your Majesty, I do not know how he returned. Perhaps the power of this strange, black pyramid we see ahead of us was responsible. I cannot say.'

The girl regarded Jack suspiciously. Surely she did not see through him! The cold sliminess of her look unnerved him far more than any number of horrors he'd witnessed in both the demon and mortal realms. 'Then let us hasten down to this place of power so that I may have my answer. I am eager to meet my bridegroom, demon, as he is no doubt eager to meet me.'

'Of course he is, Your Majesty. He has not slept since the bargain was struck. He hungers and lusts for you, Your Majesty, while being respectful of your person.'

'Need we be cautious of the denizens of these mountains, demon? What can you glean from the magician's mind?'

Jack went through the pretence of thinking deeply. 'These... Brethren... are a broken people. There is little now left to them. A mixture of illusion, bewitchment and compulsion should see us safely past such simple mortals. Should any display a magical resistance of any sort or be warded, then the animee will be able to take care of them.'

'Very well, then lead on, demon, and herald the coming of a new age for both the demon and mortal realms.'

They ghosted down into the valley. They began to pass stone cottages built onto equally stony ground. Life here looked to be hard and uncompromising. On a nearby hill line, a group of people placed the final stones on a burial cairn. A woman sobbed, keening for whoever was being laid to rest.

'Sweet spirits, they have taken another from us! We are cursed!' she wailed.

Cursed indeed, Jack thought to himself as he detected the telltale laughter of demons on the wind and sensed their energies scudding around the edges of the mortal community. The air was charged. Clearly, lesser demons had been leaking through into Shakri's realm for some time. Lightning flashed in the dark clouds swirling high above the pyramid. *The curse has only just begun. Soon, you will all wish you were buried in a cairn with the dead.* But perhaps not even the dead would be safe. These limited mortals couldn't begin to imagine what was about to befall them and their realm. And it wouldn't matter if they could. No forewarning would save them. There was nowhere they could run in this realm that could keep them safe or hidden from the all-powerful Demon-King. Even the child-like gods of this realm would not be able to last for more than an instant before the cosmic majesty he represented. All would fall before him, never to rise again. Here was the time of the Fall.

Jack was at one moment delirious with self-importance that he should be the one to open the way to His Majesty, and at another so appalled by it that it all but rendered him mindless. He knew that this would become his eternal experience of existence once the Demon-King ascended to the throne of this mortal plane. There would no longer be the apparent freedom of will that Wim maintained. There would no longer by the self-propagating circle of life and death as maintained by the magic of Shakri and Lacrimos. There would only be the defining will of the Demon-King.

Jack found he had begun to tremble, or was it the world around him that trembled? The pressure of the approaching moment, of the realms starting to converge, was already affecting the laws and concrete aspects of Shakri's realm. The Pattern moved towards a cataclysmic convergence. Even if Jack tried to step aside from it now, it was inevitable that the convergence would happen through some other means, probably the witch. At least if he led the way in these final moments, then there was some chance that the Demon-King would recognise his role and think to reward him rather than allow him to be swept away by the unstoppable tide of power released from the demon realm into this one.

'Hurry!' screamed the witch. 'I cannot wait to consummate my power with his a moment longer. Every fibre of my being yearns and burns with need and desire. Quickly, demon!'

They raced for the pyramid now. Electricity arced to the structure from sky and ground. Their hair stood on end. Their horses whinnied in fear. Jack began to chant in the demon tongue, preparing the spell that would open the way.

They jumped from their mounts and began to climb the stairs to the main portal. Guards in grey robes came forward to challenge them.

The witch cast a web of illusion. 'We are your oldest friends. You trust us more than any others. You will make way for us. Animee, kill them if they impede us, even if they but misstep.'

As they entered the main chamber of the pyramid, the air above the altar became sheer and tore. Wisps spilled into the chamber, followed by elementals. They scattered as something vast trod towards the breach. Giant, snarling muzzles pushed through into the chamber and then the heads and torso of a terrible cerberus. Riding upon its back was the horned and shining Demon-King. It hurt the eyes to look upon him, such was his power.

'Dread lord!' Jack moaned.

'He comes!' the witch gasped in ecstasy.

The Demon-King laughed, the sound becoming louder and louder as it travelled. It boomed until the world was shaken to its foundations. He was so inimical to this realm and the magic from which it was constructed, he was such an anathema to the gods, that he corrupted the original fabric of the time and space fashioned by the pantheon. A grey dragon-demon crawled out of the rent air and flew out over the Demon-King's head. Then came the terrifying archdemons of the six houses of demonkind.

'Now let the subjugation, suffering and slaughter begin!' commanded the Demon-King, and his voice and will were heard and known by every being in both realms. It caused the gods to cry out in agony and their priests to collapse unconscious or dead. As one, mortalkind wailed in fear and terror, knowing that it was the beginning of the end of days.

Chapter Ten: For mortals know no different

'We do not know the Jaffrans intend us any harm,' the old councillor who'd wanted the position of Harbour Master for his nephew decided. 'Jaris, had you strayed into their waters?'

Jaris, the young sailor Lystra had pulled from the sea looked uncomfortable. 'I can't be sure, sir. There are no markers of territory upon the sea, sir, you see. 'Tis possible they thought we were too close to Jaffra, but we was heading away from that cursed island, sir, may Maris becalm my boat forever more if I tell you the word of a lie.'

The old councillor exchanged meaningful glances with his five male colleagues – most of whom nodded their shared understanding – and sat back in his ornate chair with the sort of satisfied air that said he was sure he had got to the bottom of things.

'No!' Lystra responded instinctively, taking a pace towards the panel of elders. 'Twenty ships heading for King's Landing. We must clear the town before –'

'Harbour Mistress!' Councillor Brevis boomed. 'You will address this august council when invited to do so, and not before then! I know you are not familiar with the protocols of such occasions, but you should know when to take your lead from your betters. You go too far.'

Old Councillor Septis whispered something about women and emotion to his immediate neighbour and they shared a smile. Lystra bit her lip and couldn't stop her face from blushing, hard as she tried. 'My apologies, Councillor Brevis.'

The councillor nodded and looked at Jaris once more. 'Are you sure the Jaffrans were heading this way, man?'

Jaris shifted his weight from one foot to the other, wrung his cap in his hands and gave Lystra an unhappy and apologetic look before replying: 'I couldn't tell up from down, sir, what with it getting dark and our boat sinking beneath us. But if Mistress Lystra says –'

'Thank you, Jaris, that will be sufficient,' Brevis interrupted him, now turning to Lystra. 'Harbour Mistress?'

Lystra deliberately took a calming breath. How she hated dealing with people and their tangled-fishing-net ways. As pa had always said, there was nothing complicated about when the sun rose every morning and knowing when it was time to go fishing. Curse these men, for they would see them all dead at this rate! In a controlled voice, she said, 'Holy Maris led me to this man on a stormy sea at night so that I might save him and bring fair warning to the people of King's Landing. I speak as the Beloved of Maris now: an evil shadow has been cast upon these waters. All know that our daily catches barely sustain us anymore. Unholy creatures invade Maris's kingdom and are upsetting the natural balance. And whence comes that shadow? The evil approaches us even now. In a matter of hours, Jaffra will be here and we will all be doomed unless we leave immediately.'

There were long seconds of silence in the council chamber. Several councillors looked afraid, for the words and conviction of the Beloved of Maris were never easily dismissed. The spell of the moment was broken, however, by old Septis sitting forward once more. His small, pointed tongue darted in and out as if tasting the emotions in the room. The light from the room's fire shone brightly from his dark eyes.

'Come, come, Harbour Mistress, do you really expect these learned men to believe that an island on the other side of the sea is responsible for the size of our catch here in King's Landing? Do you have so little faith in Maris? Neither can that island be responsible for ships no longer choosing to put in here. Is it not more likely that the captains of those ships have come to realise what everyone in King's Landing has known for some time now but not quite had the courage to mention? Is it not more likely those captains see that Maris has turned His favour away from King's Landing?'

She couldn't quite breathe. 'What are you saying?'

'Is it not more likely they understand that in forsaking us Maris has cursed us? Perhaps they know King's Landing will never again see prosperity until it has got itself a new Harbour Master. Perhaps they now see that you are *not* beloved of Maris, and that it is your blasphemous claims to be so that caused Him to turn from us in the first place! There, it has been said.'

Lystra had no voice. What was this creature that faced her? She looked at each of the councillors in turn. One refused to meet her gaze, while the eyes of the others had become hard with confidence and condemnation as Septis had spoken. There was no appealing to or reasoning with such individuals. She had come looking for brave souls to lead them through the chaos that was descending on their heads even now, and all she had found were the children that had taunted her all her life. Without a word, she turned on her heel and walked from the chamber. She would keep going until she had left King's Landing and its people far behind. She would take her boat and nets and find a remote place along the coast or on a small, nearby island where she could live out her days alone communing with Maris and taking to pa.

Jaris caught her on the stairs. At first she thought he was laughing at her, but then realised he was stammering. 'Ha-Ha-Harbour Mistress! I am sorry! I did not have the courage to stand up to them. Forgive me! Please!'

She did not halt her descent of the stairs. 'Did you not hear? I am no longer Harbour Mistress, Jaris. Please address me as Lystra,' she said softly. 'You will excuse me but I will have to clear out the cottage, now that it no longer belongs to me.'

'What of the Jaffrans!' Jaris asked in panic. 'What will we do?'

'I don't know about you, but I'm leaving King's Landing. I suggest you do likewise.'

So agitated was Jaris that he half fell down the stairs. Lystra caught him and he put himself on the step beneath hers, blocking her further progress. His eyes were now level with hers and she could not avoid his intent gaze.

'Hear me!' he said desperately. 'It matters not to the fisher people whether you are Harbour Mistress. You are the *Beloved of Maris*! We know this to be true, no matter what the town elders say. The fisher people follow you and obey your word. You cannot – *must not* – desert them now! Just come and speak to them. If you tell them to flee King's Landing, they will not hesitate to do so. They will not listen to me. When we landed this morning, you instructed the fisher captains not to put to sea today. Hungry though the people are, every last captain has stayed ashore. They anxiously await your further word. They are faithful still to you and Maris. And by that faith we know Maris has not forsaken us. By that faith, I know the words of Councillor Septis speaks are twisted and false. If you *do* abandon us... Lystra... then Maris will indeed have forsaken us and the words of Councillor Septis will become true. Do you not see that he was trying to create a different world with his words, as a magician does with his spells?'

Lystra couldn't help a small smile. 'You weren't so eloquent in the council chamber, Jaris.'

Jaris looked abashed. 'I-I know. It is to my shame. There was something about the room that prevented me. I must make amends now or I feel everything will be lost. And there is something else, Lystra. You still owe me.'

'What do you mean?' she frowned.

'You saved my life, remember. So I am now your responsibility. That is the tradition of our people. And in return I will serve you, Beloved of Maris, if you will have me.'

Her face flushed hot. Damn his twinkling and mocking eyes! She roughly pushed past him, almost tipping him down the stairs again. 'I have no time for such folly! Let us find these fisher captains at once. Every second now may cost a life later. Hurry, Jaris!'

❈ ❈

The forty-eight captains of the fisher people gathered around Lystra to hear her commands. They were a tough collection of old sea-dogs, wind-burnt soaks and salt-rimed leathers, but each knew himself no more than a mortal man. If Maris had something to say to them, then who were they to refuse to listen? It mattered not one jot that the Holy Sealord chose to speak to them through a young maid. Who were they to question His divine will? Even Proud Platus bent his head so he might better pay attention.

Lystra met every eye there and found her personal fellowship with them renewed. Together, they might still frustrate the evil that challenged the holy kingdom of Maris. 'The red sails of the Jaffrans are coming,' she said simply, Jaris nodding beside her. 'They will be here sooner than any of us would like. In His mercy, Maris has given us warning, just as when He allows the fisher people to read from the water and weather when a storm is coming. When any one of us reads such signs and declares all should stay near the shore, none doubt him, is that not so?'

'Aye!' they replied without hesitation.

'Then do not doubt that a storm of red sails comes fast upon us and that we must seek shelter. This storm will batter King's Landing like the Humbling Storm of a century past. You have all heard your fathers and grandfathers tell how the Humbling Storm tore down most of the homes in King's Landing and killed a great many. That is what we face now.'

'What must we do?' Captain Sharkis asked for them all.

'We must leave King's Landing,' Lystra said in a clear and loud voice. 'We have boats enough to hold all the fisher people if we do not seek to bring possessions with us. Do not be down-hearted about leaving, for are we not all nomads upon the open sea?'

There were answering nods and murmurs of agreement.

'Yes, we are nomads that follow the fish and the will of Maris. Be not down-hearted, for we can return to King's Landing one day, once the storm has passed, and begin to repair the damage. Let us leave quickly then.'

'Where must we go?' Captain Sharkis begged.

'We could follow the Swirlfast River inland and south, for the Jaffrans would be unable to follow with their large ships, but what is there for folk such as ourselves on land and in the south? We will founder and lose our way in the swamps and bogs. Those small communities down the river have never welcomed us before and have no reason to do so now. And we would be without the protection and guidance of Maris if we go there.'

'Then we head along the coast in our boats,' Captain Sharkis anticipated.

'Aye,' Lystra nodded. 'I am sure Soldis will take some of us in, and the Spit of Tyr the rest. They will be grateful for the warning we bring, for it will give them time to look to their own defences and perhaps allow them to weather the storm when it comes for them. *The Pride of Corinus* is not due into King's Landing for another week, so will be far too late to help us. And what can one warship do against twenty? But if the *Pride* can be held at Soldis and the Merchant Guild there moves quickly enough to refit its ships for war, then we will have something of a fleet to save our kingdom. The fisher captains that travel onto the Spit of Tyr must also urge the Guild there to send an embassy to the Accritanian court of Helicon.'

Several captains muttered and spat at mention of the Accritanians, but Lystra knew better than to make an issue of it now.

'Go to your families and neighbours now!' Lystra called. 'We leave in an hour. I will lead half the boats to Soldis, and Captain Sharkis will lead the rest onto the Spit of Tyr. Captains, be in your boats in good time, for Captain Sharkis and I will not be able to wait. If –'

'I mean no disrespect, but my conscience must speak out!' Captain Platus interrupted. 'Some of us have family amongst the rest of the town, Harbour Mistress, including yourself. What of them? What of the wider population of King's Landing? They will not fit in our boats, yet we cannot just leave them to the slavers of Jaffra. We fisher people may be followers of Maris, but we are also Memnosians. What would be said of us if we abandoned our countrymen? We would be a people without honour!'

Some shouted in support of Captain Platus, while others like Sharkis shook their heads and tried to shout them down.

'This could turn ugly,' Jaris whispered in warning.

Lystra moved quickly to intervene. 'Peace, good captains, peace!' Once they had quietened again, except for the odd grumble here and there, she continued: 'We have given warning to the council of elders, Captain Platus. We will also carry word to as many as we can in the next hour. They should be urged to take to the road for Holter's Cross. We do not want them mobbing the boats, for they will put us all at risk with their panic. As you say, Captain, our boats do not have the room to carry them. But bear in mind also that some will not leave, no matter what we say or how hard we plead. We cannot risk ourselves because of such people, else all will be lost.'

'Surely the elders must be saved!' Captain Platus joined.

'Put them on your own boat and leave your family on the dockside if you're so worried about the old tartars!' called someone towards the back.

'Who was that?' Captain Platus challenged. 'Do not speak so disrespectfully of our elders! We should share the responsibility of taking them to safety. There must be other principled men here who are prepared to take an elder each on their boats.'

'I'd rather take Big Brenda from the inn!'

Laughter.

'I say it's a principled man who refuses to let those sneering landlubbers on our boats. All they do is seek to tax us on what Maris has freely given. It is a blasphemy of sorts and we would be cursed if we let them aboard.'

'Quiet, all of you! Listen!' Jaris shouted at the top of his lungs. 'Listen! The lookout, the lookout!'

The fisher captains suddenly stilled, all argument forgotten. No captain wanted to miss the call of his lookout. It could mean the difference between life and death.

A thin voice came to them on the wind from the viewing point atop the town hall. ' – sails, ho! Red sails heading for us! Four… six… more! Red sails, ho!' Then the town's alarum bell began to ring out.

'The Jaffrans!' Jaris cried in horror.

'We're too late,' Lystra whispered, her heart pounding.

Some of the captains cried out in dismay. 'What shall we do? There is no time to get our families away. Holy Maris, save us!

❊ ❋

Her mind spun like a cursed compass or a bird caught in a high wind. What were they to do? Captains shouted at each other and then at Lystra, desperate for direction.

'Let me get my bearings!' she pleaded. 'Maris, guide me!'

Damn these Jaffrans! This was her harbour and they had no right to land here without her say so. And they would not get the chance if she had anything to do with it.

'Hear me!' she shouted.

'The Harbour Mistress speaks!' Jaris bellowed. 'Calm yourselves! Are you men?'

The fisher captains slowly quietened, their faces tense with fear.

'Their ships must not be allowed inside the harbour walls. The longer we can keep them out, the longer the people of King's Landing will have to flee the town. I want twenty boats out there, forming a line and blocking the harbour mouth. Lash the boats together as securely as you can. Captain Sharkis, can you do this?'

The captain nodded. 'Aye. But if they ram us, I'm not sure the line will hold.'

'Remove weights from your nets and foul the waters beyond the harbour then.'

Captain Sharkis grinned. 'I get your drift, Harbour Mistress!'

'It'll be your biggest catch in years, eh, Sharkis?' a captain joked, forcing some laughter from the assembled fisher people, helping restore them to themselves.

'Captain Platus, I ask something of you now that no one here will condemn you for should you refuse. If at first we manage to hold them back, they will seek to land men on the harbour wall, either directly from the sides of their tall ships of via small landing boats... You will of course be supported by the few guards the town maintains, but... well...'

'But those guards are rarely sober enough to know one end of a fish from another, let alone the pointy end of a sword. My aged mother could best them with a mere piece of driftwood,' Captain Platus smiled. He stepped forward to stand beside Lystra and then faced his fellows. 'I will be proud to fight for my people. Any captain or crewman without family will be welcome at my side, as long as they do not try to steal too many Jaffrans off the end of my lunging spear!'

Captain Sharkis came forward, clapped Captain Platus on the shoulder and offered his hand to shake.

'Maris, protect us all!' Lystra whispered.

The lead Jaffran ship ploughed through the water, bearing down on the hurriedly completed line of Memnosian fishing boats. The fisher captains had set their blunt sterns facing out to the open water and then tied the boats side-by-side with their best knots. All knew that their line was only as strong as the weakest knot, length of rope or wooden tie-post.

Watching the giant warship rushing upon them now, Captain Sharkis realised he was a more religious man than he'd ever previously thought. 'Clear the decks!' he hollered. 'Get to the harbour walls if you can! Move, you sluggards!'

'Come on! Turn!' Lystra pleaded.

'Surely it cannot hold, Harbour Mistress!'

'Holy Maris, help us!'

At the last moment, the Jaffran ship seemed to slow and then move off its line. There was a cry from the tiller end of the enemy warship as the nets in the water dragged its rudder out to a wide angle. The prow of the ship swung sharply so that its body was now at a forty-five degree angle to the line of fisher boats.

'Brace for impact!' Captain Sharkis warned.

His voice was drowned out by the horrendous crash and splinter of wood and the banshee-like screaming of twisted metal. Everything shook and shuddered, some of the mortared stones of the harbour wall breaking free and tumbling down into the water. Men fell with them and were engulfed by the high wave pushed out by the impacted line of boats. Above it all was a mighty groaning that continued and continued as if the world itself had been mortally injured by the heavens falling down upon it.

'Now let the subjugation, suffering and slaughter begin!' commanded a menacing and disembodied voice all around them.

The line of fisher boats slowly bent under the pressure of the Jaffran warship, like the yew of a longbow as the weapon is drawn.

'Waaait!' Captain Sharkis urged. 'Hold!'

A rope suddenly snapped between two of the boats and the vessels jostled against each other.

The fisher people held their breath.

Then the boats became wedged and the line arced a little further. The line stopped. The longbow had bent as far as it would go. There was a moment of stillness, and then the sudden release! The line of boats flexed back, pushing the Jaffran ship so hard that it heeled dangerously and almost foundered in that initial thrust.

Ragged cheers went up from the fisher people.

'Grapnels!' Captain Sharkis called across the harbour. 'I don't want to see any daylight between our boats and that ship. Hold close, lads, as if it were your last night with your lady-love before putting to sea for the rest of your lives. Heave those irons! That's it! Tie it fast! Now the pitch, before their archers see what's afoot. Good! Now the pots of fire! There she goes!'

Hungry flames licked up the side of the warship and then leapt to dance upon its decks. Thick, black smoke billowed up and began to block out the sun.

'Let's make the sky as dark as night!' Lystra cried as her people shouted their defiance at the oncoming fleet.

⚜ ⚜

Whether it was instinct or natural impatience with the world, the Scourge wasted no time in reaching the temple of Cognis set in the Needle Mountains. The majesty of the peaks and the spectacular landscapes laid out far below were of little interest to him. As Divine Consort of Shakri, he was more than a little familiar with all She'd created, for She'd spent their early months together constantly showing off to him all She had made. He'd indulged Her for a while, besotted as he was, but eventually been unable to hide his boredom with it all. She'd sulked for a bit, and he'd felt guilty, but then She'd guilt-tripped him into agreeing to all manner of things he would normally have refused to have anything to do with. He'd accused Her of manipulating him and She'd flown into a foul rage. He'd had no choice but to respond with his own rage, a rage he'd fought to keep under control his entire life, a rage that proved to be far greater and more terrifying than anything She'd been able to display. Damn Her but She'd brought it on Herself, provoking him beyond all endurance.

She'd fled from him and he'd pursued Her. She'd begged with Incarnus to protect Her or intercede on Her behalf, but even Incarnus had been unwilling to become involved in the domestic relationships of the Mother of All Creation. Shakri had continued to elude the Scourge until his rage had finally blown itself out.

They'd made up with each other and the passion of the love-making that had immediately followed had been unlike anything he'd ever experienced before or since. He'd been unable to speak for an entire month afterwards. Even Shakri – Goddess of Love though she was – had seemed satisfied for a good number of days.

But it was at that point the vindictive cow had told him he had to leave, and had exiled him back to the mortal realm!

The hurt of it was still with him. He tried not to think about it, tried to distract himself with other things, but everything he looked at was a part of Her realm and reminded him of Her. There was only escape from it through the numbing effects of drink or finding an obsessive singleness of purpose that pushed out all other consideration.

'You!' he shouted at a young acolyte who was vaguely sweeping the floor of the temple's walled courtyard. 'Stop day-dreaming and inform your high priestess the Scourge is here and in no mood to be kept waiting. Honestly, you followers of Cognis are always so lost in your own thoughts that you don't know the first thing about what's going on around you. How is it none of you even knew I was coming, eh? And why does no one keep a lookout? I could have been anyone just riding in here unannounced. It wasn't so many years ago that a group of blood-mages laid waste to this place, you know! By the bloodless prick of Cognis, why haven't any of you thought to put a gate across the path where it is so narrow it can only take one person at a time? A single armed person could defend this place all day if they were but correctly positioned. By your god's unwashed beard, girl, don't just stand there gawping. Move! You seem some witless peasant with mud for brains rather than a student of the god of knowledge! Don't you know how to run, or must I turn the cheeks of your arse red with the flat of my blade? And get me something to eat! I've only had mouldy bread of late.'

Beside herself with fear and upset, the acolyte ran gibbering to the temple building. As she got to the door, she half collided with Larc, who was just emerging to greet the commander.

'M-Master. He... I... Scourge!'

Larc laid a gentling hand on the girl's shoulder. 'All is well, Lilia. You may help Vasha ready herself to meet our guest. Do not be affrighted by this mountain goat who has come to bleat at us. It is just his way. He is not used to company and therefore snorts and stamps whenever there is risk of coming near another. He is barely domesticated, you know.'

Lilia finally smiled, bobbed to Larc and went inside the building at a less panicked pace. Just as she disappeared from view, she turned her head and stuck her tongue out at the Guardian.

The Scourge smiled. 'Larc, you're a sight for sore eyes! You've been reading books and getting yourself an education, eh? I bet you spent a year scripting that little piece on goats for yourself.'

Larc came forward and shook the Scourge's hand once the commander had dismounted. 'And it's good to see you too... although peace and harmony rarely follow in your wake, my friend. I will not ask why you are here or speculate what your coming here betokens until you have had some refreshment and we have joined Vasha. Let us move inside, however, for the sky and winds tell me there is a bad storm coming.'

'Really? You can tell such?'

'Reading the world and its Pattern has been a study of mine for some while now. When a person lives in the same place for a length of time, they come to know the signs.'

'I'll take your word for it, for I do not think I've ever spent more than a week in the same place, and that place was probably some inn or other. I'll hitch my horse here for the nonce. Lilia or some other will see to him, yes?'

'Of course. Come in, come in. Don't worry, we will not demand you genuflect or say a prayer on entering the temple.'

The Scourge coughed. 'That's good. I was never expected to do the same when I lived amongst the pantheon.'

Larc looked embarrassed. 'Ah, yes, of course. I had… well, I guess I hadn't really appreciated… anyway, please excuse me. This way.'

As they went inside, thunder rumbled in the distance. The sky was still clear, making the Scourge wonder just what was coming if it could be heard so far away. Nothing good, that was for sure.

The temple was small, but so cleverly laid out that it felt infinitely larger. Of course, that was always the way of things with knowledge. Above the altar, there was a domed ceiling that was painted so richly and with such detail that is seemed the whole world was captured there and put on display. The Scourge dared not look at it, lest it remind him of Shakri so vividly that he be totally unmanned.

'Vasha is waiting for us through here, in the main antechamber.'

The Scourge followed after Larc and ducked through a low, curtained doorway. As he straightened up, he met the knowing eyes of the young and radiant high priestess of Cognis.

'Vasha!' the Guardian rumbled with a near paternal smile. 'How are you?'

'Scourge!' she exclaimed. 'I am so happy to see you. I was but a girl when we last met.'

'And now you are a woman fully grown. I trust the two of you have been well up here in the mountains.'

There was a sudden loud crash from outside the temple and they all jumped.

'Is it a rock fall?' Vasha gasped. 'No. Thunder, I th-!'

229

The rest of what she said was drowned out by detonations all around them. Earth and sky shook, as if clashing together. Lightning streaked down and blasted the rock around the temple. There was an awful cracking sound.

'Aiee! The dome is broken!' came a faint and scared voice from the adjacent chamber.

They staggered as if drunk and barely managed to stay upright. It was as if the mountain itself were tilting, as if the cataclysm was upon them.

The wind rose and moaned as if it were dying. A terrible voice emerged and assaulted them: 'Now let the subjugation, suffering and slaughter begin!'

With a cry, Vasha fell to the floor. Her eyes rolled back in her head, her heels and fists drummed on the ground as if she were having a fit and she began to foam at the mouth.

'All-knowing Cognis, what is happening?' Larc panicked.

'Kill me!' Vasha shrieked. 'If you love me, kill me! Quickly!'

Her hands went to her hair and pulled large clumps free. She tore her face open with her nails and then tried to throttle herself.

'Restrain her!' the Scourge yelled. 'Before she can harm herself any further. Use all your strength, you fool, as if fighting ten women. That's it!'

The Scourge bent close to the priestess's ear. 'Get used to it, Vasha, for we will not allow you death as an option.'

'Nooo! And I would not know escape even in death. Ye gods, there is no hope left! All is undone. He is here, he is here! So many, so many! The demon realm rises!'

'Who is here?' the Scourge demanded.

Vasha spoke faster and faster. 'The Demon-King, the Demon-King! I can no longer read the Pattern. It unravels. I am blind. What to do? Nothing to be done. I know nothing. Cognis is a dullard or fool. Cognis is lost! He is lost to us!'

'What does it mean?' Larc asked the Scourge in anguish.

'Shut up. Vasha, other gods are also lost to us. It is because of this Demon-King, yes? Where is he? How do we stop him? Does Saltar know?'

Vasha's words now came impossibly quickly. 'The realm knows nothing of Saltar. Absent. The Demon-King is on top of us! So many. We must flee! The three of us are meaningless alone. I cannot see what is to be done. We are all lost. There is nowhere to go, nowhere to run. We will only buy ourselves extra moments in fleeing. There are only extra moments left to us. It is the end!'

Larc, with his arms and legs wrapped tightly around the woman he loved, looked up at the Scourge in silent appeal.

The Scourge snorted derisively. 'The end? Not if I have anything to do with it, it isn't. I haven't put up with so much for so long from our own piddling pantheon then to have some demon pretender waltz in and make things even more tiresome for me! Not when I've worked so hard to get our lot finally showing some sense of decorum and self-discipline. If this Demon-King thinks he can just come along and take over with his ugly band of bravos, then he's got another thing coming. By the pulsating and ulcerated arsehole of Lacrimos, I won't have it, you hear! How bloody dare they! I'm sick to death with every cheap upstart and renegade thinking they can use this realm as their plaything or garderobe. It's so... so... well, flaming disrespectful is what it is! Vasha, stop wailing and gnashing your teeth, would you? I can't hear myself think. Right, so, we're going to leave here immediately if I catch your drift. Let's buy ourselves as many extra moments as we may. Where should we head first, eh? Are you still sane enough to tell us that?'

Vasha's ears began to bleed and her head lolled about violently, Larc only just managing to hold it up free of the stone floor. 'East...' she murmured. 'One moment to the next. We may not get there soon enough. The storm will seek to prevent us.'

'Right! Everybody on their feet. We're leaving!'

※ ※

The stone eye of Istris cracked and split. At last, the dreaming was over. The centuries of waiting were at an end. The voice of the Demon-King had finally been heard, and his will would free all demonkind from its incarceration. Their former glory would at last be restored, exceeded even. New planes of existence would be theirs.

He was so hungry. Never had he experienced such an appetite. Given how long he'd been entombed by the simple and torpid nature of this realm, it was no wonder he could barely think for the need of food.

Istris opened his other eye and slowly twisted his neck. The shell of hardened dust and sand that covered him began to fall away in chunks. He rippled his muscles and stretched. He hadn't felt anything so good in... well, centuries. He grinned and bared his lion teeth.

The ceremonial guard who'd been dozing on the other side of the hold suddenly started awake and peered through the gloom.

'Yikes! The statue moves! Or have I had too much palm wine?'

Istris growled. Where did such irreverence come from? The creature was only mortal, after all. Istris could smell its blood from here.

231

The mortal wove its way across the hold and bowed deeply. 'Holy Sphinx, I will fetch your priests!' he babbled.

Istris opened his jaws and bit the mortal in half through the waist. He swallowed head, arms and torso without even chewing. And then he ate the rest in a quick slurp. His stomach squirmed a bit, for it had been a long while since it had been put to use. Ah! That was better. The demon sphinx felt momentarily light-headed as it was flooded with new life-force.

Wonderful! If anything, it only served to increase his already demanding appetite. He sensed and smelt other mortals scurrying about not far above him. He should go devour them before the other sphinkaes managed to throw off their torpor and began to compete for the food.

�><✦

In being dragged off course, the lead Jaffran warship had cut across the path of the warship off its stern and starboard bow. The second warship had been unable to turn to port in time to cut back across the wake of the first ship, and couldn't turn further to starboard because then it would be on a direct path for the immovable harbour wall. The collision when it came saw the second ship ram into the first amidships. The flames that began to devour the lead ship then leapt to the second. The screams of crushed and dying men could be heard even from the far side of the harbour. The sea became mottled red and black like an ugly bruise.

The next ship went out wide to port and headed for a strand of beach outside the harbour walls, only to tear out its bottom on hidden rocks and run itself aground. But it was close enough to the harbour walls so that its archers could launch deadly flights of arrows to keep Platus and his men back from the end of the wall nearest the listing and burning hulks of the Jaffran warships wedged up against the boats of the fisher people. The flames forced Jaffran sailors and soldiers into the water in larger and larger numbers. Those not dragged down into the dark depths by their armour flailed towards the harbour wall and dragged themselves up the narrow landing steps.

The fisher people lunged with spears at the swimmers who came close to them, but otherwise held back for fear of enemy arrows.

'We cannot allow them to set foot on our ground unchallenged!' Captain Platus fumed. 'Harbour Mistress, with your permission, I will prevent this evil from establishing a foothold.'

'O-Of course!' Lystra stammered, her tongue struggling to work. 'I will lead the charge with you.'

Platus nodded proudly. 'You will be our figurehead, Harbour Mistress, who will steer a clear course for us through the storm.' He turned to the two dozen men standing behind them. 'Are you men of good faith?'

'Yes, Captain!'

'Will you allow these invaders to take your home?'

'No, Captain!'

'Then follow me, you proud fisher folk!'

With a roar, the brawny fishermen of King's Landing charged forward with nets, spears and knives in hand. They were led by the giant blackbeard Captain Platus and their no less doughty Harbour Mistress, whom every man loved like a mother, sister and priestess all rolled into one. Most of the Jaffrans had lost their weapons leaving their ships or in the water, so could muster little resistance as the fisher people barrelled into them. Also, the fisher people – who were used to hard, manual work – were generally thicker set than the willowy and wiry Jaffrans.

Captain Platus threw his net over one of the larger Jaffrans and then stabbed his catch with his spear. The enemy soldier screamed as his bowel was perforated and never even saw the captain's mighty fist coming in to smash his face beyond human recognition. The Jaffran was catapulted more than six feet off the harbour wall and quickly sank into a watery grave.

Lystra ducked the clumsy swing of a Jaffran's scimitar and stabbed up quickly with her spear. Her weapon failed to penetrate the soldier's metal-plated leather and snapped in two. A lean and tanned face leered at her from under a conical helmet topped with a killing spike. He had brownish, gapped teeth and smelt like an unwashed animal. The scimitar now came at her from overhead.

Not knowing what else to do, she bunched her net, pulled it taught between her two hands and pushed it out in front of her to meet the blade. The sword cut through one rope, two, three; she twisted the bunched net and pushed the weapon sideways until she was no longer in its path. Then she abandoned her net, balled a fist and punched the man as hard as she could on the nose. The cartilage gave under her knuckles and blood sprayed everywhere. Suddenly afraid of his blade because she had lost track of it, she punched him again, and again, and again, until he was down and no longer breathing. She reached for the sword in his unmoving hand, but a cruel hobnailed boot stamped down on her fingers and began to grind them under.

She screamed in pain and terror.

'Hold on, Mistress, your servant is here!'

Two spears punched through the air over Lystra's hunched form and propelled the owner of the hobnailed boot back into the melee.

'Up, Lystra, up!' Jarvis urged and took up a guard position in front of her.

She wiped tears of pain from her eyes on her sleeve and used her uninjured hand to claim the scimitar. Unfortunately, she now only had her less dextrous hand with which to wield the metal, as she couldn't even feel the fingers on her right hand.

'We are even, Jaris!'

'Nay, Mistress. Now I am as much responsible for your life as you are for mine.'

'You are a stupid, stubborn man.'

'Arrgh!' gurgled a fisherman next to them as an arrow took him in the throat.

The harbour wall was now entirely red with blood. Used to slippery and difficult footing, the fisher people largely kept their footing, but the Jaffrans in their hobnailed boots struggled on the slick stones.

Suddenly, the harbour wall was clear of Jaffrans, and Captain Sharkis and his men joined them from the line of boats. There was a fresh barrage from the Jaffran archers and the fisher people retreated back along the wall once more. They'd lost six men in total, which although was not many still saddened and angered every one of them because they had known each man by name: Ugly Jake, three-fingered Swallis, Trabis who cheated at cards, Thetis who loved other men, young Polkar with the foam-white hair and Chaldon the thinker.

The Jaffran fleet had lowered their sails and put down anchor, for they dared not come any closer to the wall of fire now engulfing the boats of the fisher people.

'My grandfather built that boat with his own hands,' one man said to no one in particular. The rest looked on in silence as their livelihoods burned.

'Maris will provide if all we have is a single thread from our clothing and a single barb,' Lystra said to console herself as much as the fisher people. 'And there are always crabs in the rock pools and seaweed to be had, although the seaweed gives me terrible wind, if the sea-god will forgive my complaint.'

There were a few smiles, but their faces fell again as Captain Platus spoke: 'See there. They are putting out landing boats. I had thought they would wait for the flames to burn themselves out, but they will want to be ashore and well into the town while the sun is still high. They will not fancy landing at night and will not be able to pursue those who flee through the dark. They dare not linger outside the harbour too long.'

'Look, more landing boats from over there!' Captain Sharkis said, raising his chin towards the more distant ships. 'I count six. Twenty men per boat. That's at least twice our number.'

'It matters not,' Captain Platus said disdainfully. 'Every man here is worth at least three of them, as Maris is my witness!'

'Jaris, you have the youngest and sharpest eyes here. What else do you see?' Captain Sharkis asked.

Jaris cleared his throat awkwardly. 'They bristle with weapons and armour, you can see how it glints. Shields. Long spears… and archers too.'

'And we have lost many of our hand nets,' Lystra pointed out.

'We must hold!' Captain Platus insisted. 'The wall is narrow and defensible. A line of just ten of us can hold it. If we retreat to the town we will be overrun in an instant.'

'Their archers will pick us off from behind a wall of shields if we wait for them here, my friend,' Captain Sharkis gently pointed out. 'We have no shields, Platus. We are not soldiers. We have done our best, but –'

'No!' Captain Platus's voice cracked like a whip. 'None of us in King's Landing are soldiers. Does that mean we should meekly allow these Jaffrans to have the town as soon as we see these sails? If we are not prepared to defend what the gods have gifted us, then surely we are not deserving of any of it! Are we so ungrateful and so disrespectful of the pantheon that we would so easily cast aside their bounty? We may not be soldiers but are we not loyal followers of our gods? Dur Memnos is their kingdom! Will we not defend it against these blood-soaked demon-worshippers? And what of the fleeing people of King's Landing we are buying time for by standing our ground? Have we forgotten them so quickly? I will remain here alone if I must if it will buy my wife and children but a few seconds more life!' he bristled and raged at them. 'Do *not* tell me we have done our best! We have *not* done our best, for we still live! Are you afraid? Be not so faithless, for all fisher people know holy Maris has a place waiting for them in the court of His wondrous kingdom.'

Many had lowered their heads in shame. Some stood tall with fire and eagerness in their eyes. Lystra nodded her head.

'Well said, my friend,' Captain Sharkis said, his voice thick with emotion.

'Thank you, Captain, you give us courage,' Lystra said. She turned to the waiting group of men and raised her hands to bestow the sort of benediction they always seemed to demand and expect of her. 'Maris, hear me! We ask your blessing this day. I bless these men in your name! We ask your protection, not in selfishness but on behalf of our loved ones, your people in King's Landing. May we stay sound this day, guided by you through all storms, until the fleet comes safely home! By your grace!'

'By your grace!' the assembled men repeated with conviction and determination. What need did they have for armour when their faith would protect them?

The first of the Jaffran landing boats reached the harbour wall, another close behind it.

'For Maris!' called Captain Platus and thundered along the wall towards them, fifty fishermen hard on his heels.

Caught as they were stepping from boat to wall, the Jaffrans had no time to form a defensive line and brace themselves against the oncoming enemy. Few of them had even managed to get their spears down or their swords up as the fisher people crashed into them. Soldiers from the first boat toppled and sank like stones to the bottom of the harbour.

Two archers at the back of the boat finally got their bows working and took one fisher person in the gut and another through the eye. Captain Platus jumped down into their boat, setting it to rocking violently and bludgeoned his way towards the bowmen.

Jaffrans in the other boat yelled in their foreign tongue, other archers seeking to bring their weapons to bear but unable to get a clear shot. One of the soldiers in the first boat clouted Captain Platus with an oar, but the captain did not even stagger. He head-butted the Jaffran's hooked nose and wrenched the oar from him. They he began to lay about him, sweeping most of the Jaffrans off their feet.

Half a dozen fishermen swarmed after Captain Platus and made short work of the Jaffrans, as if they were gutting fish.

'Look out!' Captain Sharkis called from the harbour wall.

An arrow buried itself in the meat of Captain Platus's shoulder at the same time as the second boat came in with spears levelled. They skewered the captain through his sternum and thigh.

'Noo!' the fisher people cried collectively.

Captain Platus grinned, his teeth lined with blood. 'Ah! I've never felt more alive!' He pulled the helmet off the nearest Jaffran – who still gripped the spear that had gone through the captain's chest – and smashed in both his temples. The Jaffran fell without a sound.

'And now you!' the captain coughed and reached for the other spearman. But this one was not about to be caught in the same way. He abandoned his weapon and pulled out a short stabbing sword, with which he hacked into the captain's hands and arms.

Now the Jaffran soldiers from the second boat pushed forward, spilling into the first boat or leaping from the stairs. Captain Platus was toppled and the fishermen with him were cut down.

The dark eyes of the Jaffrans glittered. They knew they would begin to prevail now that the initial onslaught of the fisher people had been broken. The Jaffran weapons had a longer reach, and their armour and shields would protect them from most of what the fisher people could throw at them.

Arrows rained in once more from the warship stranded on the rocks. The men to either side of Lystra went down at the same moment. *This is madness! Ye gods, where are you? Must we all die before you notice our plight? Sweet Maris, what have you allowed to visit our shores? If this is your punishment of us, then so be it, but if not then help us now, I pray. Pa, I'm sorry! I've failed to keep them safe, failed to look after mother and my brothers and sisters for you. I did my best, pa, honest I did. I'm scared, pa! I hope you're waiting for me, pa. I miss you!*

A curved blade raked down Jaris's side, leaving it a bloody mess. He cried out and staggered backwards. She caught him and steadied him, just as she had on the stairs less than an hour ago. He looked into her eyes and tried to smile bravely for her, but he could not hide the knowledge showing in them that all was lost.

'Sorry, Mistress, I have not been the best of servants to you!' he said sorrowfully. 'I would have enjoyed living my life with you, truly.'

She lived a lifetime in the brief seconds of that gaze. She saw that he would have treated her well… that they would have been happy together… there may have been children… there may have been love even. It was not to be, but the knowledge of it was enough. Shakri had allowed her this moment of beauty and wonder at the end, and it was enough. She was not scared anymore. She was almost happy.

Through the blur of her tears, she saw Captain Sharkis hold off three swords with just his skinning knife for impossibly long moments. But his knife could not be in more than one place at any one time, and they finally found him out, unstringing him with gleeful smiles on their faces.

'Maris, where are you?' she cried in a broken voice.

An incongruous voice sang back to her, causing her to wonder if she'd finally lost her senses in the desperate insanity of the fighting: 'Is that a fair damsel I hear calling for rescue? Are her virtue and very life in peril? Are there insurmountable odds to be faced? Are there innocents beset by dread foes and malign forces? Then fear not, good people of Dur Memnos, for your god Aa and His trusty companions are here to save the day. Come, be not amazed that I have come among you. Surely you had not hoped to keep all the fun to yourselves. You must pay your tithe to the gods, remember, to those who watch over you so well!'

'Who is this lunatic?' Jaris wondered aloud.

'He says he's the god Aa, but I do not recognise him.'

'He's good with a sword, mind you, and his arrival could not be more timely. Does Aa not favour the reckless and foolhardy? Is He not the holy champion of lost causes?'

A young lad with small, black eyes and a twitching nose joined them. 'It really is Him, you know! Excuse me, but I must enter the fray. I fancy myself one of those bronze helmets, and I've never tasted Jaffran.'

'Maris be praised!' Jaris exclaimed.

Aa's head whipped round. 'I heard that! Let us be quite clear, my good fellow, that if there's any praising to be done round here, then it will be in my name! I am not some instrument or pawn of Maris, Shakri or any others in the pantheon. Is –' He slashed an arrow out of the air with His blade, '– that –' He feinted and extended His sword so that a Jaffran rushed it into his own throat, '– clear!' He swayed so that two spears contrived to miss Him and then clashed the helmets of those responsible together, causing them to reel and tip themselves over the side of the boat without any further help.

A young boy came past. 'Don't mind Him. He just gets sensitive about such things.'

'Orastes, I do *not* get sensitive! It's a matter of propriety and reverence for the holy! Struth, lad, has no one seen to your religious education? What of piety and so forth? You should seek to emulate young Distrus there. He understands the importance of respecting your elders and betters.

'Take that, you heathen!' Aa laughed theatrically as He took the lead soldier of a newly arriving boat through his disbelieving eye.

'Yes, Aa!' Orastes sighed and then marched forward with a serious look on his face.

Then came creatures of nightmare bumping and turning Lystra and Jaris all around as they streamed past.

'What ungodly beings are these! Maris, protect us, we are surrounded,' Jaris cried, trying to keep himself between Lystra and the drooling, cackling torments from the deepest, darkest parts of the forest, places where no mortal dared to tread.

'It's alright,' a boy in a grey robe reassured them as he came past. 'They obey Orastes, demons though they are. He has told them they must not eat any mortals, and they seem bound by that.'

'Demons and children,' Jaris said faintly. 'I do not understand this world anymore. It is all upside down. Surely this is the beginning of the end.' He swayed dangerously on his feet.

'He does not look well,' the grey-robed boy warned. 'My master Ninevus waits back on the dock. He is a powerful priest of Shakri and can see to his injuries for you.'

'Th-Thank you,' Lystra said numbly and stumbled away supporting Jaris under the shoulder. After a few yards, she shook her head, picked him up and began to run with him in her arms. He was so light it terrified her. He could not die now! If he died, then surely it would be the end. Why did the gods play with them so? Why?

✄ ✄

Kate knew they all thought she was a crazed monster. They glanced at her sideways when they thought she wasn't looking. She could all but hear their thoughts as they decided the grief at Saltar's loss had unhinged her mind – she refused to believe that the palace guard had not whispered the news abroad. How could she trust any of them when they had allowed her son to be taken from her? The only way her enemies could have successfully smuggled Orastes out of the palace was if the palace guard were complicit and conspiring against her. Had they been responsible for the death of her beloved husband and the Chamberlain too?

Her enemies were all around her, as they had been her entire life. They constantly sought to undermine her, to topple her, to devastate her. Even as a child, she'd always had to fight them and remain on guard against them. Fighting and fighting, always fighting. Killing, and stabbing, and hurting, and biting, and gnawing without respite. She wore her green armour permanently now, for who knew where and when the next attack would come?

The first person she could remember being in her life, her mother, had been her enemy. And her mother had brought her bad men who were also enemies. She'd fought them off and escaped, only to be found by Wardens who wanted to eat her. The Scourge had seemed to save her, but really he'd only brought new enemies upon her – Voltar and other dark magicians – just as her mother had brought bad men to her. She'd had to fight them all. They'd allowed her a dead man as a husband – perhaps some cruel joke on their part – and even a child. She now knew why they'd done that: so that they could take them away and cause her even more pain than she'd suffered already. She'd destroyed a whole nation of blood-mages and their dark god to protect

239

her child, but still the fighting had not ended. As vigilant as she'd been, her enemies had managed to bring her grief once again.

Kate had been tempted to purge the army, but wasn't sure who she could trust to carry out the deed. The Outdwellers who had recently joined had been an option, but she'd returned from Lord Selwyn's estates only to find they'd deliberately been sent off somewhere, ostensibly to find Orastes. It was clear to her that the army commanders just wanted the Outdwellers out of the way; further proof that the commanders conspired against her. Beyond not having enough trustworthy people to carry out the purge, however, Kate also needed to keep the army largely intact if she was to march on Holter's Cross with any hope of victory.

She'd summoned the high priests of Corinus to an audience and informed them that the mercenary Guild of Holter's Cross had kidnapped Orastes and that she needed priests from each temple to accompany the army. With Sister Spike standing at Kate's side and glaring at the assembled religious dignitaries, most had immediately agreed. Ikthaeon, the priggish high priest of Shakri, however, had never been one to take orders from another, and had asked for proof of the disloyalty of the Guild. Sister Spike had then spoken of the mercenaries who'd attempted to murder herself and Kate when they'd paid a courtesy visit to Lord Selwyn and his family. Her facial injuries were plain for the high priests to see, and then she'd shown the sickening bruises on her torso from the beating she'd taken. Those who were not shocked into silence shouted out in horror and outrage. Ikthaeon had even offered to heal Sister Spike himself, and she'd had to work hard to prevent him laying his hands on her flesh.

Of course, Kate knew she couldn't trust the priests of Corinus any more than she could the commanders of the Memnosian army. Ultimately, the priests served the gods, and the gods invariably put their own interests ahead of the concerns of mortalkind. Just look at how they'd allowed war to rage for generations between Dur Memnos and Accritania; indeed, it had been the opposition between Shakri and Lacrimos that had all but defined that war and kept it going. The real victims were always mortalkind. The gods schemed and played out their petty squabbles through mortalkind, usually with dire results for any mortals the gods chose to involve. Just look at the conflict with the blood-mages of the Brethren: that had all come about because of the competing ambitions of Nylchros and the pantheon.

Yes, the gods decreed a life of constant war and suffering for mortalkind. Fighting, and fighting, always fighting. The life surrounded by enemies decreed for Kate was pretty much the life they'd decreed for every mortal being. It appeared to be in the gods' interest to keep mortals at each other's throats. Perhaps it was the fighting that kept mortals distracted and ensured they in fact remained mortal. Perhaps *conflict* was therefore the exact nature of mortal being. If there were no fighting or struggle, just imagine what life would be like… in fact, she couldn't even begin to imagine it, for it was so beyond her experience.

So she could not trust the gods or their priests – the Scourge was probably right when he said mortalkind would be better off without the pantheon. Even Sister Spike was ultimately not her friend – for she probably only remained trustworthy and reliable while Kate continued to fight and ensured Dur Memnos remained at war, keeping mortalkind subjected by itself. Incarnus thrived on it, did He not?

There were none she could trust then. How lonely and isolating was mortal existence – perhaps that too was by design, for it encouraged mortals to despair and confirm their mortality by looking to end things rather than seeking a supremacy or divinity of their own. Her enemies were all around her. They had her with her back to the wall. Well, if it was war they wanted, then it was war she would give them!

Kate had marched the collected temples and the main body of the Memnosian army towards Holter's Cross, so that she could see to her enemies on both sides being caught up in a slaughter. Although the Guild had five thousand mercenaries compared to her two thousand, the Memnosian army was used to fighting as single unit and renowned as the most fearsome military force on the continent. Yes, Holter's Cross had impressive walls to defend it, but Gart's priesthood would be able to bring them down on the heads of the Guild without much effort. Surely, there was very little that would be able to stand against a combined magical assault from all the temples of Dur Memnos. The wrath of the entire pantheon would finally descend upon the greedy and immoral Brothers of Holter's Cross and wipe them out of existence. The kingdom had suffered the running sore, festering open wound and the blight of the Guild for far too long. It was time to do something about it before it was too late, before the poison corrupted the entire body of Dur Memnos and all was lost.

Yes, the kingdom and mortalkind could ill afford to lose anymore lives. Yes, it jeopardised the balance and Shakri's entire realm. But what value did that realm have if a mother could not bring up her young family in peace and without constant threat of attack? What value that realm if she was not allowed to be a mother who nurtured that child rather than armed him and trained him to kill? What value if a mother was made a crazed and homicidal monster rather than allowed to be a loving human being? What value if a mother was denied her child and not allowed to hold him? What value when a child was denied a family? What was there? What was left? Where the meaning or value when life became naught but fading memories, then naught but vague dreams? When faces were forgotten? Feelings had no object? None.

So let such a realm come to nothing if she could not have Orastes and a loving husband. Let it whither and die. Let it burn.

Kate stared into the small brazier they'd placed in her tent and watched worlds born into and swirled away by the flames. They were so fleeting that most failed to register on her conscious mind before they were destroyed by the inferno. Was mortal existence all but the same? Sometimes she felt it was. If she did not find Orastes alive, then she cared not if the realm was reduced to embers or a burning mote adrift in the void.

Orastes was her entire hope, and her enemies had realised that, perhaps even helped bring it about. They may have allowed her husband and child so that their loss would ultimately destroy her. See what Shakri's love had done to her! See how it had reduced her life to all or nothing. If she could not find her sweet son, then that love would break her where nothing else her enemies had tried had succeeded. Ah, but it could all end here!

Kate smiled. At least there would be no more fighting after this. Here was the final fight, the great conflagration, the last battle. Either it would all be lost – her son and the entire realm – or she would have reduced her enemies to nothing via this total war. It was a relief of sorts, even gave her a twisted sense of hope.

She might still steal a march on such enemies. She'd forced the pace of her army and not allowed them rest for an entire day and night. There was no way news of her advance would get ahead of them to warn her enemies unless the Guild had some sort of magical foresight. With luck, her army would come upon Holter's Cross before the Guild had a chance to organise itself properly, but she knew better than to underestimate her enemies. She'd finally called a halt a half day's march from the enclave so that Silos Varr could send out scouts to see how Holter's Cross disported itself, and so that her army could collect itself and catch a breath before the bloody confrontation to come.

Now she waited impatiently in her tent. She continually clenched and unclenched her fists. She was eager to have it all done, desperate to have her son back or, if that proved impossible, have the rest offered by a grave. She continued to glare into the hungry brazier, meditating upon the challenge ahead, seeking the sort of calm self-possession she would need to make clear-headed decisions in the middle of a conflict. She still found it difficult, despite all her years of battle experience and all the training she'd kept up with Sister Spike over the years. *Where's your self-discipline, Kate?* The flickering restlessness of the brazier wasn't helping, she realised. She could not find any quiet centre within it, so turned away. At all but the same moment, the guard outside clashed his spear against his shield to announce the entrance of visitors. At last!

Silos Varr entered, his face as impassive as ever, dogged by Sister Spike, who had decided to adopt the same role of personal bodyguard to Kate as she'd fulfilled during the campaign against the Brethren five years before.

'What news?' Kate asked without preamble.

'Milady, the reports from the scouts are quite strange,' the soldier replied matter-of-factly. 'Holter's Cross is already besieged.'

'What? Surely not the Accritanians!'

'No, milady. The scouts report... well, they report that all manner of unholy creature besets the walled city, creatures only ever heard of in folk tales and the like. Their number is apparently without limit, for they cover the ground for miles in all direction around Holter's Cross. Child-stealers, doppelgangers, wild men o' the woods, weres, bedevilling wraiths, winged homunculi, small wyverns, boggarts and so forth. I... I do not know where they come from or what to make of it.'

'These scouts of yours...' Kate began to ask with an examining tilt of her head.

Silos Varr shook his head. 'Nay, they have not been drinking. I would trust the lead scout Verag with my life, milady. I do not know how we can fight such an enemy. Perhaps a Guardian could advise us.'

'I was a Guardian once,' Kate quietly reminded the soldier. 'Yet I have never heard of such a gathering. What does it mean? Sister Spike, surely this is temple business. Summon the high priests, quickly!'

The news was met with consternation by the eight high priests who came to crowd into Kate's tent.

'Such demons are not of the Mother's making!' Ikthaeon, high priest of Shakri, announced. 'They are a blasphemy and must be destroyed. My temple has magicks that will help.'

The large high priest of Gart demurred somewhat, however. 'My temple has always known of such creatures, of course. Some are of Shakri's making but have found themselves hunted by men and therefore hidden themselves in the remotest parts of the realm or in the darkest woods. Others though have been created by renegade magicians in defiance of the gods. And then some sound like they are new to this realm. But what has brought them all together now?'

'It seems that the crimes of mortalkind are finally catching up with us. These creatures, many born of our misdeeds have returned to haunt us with a vengeance. They are here to punish us,' the unnerving high priestess of Lacrimos whispered. Sister Spike nodded her head at mention of the word vengeance.

'They will certainly punish Holter's Cross,' Kate said with some satisfaction. 'Perhaps we should wait until they have had their way with the Guild. Is my enemy's enemy not my friend?'

'You cannot seriously be suggesting we stand idly by while these demons attack the Mother's children in Holter's Cross!' Ikthaeon protested. 'And what of your son, milady? If the demons manage to take the fortress…'

Silos Varr cleared his throat to pre-empt the argument that was about to erupt amongst the leaders of Dur Memnos. 'Are we not all sinners?' That quietened them. 'This kingdom is under attack. Shakri's realm is also under attack. Yes, the mercenaries within Holter's Cross are sinners, but surely we are at fault for having let things get this far. We are at fault for our lack of vigilance and for not having attended to the sinners of Holter's Cross long before now. Will we repeat the same fault now by not attending to these demons who surely threaten all the inhabitants of Shakri's realm? Will we?'

The high priests clearly did not appreciate being spoken down to by a mere soldier, but apparently had no arguments with which to belittle him. There was an awkward silence in the tent. After some seconds, Sister Spike said: 'We are relatively few in number, while they are a vast host. We have priestly magicks on our side, but who is to say what powers they have at their command? Our goal, therefore, should be to punch through them and make it to the gates of the fortress, yes?'

Silos Varr nodded.

'What if the Guild will not open the gates, however?' the high priestess of Incarnus asked.

'Then we will die and the Guild will have proven itself to be as without soul as the demon host,' Kate shrugged. 'If they were really so, however, they would already have opened their gates and joined their demon brethren, I would hazard. So perhaps there is yet some hope for the souls of Holter's Cross. Surely, Sister Spike, if we cannot place our faith in the mortal soul gifted to us by the gods, then we cannot place our faith in any of the pantheon either. And none of your priests would want that, now would you? So I am satisfied. Go to your people, for we march at once.'

Each of the priests left with a nod, and Silos Varr went after offering her a smart salute. She smiled. She appreciated the irony of her enemies in Holter's Cross being forced to let her enter the enclave. Once inside, she would find her son and give no quarter to those responsible for the kidnapping. In fact, she intended to make sure they ended up wishing they had embraced the demon host rather than letting her through their gates and in amongst them. To her, her enemies were all the same.

❈ ❈

It was a scene from the sickest of imaginations. Not even a priest of Lacrimos at their most inspired could conjure up such an image of horror with which to warn mortals against sin and a lack of faith.

Terrifying creatures copulated with those they also sought to devour or murder. Others danced to the bray and cackle of smaller demons being tortured, while some simply played harmlessly. One particularly ugly brute with tusks at the side of its porcine snout and a thick, hairy hide actually slept undisturbed in the middle of the chaos. A large, flying serpent flapped lazily overhead and began to descend towards the battlements of Holter's Cross, untroubled by the salvos of arrows that were launched at it every few seconds by the defenders. It was bristling with shafts by the time it landed. It lashed back and forth, knocking soldiers to theirs death and crushing others against the stone walkway. There were distant screams of death, and finally hisses of rage from the beast as spears and swords came to bear. At last, the beast was vanquished and its body seemed to collapse in on itself.

'At least six men killed by just that one demon,' Silos Varr observed. 'Imagine the carnage that will result if these creatures manage to organise themselves or become provoked. At the moment, they hardly seem bothered with the fortress. Are we sure we want to do this, milady?'

'We will do this,' Kate said without hesitation. 'My son is in there.'

'Then we should not delay or the men's courage will desert them, let alone my own.'

Kate and her army watched from amongst the trees to either side of the King's Road that led to Holter's Cross. The sight of what lay before them touched on deep ancestral memories, made them recoil and want to run screaming back towards Corinus. Added to that, they'd suffered the blow of their horses rebelling as they'd approached the edge of the trees. Riders had been unable to control their mounts, and even the priests of Shakri had been unable to gentle the panicked animals, most of which had fought loose and gone into full flight. The Memnosians were now without a cavalry, and the army's confidence was shaken.

'Shakri preserve us!' Kate found herself whispering to work her jaw loose. 'You are right, Silos Varr. To delay now will see us dismayed and in full rout before we have made a single charge. We must act before we lose the advantage of surprise. Are the priests of Gart ready?'

'We are, milady,' answered the high priest at her shoulder.

'Then let us pray to the good god of the earth.'

A dozen priests of Gart picked up the prayer started by their high priest and began to chant, their words tumbling louder and louder like a rockslide picking up momentum. The quarter of a mile of ground between the trees and the walls of Holter's Cross began to tremble. Then cracks started to shoot out like lightning through the ground. The world shuddered and then a chasm opened wide, stretching from the feet of the high priest in a straight line towards the enclave. Flames licked up from the depths. Demons, ancient fiends of yore, snarling wights and all manner of blasphemous beast fell shrieking into the earth's maw. Then the high priest brought his hands together and the chasm crashed closed. The ground was whole once more and a clear corridor thirty feet wide now lay before them.

'Forward! At the double!' Silos Varr commanded loudly. 'Priests in the van and to the sides of the column!'

The Memnosian army charged out of the trees, screaming their battle-cry as much in fear as defiance. Some of the demon host turned to watch them with little apparent comprehension; the rest continued to indulge in their vile acts without even noticing the mortals. Those demons that came close out of curiosity found themselves splashed with holy water by priests of Shakri and their flesh set aflame; which then had them roaring in anger, crying like children and laughing insanely. The cacophony began to excite the wider host and an increasing number of burning, ravenous eyes turned towards the mortals who raced for the fortress.

Winged lizards banked towards the army. Priests of Incarnus threw sharp-edged destruction while priests of Shakri forced grasping vines from the ground to snatch the demons out of the air and tear them apart. Black ichor began to rain from the skies. The smell of the demon blood attracted more and more attention, until the will of the host began to coalesce and become one. The voice that boomed from the heavens was the most terrible and soul-withering ever heard in the realm.

'Now let the subjugation, suffering and slaughter begin!'

Kate could not see, could not hear. Her legs buckled and she fell to the ground. She vomited herself inside out and wanted to die.

Somewhere, Silos Varr was shouting. 'Don't stop! Quickly!'

Hands grabbed her roughly and dragged her forward. Her head began to clear and she pushed the support away.

'Hold your formation!' Silos Varr yelled behind her. 'You priests, protect milady!'

'I need no protection,' Kate mumbled and released her crossbow into the face of a lude fury at point blank rage.

The naked wild woman flew backwards and then clambered back to her feet, Kate's bolt sticking out of her face. 'The Green Witch!' she choked, the demons around her echoing and amplifying her voice. 'We know you. We have your child.'

Kate slowed in shock.

'Yesss, that'ss right, we have the boy!' the fury hissed seductively. 'Join usss and he will be yours again. Resist us and dies, his head our trophy and his skin our banner. The Demon-King is in want of a bride and admires the Green Witch.'

'I'm married!' Kate said weakly.

The fury laughed and laughed.

Shut up, shut up! Kate released another bolt and took the possessed woman through the throat, finally silencing her.

'You have shown the wretch a mercy,' Silos Varr observed.

'But perhaps doomed us all.'

The vast demon host reared as one and descended upon the Memnosians.

His old heart close to bursting, Constantus staggered towards the end of the Worm Pass and looked down upon the green hills and valleys of Dur Memnos. The afternoon sun glittered prettily on a lazy and meandering river. It all looked tragically peaceful, idyllic and completely unprepared for the horror about descend upon it. The irony sickened him to his core. He had led an Accritanian army this way a decade or so before, intent upon the destruction of this very kingdom, but had ultimately been thwarted. Now, when the two kingdoms were at peace, he ran before and unwillingly led a malign force that was more than capable of destroying Dur Memnos. How had it come to this? How had the realm become so perverted, so corrupted? Had it always been this way and he just too ignorant, limited and wistful to see it? As the leader of an entire kingdom, surely some of the responsibility was his. He was ready to sacrifice whatever was required to put things right, but he would need to stay alive beyond the next hand of minutes if he and his men were going to be of any use.

With the lord and his family, Constantus and his men had hurriedly left the Ristus estates and headed for the Needle Mountains. With most of the children, women and old people on horseback, they'd made good time and assumed they were relatively safe when they'd made camp. Yet they'd slept within a dreamless void, with only a terrible voice for company, a voice that demanded subjugation, suffering and slaughter. And then half way through the night, a mounted guard who'd been stationed about a mile back down the road had come riding hell for leather into camp and started screaming that the possessed had walked through the night and were minutes behind him.

There'd been a mad scramble, during which they'd lost most of their bedrolls, and then they'd taken to the road once more. The dawn had found them strung out in a long line, all looking haggard and exhausted. The day that followed had been a hellish, waking nightmare, constantly looking back over their shoulders or just concentrating on placing one foot after another without faltering.

Around midday, figures were sighted on the horizon just a few rises behind them. Constantus knew there was no way they would make it to the mountains if they carried on like this. The possessed were close to overtaking the stragglers, and they would soon be amongst the rest of them. They needed to get organised and bunched up if they were going to have any chance of survival.

'Vallus!' Constantus croaked.

The Colonel managed to pick up his pace ever so slightly and join his superior. 'Yes, General?'

'You need to buy us some time.'

Vallus almost looked relieved. 'It has been an honour serving with you, General!'

'Shut up, you idiot! I'm not asking you to sacrifice yourself.'

Vallus looked confused, even disappointed.

'Just listen. Get those people off the horses. Then you and as many men as the horses can carry ride back and make a stand against their front-runners. Hold as long as you can, so that the rest of us can make some good distance towards the Worm Pass, and then ride back as fast as you can.'

'It will be the end of the horses. They cannot take much more.'

Constantus nodded. 'Discard your shields and armour on the way back so they have less weight to carry. No, don't protest. I don't want to hear how the men would prefer to die with their shields on their arms. I'm trying to see to it that as few men have to die as possible. Get me?'

Vallus saluted smartly, his old smile returning. 'Yes, General, sir! You and you, off that horse! Men, to me! We have orders.'

They'd stumbled into the Worm Pass with dozens of the possessed less than a hundred yards behind them. They'd then fought a rearguard retreat for an entire mile, the narrow confines of the pass preventing the steadily increasing numbers of the enemy from overwhelming them. Although the possessed were little more than skin and bone and they hardly shared a weapon between them, their attacks were frenzied in the way of those that had no concern for their own safety, and they only needed to scratch a soldier in order to infect him. And whenever one of the defenders was turned, they would invariably attack their own comrades and often kill or infect several others.

Constantus and Ristus lost several dozen men before the second rank of troops to the rear properly learned to keep a close eye on those fighting in front and to cut them down without hesitation if it appeared there had been even the slightest of physical contacts with the enemy. There was no doubt that in the madness a few innocents were hacked down by their own comrades.

They inched backwards, swapping men as they tired but having to use men again before they'd fully recovered their wind. The defenders began to make more and more mistakes, and at one point it looked like they would break entirely, when there was a sudden and blessed lull. There were distant echoes as more of the possessed began to enter the Worm Pass.

'This is our only chance of getting out of here!' Vallus shouted. 'Every man for himself. Run!'

They raced past the Only Inn, where Constantus remonstrated with Mistress Harcourt and her husband Talon but eventually had to abandon his attempts to persuade them to flee. At last, the remains of the Accritanian army spilled out onto the slopes of the Memnosian side of the Needle Mountains and milled around in panic for some minutes as they assessed who was lost and who was still with them.

'Form up with your sergeants!' Colonel Vallus began shouting once he'd caught his breath. 'Encircle the end of the pass. Civilians carry on into the foothills!'

Constantus pulled his sword from its scabbard and took his place in the front rank. If this was to be their last stand, then he would face it as bravely as the proud men he led. Lord Ristus took his place at his side, his face calm.

'I see that we ultimately fight for the same things, General. Perhaps it doesn't matter who sits the Accritanian throne, as long as they are prepared to fight for such things, eh?'

Constantus smiled. He'd discovered a certain liking for this man, even though they'd always been political enemies. 'Indeed, milord Ristus. It gives us hope that, even if we die here, there might still be a future for our beloved Accritania.'

'That is a good thought. I shall hold it with me. And I would ask a favour of you, General.'

'If it is within my power to grant it, then it will be done.'

'Should you survive, and I not, then look to the welfare of my afflicted wife, try to restore her to herself.'

'I would do the same for anyone, milord Ristus. Be sure I will do whatever I can.'

'I thank you. Then I am content.'

'Here they come!' Vallus shouted hoarsely as wild-eyed, maniacal men, women and children came pouring out of the pass with clawed hands raised.

Constantus heard the rumble of horses – it was said that those who were about to die would sometimes hear the approaching thunder of Shakri's divine battle-steeds. It was a blessing of sorts, for it allowed a man to prepare himself, to make peace with himself and the gods, before the storm and darkness engulfed him. He closed his eyes for a second, raised his sword and then struck his first blow, a grin on his face and a paean in his heart.

A familiar voice rang out: 'By holy Wim's crazed appetite for goats, Constantus, what have you got yourself into now?'

The Scourge! Here? It could not be, surely. His mind must be playing tricks on him, here at the end, recalling memories of better times and friends.

'Lacrimos and Cognis have sent me to save your woebegone Accritanian arse, that or to put it out of its misery. What anti-social creatures are these? Friends and relatives of yours?'

'Possessed… by… some… demon… called… Cholerax!' Constantus called back, blinking and turning his head to the side so that the red spray of a limb he'd just amputated didn't get in his eyes. 'Help?'

'Demons, eh? There's been a sight too many of them around for my taste. I might be able to help you out. Let's see.'

Water sprinkled on the heads of the first rank. What was this? Several of the possessed were also splashed and they stopped in their tracks, bewilderment on their faces and intelligence beginning to return to their eyes. These were promptly torn down by those coming on behind them, but a few more of the possessed were returned to themselves by the contact.

'It's a miracle!' Lord Ristus cried.

'Not really. If more of you Accritanians were to have yourselves properly baptised by a priest of Shakri when you were young, then you wouldn't have half of this trouble with every passing demon. But, no, you've always been far too tolerant of necromancers and so forth.'

'Spare us the sermon, Scourge, it really doesn't suit you!' Constantus panted, shrugging off a spitting, drooling old man and shoving a blade down the throat of the possessed. 'Or are you Her Divine Consort once more?'

'A simple thank you would suffice, Constantus, or a friendly measure of Stangeld brandy from the flask you usually have about your person.'

A half hour later and the dead were clogging up the entrance to the Worm Pass. Now they had been anointed with water blessed by the temple of Shakri, the Accritanian soldiers fought without fear of being possessed themselves and held the vehicles of Cholerax at bay with relative ease.

The Scourge passed the flask of Stangeld brandy back to Constantus. 'I wouldn't bother, it's empty,' he smirked. Then his face became serious: 'And I'm all but out of water too. By the insatiable lust of Shakri, how many of these possessed are there, Constantus?'

Constantus sighed heavily. 'An entire nation, I fear.'

The Scourge was appalled for a long second. 'By the diseased breath of Malastra, there will be no holding them. My friend, for the first time in a long time, I am afraid for the realm.'

Constantus's face couldn't have looked more wearied, pained and broken. 'Surely the gods must take a hand,' he pleaded.

'I do not know what is amiss, but many of the gods are now lost.'

Constantus struggled to hold off the panic clawing at his throat. 'What?' he breathed. 'These things are too much to bear, Scourge. Do not mention them to my men. It will destroy them. Where is Saltar?' he suddenly demanded. 'I cannot believe all is lost if he can lead us. And Kate and Mordius, and even the Chamberlain? They are not trivial in all this, surely!'

Larc now brought Vasha forward, care and worry on his face for the distracted and distressed high priestess, the woman he loved. 'Vasha must speak,' he murmured, to help her enter the conversation with all their attention.

'Saltar is no longer here,' she said unevenly. 'Only moments remain to us now. We must not tarry here or we will lose those last moments for naught.

251

We must head south, for *He* is coming!' Then she shouted hysterically: 'He is terrible!'

Soldiers resting not far away looked up with concern at the sound of her voice. Larc quickly gentled her with reassuring noises and a hug so that she would not cause wider alarm and panic.

'We must march south with all speed,' the Scourge asserted. 'Do not ask why, Constantus, for it is enough that the high priestess of Cognis says it is so.'

'Wait, wait! How can we leave?' Constantus insisted. 'If we withdraw, the possessed will overrun us and the entire north of Dur Memnos.' Then he made a decision. 'We Accritanians will remain here and hold them while you head south. After all, it is we who are responsible for bringing this trouble upon you.'

'Nay, good General, it is not so,' Larc interrupted. 'The demon realm is rising and all mortalkind faces that same threat. We must all share the responsibility and burden for having allowed the Demon-King egress to this realm.'

'Demon-King?' Lord Ristus echoed in a shaky voice. 'None of us has been able to sleep, for a truly dreadful voice haunts us. Is it He?'

The sound of horse hooves echoed off the rocks and they looked down the slope.

'About bloody time!' the Scourge spat.

'Who is it that comes?' Constantus frowned. 'My eyes are blurred.'

'Why, it is Strap… and Lucius!' said Larc with genuine joy.

'Just when I thought things couldn't get any worse!' the Scourge harrumphed. 'Still, perhaps not even the possessed will be able to stand his inane prattle. It might send them all running back where they came from.'

They waited a few minutes as the riders hurriedly ascended.

'Have you brought blessed water?' the Scourge shouted as they approached. 'We have men fighting here who need their blades anointing so they can keep back the demon-possessed.'

'And perhaps my wife could be spared a measure?' Lord Ristus interjected.

'Nice to see you too, Old Hound,' Strap replied as he vaulted from his saddle and ran towards those defending the pass.

The Scourge glared at Lucius as the one-eyed musician clambered down from his mount and unwrapped his greater lute. Strap's tall companion hunched slightly as if he didn't want to be noticed.

'It's good to see you, Lucius,' Constantus offered. 'It has been too long.'

Lucius gave the General a watery smile and picked his way over to where Strap fortified the Accritanian soldiery. The musician began to pluck at his strings to tune them.

'What are you doing, Lucius?' Constantus asked curiously, moving closer.

'He's ever been in want of an audience!' came the Scourge's sour rejoinder.

Lucius struck a gentle, mournful chord and it travelled over the rocks. They seemed to resonate in harmony. Another chord and they began to sing, their voices as haunting as a lost love. It was more than mere acoustics, so much more.

The defenders slowed and, more wondrously, the possessed stilled, as if enchanted. Their heads tilted and a sadness touched their faces.

''Twas my music that caused these people their malady,' Lucius whispered to Strap and Constantus, although all could hear him. 'I pray that there is something I can now do to ease their suffering. I will spell them here with my music as long as I may. It will be some small atonement for the tragedy I have wrought. So go, my friends… and forgive me if your hearts will allow it.'

'Truly, this is the music of the gods,' Lord Ristus murmured. 'I cannot believe the pantheon is entirely lost when I hear such.'

His face an unreadable mask, the Scourge began to issue orders. 'General Constantus, if you will march to the aid of Dur Memnos as friend and ally, then I ask you to gather your men and pretty lord now and take your leave for the south. If you could also see to the safety of the high priestess, her companion and their acolyte, I would consider it a favour. I hope to overtake you on the road soon. There are some final things I must see to here first.'

The General smiled and nodded in understanding and went with the Lord Ristus to marshal the men for their departure. Larc guided Vasha in their wake and took her towards their waiting horses and acolyte. In short order, only the Scourge and Strap remained at the top of the slope, not far from Lucius.

'Scourge,' the younger Guardian said gently. 'You are my commander, but also my friend. It is as friend that I ask you be not uncharitable to Lucius here at this end-point. He has suffered much in ways you and I could never understand. But he has suffered most in his own judgement of himself and *your* judgement of him, for you are a man and friend he has always respected. There is no trace of malice in his heart. You have known him long enough not to dispute this. And he spares these people now where you and I would have ultimately failed. So be not unkind. I ask this as a friend.'

'Thank you, Strap,' the Scourge said quietly. 'I hear your words, be assured. Join the others now.' He turned away from Strap, who moved off towards his horse.

The Scourge stood alone and surveyed the scene of devastation. The dead lay everywhere, some twisted and gruesome, others calm and at peace. The wind moaned in counterpoint to the music playing through the mountains. Ah, but Lucius was in tune with Shakri's nature and creation. He provided vivid accents and phrasing that allowed the Scourge to see the beauty and passion here that he had contrived to miss when Shakri Herself had displayed it to him. *What a fool I've been.*

'Ah, Lucius, I have mistook you,' he said, and the musician was finally able to meet the commander's eyes without fear or trembling. There was only apology and empathy there to see.

'I ask your forgiveness, here in this realm,' the Scourge continued, 'and will ask it of you again when we meet in the next realm.'

Lucius smiled, pure joy in his face.

'How long do you think you can play on?'

'Some hours, I think. Longer, if holy Mellifluer will guide my hands when I weaken. I pray it will be enough for you.'

'Goodbye, my friend, goodbye.'

'Farewell, Guardian. Be well. And god's speed!'

'I will give the cursed Demon-King your regards, fair Lucius, and see him weep for the rest of eternity. You have my vow on that. Until we meet again, good Lucius, until we meet again.'

※ ※

Ja'rahl crouched in the deepest and dankest hold of the flagship. The strong winds and salt of the sea air had dried the wet blood protecting his papery skin in mere seconds, so for the duration of the voyage he'd been forced to stay below decks, within the ship's bowels. Even the light that played across this grey expanse of water and fractured sky seemed to weaken him, penetrating his core and draining him of the life-force he clung to and so jealously guarded.

He'd required an almost constant stream of blood-slaves coming to the hold to maintain his strength. It was a pity he'd been unable to risk bringing one of the Memnosian gods with him: but a ship could never be secure enough to hold a deity; and one getting loose to warn the others would see him fighting the entire pantheon at once. Even worse, he felt weaker the closer the ship got to the cursed lands of the pantheon – lands where Istris and His priesthood were not a defining force.

And so Ja'rahl had crouched in a limnal darkness and misery for long days and nights, feeling sicker and fainter, less a part of existence, than at any other time in all his long centuries. Yet at last they'd arrived and he'd felt tides of power moving back and forth. At one moment his being had waxed stronger, at the next fallen back. Then some sort of breakthrough had happened and he'd shuddered with an orgasm of power, his every fibre enacting a satisfying subjugation, suffering and slaughter of sorts.

Then came the miracle! He sensed the divine presence once more. *At last, Istris wakes! Oh, sweet Lord!* His nausea now gone, he rose and loosened his stiff and ancient limbs. He drank deeply from a nearby bucket of blood to lubricate his throat and then creaked towards the small door that led up and out of the hold.

'Priests, to me!' he gurgled, calling them with his mind more than his voice.

He took to the deck and every Jaffran priest, soldier and sailor fell to their faces, hundreds of them not daring or wanting to look upon the Eternal who defined their lives, dreams and nightmares. One sailor descending from the high rigging fell in his haste and hit the deck with a soft thud. Ja'rahl ignored the ruined sack of blood and bones and turned his malevolent gaze on the small Memnosian port of King's Landing. There appeared to be ships and boats burning, some of them Jaffran.

'Captain, why are we still outside their harbour walls? Divine Istris awakes and His new kingdom must be ready for Him.'

The captain, an old, stocky man with a salt-and-pepper beard shook in terror with his forehead planted hard against the planks of his deck. 'E-Eternal, the Memnosians, in their wickedness, were prepared for our arrival. They say a demonlord fights with them, one they worship as a god, and... and a host of terrible lesser demons.'

The deck on which they stood suddenly heaved beneath their feet. Ja'rahl fell to his knees, feeling the dead flesh squelching and bursting there. He cursed and ordered his priests to lift and protect him.

Deck planks buckled violently towards the other end of the ship.

'Istris is breaking free! Captain, steer straight for the harbour walls. Quickly, you fool!' Ja'rahl screeched, his customary calm and self-possession deserting him. He felt soft tissue tearing within his chest, but did not have time to pay it any mind.

Istris, King of the Jaffran gods, largest and most majestic of the sphinkaes, roared and shook His mighty mane. With a powerful thrust of his hind-quarters, he surged up and out of the wooden ship that had been little more than a floating coffin for him and his kind. He blinked momentarily against the sun and then snatched up a mortal in his jaws. With a snap and crunch, the struggling morsel was gone. Istris swung his large head round and devoured another Jaffran. He swatted another almost casually with his paw, ripping open its chest and filling the air with the pleasing scent of and taste of blood. Ah! Now the others were beginning to wake too.

Ja'rahl was carried forward by his panicking and terrified priests and placed on his ruined knees before the towering sphinx.

'Sweet Lord, it is Ja'rahl, your high priest! We have carried you across the great sea as you have commanded, for *the return* is at hand, just as you said it would be. There lies our enemy, the dark kingdom of Dur Memnos. See! One of their renegade demonlords seeks to defy your will. There, with the womanly hair and wide, red hat and coat! We head straight for him and will make him a meal for you!'

❉ ❉

'Er... Aa, that ship is coming straight for us. And what monster is that at its prow?' rat-boy asked as he dodged a Jaffran's clumsy thrust, and stabbed his blade through the soft underside of his attacker's elbow.

Aa stood poised and waiting. Two Jaffrans slashed at Him while another hung back to follow up on the opening he was sure would appear. The Divine Libertine batted the two swords aside as one and hung His coat out for the third to hack through, which he obligingly did only to find his blade entangled and his head suddenly covered. Aa had reversed out of His jacket to befuddle and ensnare His opponents. He riposted with lightning speed and precision, unencumbered by coat or armour. The three Jaffrans fell dead and the few soldiers left on the harbour wall now hung back, unwilling to engage. They were unaware of the ship's prow bearing down on them.

Aa looked up. 'Oh dear!'

'What do you mean, *Oh dear*?' Orastes asked nervously. 'Pug, what is the matter? Why are you now holding back?'

'I mean that retreat is the better part of valour, live to fight another day, and all that. I mean run! Come on, my brave boys! And you smelly fisher people. Run!'

The sphinx leapt high off the ship and landed on the Jaffran soldiers below, all but killing them. Then He bounded forwards after the fleeing god Aa.

'No, faster than that, Orastes!' Aa tutted. 'Come here!' the god called, put the little warrior under his arm and showed Istris a clean pair of heels.

The Jaffran flagship smashed into the harbour wall with a rending, bone-crunching, teeth-jarring sound. The entire fleet was now moving to follow suit.

'In the wake of your god Istris, you dogs!' screamed an aged devil who glistened with blood from the same prow from which the sphinx had come. 'Priests, I want that demonlord brought to me at once! Soldiers, you have been seriously lacking thus far. If you do not take this town at once, then every one of you will be fed to holy Istris and His court.'

Aa and His companions, the fisher people and the demons commanded by Orastes fled back along the harbour wall toward the dock. Istris was not far behind them, snapping up the imps and spirits who were too small to make sufficient distance to escape. Then the sphinx got amongst some of the exhausted fisher people who lagged behind and began to decapitate them, bite out spines or crush them underfoot.

'Quickly!' rat-boy cried to Distrus.

They rushed past Ninevus, who stood where the harbour wall joined the dock and unusefully waved them on.

'Master, run!' Distrus cried, pulling on the priest's sleeve.

'Leave him!' Aa said with an exasperated shake of His head.

'I can't!' Distrus wailed as rat-boy and a fisherman wrestled the acolyte away.

The sphinx came storming up to Ninevus, who immediately cowered in fear and began to pray. Instead of tearing the mortal to pieces, however, Istris reared back on his hind legs and roared rage and frustration to the sky above.

''Tis a miracle!' an agog fisherman exclaimed.

Istris prowled back and forth across the width of the harbour wall like a beast in a cage. He lunged and swiped at Ninevus, but always stopped short of touching him.

'First rank, fire!' came a command. 'Spears advance and help the priest fall back.'

Arrows peppered the sphinx, not doing any real damage but forcing it to retreat back along the harbour wall.

Orastes, who had now been placed on his own two feet and behind whom a hundred demons clustered for protection, looked round happily at all the Memnosian soldiers who had just arrived on the dockside. 'Where have you all come from?'

The small soldier who'd just given the commands came to attention and saluted Orastes smartly. 'Lieutenant Sotto of the Outdwellers at your command,' he smiled. 'You are Orastes, son of the Green Witch, yes? The Green Witch sent us to see to your safety and return you to her, you see.'

'She did?' Orastes asked, crestfallen. 'She's not mad, is she?' Then he turned to the deity who was all but becoming lost in the press. 'Aa, you said you asked mother if it was alright! You did ask her, didn't you?'

Lots of eyes turned towards the deity and with a sigh He came forwards. 'Well of course I did! You know what mothers are like. They'll always worry anyway.'

A giant Outdweller came to join the small Memnosian commander. 'Sotto, can I go play with the big pussy-cat, can I, Sotto?'

'Maybe later, Dijin. I don't think it's particularly tame. Right, you men! An orderly retreat, at the double, before these Jaffran devils get themselves organised. Through the streets and to the high ground above the town. Move! I'm not going to tell you twice, you godforsaken indolents!'

In the semi-organised flight from King's Landing that followed, Aa drew up alongside Sotto and casually asked: 'Just how angry is Kate, do you think?'

Sotto smiled. 'Oh, you know the Green Witch, holy one! She will be as happy and relieved to see her son again as she will be displeased with those responsible for his disappearance.'

Aa laughed, but the sound was not a happy one. 'Verily, this is what I was afraid of. I knew I shouldn't have let them talk me into any of this!'

Chapter Eleven: And deserve no more

Lebrus had used his longbow to bring down the first Elders that came for them. Then he'd led the Chamberlain, who carried Saltar's body, at a flat run down into the sanctuary of Marsby, knowing that the dead they'd left behind them would buy them the time needed to get to safety.

The Chamberlain had left Saltar's body in Lebrus's stable and then followed him into the main room – the kitchen – of his home. The Chamberlain had bowed smartly and presented himself to the lady of the house, Astraal, who stirred a pot on the stove with one hand while cradling a babe in the crook of her other arm.

Astraal had no smile of welcome for the Chamberlain. 'Husband, what creature is this that you have brought into our home? I do not like the look of it, as ingratiating as it attempts to be. It is not natural in the way of Shakri's creation, that is certain. It is one of Voltar's foul conjurings then?'

The Chamberlain stretched a smile as wide as he was physically able across his face. 'Good woman, you do well not to trust me, hmm? Your senses are unusually keen, yes? I am not originally of this realm, it is true. But I am far older than Voltar, so not of his making, hmm? You may thus be sure that if I had any intent that were not in the interests of this realm, then all would have known about it long before now, particularly beings like the Keepers, hmm?'

The look of distaste on Astraal's face only increased. 'Husband, how can we trust one who twists words and corrupts meaning so? No good can come of one who wefts and weaves truth and reality to the design of its will. Its tongue should be pulled out to safeguard the realm.'

This was not going well, not at all well. The Chamberlain wondered if he'd be better off remaining silent. Or should he attack them? No, the Keepers were too much of an unknown quantity for him to take such a risk. 'I am here to see the witch, hmm? I need a cure for the basilisk venom, to restore the life of the man who will ultimately defeat Voltar and save the realm.'

Astraal considered the Chamberlain in silence for a while. Lebrus shifted nervously, but kept silent. 'Soup?'

The Chamberlain blinked. 'I'm sorry?'

'Do you eat soup?'

He was thrown. What test was this? 'Err... yes,' he replied cautiously.

'Then you cannot be entirely alien to this realm,' Astraal opined. 'You will have soup and then be on your way with the first light. But if you are lying and you do not eat the soup, then your life will be forfeit, agreed?'

This was as far beyond the Chamberlain's experience as anything in Shakri's realm ever had been. How could his life be forfeit for not eating some peasant's soup? What magic was being used here? He couldn't sense or fathom it. Did it lay in just the words of his agreeing to it? Was he actually binding and bespelling himself? He was terrified. He was suspicious. He felt exposed. Never had he felt at such a disadvantage when dealing with a mortal being of Shakri's creation.

'I-I agree,' he stuttered, suddenly feeling like he'd lost all ability to read the Pattern. The disorientation he suffered was so bad he even wondered if he knew himself anymore. What had she done to him?

Once they were seated, Astraal placed earthen bowls in front of each of them and then spooned a helping of vegetable broth for each of them out of the pot on the stove. Lebrus and Astraal watched the Chamberlain as he raised a spoon towards his mouth. It suddenly occurred to him that the woman might have put something in the soup! His hand shook violently.

'It will make you stronger,' Astraal promised.

Close to tears, the Chamberlain sipped the soup and swallowed. He waited. Nothing happened.

'Not enough salt?' Astraal asked with her first smile since the Chamberlain had arrived. 'It's hard to get it here in Marsby. I complain to Lebrus that he should make more effort to trade with the other communities, but there's always some reason why he can't.'

'Beloved, nothing can improve on your cooking,' the bear growled affectionately.

Mystified, the Chamberlain ate his soup in silence while the couple carried on with their domestic banter. They must have played out a similar conversation on countless occasions in the past, and no doubt always with the same degree of enthusiasm, enjoyment and love. Why did they do it? What made it necessary? What did it do for them? It was a repetition of sorts, although with slight variation and development each time. In the same way, mortals had children who were similar to their parents, with slight variation and development with each generation.

Yes, he began to glimpse it now. Just as the cycle of birth and death allowed Shakri's paradoxical creation to self-propagate and be self-sustaining, there was a sort of magic in the day-to-day repetition of feelings and ideas. It confirmed and consolidated meaning, identity and reality. Similarly, the apocalypse and salvation represented by the coming of Voltar, Nylchros and the others in the future were also inevitable if the realm was to have consequence. Life and death, day and night, light and dark, destruction and civilization, repetition and difference. There *was* a magic of sorts at work here in the home of Lebrus and Astraal then, but one so subtle and implicit that it was all but invisible and all but impossible to detect. It seemed that the mortals of Shakri's realm were far more magical than he'd ever suspected. Each of them had magic that could be commanded, did they but know it.

The trap that was the Chamberlain's mind realised that here was a key to cosmic power. He began to plot and scheme. If he could but master this magic and find a way to wrest it from the mortals of Shakri's realm, then surely there would be none who could ever stand against him.

'May I have some more soup?' he asked hungrily.

❈ ❈

The swamp around Marsby was an oozing, sucking, dripping thing. It seemed to drain life more than support it. Skeletal trees lay broken and half-submerged on the slightly higher areas of ground, their roots having become so waterlogged that they'd rotted. Thick reeds clogged and strangled the deeper channels; halting the flow of water and causing it to stagnate; thereby killing the eyeless fish and monopods that had once fed the people of Marsby; and even starving the fearsome snaggle-toothed lizards that had once roamed the area. There wasn't even much for flies and mosquitoes to live off, which in turn meant there were precious few spiders, birds or water rats. It seemed and felt to the Chamberlain that the swamp was a creeping blight and that he watched Shakri's creation dying before his very eyes. Such had been the state of the realm under Voltar's reign.

Noxious fumes were released every time he pulled one of his feet free of the clutching mud and placed it down again. The marsh gas made him feel faint and had a strange effect on his thoughts. He fancied he walked across a bloated and decaying corpse the size of the realm. His limbs began to feel heavy, and his movement sluggish.

Curse this place, but it threatened to overwhelm him too! The Chamberlain fumbled one of his special needles from the seam of his tunic and injected himself with a stimulant. He blinked his eyes wide and surged forwards, knowing he needed to make as much distance as he could before the drug was no longer effective.

He'd almost forgotten – to his cost – just how dangerous the swamp witch of Marsby was. Of course, the lapse wasn't simply down to his memory, however; for the witch was so powerful that – even trapped at the centre of this murderous place – she managed to cast an insidious influence across the whole region. It was by such means that she inexorably drew Elders towards her home, so that she could feast on them and continue to survive.

The Chamberlain shrugged his shoulders slightly, to rebalance Saltar's stiff body, which was laid across the back of his neck like a staff, and pushed on. He began to spy old bones everywhere and knew he was getting closer to her lair. He wondered with some anxiety what sort of reception he'd get from the witch, whether she'd be angry he'd stolen from her millennia ago and run off. He'd been young and foolish, but surely the hag hadn't had a heart to be broken… had she? What was it mortals said about *a woman scorned*? He shook his head. The hag was no woman in any meaningful sense. Then again, she was a spiteful and vengeful being, as he recalled.

Refusing to let his steps slow, he came to the fence of bones that marked the edge of her territory and prison. And there was the terrible house of skulls in which she lurked. Several thousand empty eye sockets watched him and his skin prickled. She knew he was here, but still did not show herself. She waited to catch him off-guard, no doubt, and had probably placed wards and webs everywhere. She should know better than to try and catch a spider in such a manner.

His nerves jangling, the Chamberlain edged towards the gap in the long fence of bones. He constantly sensed and checked for any sign that he was about to trigger a snare or trap, ready to leap back in the instant. He eased himself and Saltar through the fence and looked up towards the gruesome house and its shadowed windows and doorway. Did he see something move within? He waited for long moments, hardly daring to breathe. She was not going to come to him, he could tell. He forced himself to take a small step forward. And another. He had been wrong to treat her in the way he had. He saw that now.

'Beloved, I am sorry, hmm?' he called, his voice and words sounding feeble and thin.

His chest hurt and the roots of his hair pained him. His teeth felt like they were being prised out of his jaw and he tasted blood on his gums.

Suddenly she hunkered in the doorway at the top of the path and he gulped. She wore a glamour, whether to beguile him, whether because of vanity or because she felt he had no right to look upon her, he was not sure. Perhaps it was all those things. Whatever it was, he knew better than to use his own magic to pierce the glamour. He was content to look upon the spiderlike creature she presented to him, perhaps even excited by the image. He knew that beneath she was all spoilt fruit, putrid mud, fish heads, sticks and beetles, anything that could be gleaned, lured or stolen from the swamp and fashioned by magic to give her life-force a vessel.

She belched like a toad and laughed. 'And so you are forced to return! Is that a present you bring me?'

'Nay, beloved!' he shrugged awkwardly. 'His flesh is poisoned, yes? You would not be able to stomach it, hmm?'

'Well, come closer. I won't eat you, you know. You're quite unpalatable, are you not? In fact, you're probably the most poisonous being in this realm. What present did you bring me then?'

'I... er... have nothing with which to... er...'

'Make amends?' she buzzed angrily. 'You are a fool and a betrayer! Far less clever than you think yourself. Far, far less. Less than you could have been and less than you will ever be. And you have done it to yourself. Ultimately, you have fooled and betrayed yourself, for your character had played itself out and created its reality and end. It gives me some satisfaction to know it.'

Her words troubled him like gnats, mosquitoes and hornets. Bit him, stung him. What did she mean? 'Beloved, do you remember you had a measure of basilisk venom, hmm? Do you have the antidote? I need to save this being here, so that he can save the realm.'

The witch laughed so hard with contempt for him that her glamour failed and he saw cracks appear in her skin. 'Still you do not see, you pitiful creature. You have always been so arrogant in your ignorance. I deliberately placed the basilisk venom within your reach all that time ago. It was a test to see if you stayed with me out of a genuine desire for my company or in order to steal my secrets. Furthermore, I'd also been hoping you would take the venom out into Shakri's realm on my behalf.'

The Chamberlain couldn't help asking the question, but already knew he didn't want the answer. 'What? W-Why did you want me to take the venom out into the realm? For what possible... unless...?'

The witch cackled. 'Yes, my dear, simple creature. I wanted you to take it out into that realm in order to use it. And, of course, you *have* used it, haven't you? Why else would you have taken it if it wasn't to use it? Why else would you now be here asking for an antidote? As soon as you took the venom, I knew you would either die or be forced to return here one day. Do you not see you have ensnared yourself, dearest? And that you will never be free of me until I will it so? And I will *not* will it so until *I* am free.

'Trapped here, there was no way I could use the venom in the wider realm myself. The substance that had the potential to see me freed was similarly trapped and kept impotent. But then you came along.'

'Beloved, how will it see you freed, hmm?'

'Why, it will destroy all life in Shakri's realm. The pantheon will thus fall and I will be free. Come now, dearest, you should know there is no antidote to basilisk venom. It is inimical in this realm. It cannot be resisted by any mortal of Shakri's making. It is always lethal, *always*. Better, its potency never fades. It will kill one mortal and then wait for another to touch that body, kill them, and so on. Once released into Shakri's realm, the venom should see a majority of mortals dead in a matter of weeks.'

If he'd worshipped gods, the Chamberlain would have offered any number of prayers at this point. What had he done! The four Wardens had been killed by the venom, and one of them had then been eaten by Elders, who were now sure to die in turn. Would it end there or had he just seen to it that all life in Shakri's realm would soon cease? As corrupt and polluting as he knew the creature before him to be, he still found it incredible that she would happily bring about the end of the entire realm and all its beings in order to secure her own freedom. No wonder he'd heard of her referred to as the Ungod on occasion. 'There is no antidote, beloved, hmm? How is it I have become inured to the poison then? Is it because my origin lies beyond this realm?'

The animated bundle of sticks, clay and decaying blossoms shrugged carelessly. 'No doubt. Besides, there is already something poisonous about you, at the core of your being. I would have been able to feed off you in the past otherwise. Something of you shares its nature with the basilisk venom, I suspect. I'm surprised you yourself haven't destroyed this realm before now. Still, you've finally done so, now that you have used the venom. I wonder: how does it feel to be responsible for destroying an entire realm, dearest?'

She was right. He was as bad as she was. He should have known better than to use the basilisk venom, but it had always been in his nature to put his own selfish plans and desires first. Perhaps he and the witch deserved each other then. Should he stay here with her forever more? It would mean the venom he and Saltar carried within them would once more be trapped here. And as long as none came across the bodies of the dead Elders and interfered with them, then the venom wouldn't spread any further... or would it? Maggots, flies and small forest creatures would inevitably feed and carry the venom beyond this region, unless they died almost immediately. Even then, more would feed on them, and more on them. The death would grow slowly like a canker across the land. It might not happen in the few weeks the witch asserted, but after a few months, a few years...? Then his heart leapt as he realised that in a few months from now, Voltar would have ended nearly all life in this realm anyway. Balthagar, or Saltar as he preferred to be called, would be facing and defeating the tyrant in his throne room, and then recreating the world anew! The world would be remade based on its original, life-affirming design, no trace of a spreading venom within it.

The Chamberlain became giddy with relief that he wouldn't now be responsible for the extinction of every species and race of life, for the consequent collapse of the realm of the dead and the eventual deicide of the pantheon. More than that, it gave him great and malicious satisfaction that he would not end up allowing the Ungod her freedom. He smiled broadly. 'Beloved, it gives me joy beyond description to be responsible for the destruction of this realm if it gives you your freedom.'

Her mollusc eyes widened and she moistened her tree-bark lips with mucus. 'It gives me pleasure to hear you say such, dearest, although I can hardly believe it. I should be angry at how you once treated me, but it is true you have ultimately freed me. Perhaps I should now be grateful for that. Have you seen the error of your ways, dearest? Do you think you have been punished enough? Shall we start a new life together, a life that will see us together for the rest of eternity?'

'Beloved!' the Chamberlain declared, apparently overcome with emotion, and took her in his arms. He steeled himself and planted a kiss on her rough lips, praying that she was not inured to basilisk venom herself and that he had just given her the kiss of death.

How long before he would know if he had succeeded? There was little point in waiting anyway, for if this didn't work he would be unlikely to be able to defeat the witch by any other means in her own home. There was no point wasting any more time here – he needed to return to the future version of Dur Memnos as quickly as possible, before anyone found his body in the tower of the White Sorceress, touched his skin and thereby began the spread of the basilisk venom for a second time.

The Chamberlain sighed. 'Ah, beloved, you do not know how long I have dreamed of this, hmm? I knew you would be angry with me, and you were right to be, but therefore I feared to return to beg your forgiveness, yes?'

'So it was not need for the antidote alone that brought you here?' she hummed suspiciously.

'Nay, beloved, never! To prove my good faith, I have now thought of a present I wish to bring you. I will not be gone long. I will also take this dead mortal's body with me so that its basilisk venom can be spread more quickly in the realm beyond, you can be freed all the sooner and we can be together forever.'

He gently released her, hefted Saltar's body up and across his shoulders once more and then moved back through the bone fence.

'Hurry back!' she called.

The Chamberlain moved deeper into the swamp, praying he would never have the misfortune to meet the despicable Ungod again. He had singularly failed to discover an antidote for the basilisk venom, precisely because there was no such thing as an antidote. However, he knew more now than he had before, including the fact he needed to get back to the right version of Dur Memnos without delay. With luck, he'd return before his body was discovered. The alternative didn't bear thinking about. He suspected Saltar's body in the correct Dur Memnos wasn't actually tainted with basilisk venom, since it was only in the Prison of All Eternity that the Battle-Leader and Chamberlain had come into contact, but there was no doubt Balthagar's essence had been touched by it. The Chamberlain had no idea how to go about saving Balthagar-come-Saltar, but decided he could only deal with one problem at a time. As long as he worked something out before another threat like those posed by Voltar and Nylchros came along, then all would be well.

He found a relatively dry area of matted reeds and lowered Saltar's body. He pulled a small, concealed knife out of his boot and sliced Saltar's wrists open with deep, long cuts. Then the Chamberlain turned the knife on himself. It was the first time he'd done anything like this to himself and had to fight against his every instinct for survival. His hands shook and he botched the job slightly, but soon his blood was running down to the water with Saltar's. He lay back, closed his eyes and floated away.

※ ※

A rat squeaked in his ear and the Chamberlain's eyes snapped open. He sprang to his feet, instantly alert for any sign of the Grim. The infinite corridors of the Prison of All Eternity stretched with an echoing silence in all directions. Saltar's inert body lay nearby, his skin as white as marble.

'Thank you, Samuel, hmm?' the Chamberlain bowed to the lesser god. 'You have our gratitude, yes? One day, we will look to demonstrate that gratitude through actions and favours rather than words, hmm? Until such time, might we prevail on you to show us to the correct trapdoor this time?'

The rodent sat back on its haunches and chittered in what appeared to be an angry manner. It certainly showed its teeth and spat.

'We apologise!' the Chamberlain hurried to reply. 'No offence or criticism was intended, hmm? We do not have a proper understanding of this place. We are less than rats, that is clear, yes? It could well be that the trapdoor you chose for us last time will prove to be our salvation, but we cannot know that, hmm? Forgive us our ignorance.'

The rat spat one last time and led the way to a trapdoor with a telltale crack in the ceiling above it. The Chamberlain yanked on the pull-ring and opened the way back to the version of Shakri's realm to which he felt he belonged. With his foot, he pitched Saltar's body into the dark. Then he saluted Samuel and threw himself off the edge of eternity.

※ ※

Saltar had been dead many times before, but he had no memory of it ever having been like this. He'd been hacked to pieces and burnt, pierced through the chest by a spear, sliced in two by a scythe, crushed to a pulp and caged, thrown into chasms, buried amongst the roots of the earth, plunged into a volcano's heart and all manner of unpleasant endings beside. Death to him had always been synonymous with pain and being unmade, but here was something different. Maybe this wasn't death then, or, if it was, nothing he'd experienced before had really been death.

What he experienced now was a *feeling* as much as anything else, a feeling of floating, of being weightless. He didn't know if his experience was something he partly saw or whether it was all perceived in his mind's eye; and perhaps it didn't matter. He felt carried along by a river. It could have been the poison that carried him so gently. A river of poison. He wondered where it took him, whether it was some place bad, perhaps somewhere just different... or simply no place at all. Good or bad, he feared he would not be able to return, feared that Shakri's realm would now be left to fend for itself, that there would be no one there to look after his darling Kate, their sweet son Orastes and his dear friend Mordius.

He lost his sense of physical self, which wasn't so surprising given the numbing effects of the basilisk venom and the way he was floating away. At least his sense of self had survived without its physical definition – since he'd always feared he'd begin to dissipate without some sort of anchor in either of the realms of Shakri or Lacrimos. There was more to him than just a mound of heavy, lumpen and quick-to-spoil flesh then. It was a relief to him in many ways. Still, the floating sensation was beginning to lull him and make him feel sleepy. What if he never woke again? That made him panic a bit and he tried to struggle against the flow.

Saltar raised his head out of the river of poison and looked at the shadowy banks some distance from him to either side. Whether he saw or felt his surroundings, whether they were real in the way of Shakri's realm or not, he didn't care. He simply needed a narrative within which he could survive, respond and perhaps make progress in freeing himself. He was caught in the fastest flowing part of the river, he realised, probably not the best place to be if he wanted to be able to control his travel and avoid the jagged rocks and huge waterfall that no doubt loomed ahead.

Numb with the cold as he was, he could do little more than angle his body slightly so that he lay across the current and slowly got dragged out to the side, where there were swirling pools and dead areas of water. His head bumped against something, and again. It hurt like crazy, which was perhaps a good sign. It was probably a sharp rock. If such a stimulus didn't create the wherewithal in him to move, then his brains would be bashed in and that would be the end of it. So he would win either way... or lose, depending on how you looked at it. The rock dented his skull again, this time in a slightly different place, and it caused his entire body to spasm in an autonomic reflex. Synapses were triggered and more feeling returned. He began to thrash about.

He flopped onto the bank like a fish that has stranded itself with an ill-timed jump and is too exhausted to do anything more about its predicament than wait for death. And so he waited, poison tugging at his lower legs because they remained in the river.

He had no idea how long he lay there, how fast or slow his experience of everything had become, or the relative speed of his thoughts. At some point, he cranked himself up and tottered in amongst the evenly spaced and apparently uniform trees along the bank. Their vaulted branches supported a flat and unilluminating sky above. It was all reminiscent of the endless pillars in the Prison of All Eternity. He wondered if terrible creatures like the Grim hunted these lifeless forests or whether he was completely alone, trapped in this strange hinterland between realms, or within his own mind.

Saltar realised he was lost. There was no way of telling in which direction the river of poison now lay, no sound or smell he could detect. He extended his senses as far as he could, but encountered not the briefest glimmer of life-force. In fact, when he examined himself, he detected nothing either. Was this the last-gasp, haunting image that was all his ravaged mind and body could create for him here at the end? Was this his dying moment – just an empty and enfeebled impression of the individuality and therefore ultimate isolation of spirit and consciousness? Where were the gods with all their promises of a rich after-life? He would even welcome the Grim right now, rather than be left like this. Perhaps he should have stayed in the river after all. Sleepiness crept over him again, so he forced himself to walk farther, just to stay awake, perhaps to extend his final, lingering moment.

'Hello!' he called desperately. 'Is there anyone there? Kate, can you hear me? Orastes, are you there? Mordius, now would be a good time to forget that necromancy is forbidden! You've done it before. Chamberlain? I fear something's gone wrong. There are no more moments, no more grains of sand in the hour-glass, no more last reprieves and resurrections, no more irreducibles.'

Nothing came back to him, no mournful wind, no growl of danger, no cry for help, no sound of battle, no death anthem, no prayer, nothing. He stopped and sat down with his back against one of the countless, identical trees. His eyelids began to droop. It would be good to rest at last, after so long. Just how long had it been? Thousands and thousands of years. Faces floated to the surface of his memory, some he recognised, some he half remembered and some that he could not say he'd seen before. Some were human and others were not. Mortals, gods, demons, other beings, he'd seen them all in his time. Feeling, beauty, the divine and the defiant, and every aspect of faith, belief and philosophy. The only gap or curiosity left lay around the demons, where there was still something he could not quite grasp. What a troublesome race they were, had always been! How was it that they could seem so familiar and yet so twistedly *other* and unknown? They intruded, disrupted and corrupted where otherwise there would have been absolute cosmic harmony between the gods and their mortals, an eternal and immortal continuation, an unvarying, soulless continuation that was like the forest in which Saltar now found himself. No, the demons would not be quelled. There was something *necessary* about them that refused it, just as the Scourge challenged the pantheon, as Saltar fought the aspiring omnipotence of the likes of Voltar and Nylchros, just as the free will of mortalkind resisted – and often greatly annoyed – all those who sought to rule.

As if in answer to him, a pure voice of chaos shattered the sky: 'Now let the subjugation, suffering and slaughter begin!'

Trees were blown over, torn out by the roots, vast swathes of the continuum annihilated. Saltar tumbled over and over until he was wedged into a forked branch and held in place against the tumult. He shook his head and stood up, feeling much better. It was like someone had slapped his face to bring him round. The onslaught had actually been bracing. It had put a new strength into him, added to him somehow. Yes, he was more now than he had been before.

The part of him that had always been closed off and denied him was now all but within reach. He'd been partially restored by… the Relic, was it? Did that make sense? It was something to do with demonkind apparently. He felt like he really knew himself for the first time in eons. He'd been blindfolded but now he could see. His ears had been stoppered and his hearing muffled but at last he could make sense of the noise around him. He'd slept for so long, but now he was waking up, at last free of his troubling dreams.

⁂

His terror absolute, Jack quailed before the majesty of the Demon-King and his shifting court of hulking archdemons. As only a demon of the fourth sphere, Jack could not hope to last any longer than it took him to apologise for not having more meat on his bones and for being a disappointing snack at best.

Jack wanted to hide more than anything else at that moment, but one could not hide from the superior knowledge of the higher spheres, and any attempt to do so would only excite their appetites. If only the witch would distract them. He cringed and cowered within Mordius, desperately wishing he was somewhere else.

On the back foot, Jack was suddenly shoved aside and the psychic being that was Mordius reclaimed something of his natural place. Jack scrambled to fight back before he could be completely expelled from the magician's body.

Mordius, wait! Jack thought frantically. *See what confronts us! Neither of us can survive this alone. Wait!*

Thief! Get out! Begone!

I cannot! Mordius, please! You do not know what it is like to live like this, how terrible it is to be a demon, hunted for food in your own realm and reviled and persecuted in Shakri's realm. I want to be more, you know that! I helped you topple the Brethren, did I not?

You consigned me to the terrible darkness, you liar! If I hadn't caught you unprepared just then, you would never have let me out, never! You are an evil and selfish creature unworthy of any pity. In fact, you exploit the pity of others and sneer at them for weakness. Oh, what a fool I have been always to try and see the good in others, and in a demon of all things! Why didn't I listen to the Scourge from the beginning? Was I temporarily mad, influenced by Wim's divine will, Him you profess to worship, or had you placed a demonic charm on me? Now, once and for all, get out! I reject you with every fibre of my being. I pray to Shakri that She will see you gone, for you have no right to this body or Her divine spark! Begone succubus!

It felt like the skin was being pulled from around his eye sockets, his lips pulled back and torn away. *Mordius, no! You will kill us both! I did not know that you would be consigned to darkness. I thought you would be a silent watcher. I have hid nothing from you, and sought to show you how I have manipulated this awful witch. At the same time, I have hidden you from her and kept you safe. More than anything, she wishes to suck the soul out of you, from the marrow of your bones, you know that is true. I have always been slippery when it comes to the truth, Mordius, I know, but it is not in my nature to be completely dishonest. It is impossible for me. You must hear the truth, even if it is just partial, in what I say. And I ask you to be as honest with me when I ask you this final question: if you were in my position, would you not have done much as I have done?*

I would – I would... not behave as a demon. I would not be slippery with the truth. I would not –'

Really, Mordius, would you not? You are a necromancer, are you not, a breaker of the natural laws of both Shakri and Lacrimos? Even when you knew of the damage your magic did to the balance, you still raised Strap, did you not? In possessing a body and animating it with my will, do I not do the same as you? Do not necromancers exert their will on and through the bodies of those they possess? Mordius, you are *a demon, but you are not as honest as I am when it comes to admitting it.*

Mordius spluttered in outrage. *You fork-tongued serpent! Perverter of truth! Corruptor!*

'I know you!' boomed the Demon-King, shaking the mountains, drawing lightning down from the clouds and causing every creature for miles around to cower in fear for its small, precious life.

The two entities within the body of Mordius lost control of the body's bladder at the same time. Mordius whimpered, while Jack just about managed to squeak a response: 'Dread sire, it is I, Jack O'Nine Blades, your faithful servant who opened the gateway to the demon realm! I bring you this most powerful being who has until recently been cruelly imprisoned by the cursed pantheon. She wishes to be your b-b-b-b…'

'Bride!' shouted the witch with a stamp of her foot and her fists on her waist.

The Demon-King ignored her. 'Jack, yes, I remember. And the body you occupy is also known to me. Why, it is little Mordius, the cowardly magician.'

'I brought him here!' the witch shouted up at the Demon-King, who stood thirty feet tall. 'I command the magician and have bound the demon to my will. The necromancer can give you command of the dead… if I choose to allow it. But I will have my price, Demon-King.'

The Demon-King turned his bloodied gaze upon the witch, the mosses and scraggly grass around her withering in an instant. Her girlish face suddenly looked older. He smiled knowingly and looked almost human. He rolled his head around on his corded neck, his long, spiral horns slashing and stabbing the sky, and his wide nostrils releasing smoke while he flexed his chiselled, naked chest. 'So you presume to bind one of my subjects and then offer him up as your dowry. Insult and injury. A clumsy overture, more blackmail than proposal of marriage, is it not, small being?'

An archdemon laughed mockingly at the witch until the Demon-King's tail casually flicked out to snap its head back and break its neck. But the witch was not about to be cowed by vain displays of strength and unhesitating cruelty. Quite the opposite. If anything, she was aroused by the things he did to impress her.

She slowly licked her lips with her tongue. 'By what measure do you call me small? Test me and you will find me as much as you can handle. I know the pantheon of this realm far better than they would like, for I am their Ungod. Now that I have won free of my imprisonment, I will see them destroyed or moulded in my image. You will struggle against the realm and power of Lacrimos unless I command Mordius to aid you. I will struggle against the realm and power of Shakri, however, unless I have your army behind me. Together, none can stand against us. If you will not acknowledge me as Demon-Queen, perhaps I will accept you as my Prince Consort… or chamber boy or bed slave.'

The Demon-King laughed, but the way his tail lashed forbade any of those present to echo him. 'Your thinking is so limited and simplistic, it is laughable. I have no need of this mortal, and therefore inconsequential, magician to conquer the realm of the dead. Once Shakri's realm falls, then so will the balance and so will Lacrimos. You offer me nothing, witch. You seek to create an ultimatum so that I must accept your will. It is nothing more than the noise and trickery, distraction and slight of hand, one would expect of a fairground conjuror who entertains children. Enough of this sideshow now! The Demon-King shares his rule with no one. Servants, bring me my cerberus and we will progress towards the throne of the mortal realm.'

'Wait!' the witch demanded. 'Such a throne is not easily taken. The Builder is formidable, I have heard. Yet he has some excessive affection for this magician, which will be his weakness. With my aid, you will have an advantage. Otherwise, as many as you have brought with you, your power will dissipate quickly once the realm rallies against you. Accept this offer now or my price will be far higher in the future. Perhaps I will not even need to make you an offer in the future.'

On his cloven hooves, the Demon-King swept past her and knocked her to the dusty ground. She coughed and spluttered, tears of anger and frustration in her eyes. He thumped the most aggressive head of his canine mount on the nose and then vaulted onto its back. The Demon-King gave the witch one final look, adding another ten years to her age. 'Now you seek to snare me with fantastical visions and fears. We number in the millions compared to the paltry thousands of this realm's mortal population. The Builder effectively leads no one. He will bend his knee along with the realm's pitiful pantheon, if I even allow them to exist that long. Should I run out of amusement, I will then turn my attention to you. You will wish I had not, for I will brutally take whatever I want from you. My archdemons will bear you, the magician and the animee along in our wake. If you do not do precisely as I command, and without hesitation, then I will allow my archdemons to take their pleasure of you until you are unmade by it. And before you are permitted to end, you will thank me for the lesson and wisdom I have allowed you. The philosophy of the Nihil is thus supreme.'

※ ※

It was like fighting through madness, through every nightmare and irrational thought she'd ever had. A sick mind had been overlaid on Shakri's realm and mortalkind was now forced to become a part of it or accept extinction. Perhaps she'd finally gone mad with grief at the loss of her son and husband, and this torment was all in her head. In some ways, she hoped she was mad, for otherwise the reality of it would surely be more than any of the mortals of Shakri's realm could bear. It would be the end.

The dark host of creatures from Memnosian myth had descended hungrily on Kate's army, and would have devoured every last human within a hand of minutes if the priests of Shakri had not used their entire supply of temple-blessed water. Then Ikthaeon's priests had attempted to use their knowledge of beastlore to bring the creatures under their sway, but they only had success in one or two instances, for the host was frenzied and beyond taming. They were so rabid that, even if they had once been a part of Shakri's nature, they now rejected their creator and were a danger to themselves and every other living thing. They fought each other to have the chance to claim the flesh of the humans.

Ikthaeon gasped in horror and pointed a shaking finger at the dark, antlered figure who stalked through the host and constantly increased their bloodlust wherever he passed. Beastmen who couldn't get through the press to reach the humans began to chew off their own limbs.

'What is it, priest?' Silos Varr demanded urgently as he put his shoulder behind his shield and slammed its boss into the face of a leaping warg. Then he rammed his shield downwards, its sharp metal rim all but decapitating the beast.

'It cannot be, but I see it with my own eyes. The feral god that the savage tribes of the wilderness worshipped in ages past! The corruptor of Shakri's order! Where the Mother is growth, abundance and renewal, he of the unspeakable name takes and takes until there is nothing left, until the cycle of life is broken forever. Do not mistake me. He is not a predator who hunts so that he may survive – he simply kills for the joy of it. The feral god is the antithesis of civilization. It is no wonder that our cavalry could not hold their own mounts and that my priests were unable to command these possessed and perverted forms of Shakri's nature. The goddess is love and life, but he is more than hate and death. He is something far, far worse. He is extinction.'

'Great!' Silos Varr responded. 'Well, Shakri is his nemesis as much as he is Hers, yes? So do something, High Priest Ikthaeon! And do it quickly, for all our sakes!'

Trembling, Ikthaeon began to chant the most powerful magic he knew. It was a spell he'd never dared cast before so dangerous was it for the wielder, the being at whom it was being directed and just about every living thing for miles around. The feral god raised his head and the smoking, red coals of his eyes met the priest's. Ikthaeon was caught up in the mad gyre of the god's influences. He cried out and fell away.

Seeing their high priest go down, the other priests of Shakri lost confidence and co-ordination. Only a dozen or so of them had been brought from Corinus with Ikthaeon, hardly enough to defend the several thousand Memnosian troops effectively, and certainly not enough to keep back the hundreds of thousands on each side.

'Keep moving forward!' Kate yelled. 'Sister Spike, we need your priests to keep our flanks now, not just as the fist at the front!'

'We will lose momentum going forward!' the High Priestess of Incarnus shouted back.

'That won't matter if we are overrun and they get amongst us. I am not making a request, Sister Spike. I am ordering as beloved of Incarnus.'

Sister Spike scowled but gave a sharp nod and then detailed some of her warrior-priests out to the flanks. The priests wore armour made of overlapping metal leaves, each leaf inscribed with a rune painted in the priest's own blood. Savage blows from the enemy host deflected away harmlessly, stones and missiles failed to penetrate and grasping hands were consumed by holy fire. The priests launched their quarrels, knives, axes and throwing stars and scythed down hundreds of living nightmares to either side. The warriors danced back and forth with long blades, bladed poles, maces, flails and hammers. Where a priest of Incarnus looked over-matched or daunted by a troll or ogre, a priest of Gart would liquefy the ground beneath the enemy and trap them at the ankles so that they became easy targets.

Insane and careless of life though the enemy host was, it actually seemed to retreat a step in the face of the merciless priests of Incarnus. Then the feral god blew a great, winding horn and roared his servants forward as one. The priests of Incarnus were pushed back by sheer weight of numbers and were no longer allowed the freedom of movement they required to remain effective. They were crushed against the body of Memnosian soldiers, immobilised and then devoured face-first.

'Close up!' Silos Varr hollered. 'Form a shield wall! Close up there! Men in the middle, watch for any gaps. Keep your feet under you or you will be trodden under! Keep moving forward in step!'

Even so, the forward progress of the Memnosians began to slow and they were sorely pressed on both sides and to the rear. A Memnosian solider might cut down five or six of the leering enemy before being overwhelmed, but that would still see the humans finished without any significant loss to the overall size of the enemy host. And the humans were becoming exhausted.

'Keep moving forward!' Silos Varr urged. 'If we stop, we are surrounded and we die. None here fear death, but will you have it said you did not give a good accounting of yourselves? The Accritanians will laugh to hear it told!'

'Stand aside!' whispered a voice that made them all shiver.

The High Priestess of Lacrimos swept forward and cast a death spell ahead of the Memnosian force. Black tendrils of power curled from her fingertips and created a miasma and then a dark pall across the battlefield. The darkness strangled and asphyxiated the enemy; pushed down their throats to choke them and up through nostrils to reach and crush brains; and applied pressure to rupture ears and burst eardrums. The howls of agony were a torture to hear, and more than one soldier sheathed his weapon to stop his ears.

'You are undeserving of the life allowed you,' the priestess murmured. 'All must bow to my master's divine judgement.'

The feral god came charging out of the dark miasma with antlers lowered. His rack speared through the priestess's body in multiple places; through neck to shower the scene with blood; through abdomen, from which a milky substance leaked; and through bowel, releasing steaming urine. He pulled his bullish neck back up to call his victory and her body was raised aloft, where its own weight impaled it further. Then she was dashed back to the ground and stamped upon and gored until her form was an unrecognisable mush.

Kate released a bolt and it punched into the feral god's skull between his eyes. But the thickness of the bone he had there prevented her from killing him. He turned magma-filled eyes towards her scraped the ground with a hoof-like foot. A sasquatch started to lumber towards Kate, but an aggressive command from the feral god pulled it up short. She belonged to him.

Seeing the god was about to charge and that she would not have enough time to reload her crossbow, she threw it aside, picked up a shield near her and pulled the longsword she wore across her back.

'I am with you,' Sister Spike said.

'Come on then!' Kate urged. 'What do you want, an invitation, you ugly, cow-rutting turd-eater!'

The feral god rushed her and bellowed its apocalyptic joy. Kate crouched behind her shield and extended her sword so that the god would run onto it and impale himself.

'No!' Sister Spike cried and barged Kate aside. 'You may skewer him, but he will trample you – aieee!'

The god smashed into one side of the high priestess, spinning her like a child's toy. The god caromed off her with a momentum that made it impossible for him to finish her there and then. Sister Spike deliberately kept spinning to absorb the impact and reduce the damage. Then she sprang up onto the god's back and smacked her elbow high between his shoulder blades. The blow made the god seize up and he pitched forward. Sister Spike somersaulted over the god's lowered head and then turned to meet him again... not anticipating the headlong and suicidal leap he would make. If she'd stayed on his back, he would have broken his neck against the ground – instead, she cushioned his collision.

'No!' Kate raged as the god's antlers tore through Sister Spike and ploughed her into the ground, the priestess's limbs flying like a rag doll's. 'I cannot allow this! The gods cannot allow it!'

Tears burned down Kate's face like acid. Words did not even begin to form. There was no thought. Only rage. White rage that wasn't a feeling, just a state of being and need.

Are you there?

I have always been here, you know that. But you never share your will with me. Command me! Incarnus boomed in her mind.

Smite him to nothingness. And even that will not be vengeance enough!

Kate pointed at the feral god and the massive hammer of the unseen juggernaut descended upon the feral god, who had risen to proclaim his might to the echoing hills. The hammer fell again, and again, smearing what he'd been and then wiping him out of existence. And still the hammer fell, pounding mud into slurry and then a trembling lake.

Silence and stillness fell over the field. Kate walked slowly to the remains of Sister Spike, the only person she'd ever known as *friend*, whatever she meant by that. It was something unique. *Friend* was Sister Spike, and only Sister Spike. Now she understood Incarnus and the desire to see the world hammered down and into something new. She understood Saltar's beserker rage. And then there was a rage beyond all of that; a hatred of everything that stood between herself and her son. The feral god had deserved no less for standing in her way. She'd have castrated him and eaten his member before him as he died, if she'd had the chance.

She found the invisible hammer of Incarnus in her hands. She was his avatar. She smashed it through a group of a dozen kobolds and then down on a suddenly repentant wild man of the woods.

'The Green Witch!' came a rallying cry behind her, but it hardly impinged upon her wider awareness.

The enemy before her began to back away. The single will that had driven them on before had been destroyed with the feral god. On another part of the field, the larger members of the enemy host began to fight amongst themselves for the right to lead. Rival factions formed and stood against each other. Wraiths and the enemies of humankind now fought to get out of Kate's path.

'Forward, after your leader!' Silos Varr commanded. 'Keep your formation! In the name of Dur Memnos!'

Then the gates of Holter's Cross opened and a thousand men on horseback charged forth. The mounts were unruly, but were blinkered and could be controlled now the feral god was gone and the atmosphere of primal terror had faded.

The Memnosian army cut a wide swathe through the enemy, who were largely weaponless and in disarray. Kate led her people into the enclave and the gates were shut tight behind them. Her hammering heart, grief and need for vengeance did not abate in any measure, however.

She looked down on the smiling mercenary captains and Guild Brothers before her and they suddenly looked affrighted. 'Bring forth my son, or Incarnus will dismantle this place. No, do not speak. Fetch him here to me, at once!'

She raised the invisible hammer and all felt the weight of it and their imminent destruction, even if they could not see it. Several Brothers fell to their knees and begged for mercy, tears streaming down their cheeks. They meant nothing to her. Only her son was important, and her memories of Saltar and Sister Spike. She prepared to lay about herself indiscriminately. Incarnus cared nothing for these trivial and conniving mortals.

'Hold, witch!' came a sharp voice. 'None may wield a weapon within Holter's Cross without the Guild's leave. We have your son and will produce him once you give over this magic you have raised. As Grand Master of the mercenary guild, I am more than familiar with the power of holy Incarnus. You must lay it aside… milady.'

'Grand Master Thaeon,' Kate said in flat and hollow tones. Unsurprisingly, Incarnus had always favoured the old crow, and was inclined to listen to him. The power she held began to fade, no matter how hard she tried to hold onto it. She found her own voice: 'Bring Orastes to me, or you will die first and then I will take this place apart brick by brick, until I find him for myself.'

The shrunken, old man, who sat unmoving in his palanquin, cawed in derision. 'Empty threats now, are they not, milady? In my own way, I am a servant of the Divine and Righteous Rage. He would not turn on me now, not when we are surrounded by so many enemies of the realm and the pantheon. Besides, the Guild does not have your son, nor have we ever had him in our keeping. Why would we? The Guild is not so imprudent, and knows it can never challenge the Memnosian throne. The people and temples simply would not allow it, never mind the Builder, the Chamberlain, the Necromancer, the Scourge and, worst of all, the Green Witch herself. Put simply, the gods would not allow it.'

Kate blinked, more her own truculent self now. 'But you said you had him before. And your men backed Lord Selwyn. They tried to kill me... and Sister Spike!'

The Grand Master managed to shrug, though the effort put a spike of tiredness in his eyes. 'Saying we had your son distracted you long enough to allow the divinity to leave, to find where He is actually most needed. He never rests, you know – of course you know – so your hesitation lost the Divine and Righteous Rage its momentum.' He paused to catch his breath. 'As to your Lord Selwyn... well... he is not a direct client of the Guild, you must understand. Yes, a mercenary captain and his crew undertook the Lord's contract, but the contract was agreed by the captain, not by any Brother of this Guild. We had the captain incarcerated once we discovered what had been going on...'

'Once you had discovered what had been going on *after the fact*, Grand Master Thaeon,' Kate clarified. 'If what are you the Grand Master if not the mercenary captains of the Guild? Of what use is *after the fact*, Grand Master Thaeon? Of what use would your discovery be if this captain had succeeded in murdering Sister Spike and myself? Who would then have come to the aid of Holter's Cross in its hour of need? I had to bring your captain into line, Thaeon, because you could not keep him so. Perhaps it is now time the throne took over the administration of Holter's Cross. Left to you, Thaeon, we would have lost the realm already. After all, you are *so* old, and cannot be expected to keep an eye on these young and hungry captains!'

The half dozen Guild Brothers in attendance on the Grand Master shouted and blustered in outrage, but none of the mercenary captains reacted or betrayed an opinion. Their eyes and ears moved back and forth, trying to judge where the power was about to lie.

Grand Master Thaeon allowed the awkward moment to stretch, until all waited on his words and will. He gave a small smile. 'As I was saying, we had the captain incarcerated once we discovered what had been going on. He was put on trial, found guilty and about to be summarily executed... when these unwelcome visitors came to our door. We needed every fighting man available, so his sentence was commuted. He died on the wall along with a good number of his men this morning, I believe. He is dead, milady.' He smiled again. 'As to the administration of Holter's Cross and the care of the realm, surely the host outside was incited by those who rule Dur Memnos rather than the Guild of Holter's Cross. The actions of one usurper after another have threatened the pantheon time and again and destabilised the natural order. How can such rulers be fit to sit the throne, let alone be allowed to bring the power of Holter's Cross under their administration?'

Kate clenched and unclenched her fists. If she'd been holding a crossbow just then…

'But this stand off will do none of us any good when it comes to facing this common enemy,' Grand Master Thaeon observed reasonably, prompting universal nodding from his Guild Brothers and now the mercenary captains. 'We can discuss the politics of Dur Memnos once we have faced the enemy without…'

A vast and cold shadow swept over the enclave, plunging them all into near darkness. The sky echoed with the scream of a giant, two-headed dragon. Its grey bulk all but blocked out the sun.

'… which may be far sooner than any of us would like,' the Grand Master finished.

A call trumpeted from the host in answer to the winged serpent, and then issued its challenge to Holter's Cross.

Silos Varr wearily pulled the nose and faceguard of his helmet back down and then began to issue orders. Even the mercenary captains were happy to follow his orders, for although they were veterans of an untold number of sieges and pitched battles, few had ever been called upon to organise and direct such large numbers of men before, and never with the survival of the entire realm at stake. They listened to him as attentively as if he were Lacrimos Himself.

⚜ ⚜

Despite calluses formed over a lifetime of playing, his fingers had eventually cracked and blistered. Blood had begun to smear the strings of his greater lute, then run freely in bright, red beads. Far from ruining the timbre of the instrument's sound, the blood gave it a new animation and mellowness, increased life and body. His life-force bled out into the music, as a necromancer's power imbued a corpse and made it dance.

His tired mind and eyes saw his shadowy creation leap and skip around the mountains. The legions of the possessed gathered around him also watched it with childlike wonder. The figure became more solid the longer

Lucius played. He could discern elfin features and a lyrical smile. As the royal musician weakened, so the other became stronger.

The musical spirit began to beat a counterpoint with its feet to Lucius's melody, and then sing in sweet, ululating tones. The aching beauty of it brought tears to the eye of listener.

'Mellifluer!' Lucius mumbled joyfully. 'At last! I thought I would never meet you, only ever hear you.'

The god gave a flourish and bow, all syncopated to the music that bound them, the beat of the musician's heart, the rhythm of his breathing, the timing of his blinks, the rise and fall of the wind, the flow of the clouds above, the wheeling of the eagle in the sky, the leap of the mountain goat on the next peak, the rattle and bounce of small stones and the trickle of water down rocks.

Mellifluer began to conduct the world around Him and soon had the possessed moving around in a complex, weaving pattern that was much more like a formal dance. Their eyes began to lose their glaze and they smiled at being returned to their own selves.

Yet it couldn't last, just as a song always has to come to a close and just as life always comes to an end. Lucius's strength was entirely spent, so that he could not even support the greater lute anymore. He collapsed to the ground, with the instrument lying across him. Mellifluer looked mildly disappointed but, as He faded, smiled fondly at His priest, Lucius.

The last notes echoed for a moment and then were no more. He'd held the possessed all through the night and well into the dawn. He could do no more. The Scourge, Strap and his company should be half way to Corinus by now.

'I am content and ready to die,' he sighed as a plain-faced man in the uniform of an adjutant of the Accritanian army came and stood over him.

'Cholerax will not allow that,' the Adjutant said without emotion, 'for the Demon-King and his court will be in want of all manner of entertainment. We will carry you to him and you will be punished beyond all measure for delaying us here and thereby denying his will.'

Lucius tried to wish himself dead, but the wishes of a mortal were no longer of any significance whatsoever in this realm.

※ ※

Men slumped against the parapet of Holter's Cross and fell into an exhausted sleep where they were, wearing their armour and still with weapons in hand.

They'd fought through the night, staring one horror after another in the face. Most continued to see horrors in their sleep, judging by the way they twitched and moaned. The few that didn't sleep looked like they never would again, their faces stricken and their eyes unblinking.

The enemy had swarmed the walls in such numbers that the defenders couldn't slash and cut quick enough to keep them all back. The western wall was the first to be overrun, and the enclave would surely have been lost if Kate and Silos Varr had not led a charge with the reserves, and the priests of Gart had not raised crags of earth just beyond the wall to prevent temporarily any further enemies from joining those who'd already reached the top of the wall. The fighting had been savage, and Kate and the few remaining priests of Incarnus had only just prevailed. And now there was no reserve left, for those men were required to take the place of their fallen comrades on the wall.

Then the southern wall had begun to buckle under a bombardment of boulders thrown by hill giants. It had been all the rapidly wearying priests of Gart could do to keep the wall knit together. A number of the priests had already collapsed, and even the burly high priest of the earth god was trembling with the strain.

As evening had come on, new types of creature had drifted out of the woods to join the dark host. Here were the night-stalkers of legend, the bogeymen and child-stealers, the vampires and restless ghosts. They had glided up to the fortress, and then risen on the air or simply passed through the walls. As steadfast as the defenders were, they could not help be afraid of the beings their mothers had always warned them of. The night-terrors were everywhere, and nowhere, materialising behind shoulders and always just beyond the corner of the eye. Soldiers began to shout in panic, spin in circles and slash widely about them.

'Ikthaeon!' Kate shouted urgently as she faced a gruesome spectre who carried his own head under his arm. 'We need that water, and now! Douse the walls before any more come through!'

Working with the Guild Brothers, the priests of Shakri had ferried skins and buckets of water along the walls and then began to pour it down the stonework. But they were few and the task was enormous. Ikthaeon had been blessing water non-stop since he'd been brought inside the walls and restored by his attendant priests. Water had been needed for the edge of every blade, else they'd been ineffective against most of the enemy, and every defender had needed baptising so that they could not be tempted or possessed. The Guild Brothers could not draw water fast enough from the enclave well to meet the demand. And now the walls needed soaking. A great many died before the enemy were pushed back outside the walls.

And then the stars above them had started to disappear. With a great roar, the dragon-demon had descended upon them out of the night. From one terrible maw came the blast of a magical breath that turned men to ice where they stood, and from the other came some sort of stomach acid that dissolved flesh on contact. Silos Varr placed himself between Kate and the dragon, and raised his shield just in time. The shield turned to ice and shattered as the first head spat its ire. The second head whipped round on its long sinuous neck and gouted lethal liquid towards them. Kate squirted the skin of blessed water she held, to create a stream to meet it, and there was an almighty explosion. Silos Varr and Kate were thrown backwards, the soldier hitting a stone wall and then lying still. The dragon reared back in pain, one of its heads lashing backwards and forwards to try and clear its eyes, but it was blinded. The head hit a wall and a large section of brickwork collapsed on it, to add to its wounds and distress.

Kate picked herself up and deliberately took up the water skin again. She shook it and heard it slosh. There would be enough – there had to be. She stalked towards the first head, which arched up high and wove like a snake preparing to strike.

'By what right do you do this?' she yelled angrily. 'You are naught but an unholy worm. This is Shakri's realm. There is no place for you here. Begone!'

Ikthaeon, his knees shaking, came forward with some few of his priests. 'Y-Yes! You are not welcome here, serpent! In Shakri's name, I banish you from this realm.'

'What are you doing? Stay back!' Kate warned.

The dragon hissed at the high priest and its forked tongue flickered around its long teeth. 'Shhhhhakri is dead, mortal!'

'No!' Ikthaeon denied, with a catch in his voice. 'You lie!'

The head wove forwards and its large, glowing eyes mesmerised the high priest. Too late, Kate shouted a warning. The priests next to Ikthaeon were too slow or petrified to pull him back in time. The dragon's head snapped out and bit the high priest around neck and shoulder. It tossed him into the air and waited with jaws wide to swallow him down. Kate hurled her water skin as high and as far as she could.

'Holy Wim aid me!' she screamed desperately.

Ikthaeon actually laughed as he fell to his death: 'I have drunk to the brim of Her holy water, demon! You have undone yourself!'

Priest and water skin disappeared down the dragon's throat and almost immediately it began to writhe in agony. It gagged, trying to bring up what it had just taken down, but this time the acid of its stomach had worked too quickly for its own good. Already, the magic of Shakri was destroying it from the inside out. Spears of light and heat began to burst out through the dragon's scales and it screamed its death to the mountains so that its master would know what had happened. Then it burst into flame and its skin turned to ash. It collapsed in on itself until all that was left was a wide area of grey residue, which began to blow away on the wind.

The first rays of the dawn began to show in the sky.

'Some of the creatures are returning to the woods!' a soldier called weakly.

'Shakri be praised!' Kate said numbly and half sat, half lay against a set of stairs. A Guild Brother came to see if she was injured. 'Get away from me. See to Silos Varr, if he still lives. Then spread the word that all should rest while they can... or eat if they have the stomach for it.'

The Guild Brothers and the grieving priests of Shakri began to pick their way through the gore decorating the walls. They brought down the dead and laid them out in rows beneath the parapet. They brought water to the lips of those who were without the strength to raise a beaker. They whispered words of benediction and comfort to those who would not last long enough to see the sun rise. And they brought healing to everyone else, for not one soldier had been able to stay completely free of harm. If they could, they would also have brought hope, but they did not know how.

As the sun struggled to rise, a distant trumpet sounded.

'What is that?' Grand Master Thaeon demanded. He'd come out of the Guild House now that there was a lull in the fighting and had positioned himself near Kate as he organised the Brothers and listened to their reports. Silos Varr had been tended and propped up on a pallet, where he drifted in and out of consciousness.

'Memnosian colours to the east!' shouted a sharp-eyed Brother from where he kept watch on the elevated walkway. 'Five hundred or so... and demons with them. Led by... what looks like a young boy, though it could be a dwarf or halfling.'

'And men from the north,' shouted a runner. 'Half a thousand Accritanians!'

Grand Master Thaeon frowned and shook his head. 'Far too few. They will never make it through to us.'

'Nay, master!' called the Brother again. 'The enemy look slow and sluggish in the new light. There is little organised resistance.'

Kate crouched down and hugged her son fiercely, squeezing him until he yelped.

'You're not angry, are you, mother?' Orastes whispered in her ear.

She looked him in the face and smiled. 'Not with you, Orastes, no. And even when I seem to be, it's only because I love you and want you safe. But where have you been?'

'I went on an adventure with Aa and rat-boy!' Orastes said enthusiastically. 'And then we met Distrus and Master Ninevus. We fought some monsters who then became our friends, like Pug. And then there was fighting in King's Landing. There were Jaffrans and a giant sph... sphincter, I think rat-boy called it. Then Lieutenant Sotto and his big friend Dijin came and said you wanted me to come home now, except we found you here in Holter's Cross.'

'Aa, you say?' Kate said evenly, glaring round the gathering of newcomers. 'I can't see Him anywhere.'

'Oh. He was here a minute ago, honestly He was,' Orastes said in confusion.

'I believe you, Orastes, I believe you. I'll just have to have a word with Him some other time.'

Then Kate stood and welcomed the Scourge, Strap and General Constantus. 'Well met, my friends! It is good to see you again, short-lived though it may prove to be. With your help, we may live through one more night, however.'

'Kate, where is Saltar?' the Scourge asked. 'There is no time to explain.'

Kate covered her son's ears. 'H-He is... he is dead.'

The Scourge sighed. 'Then all is indeed lost.'

'We must find him!' a young, wild-eyed woman wailed.

'Is that Vasha? And Larc?' Kate asked. 'His body is in Corinus. I'm not sure we can make it there though. We may have a better chance here, behind these Shakri-blessed walls.'

'We have no choice, Kate,' the Scourge replied.

285

Chapter Twelve: Than to suffer for their presumption

'Now let the subjugation, suffering and slaughter begin!' commanded a terrible voice.

The corpse opened its eyes and stared uncomprehendingly at the stone roof above it. The first breath it took with its torpid lungs was an agony that made it spasm and thrash against the floor where it lay. Fire burned along its limbs, into its muscles and through its veins and arteries. Sparks of life ignited the engine of its heart and set it to pumping blood, although every breathe was torture. Thoughts began to crackle through its mind and it began to become aware.

'Ahh, it's almost better to be dead!' the Chamberlain groaned as he awoke in the tower of the White Sorceress.

Yet he had heard and recognised the voice of his brother and could not refuse the summons. He feared the inevitable confrontation, but knew it could not be avoided. The Nihil would find him whether he hid in the realm of Lacrimos or Shakri. If he fled, the realms would be lost and then his brother would have even greater power with which to hunt him down and destroy him.

'Vidiussss!' the Chamberlain hissed. 'I should have had you imprisoned long ago, hmm? Yet without you, we would perhaps have lost these realms before now. It was the original fall of demonkind that set all of this in motion, so many aeons ago, can you not see that? That fall has brought us to this point now, set us in fatal opposition to each other. All will be destroyed Vidiussss, but that has always been what the Nihil wanted, hmm? Nothing can persuade you to lay aside your weapons and power, can it? Then I must do all I can to see you annihilated.'

His arms and legs finally found some co-ordination and he got shakily to his feet. He looked across at Saltar's dead body and shook his head.

'Balthagar, you have been a fool. Too long have you played at being mortal, acting the part of a noble being, but never really understanding it, hmm? Airs and graces, prancing and posturing. A wife and a child, of all things! They are sops with which the weak gods of this realm have plied you to keep you their lackey! What were you thinking? How much time was wasted on these trappings, on indulging your ego? Such nonsense contributed to the fall of demonkind in the first place, yes? And we will remain fallen until the Arachis at last assume their rightful place as rulers and engineers of the new cosmic order. We will be lackeys to no one! You Spartis are meaningless and always have been.'

The Chamberlain turned his back on the dead Battle-leader and strode from the room. A lone guard standing outside jumped in terror as the man-spider came through the door.

'M-M-Milord! We thought you were d-d-de…'

'Well, rejoice, for I am risen anew, hmm?' the Chamberlain replied, eyeing the man hungrily. It was a shame he would need every soldier available in the coming confrontation, for he was famished and his mortal body was in desperate need of nourishment.

'Why, she has taken the army and the temples and marched on Holter's Cross, milord.'

She had? What had possessed her. Never mind, it was one less difficulty with which to contend. He was sure he would have been able to kill her anyway, but she had an annoying habit of calling on the gods when he least expected it. 'And neither Mordius nor the Scourge are in Corinus?'

'N-Not that I know of, milord. No, I don't think so.'

'Then who commands?'

'Well… I… er… the thing is, milady didn't really leave instructions as to that when she left. I guess, I guess it would be the captain of the city guard.'

'Then I am taking command. You will take me to the captain and then we will arm the city, for the greatest threat this realm has ever known is heading this way. I want every man, woman and child, priest, Indweller and Outdweller alike, out on the field below Corinus. We will make an army of the people yet. Do not take no for an answer from anyone, for now we fight in the name of Shakri, and that is the duty of every mortal. You will force them from their homes and beds at sword point if necessary. And if any resist, then they must already be in league with demons, and you know what to do, soldier!'

The man's mouth hung open in abject terror. The Chamberlain gently took his arm, turned him and propelled him along the corridor. It was good he was scared, for scared people were more inclined to do precisely as they were told. In the same way, mortals only worshipped the gods and carried out the pantheon's will because they were scared what would happen to them if they didn't.

The people of Corinus would do as he told them. They would line up like sheep to the slaughter. And then the gods would be forced to appear and intervene, else it would be the end of their realms and the pantheon itself. They would confront the Demon-King for him. The Prince of the Arachis laughed to himself. At last, he would no longer be their pet. Instead, the gods of this realm would serve him!

⚛ ⚛

The Memnosians tried to move along at pace, but they had one horse to every four men, and the horses were usually required to carry one of the injured each along with their usual rider. Those on foot shuffled along as if they were wearing chains, so exhausted were they from the fighting in Holter's Cross or from the long march from Accritania or King's Landing.

Grand Master Thaeon had tried to stop any of them from leaving, but Kate, the Scourge and General Constantus had ignored him, which had made him apoplectic with rage and caused him some sort of seizure. There'd been much fuss and to-do and Master Ninevus had been forced to attempt to heal the old crow. After long minutes of trying, he gave the assembled Guild the bad news:

'I've made him comfortable and he's no longer in any pain, but I'm afraid there's little more I can do for him. His body is old and in decline. It is the natural way of things. It is the cycle of life and death.'

The Guild Brothers had wrung their hands and been unstinting in their public displays of grief; while the mercenary captains had wasted no time in gathering together their companies and readying themselves to leave with the Memnosians and Accritanians. The Brothers had shouted that it was the Grand Master's command that they stay, and that they risked being thrown out of the Guild if they disobeyed, but the mercenaries knew that their best chance of survival lay with Silos Varr and Kate, whose leadership had kept them alive through the night. The Brothers had then shouted that they too would leave Holter's Cross, but that the host had to wait until the Guild's vast treasury had been loaded into wagons.

'There will be no waiting,' Kate informed them. 'Those who wish to live will leave now, before the enemy outside fully wakes up and realises it's

288

time for breakfast. Your treasury will be of no value to you if you are dead, Brothers.'

And so the mortals had left Holter's Cross, and the Guild of mercenaries that had so long been a bane to the kingdoms of Dur Memnos and Accritania was no more. There were about five thousand of them in total, but not all of them were soldiers, for there were also families, Brothers, fisher people and some citizens of King's Landing amongst them. The refugees had set off down the King's Road and been largely ignored by the squabbling, sleeping and disorientated enemy, who were still so numerous and covered the ground so thickly that, upon occasion, the humans were forced to cut themselves a way forward, but at no point did an organised group of the enemy stand in their way.

By the time the sun was properly above the horizon, Holter's Cross had disappeared from view behind them. Kate rode tall in her saddle at the front of the column, Orastes sat in her lap before her. She hadn't let him out of her sight for a second since he'd been returned to her.

'How is it you are here now, Scourge? And with Constantus? Why is it Sotto and Dijin arrive with my son at the same moment? Don't get me wrong, I thank the gods it is so, but the timing cannot be coincidence. Indeed, it feels… ominous.'

The Scourge half smiled and half pulled a face. 'Like you, I am glad to see my old comrades, but fear it cannot signify anything good. It feels like the sort of convergence we have been through before, with Voltar and Nylchros. What's that term Mordius always uses for it? A nexus in the Pattern, or some such. All I know is that great powers are coming together and it rarely means anything good for us mortals. Even Lacrimos was nervous when I saw Him not so long ago. He spoke of gods going missing and so forth. And Vasha said Cognis was gone too.'

'It is this Demon-King then? And he threatens to end us?'

'I doubt he's coming to pay us his respects and give us a big kiss, eh?' Strap observed to Larc.

Larc frowned slightly and moved his horse closer to Kate's. 'Sorry to interrupt, milady, but have you spoken to Mordius on these matters? Did he reach Corinus before you marched on Holter's Cross?'

'Yes, mother, is Uncle Mordius waiting for us at home, with father?'

Kate looked queasy. 'Err… no… they are both still… away.'

'You mean Mordius didn't return with his warning?' Larc asked worriedly.

'No, he did not,' Kate said softly, stroking Orastes's hair.

'Oh! What can it mean?'

'He probably got his nose lost in some book and lost track of time. He'll turn up, you'll see,' Strap laughed.

The mountain man turned on the Guardian angrily. 'These are serious matters, I'll thank you to remember. The demon realm is rising. We speak of people's lives, or does that mean nothing to you!'

'Larc, what is it?' Vasha asked vaguely from where she rode behind her life-mate.

'Easy!' General Constantus warned.

The Scourge gave an exasperated sigh. 'Larc, don't listen to him! He never stops his yap. Years, I've been trying to shut him up. I think it's just how he gets when things are tense.'

'Look, I'm just trying to keep our spirits up,' Strap explained.

'Master Ninevus!' the Scourge called back down the line.

The priest, who rode with both rat-boy and Distrus balanced precariously behind him, flinched and hurried to come forward. 'Yes, commander? May I be of some service?'

'You are familiar with the blessing of sleep, yes? Then be so kind to bestow it upon this young Guardian at once.'

'Scourge! Don't you dare! That's not funny!'

'I'm just trying to keep our spirits up,' the Scourge nodded to the priest.

The only response that came back was Strap's gentle snores.

***

They crawled along the King's Road, and when night came most of the men collapsed where they were, without even the strength to move onto the softer ground on either side of the road. The Outdwellers were in the best shape, and these were detailed to set a guard perimeter, build some fires, coral the horses and carry out the other duties required to establish a professional military camp.

Dijin opened his mouth to speak.

Sotto raised his hands to forestall him. 'I know, you're hungry! You want to know when we're going to eat. Go harass the Guild Brothers for me. They brought quite a few provisions with them from what I could tell. Make them share, Dijin. Take rat-boy with you if you need someone to help you.'

'Yes, Sotto,' the giant said happily.

A fire imp crept out of the woods and the Scourge growled a warning.

'It's alright, Uncle Scourge, it's only Pug. He's been travelling with the other demons in the woods so as not to scare anyone here. He's a friend.'

'No, lad. It's a demon. Demons do not understand friendship. They only understand need and power. They bow to those they fear and they torture and consume those they need not fear. Let me destroy it, and we will all sleep more soundly for it.'

Pug cringed in terror.

'Please don't, Uncle! Mother, tell him not to! Pug does what I tell him. He helped us fight other demons when we saved a village before. He's very useful. He can help light the fires and hunt for food if I ask him to.'

Kate waved the Scourge away tiredly. 'Leave him be, Scourge. From what you say, there are more than enough demons coming to keep us all busy. One more can't hurt.'

'I will not rest while one of them remains in this realm,' the Scourge insisted. It only takes one. I'm sure Jack O'Nine Blades has much to answer for concerning the Demon-King's arrival in our realm. If we tolerate just one of them amongst us, then we tolerate them all.'

'The commander is right!' Master Ninevus – who'd been conspicuously eavesdropping – dared to interject. 'They are a corrupting influence that must not be tolerated.'

Almost bent double, Pug hid behind Orastes's legs and pulled on his sleeve to get his attention. 'Mahgter, we ghould not gshtop here! He ig coming. And thege woodg are bad plage!'

'See!' Orastes said defiantly. 'Pug has brought us a warning. We should keep going. These woods are bad.'

Kate and the Scourge exchanged a look. Kate shook her head. 'Look at these men, they could not keep going even if they wanted to. It would kill them. And we cannot afford to lose any more if we can avoid it.'

Strap, who'd recently awoken with a harrowed look on his face, said groggily: 'These are the Weeping Woods, are they not? There are many unsavoury stories about them.'

'I vote we rest here for a hand of hours and then start out again,' General Constantus said as he joined the command group. 'Just a bit of rest and food. We needn't stay the whole night.'

Kate looked to the Scourge and Silos Varr, both of whom nodded. 'Very well, spread the word that we will take a brief respite.'

Those who entered the realm of sleep found only nightmares waiting for them. A vast presence bore down on them and slowly crushed them. They were pinned, and there was no escape.

'Bow to me as your King and you may live!' echoed the voice of the Demon-King and all saw the world of order and given place that he intended. All would know their purpose, for it would be to serve the Demon-King. None would suffer the agony of doubt and the consideration of life's meaning. Families would be secure and all their members would seek to achieve the same things for the Demon-King. There would be no division and fighting. See! Many had pledged themselves to His Majesty already and they were happy. See all the happy faces of loved ones. See Mordius and Colonel Marr happy at the Demon-King's right hand. 'Leave off this flight, for there is nowhere to go. It is senseless. Come to me and bow instead and all will be well. Continue to flee and you will be an enemy of the order and I will not be able to protect you.' All saw the war to come, and the cruel acts that would be perpetrated to undo the morale of dissenters. Parents would be set against their children, lovers at each other's throats and siblings to carving out each other's hearts. Virtue and innocence would be ruined, fidelity and dignity turned into parodies of themselves. It was all so unnecessary! The people were used to the protection of a ruler, so they should know to turn to he who loved them best and was stronger than those rulers who would not be able to protect them adequately. Weak rulers themselves needed the protection offered by the Demon-King.

Kate fought her way gasping out of sleep and took large, shuddering breaths. Her hands were pale, even bluish, and she knew she'd been close to capitulating her will and life. In a sudden panic, she turned over and tried to shake Orastes awake. He was slow to respond, but finally opened disorientated eyes. 'Shakri be praised!' she hiccuped in relief and hugged her son as he began to sob.

The Scourge started awake, all but leaping off the ground. He was drenched in sweat and his hands shook as he pulled a knife and glared around him. 'By the menstrual moods of Shakri!' he swore as he got to his feet and kicked Strap and Constantus up.

Somewhere, a woman started screaming hysterically.

'If that doesn't wake everyone up, nothing will,' the Scourge grimaced.

'We must wake as many as we can!' Master Ninevus contributed shrilly. 'There are unholy forces at work.'

'You don't say, priest!' the Scourge said with a shake of the head. 'I bet Shakri's proud of you.'

'None of the people of King's Landing are moving!' rat-boy called.

'Idiots have probably never been anointed with water blessed by the temple of Shakri. They're all besotted with the god of seaweed and tentacles, aren't they? Priest, take your acolyte and get to work. Move! The Divine Consort of Shakri commands you, and the Consort is not in a good mood right now. And while you're at it, start blessing as much water as you can find. I think we're going to need it. People are only to drink beer, wine and liquor from now on.'

Master Ninevus squeaked his understanding and hurried to lead Distrus away from the terrifying warrior of legend who was the Scourge.

Strap grinned. 'Only beer, wine and liquor, eh? There's some benefit in all this then.'

'What time is it?' Kate asked. 'We seem to have lost half the night. Someone build the fires higher – we could all do with the comfort.'

'And someone shut that woman up, she's starting to give me a headache,' the Scourge groused. 'Strap, where's your devilberry liquor?'

'I think it's High Priestess Vasha,' Silos Varr murmured, peering into the murk.

'That's not good,' General Constantus said for all of them. 'Damn, but it's a dark night, as black as the depressions of holy Malastra. It cannot be natural. It's as if we are adrift in the void. Colonel Vallus, have our men check on the guards and relieve them as necessary.'

There were ferocious snarls and howls away in the woods, inhuman sounds that made the hair stand on the back of the neck. Distant flares of red and green magic could be seen here and there. The horses began to whinny and bite at their tethers. They kicked and jostled each other. A stampede looked to be seconds away.

'Mother, it is Pug,' Orastes said in a small, sad voice. 'There are too many for him to hold back.'

Larc ran through the camp towards them. 'We must leave at once! Vasha has foreseen we will know only slavery and death if we stay.'

They needed no second bidding. 'We will leave in good order!' Silos Varr shouted. 'Priests and the main Memnosian troops first, followed by the men of Accritania, then the mercenary companies, civilians and Outdwellers to the rear! The same marching order as before. Quickly!'

In a daze, the humans stumbled in their ragged ranks out of camp. Several hundred of them had failed to awaken, and more than a few civilians had tried to pick up friends and loved ones who lay in a coma. Exhausted as they were, however, they'd been unable to carry the bodies far. In the end, a woman called Lystra and a man called Jaris – who appeared to lead the people of King's Landing – had ordered the grief-stricken individuals dragged away and the bodies left behind. In respect or fear, the soldiers looked away.

'Can we pick up the pace?' Kate asked Silos Varr.

'Only if we are intending to march straight through the gates to holy Lacrimos's realm, milady,' he replied. 'Our rest has fatigued us even further, unless I am very much mistaken. Many will not see the morning.'

Orastes sniffled. 'Poor Pug is gone,' he whispered.

The Scourge patted the boy awkwardly on the back. 'He was the bravest demon I ever knew, lad. I am proud to have known him.'

Orastes cried freely and tried to smile. 'Yes, he was brave. I'm glad I knew him too.'

'Master Ninevus,' Kate said over her son's head. 'There are some several priests of Shakri still surviving, are there not? Can they not strengthen us?'

The priest immediately looked apologetic. 'Milady, I'm sorry but the priests are as spent as the soldiery. They fought at Holter's Cross and were severely weakened by that. Plus, they would never be able to help so many and, even if they did, it might do more harm than good. The extra energy given always needs to be paid back at a later date, for that is as the balance demands. If the energy given them causes them unwittingly to exceed their physical limits, then they surely will be unable to recover when the extra energy is used up. It is kinder to be cruel in this instance.'

'Lights to left and right! Ghostly figures! Night beasts!' reported a runner who'd come up from the Outdwellers at the back.

'We need to make a decision, Kate,' the Scourge said sourly. 'We either make a stand or we pick up the pace and let the devil take the hindmost.'

'We dare not stop!' Larc insisted.

'I can take five hundred men and buy us all some time,' Silos Varr volunteered.

Kate shook her head. 'It would be a wasted, if heroic, effort. If my son's demons could do next to nothing to hold them back, then I doubt your men could offer much resistance either. We are at our strongest when we stay together. We must increase our pace then. We must race for the dawn and place our faith in the gods. Pass the order back down the line.'

Kate spurred her horse forward into a canter and her command group followed suit. They could not push the horses too hard because each mount bore the weight of several riders and tire quickly, but also because they did not want to leave those on foot too far behind. She felt slightly guilty to be riding where others did not, but she needed to remain a figurehead, she was hardly strong enough to stand after the fighting in Holter's Cross and, most of all, she now had her son to think of. She could not find it in herself to apologise to anyone for sitting with him here in her arms.

※ ※

It was a mad, pell-mell dash through the darkness. Kate could hardly pick out the road in front of her, but knew those who followed blindly behind relied on her to steer a clear course. Her eyes pulsed with fatigue and her mind was reduced to a pounding headache. At one point, she nearly slipped from her saddle, and it was only Orastes's yelp and slapping on her thigh that kept her upright. She rubbed at her eyes, but the grit there pained her and blurred her vision.

'I need some water to splash on my face,' she croaked to Orastes. 'Give me the water skin.'

'No! Give me that,' the Scourge barked and wrested the skin from the boy. 'We will need this. Priest, get this blessed and passed back to the Outdwellers. Kate, lick your fingers and rub them on your eyes if need be.'

Cries suddenly went up from the back of the host.

'We're under attack! Darts and arrows!' came a cry.

'There in the woods! Running figures. Dark elves!'

'What's that?' the Scourge asked, cocking his ear.

'Hearing going, Old Hound?' Strap asked. 'He said there were dark elves. You know, pointy ears and no sense of humour. They hate humans over all other creatures, they like to hunt us with their dark hounds, and so on.'

'Keep going!' the Scourge barked at Kate. 'I hear running water up ahead. Let me deal with this. Much as I dislike the idea, it's probably time I started acting like the Divine Consort of Shakri. Strap, once we're past the water, you and I will be stopping, so make sure that bow of yours is limber. Master Ninevus, you and your priests will be joining us. Silos Varr, I will be taking control of the Outdwellers, but you must make sure everyone else keeps going. I don't want to be going to all this trouble for nothing.'

Silos Varr nodded and saluted, one soldier to another.

'No!' Larc pleaded. 'You cannot stop now. Cognis has said that any who stop will die.'

The Scourge spat. 'Cognis? That bookish wimp? What does he know about living and dying?'

Strap smiled. 'Besides, many of us are already dying. It probably makes little difference either way if we stop.'

'A stream! There it is,' Kate shouted, as the dying screams of her people rang in her ears. She gave the Scourge a final glance as she raced onwards. 'If you see Lacrimos, old man, give him my regards!'

The Scourge smiled savagely and pulled his destrier up and to the side. Strap and the priests of Shakri joined him. The humans splashed across the wide, but shallow, stream, only a vague semblance of order left to them in their panic. Their fear was primal, for all knew the folk tales of the Elf Queen who had been betrayed by her human paramour and then declared war on all humans for their faithlessness. The elves has become dark and twisted with hate; and tradition had it that with the turning of every season, the near-immortal Elf Queen would ride out on her Great Hunt in search of her lost paramour and vengeance on humankind. Every human forester knew better than to venture into the deepest parts of any forest, and every human knew to move as quickly as possible when forced upon a shadowy path through any woodland.

'Quickly!' the Scourge shouted as hounds as large as wolves began to course out of the trees. They yipped and howled in excitement upon seeing their prey. 'Strap, your bow!'

'I'm ahead of you,' the younger man replied as he unleashed an arrow with an accuracy that would have made an elf proud.

General Constantus came past and demanded to stand with the Scourge. The Guardian spurned the offer and replied that this was no place for Accritanians, that the outlanders were too soft and likely to be more a hindrance than a help.

'Besides, you are guests in this realm so we would not wish to make such rude demands upon you. Just don't finish all the brandy before I get there, old friend, agreed?' the Scourge said gruffly.

'I will save you little enough, for it is well known Memnosians cannot handle more than a sniff of alcohol. Oh, they whine and complain, but that is the only thing in which they excel.'

The Scourge pushed the General on, with a wave and a kick to his posterior. The General's shouted rejoinder was lost in the crush and then he was gone.

The Guardian turned on the priests: 'Well, don't just stand there! Start blessing the stream for all you're worth!'

They stared at him as if he were crazy. 'M-Milord,' Master Ninevus ventured. 'We cannot bless an entire stream. The water needs to reside in a sainted or blessed vessel. Here, the blessing will just be swept away.'

The Scourge drew his two long daggers at once. 'Just try it! Alright? The Divine Consort says so. Got it? Ah, Sotto, there you are. You took your sweet time. Get your men lined up along this side of the stream, quick as you can! Tell them to use the water skins of blessed water.'

'Right you are!' Sotto bobbed. 'You heard him, lads! About face! In a line along this side of the stream. Chella, get your men out to the right. Slow Shento and Teeler out left. Dijin, you stay here with me in the centre.'

'What's happening, Sotto?' the ogre panted. 'No more running? That's good, cos it makes me hungry.'

'See all those dogs? Look, some have riders on them! We're going to fight them now.'

'Ooo! And am I allowed to eat them, Sotto? I am mighty hungry, you know.'

'As many as you like, Dijin, and the more the better.'

'Really?' Dijin replied with eyes as big as plates and drool stringing down his chin.

'Here they come!' the Scourge shouted and hurled his knife straight at the leaping pack-leader. His blade sank up to the hilt in the giant beast's chest, but missed its heart, and then the hound's momentum bore the Scourge to the ground.

Jaws snapped at the Scourge's face, but he'd already moved his head to the side. With one of the hound's mighty paws pinning his shoulder to the ground, the Scourge could do little more than try to stick his second long dagger into the dog's side, but the blade skidded along its ribs and did little real damage. The hound's jaws founds the join of his neck and shoulder and clamped down just as his free hand found the handle of the dagger still protruding form its chest. He pulled the handle up and down viciously while screaming in pain as the jaws ratcheted tighter and tighter.

'That really hurts!' the Scourge hissed between gritted teeth and gave up on the first dagger. He yanked the skin off his belt and squirted water into the dog's eyes. It whimpered deep in its throat and then the flesh round its eyes and muzzle began to sizzle and slough off. Tortured beyond endurance, it had to release him, and then scrabbled at its maw with its claws, tearing away more flesh. Appalled, the Scourge threw water down its throat and a fountain of blood erupted everywhere. He kicked the thing away and struggled back to his feet.

'Thanks for the help!' he coughed at Strap.

The Guardian released another arrow, and another. 'In case you hadn't noticed, I'm busy. Besides, I knew that a Guardian as big and ugly as yourself would be able to look after himself. This was your idea after all, wasn't it? And you are the Divine Consort, are you not? I would never question Her divine taste or commit the blasphemy of suggesting She must be desperate to pick someone who can't even defend himself properly.'

'One more word and I'll set my priests on you,' the Scourge threatened, holding his wound to try and stop the bleeding.

'Divine Consort!' Master Ninevus warbled. 'Blessing the stream is not doing anything to prevent their assault. It's not working. Shakri, save us!'

A hound that stood at least four feet from claw to shoulder, and carried a slight figure on its back, powered through the stream towards the priests. At the last moment, Dijin pushed his way in front of the priests, grabbed the beast's front legs and yanked them apart. The hound died instantly as its chest was pulled open and its heart and other internal organs fell out. The elf pitched backwards from its perch but landed lightly on the water and skipped upon its surface before launching a flickering attack at the human giant.

Millennia of rage had permanently warped the elf's features and made it look more demon than anything of Shakri's creation. But its face was only glimpsed briefly, so quickly did it move. In the time it took to apprehend where it had just been, it was already gone. A small blade flickered like a fire-fly and lanced Dijin in chest, side and thigh.

Sotto spread his arms wide and rushed at where he thought the elf to be, but he met only air and fell face first into the stream. Dijin had stood stock still since killing the hound. Now, his hand shot out and closed a mighty fist round the elf's neck. It raised the elf off the ground, squeezed and broke its neck. The body was casually thrown aside as Dijin leaned forward to haul Sotto out of the water by the back of his belt.

'Sotto, what are you doing?'

'Dijin, are you alright?' spluttered the lieutenant. 'How did you…? Don't tell me, your nose, right?'

The giant nodded and deposited his friend back on the side of the stream. Elsewhere, the Outdwellers were not doing so well. To the left, Teeler had already died with two elfin arrows through his throat and the rest were only just managing to keep a group of six hounds at bay with gouts of temple-blessed water. Meanwhile, elves with bows in the trees on the other side of the stream picked off the humans almost at their leisure. 'Cowards!' Slow Shento shouted at them, which brought most of them forward with ominously glowing blades.

On the right, where the trees crowded more thickly and had provided the humans with cover from most of the arrows, the elves had already charged and begun to decimate the Memnosians. The Outdwellers simply could not lay a blade on their eldritch attackers. The only one who seemed to be having any success was Crazy Chella, who threw the precious water all around carelessly and slashed at the air with quite random and abandon, as if possessed by the holy spirit of Wim Himself. Others began to copy him as best they could, but dozens had already fallen, and others were falling just as quickly.

'Scourge, we're in trouble!' Strap said as he took rapid steps backward to give himself enough room to get a shot away at a surging hound that was almost upon him.

'By the flea-ridden armpits of Wim, I'd hoped it wouldn't come to this,' the Scourge said with ill temper. Then he sighed. 'Very well, I cannot put these lives before my own pride.' He cleared his throat. 'Beloved, hear me! Shakri, Mother of All Creation, Divine Lover and Boon Companion, on behalf of your children, I pray for your benevolence and intercession. This is our hour of need, answer our prayer. Bless the waters of this stream, just as you have blessed all mortalkind and this realm with life!'

There was a brief lull in the chaos and most eyes, including those of the elves, turned towards the Scourge. Nothing happened. A blush of embarrassment rose in his cheeks, which could be seen even in the darkness.

Strap couldn't help snickering, despite their desperate plight.

'Oh, for crying out loud, woman!' the Scourge grated. 'What more...?'

Suddenly, the waters of the stream burst with a blinding radiance that lit the entire sky. The Memnosians shielded their eyes, which wept with joy, and found themselves flooded with a healing energy and a sense of peace. Their fears, their tiredness and their wounds were all gone. The sense of well being that suffused them had them laughing like children, had them as happy to be alive – no matter what darkness lay about them – as they'd ever been.

Master Ninevus and his priests were transported to a state of ecstasy, their eyes shining as bright as the stream and projecting beams of light wherever they looked. 'It is a miracle!' they chorused. 'She is amongst us.'

As wonderful as the *deus ex machina* was to the Memnosians, it was devastating to the dark elves and their hounds. Those caught in the stream were reduced to nothing and those bathed in its light were shrivelled as if burnt. So quickly did it happen, they did not even have a chance to cry out.

Then, out of the glare emerged a diaphanous female form. The Memnosians fell to the ground in adoration, all except for the Divine Consort.

The Scourge rolled his eyes. 'All a bit dramatic, don't you think?'

She turned her perfect eyes upon him and gave him a tolerant look. 'A thank you would suffice, dear one.'

'Thank you?!' he said in disbelief. 'Hundreds of men – nay thousands of people! – dying to protect this goddamn realm of yours and you want us to fall over ourselves in gratitude for the privilege? Of all the selfish and conceited…'

'Hush, Janvil!' She whispered and put a divine finger to his lips. 'All you had to do was ask, you know that. I will not demand an apology of you.'

'Apology!' he near-exploded, lost for words in his outrage.

'Shhh!' She said, nothing but love in Her eyes. 'Now is not the time. I am as humbled in this as you are. I fear we will not survive, dear Janvil. I do not want us to end fighting each other.'

'Traitor!' screamed a female voice. 'How dare you do this! How dare you murder my people!'

Across the stream and at the top of a slight rise in the King's Road so that she was silhouetted against the sky, the Elf Queen sat upon a slavering hound as large as the Scourge's destrier. She wore a glowing crown of thorns and human souls, and the long tresses of her hair floated around her on waves of magical energy. Her face and eyes had a malign and unforgiving beauty that instilled fear in those who looked upon her. The radiance of the stream dimmed slightly as her hound padded closer.

'Murderer!' the Queen spat at Shakri. 'We elves have as much right to existence as any other. You are no longer the goddess of life in this realm, for you have broken the balance with this act! Your rule is at an end!'

The Scourge looked at Shakri in horror. The goddess refused to meet his gaze and nodded imperceptibly in answer to his question. She had ended the balance to save them… to save him! What madness was this?

'What have you done?' he breathed.

Shakri had locked eyes with the Elf Queen. 'You forfeited your right to the existence I gifted you when you turned away from the ways of life and love, Alagreine. Once, I shared your grief at how you were betrayed and your heart was so cruelly broken. But you took that grief to you as if it were a lover and made it the core of your being. All you are now is an embodiment of grief who has long outstayed her welcome. Surely you know your paramour died millennia ago. Why do you pursue this still?'

'Me, the embodiment of grief?' Alagreine sneered. 'Is it not love that engenders and frames such grief? *You* are responsible for this! *You* are responsible for the destruction of this realm! And let the realm of the dead be broken open too, for then the human will no longer be able to hide from me there. He will be mine! He had been promised to me.'

Shakri looked infinitely sad. 'Promised by the Demon-King, Alagreine?' She asked softly. 'The King of Lies? The Great Deceiver? How do you know he is not that same paramour who has already betrayed you? Will you be betrayed forever more?'

'No. It is you has betrayed elfkind with this act. The Demon-King will have me as his Queen.'

Shakri shook Her head. 'As his slave, Alagreine, as his slave. I ask one last time: will you not give this over?'

The Elf Queen lifted her chin proudly. 'Better his slave than your subject, tyrant! I will be at his side when you and the pantheon are thrown into the dust, ground underfoot and torn limb from limb by the four winds.'

A pained expression came across Shakri's face. 'Then, much as it grieves me, you will now return that which I gifted you, daughter. Perhaps it is fitting that I take this grief upon myself, to ensure that your own grief is finally ended and you can no longer do any harm.'

'What? No, you cannot do this! I forbid it! Bitch goddess!'

'Little enough is left to me in this realm, but this I can do. This, I must do. Perhaps it is something I should have done long ago, so you would not have suffered for so long. Forgive me, Alagreine.'

Alagreine threw back her head and screamed in grief for her own life, the sound piercing every heart there and causing the Memnosians to shed tears of pity. Her ghost rose out of her body, drifted into the radiance of Shakri's stream and disappeared. Then Elf Queen and hound fell gently to the ground, never to move again.

Shakri turned to the Scourge and gave him a wan smile. 'Now you must go, beloved, for he will be here with the dawn.'

The Scourge looked at the sky. On the horizon, a fierce light was beginning, but it was not the rising sun, it was a line of fire. The sky itself was burning. Dark shadows like smoke rose above the flames and flew towards them on mighty wings that spanned the vaulted heavens.

'He is coming, beloved, and there is nothing the remnants of the pantheon can do. The balance is undone and the magic of this realm is ended. I have replenished you and your men and also Kate's people, so that you will be able to reach Corinus, but I do not think there is anything beyond these dying moments left to us now.'

Then She kissed him ever so gently on the lips and he embraced her, nuzzling her hair. She pulled away and moved into the stream. 'I will join you at Corinus if I may. Otherwise, be well, my children,' and She faded from sight.

Strap eyed the Scourge and gave him a wink.

'Shut up!'

'But I didn't say anything!'

'You may as well have done. Anyway, you heard the lady, we don't have time for any of this. Pick your feet up! Let's go… Dijin, must you?'

'I'm hungry!' mumbled the giant around a mouthful of dog flesh.

'I sometimes think he must be the god of hunger,' Sotto observed.

'Is there such a thing?'

'If there is, then Dijin's it. Come on, Dijin, leave that. There's something even bigger and hungrier than you coming. Time to go!'

The sky roared like a beast of the inferno, sending the Memnosians fleeing for their lives down the King's Road towards Corinus.

※ ※

At first, Ja'rahl had been overwhelmed and awestruck by the dozens of giant sphinkaes that had moved amongst the Jaffrans. He'd hardly had the courage to suggest to them that they eat the Memnosians of King's Landing rather than their loyal people, but he'd been forced to intercede with Istris or see his entire army consumed. Fortunately, the god had deigned to listen and had directed his kith and kin towards hunting down those mortals who fled through the town.

They'd lost a lot of time rounding the ravenous sphinkaes up again, and by then it was full night. There'd been no chance of catching the Memnosian soldiers, the boy-warrior, his pet demons and their ridiculous god, so Ja'rahl had decided to spend the night in the town. That at least meant he'd been able to see all four thousand of his men safely landed and the injured tended. He'd also ordered that those close to death be drained of their blood so that he could properly bathe himself.

They'd then set out with the dawn, the majestic sphinkaes leading them. They were an awesome sight, but the gods constantly grumbled of hunger and feeling weak. More than one of the Jaffran gods had been unable to resist looking back over their shoulders, tongues lolling out, to eye the mortals with appetite. Istris had growled a warning at the wayward sphinkaes and they'd roared back in ill temper, although they'd stopped short of challenging him.

It had been such displays of petulance and pique that had started the blasphemous thoughts in Ja'rahl's mind. Where were the divinely noble beings he remembered from Jaffra's past? Had their long sleep seen the sphinkaes so diminished? Or was it that he'd only ever seen the sphinkaes in the context of an abundant environment that saw their every whim and desire fulfilled? They were almost like spoilt children or a pampered mistress who had become obese. He was aghast. How could he think such things? Had his own mind become corrupted? Had the flesh in his brain-pan finally begun to rot?

Perhaps sensing His high priest's inner turmoil, Istris had called Ja'rahl forwards, and the Jaffran had order the deaf and mute slaves carrying him in his priestly throne to hurry him to the god's side.

'Command me, holy lord!' Ja'rahl pleaded.

'Ja'rahl, you have done well. You have brought us to the place of convergence in time for the return. I am well pleased.'

'Thank you, holy lord. I only seek to be your faithful servant and to serve you well.'

'And is that all you seek?'

Ja'rahl froze. Did Istris know? Had the god read his thoughts? 'H-Holy lord?'

'Come, Ja'rahl, you must be honest with yourself so that you may then speak honestly to your god. You *must* seek more, for even the gods seek more, and surely you must seek to emulate the example of your gods. Is that not so?'

'Y-Yes, of course, holy lord!' Ja'rahl rushed. Then he hesitated slightly. 'Holy lord, may I be so bold as to ask what more the gods could want, for if I am able to help them in that respect in any way, then it will be my holy duty to do so!'

Istris nodded slowly. 'And it is right and proper that it be so. It excuses the temerity of your question. Then I shall reveal this to you: all beings are servants in some way, even the gods.'

Ja'rahl was agog. If any Jaffran had dared say such a thing, then Ja'rahl would not have hesitated to see their tongue torn out and force-fed to them. 'H-How can that be, holy lord? Please forgive your witless servant.'

Istris smiled indulgently. 'Just as you serve the gods, then in some fashion the gods serve and protect their people. It is in the interest of the gods to see their servants prosper and become more powerful, for then their servants are more capable and useful as servants. Thus, I have allowed you to exist for so long and to grow in your command of magic, Ja'rahl.'

'Holy lord, there are no words for my gratitude or your divine wisdom.'

'Indeed,' Istris acknowledged. 'I have indulged you, Ja'rahl, so that you might better serve me.'

'Anything, holy lord, just name the task!'

'As you serve me, I have served the people of Jaffra. I also serve one other, Ja'rahl: he who is the King of the gods. It is he who returns to this realm to begin his rule. In his absence, of course, pretenders have claimed his throne, and they must needs be removed. I speak of course of the Memnosian pantheon of so-called gods, who are little more than confidence-tricksters. These upstarts must be destroyed, as must their servants, the mortals of both Dur Memnos and Accritania. In the time ahead, all mortals must be destroyed. Do you understand this?'

'Oh, yes, holy lord, and I will not hesitate to make it so. I have already imprisoned a goodly number of Memnosian gods also.'

Istris's massive head whipped round, a mixture of alarm and surprise on His usually serene face, which caused Ja'rahl to lean back in fear. 'You have? Tell me more of this!' demanded the god.

'W-Why I assumed you would already know, holy lord! I summoned a number of the lesser Memnosian gods to me on Jaffra and ensnared them with spells of blood. Th-Then I had them interred in a godhouse. D-Did I do wrong?'

The mighty sphinx schooled his features once more. 'No, of course not. Again, you have done well, faithful Ja'rahl. I am pleased. You may leave me now, to prepare yourself for the King's return and the time of slaughter ahead, when all mortal existence will end.'

The audience had left the Eternal High Priest of Istris utterly shaken. All the assumptions upon which he'd based his faith, and based on which he had punished the people of Jaffra for millennia, had been overturned in just a few brief minutes. He had always believed Istris to be the King of the gods, but now it appeared He had never been so. Istris had described Himself as a mere servant to the King, so what did that make Ja'rahl and the Jaffrans?... And then he realised the truth of it – the only thing that was less than a servant was a slave. Ja'rahl had never been more than just a slave to a servant. It appeared that Istris wasn't even a god, although the sphinx was clearly powerful. Istris was not divine, and could neither be omnipotent or omniscient. Just see how *fear* had transformed the sphinx's face into something ugly when Ja'rahl had mentioned holding the Memnosian gods captive!

And now the sphinx demanded Ja'rahl oversee the slaughter of all mortalkind, to aid the King's ascension to the throne of this realm. But why would this King need help from one as insignificant as Ja'rahl, one who was nothing more than a slave? Was Istris not capable of conducting the genocide Himself? Perhaps Istris lacked the necessary power – just look at how He had cowered from the mortal priest of Shakri at the dockside in King's Landing!

Could Ja'rahl really conscience the slaughter of all mortalkind, including the Jaffran people to whom he'd dedicated his existence? Perhaps. But to what end? Here, then, was the selfsame question Istris had asked him. What *more* did he want for himself? He now knew that he wanted to be more than just a slave to the will of Istris. Perhaps he would now be an equal to Istris... perhaps... Istris would be the slave to Ja'rahl! He shut his eyes, waiting for divine and righteous punishment to descend on him for just thinking such a thing, but nothing happened.

It was then that Ja'rahl dared to start dreaming. After all, it was Ja'rahl who had toppled half of the pantheon, where neither Istris nor the King had done so. It must be Ja'rahl who was the most powerful of them! He decided that he would have to watch and wait for his moment. His ancient and cunning mind began to scheme around seizing the throne for himself, he who understood the ways of power and the gods better than any other. Should it not be such a one who ruled over all others? At last, the blindfold had been removed from his eyes, the shackles from his wrists, and now all would come to know and fear the eternal blood priest of Jaffra.

Thinking to be the first to the prize, Ja'rahl therefore ordered his army to increase its pace. Soon, all the sphinkaes except for Istris had fallen back to tag along behind the humans. Ja'rahl no longer feared so-called gods, nor did he pay any mind to their pathetic demands to be fed. They could starve for all he cared. If it hadn't been for the potential value to him of the sphinkaes in the battle that was sure to come, he would actually have considered running them off or putting them down. As it was, he was content to have his back turned to them and see them languishing in his wake.

They came to the enclave of Holter's Cross that evening. Thousands upon thousands of bodies littered the open ground outside the walls, precious few of them human. The sphinkaes fell hungrily onto the putrefying flesh regardless, leaving the Jaffrans to pass through the open gates to confirm that the enclave was indeed deserted. The human dead within had been laid out in neat lines, as if sleeping in their battle gear so that they would be ready to man the parapets when summoned. Istris, the only one of the sphinkaes to accompany the army inside, turned His nose up at the bodies and proclaimed them tainted. Then, the eldest of the sphinkaes disinterestedly padded out of the fortified town to join his kind in their feasting.

Carrion-eater! Ja'rahl thought disrespectfully and went back to his inspection of the ranks of the dead. There were Memnosian soldiers amongst the corpses of the mercenaries, but none looked like those he remembered from King's Landing. They'd escaped him again then. And the defenders of this place had apparently defeated the hideous and deformed horde besieging them, joined with the boy-warrior's force and headed south. Curse them and their gods, but they would reach the throne before him and be in good position to defend it against him if he did not move quickly.

'We will begin our march towards Corinus immediately,' he informed his priests, who bowed to signal their understanding and started to issue orders to the legions.

As the Jaffrans took to the road leading south, it was Istris who came to Ja'rahl, rather than vice versa.

'We have not finished eating!' Istris half yowled and half growled. 'And when we have, the sphinkaes will sleep.'

Ja'rahl did not shy from meeting the sphinx's eye. 'Our enemies have not stopped to gorge themselves, holy lord. Surely, once the King has assumed his rightful throne, there will be all the flesh of mortalkind for the sphinkaes to gorge themselves upon. Or did I fail to understand your divine wisdom, holy lord? Forgive your witless servant.'

Istris glared at the high priest, knowing He was being challenged. He deliberated for a few long moments and then said, 'I shall call the sphinkaes to me and we will lead these mortals for the glory of the gods.'

Ja'rahl allowed himself a secret smile of satisfaction. He wondered if the sphinkaes bled when wounded. He wondered what their blood tasted like.

❄ ❄

Children cried and hugged their parents, but there was little comfort the adults could give apart from bodily contact, as they were as distraught as the youngsters. They clutched an assortment of cooking and working implements – paring knives, awls, eating forks, long-handled skillets, pokers and skewers, and so forth – as if their lives depended on it. The contents of the royal armouries had also been passed out among them, but few knew how to use the longbows, morning stars and stranger looking weapons with any competence, so most had been laid aside out of preference for the familiar domestic tools the people of Corinus had brought with them from their homes.

Nobles stood side by side with merchants and labourers. Indwellers rubbed shoulders with Outdwellers, the sick did their best to stand amongst the healthy, and priests were forced to mingle with their congregations. Ten thousand Memnosians stood in the gloom of the pre-dawn along the higher slopes of the plain beyond the walls of their capital city. The thousand or so city guard that Kate had left behind were all mounted – some on horses confiscated from the populace – so that the host had five hundred cavalry on either flank.

Along with the sobbing, prayers were offered up to the gods. A grey-haired man with a bent back tried to sing a song from the kingdom's heroic past, but none took up the tune or words and he eventually gave it up. Family members and friends hugged each other, business rivals and acquaintances shook hands one last time, and lovers kissed each other tenderly.

The Chamberlain yawned and tried to ignore the gnawing hunger in his gut, but it was difficult when he was surrounded by so much fresh meat. He could hear and smell hearts pounding with sweet blood all around him. Ah, nothing could beat the taste and experience of that organ when it was still hot and quivering with some last vestige of life. In some ways, it would be a shame to see an end to the mortals of this realm, but he no doubt only thought so because he'd become so used to the animal wants, appetites and functions of the mortal body he'd been forced to inhabit throughout the ages in order to stay in this realm. The fact that he'd allowed the bodily cycle of consumption and evacuation to become some sort of festishized pleasure for him was a sure sign that his psyche had become limited and lessened by his time in this realm. It was time he broke free of this physically dependent realm, and if he had to break the realm in the process then so be it. After all, the realm had served its purpose now, in enabling demonkind to break free of its own confining realm, so there was little point in trying to save it, was there?

The bottom of the sky began to glow and the mortals cried out in panic. This was no normal dawn of the rising sun – this was the dawning of the age of the Demon-King, when reality and existence would be determined by his will alone, when there would only be one god rather than an entire pantheon.

The Chamberlain smiled in anticipation. Here was the final battle, when one amongst the Princes would emerge triumphant. Vidius might have possession of the crown, and might have a vast army to command, but he still had not completed his coronation in this realm. He was proceeding towards the throne where he would be invested as ruler of this realm, but he might yet trip upon his ceremonial robes and break his royal neck, particularly if someone were to give him a well-timed push from behind.

Shadows and tendrils of illumination rose up from the horizon, bathing the plain in an eerie, shifting light. Now they could see forms scurrying forwards towards their position. The Chamberlain frowned in consternation

– these were not the terrible demon forms he'd been expecting – these looked more like mortals.

The cavalry to each flank were calling for orders. Then came a call he'd been dreading…

'The Green Witch!' the voice piped, almost questioning, as if it did not believe itself.

But the assembled Memnosians were so desperate that if they'd been a drowning man offered only a naked blade to cling to, they would not have hesitated to cut their own wrists open while pulling themselves free of the water. 'The Green Witch! The Green Witch!' They took up the refrain with a fever of jubilant salvation that echoed off the sky, the city walls and right across the plain.

Curse that meddling and trivial woman! Once again, she'd contrived to interpolate her mundanely mortal self into his scheme of things at the worst possible moment. The Chamberlain gnashed his teeth in livid anguish. He could scuttle down there and kill her in the blink of an eye, but the consequences, the consequences! Confound her and every other mortal that had ever drawn breath or known a thought! If he touched a hair on her head with malicious intent, the mortals were sure to turn on him. Yes, there was Silos Varr at her side – the man was tediously loyal to the throne of Dur Memnos and simply could not be seduced and suborned. And General Constantus! And was that Orastes, the detestable child of the Green Witch's loins?

Yes, there was no doubt he'd have a fight on his hands if he snapped her fragile neck. He might survive, might defeat all these mortals, but that would ruin all his plans. Think, think. Recalculate. Tick, tick. Engineer things differently. The Pattern had just spun out differently, but there were still threads and nodes to anticipate, tighten and loosen. He'd worked his will through Kate before, he could do it again. Careful, careful, here she comes.

'What are these people doing out here?' she demanded of the Chamberlain. 'They're terrified.'

The Chamberlain shrugged. 'I am terrified, milady, hmm? We are all terrified, yes? But I am glad to see you well, milady.'

'No doubt. I am sure you cried yourself to sleep every night I was away. Why aren't these people behind the walls? They would have no chance meeting an enemy head on. See, most of them don't know one end of a sword from another.'

The Chamberlain smiled and nodded incongruously. 'Yet their considerable number might give an enemy pause, hmm, buying you more time to relieve the city? Failing that, they would at least find a quick and final death in battle, rather than risk being captured with the city and becoming a prisoner of the Demon-King for the rest of eternity, hmm?'

Kate's eyes narrowed and she clenched and unclenched her fist. 'Then they're not just cattle you've staked out in an exposed place to draw out the predator that stalks them?'

'I would never suggest such a thing, milady, although your grasp of the strategy of war is clearly more advanced than mine, hmm?'

'Chamberlain, I do not know how I have suffered you for so long.' Then she suddenly realised: 'How is it you now live, when I saw you dead before! Where is Saltar?'

'There are others coming!' came a warning. 'I think it is the Scourge and the Outdwellers, but they are being pursued by... by giant cats with human faces!'

'Tell me!' Kate pressed. 'Tell me or so help me I'll command my demand in your forehead!'

'Milady, we must organise ourselves,' Silos Varr interrupted. 'We need to get most of these people out of here.'

The Chamberlain pouted and shook his head sadly, although the expression of his eyes did not change. 'He is lost to us, hmm?'

'Milady...'

'So organise them!' Kate screamed in Silos Varr's face. The soldier blinked, nodded and turned away to confer with General Constantus and the mercenary captains. Kate whipped back round to face the Chamberlain again, only to see his back disappearing amidst the throng. 'Come back here!' she shouted, pulling her crossbow out and then working to crank its mechanism.

'Mother, where's father?'

With a shout of frustration, she gave up on her crossbow and looked down at her son. Her rage drained away and she managed a brave smile for him. 'We'll see him soon, Orastes. He loves and misses you, you know. But there are demons coming and he's getting ready to sort them out.'

'I'm very good at killing monsters,' her son said proudly. 'I've killed lots of them, just ask rat-boy when he gets here, and Aa when you see Him.'

'I'm sure you have,' Kate nodded. 'But I'd be happier if I knew you were safe in the city. It would save me worrying about you. Orastes, I want you to go with Larc and Vasha here and stay with them until this is over.'

'But mother!'

'Orastes! Please, don't argue. Now is not the time. Be a good boy and do as your mother tells you.'

Orastes was determined not to cry, but his eyes filled with tears anyway. 'I don't want to go with them! I want to stay with you, to fight the monsters.'

Kate picked her son up and let him put his small arms around her neck. 'Oof! You're getting heavy. You're all grown up and a proper soldier now.' She kissed him on the forehead. 'I'm proud of you, Orastes, and know you will be a fine leader of the army one day. In fact, I'm promoting you right now. You're now General Orastes. Generals don't cry, you know, so stop that now, or you'll make me cry, and then all my soldiers will cry because I'm crying, and then soon everyone in the kingdom will be crying. That's it!

'Generals are also the best in the army at following orders,' she added gently. 'It sets a good example to all the other soldiers, you see. So will you follow the orders I give you, General Orastes?' He hid his face in her neck but gave a small nod. 'I need you to go with Larc and Vasha into the city. They're not trained soldiers like you, so will need you to protect them. Can you do that for me? Can you protect Larc and Vasha, General Orastes?'

The boy nodded again and let Kate pass him over to Larc, who then hurried to get inside the city gates before they were closed and sealed. Kate wiped a tear from her eye and prayed she would see Orastes again. She prayed that he would get the chance to grow up in a world that didn't need walls, soldiers and armies. Taking a deep breath, she went over to join her commanders.

'I am sorry to have spoken to you in such a manner before, Silos Varr. Gentlemen, how do we stand?'

'With the mercenary cavalry from Holter's Cross, we now have a thousand on each flank, a goodly number although many of the mounts are not battle-trained. And four thousand infantry in the centre, including five hundred Accritanians, Memnosian legions and mercenary companies. The Scourge and the Outdwellers will be overtaken before they reach us if we simply hold our position.'

'General?' Kate asked, bowing to the Accritanian's greater battlefield experience.

Constantus shook his head ruefully, 'If anyone had told me I would one day fight for Dur Memnos, I would have told them they were a prophet of the mad god or they'd been drinking too much devilberry liquor. As it is, there seems to be some worse creatures in the cosmos than Memnosians, although sometimes the difference doesn't seem that great.' One or two of the mercenary captains chuckled. 'Yet we have common gods and common enemies right now, so must put aside our differences if any are to survive. I will lead the infantry of humankind in the centre, with Colonel Vallus as my second and bannerman. Kate, you should lead the left flank of cavalry and Silos Varr the right. The centre will advance until our rank of archers can be brought to bear. The flanks will charge when the Outdwellers are out of time – Vallus will lower the banner as signal, agreed?'

All nodded. A few smiled, relieved that battle would finally be joined and that their fear and tension would soon end one way or another. Kate and Silos Varr became grim and stony-faced, preparing themselves for the horrors ahead that they would both see and perpetrate. One mercenary captain offered up a soldier's prayer to Lacrimos, looking around himself and saying a final farewell to Shakri's realm. And Vallus rolled his head on his neck, looking to relax and loosen himself so that he would be able to kill his enemies with greater ease.

'Then may Shakri and Lacrimos bless us all,' General Constantus said with ardour. 'Offer them your hearts, minds and bodies as kingdoms for their will! For the pantheon!'

'For the pantheon!' they shouted passionately with fists raised and the fiery maelstrom swirling in the skies above them reflecting in their eyes as storms of human pride and purpose.

'Sound the drums and blow the horns, for now we go to war!' General Constantus boomed, his voice sounding like the cataclysmic thunder of Lacrimos Himself. The army roared back in answer and set up a clamour to shake the very hills.

⚔ ⚔

Ja'rahl could not have reined in the sphinkaes if he'd tried. The chase was on, they had the scent of their prey in their nostrils and they had the unreasoning hunger of starving beasts. Besides, it was right and proper that the gods of Jaffra lead their people into battle rather than cowering behind them any longer. It inspired the Jaffran soldiers and instilled a belief in them that they simply could not lose, for they had divine right on their side. There would be no problem with Jaffran troops fleeing the battlefield while all was still in the balance, and that meant the balance should come down in Ja'rahl's favour and allow him to reach the throne of power before the Demon-King. So let the sphinkaes lead the charge and hurry the issue for him. And if a few of them should tragically die in the process, then so be it, for it would make things less complicated for him later.

Istris outpaced His smaller brethren and roared them on. The sphinkaes were less than a hundred yards behind the fleeing mortals. A large human host was coming down the slopes towards them, and riders came from the sides, but what threat could mere mortals pose to fifty divine sphinkaes, each of whom stood taller than a man on a horse?

Arrows came sheeting down, pricking the sphinkaes to greater anger. Not one was felled or even staggered. Istris and his kind began to fix the mortals with hypnotic gazes, and then made larger leaps and bound with ever greater speed as they anticipated the kill.

Ja'rahl had ordered the four thousand Jaffran troops to rush in behind the gods, and the mortals were largely protected from arrow fire as a consequence. He, however, hung back with his priesthood, to watch the annihilation unfold.

❄ ❄

Once inside the city, Larc put Orastes down so he could better guide and support Vasha.

'Phew, quite heavy that armour of yours, isn't it, General Orastes?'

Orastes nodded and sighed. 'Yes, and it makes me a bit slow, I'm afraid.'

'You could take it off.'

'No!' Orastes replied indignantly. 'A general has to wear his armour. Don't you know anything? Now, I want to go up on the walls to watch the battle.'

'I don't think – '

Vasha suddenly wailed. 'Leave him, Larc! Take me where I may rest in these final moments. There are things you and I must speak of alone before the end.'

Larc looked panicked. He glanced back down at Orastes, clearly torn.

'I'll be fine,' Orastes said, lifting his chin. 'I'm a general, you know.'

Larc nodded. 'Well, as long as you'll be alright on your own…'

'Yes, I order it! One of the guards will look after me. Go!'

With a half apologetic and half grateful smile, the mountain man led his beloved high priestess into the crowds streaming up into the city.

'Masterfully done, my young general!' said a figure from the shadows beneath the city walls. He wore a large, feathered hat a jaunty angle.

'Aa!' Orastes exclaimed in delight.

'You did not think I would abandon my blood brother, did you?'

'No, never. We are sworn to defend each other through thick and thin.'

'Precisely. And yet we leave our other brothers in blood, rat-boy and Distrus, to face overwhelming odds without us. Is your mighty sword Monster-cutter still sharp, General?'

'Yes,' Orastes said quietly.

'Is there still courage in your heart, General?'

'Yes!' Orastes declared.

'Will the Green Witch be proud of her son once he helps her defeat the worst monsters ever seen in this kingdom, General?'

'Yes!' the boy-warrior shouted.

'Then follow me and we will take this fight to the Jaffrans once more! Onwards!'

❈ ❈

The Scourge's destrier thundered up the start of the rise towards Corinus and Kate's advancing army. He looked back over his shoulder and saw that the Outdweller foot-soldiers were moments away from being caught by the giant sphinkaes of Jaffra. They pounced as if chasing mice. Arrows had been launched but done nothing to slow the enemy. The Memnosian cavalry had begun to charge, but he could tell they would be too late.

'By the idiot judgement of Win!' he sighed and pulled his trusty destrier round. He targeted the lead sphinx, which was also the largest, guiding his steed with just his thighs. He pulled his long daggers, wishing he had a lance instead.

'Why do they always have to be so big?' the Guardian complained, pulling one of his feet out of its stirrup and planting it on his saddle. 'Steady!' he murmured to the horse.

As they raced up to the sphinx, the Scourge placed his other foot on the saddle and rose to a standing position. Then he launched himself through the air so that he would come down towards the sphinx.

The sphinx roared and opened its mouth wide. It jumped with its front paws so that it rose to meet the mortal who was so eager to feed himself to the divinity that was Istris.

The Scourge's fearless destrier rose a second later and slashed with its metal-shod hooves at the underbelly of the god. The horse bit hard, drawing holy blood. It was enough to cause Istris to bring His head down slightly at the last second, saving the Scourge from flying straight down the sphinx's gullet. Instead, the Guardian skewered a knife through one of the god's cheeks and managed to land the toes of his boots just before the god's bottom row of teeth.

'The Jaffrans worship the likes of you, don't they?' the Scourge grunted as his forward momentum saw him head butt the sphinx's nose.

The god yowled.

'Well, I've got news for you… I'm in the habit of slaying both demons and gods!'

The sphinx whipped its giant head back and forth and the Scourge found himself hanging in space. He jabbed forward with his second blade, driving it home into one of the sphinx's giant golden eyes. Then he was falling, falling.

Istris screamed as the Scourge hit the ground and all of the air was driven out of his body. Winded and paralysed, the Guardian waited for giant claws to rip him apart, but his horse – trained to shield him with its body when he was unsaddled – placed itself between him and the Jaffran beast. There was the wet sound of flesh tearing and ribs breaking, and then blood and horse entrails splattered down on the Scourge. The horse gave one last snort, almost sounding derisive, and then it folded and toppled into the sphinx's forelimbs.

'You'll pay for that, you bastard!' the Scourge choked as he rolled away and got knee and foot under him.

'Wretched mortal!' Istris bellowed.

'Ah, so the cat hasn't got your tongue after all.'

With His one good eye, Istris fixed the Scourge with His hypnotic gaze, crouched and prepared to spring. The Scourge tried to tighten his grip on the one blade he still held, but his body didn't want to obey him. All would be well. There was no real threat to him from the Sphinx in truth. See, it was smiling at him really with those massive teeth. Its descending paw and claws were merely going to caress him. The spell broke as his flesh was pierced and raked. He threw back his head and screamed in agony. The sphinx tried to retract its claws slightly so that it could rend the Scourge again and finish him, but one of its claws got snagged on the mess of the Guardian's leather armour.

Istris flicked His paw and the Scourge was thrown a dozen feet. Blood bubbled out of one of the Scourge's body wounds and came up into his throat, telling him at least one of his lungs had been punctured. Ever so slowly, he put a hand to the hole in his upper chest and sealed it with his palm. He managed to draw a vital breath to keep himself alive for a few seconds longer. The sphinx stalked forward.

❈ ❈

Kate's cavalry crashed into the sphinkaes on the left and knocked a dozen of the rampaging beasts down, although they then clambered back to their feet despite the lances hanging from their chests and sides. A good number of her cavalry's mounts had reared or shied in panic just as they'd been about to reach the huge and terrifying predators, throwing their riders or crushing them when they fell. The chaos of dying and bucking mounts then became a barrier to the cavalry that had successfully driven home and were then looking to peal away to regroup and launch a second strike at the sphinkaes.

'Disengage!' she shouted, but it was impossible.

She released a crossbow bolt straight into the mouth of a snarling sphinx and saw the missile punch into and through the upper palate of its maw. The sphinx trembled and blinked. It clumsily swatted at her with a paw, which she just about fended off with her round horse-shield, and then its eyes crossed and it pitched into the earth face first.

The cavalry led by Silos Varr on the right flank should have worked to crush the sphinkaes between the two arms of the Memnosian army, but his host arrived slightly late and the sphinkaes were waiting for him. The mesmerising magic of the Jaffran gods stopped the horses in their tracks, and kept them rooted no matter how hard their riders tried to spur or lash them on. Then the sphinkaes fell on the Memnosians and wrought carnage.

Kate saw a sphinx bite the entire head off Silos Varr's mount and then casually dash the brave soldier into the ground. She knew that this time he would not recover from his injuries. And she was more affected by his loss than she would have expected. He'd been stoical and dependable where so many others had been untrustworthy. Kate grieved for his loss, not just for herself or the kingdom, but also the realm and the pantheon. Tears came to her eyes, although she could not name the precise emotion that caused them.

'Incarnus, hear me!'

I am here. We are one.

A sphinx looked up from where it was worrying a soldier's corpse out of its breastplate. It hissed as it sensed the power Kate drew to her. Then it sprang for her.

From where she sat on her horse, Kate swung the giant hammer of the Divine Juggernaut down and back like a pendulum. She nudged her horse into a canter with her knees at the same time. The hammer of power reached the height of its back-swing and then she drove it forward and up so that it smashed into the sphinx under its chin. All four of its feet left the ground as it sailed backwards, to land on its spine with a crack. Then she brought the hammer down and pulverised its head into the ground. Hot blood and gore splattered her but she hardly noticed as she looked for another target.

Seeing the Scourge turn to face the sphinkaes and Kate leading a charge on the left flank, Sotto managed to call the Outdwellers to a halt and had them about-face. 'The Green Witch!' went up their cry and they led the Memnosian infantry into the battle at a run.

'Dijin, you can eat as many of these cats as you want!' Sotto shouted at his ogrish friend.

'Really?' Dijin asked with excited eyes. 'They don't smell that good, but fighting always makes me hungry. Look out, Sotto!'

A sphinx leapt at them with a sudden turn, but Dijin's nose had anticipated its coming. With both hands reached up, the giant Outdweller caught one of the sphinx's paws and used the beast's momentum to haul it over their heads and to bring it crashing down on its side. Dijin had kept hold of its leg in his vicelike grip and the twist of the sphinx's fall snapped its forelimb. The Jaffran god roared like an angered lion and then whimpered like a mortal child as it struggled – and failed – to rise.

Dijin had been pulled from his feet by the weight of the sphinx, but he was unhurt and lumbered without fear towards his prone enemy. The sphinx's nostrils flared as it sensed him coming, but too late did it realise its throat was dangerously exposed. Using his flat hand like a blade, the Outdweller stabbed his thick fingers through the skin and flesh of the sphinx's neck and then used both hands to pull the tear wide open. Dijin buried his head in the wound and ripped the god's throat out with his teeth. Blood fountained everywhere and Dijin hung his mouth out to swallow several large mouthfuls. He wrinkled his nose and shook his head.

'No good, Sotto. Don't drink too much. It will make you ill.'

Sotto nodded. 'Understood, Dijin. Come on, there's more of them!'

Three of the sphinkaes came for Dijin at once, moving in deliberate concert rather than leaping in recklessly and allowing the mortal any chance to tackle them individually. Dijin turned this way and that, trying to keep all three in sight at the same time.

'Get back!' Sotto shouted. 'Strong as you are, you cannot stand against all of them, my friend!'

Yet Dijin stubbornly shook his head. 'No, Sotto, I must protect you. I am the strong one and you are my only friend.'

'Dijin, no!' Sotto cried. 'That is an order! Get back!'

But it was too late.

⚔ ⚔

Kate cracked open the skull of another sphinx and did not wait to see its brains spill out and its body fall. The way the cavalry was being decimated on both flanks meant that any hesitation on her part would see more of her people die and a little more of Shakri's power and realm disappear. She worked with an almost mechanical efficiency despite the savage glee of Incarnus filling her mind.

Then the sphinkaes began to avoid her, and the momentum of her killing began to fail. Annoyance and frustration soon replaced what had been bloody battle and sadistic satisfaction, and disrupted her fighting forms and precise poise. Kate began to lose direction and impetus. Incarnus sounded farther away.

She looked about, feeling strangely detached from it all, as if she saw it from outside her own body. Here was luridly coloured and shadowy death, side by side with the brightness and despair of life. Here were men fighting desperately on their own for survival, there were whole legions marching together as part of a greater force. Whole nations lived and died in these moments. In some ways, it was all a meaningless waste, in others a poignant and glorious wonder. Was this the sort of surreal ambivalence the gods experienced by way of existence or when regarding mortalkind? Or was the realm beginning to lose its coherence and fragment, all to be blown away on the cosmic winds leaving nothing?

Did any of it matter? *Really* matter? And then she spied a familiar wide-brimmed hat, a large and outrageous red feather bouncing and bobbing as its wearer moved.

'Aa?' she wondered.

At His side was… The realm suddenly slammed back into place and everything was more real and immediate than it had ever been. Never had she felt the physical limits of her body so keenly. If that wretched god allowed a single thing to happen to her son, even if it was just to become afraid, she would not hesitate to commit deicide, no matter what quips and reasons He tried to bleat as she rammed a sword down His miserable throat and waggled it around!

Now the Jaffran soldiery were reaching the edges of the battle and launching javelins and hurling stones. Orastes!

Kate seized the divine armour and weaponry of Incarnus once more and spurred her horse forward. The sphinkaes kept out of her path and she hurtled forwards to face the Jaffran troops alone. Yet Incarnus seemed to pull back. *I cannot! Shakri has forbidden us to kill any more mortals. The pantheon will take no part in destroying the last of the mortals, as it will only speed the demise of the realm and the pantheon. The balance is broken, Kate.*

'You must help me!' My son!' Kate screamed. 'What of Aa? He must protect Orastes!'

I am needed elsewhere on the field, so must leave you. I must go to continue the fight against the demons.

Then Incarnus was gone. Just when she'd needed Him most, He'd deserted her. A javelin came dangerously close, whistling just past her ear.

❈ ❈

Istris prowled forwards, His one good eye promising the Scourge an eternity of torture.

'I've always hated cats!' the Scourge coughed. 'Hey, squinty, where's this Demon-King of yours?'

'You will see soon enough!' the sphinx snarled. 'I've decided to eat you bit by bit, so you might still be alive when he arrives, although you will most certainly wish you were not.'

'You're boring me, squinty! If you take my legs first, be careful not to kiss my arse, because it might be busy doing something else!'

Beside Himself with rage, Istris threw back His head and roared. As His head came back down, an arrow flew in and took Him in the middle of His good eye. Clear fluid and blood poured out and He mewled and cried for help. He scraped at His face with a paw and tore large scratches down His forehead and nose. He rolled and thrashed about, knocking other sphinkaes down. Some slashed at Him with their claws and jumped back so that they would not get tangled up with Him. Then His voice rose in pitch and distress as He rolled onto a lance sticking up from the ground, impaling Himself. It took a seeming age for Him to die, but His movements finally slowed and He fell silent, and then still.

'Can you stand?' Strap shouted down from his horse, loosing another arrow at the nearest sphinx.

'Might have known you'd turn up once all the hard work was done,' the Scourge groaned as he struggled into a sitting position. 'By the stinking urine of Malastra, I think that's all I can manage! Help me up.'

Strap quickly checked there was no aggressor about to descend on then, hung his bow on the horn of his saddle and then leapt down to help his commander. 'You're losing so much blood, I can't believe you're still conscious. We need to get you off the battlefield.'

'Idiot!' the Scourge exhaled as he rose. 'If I'm going to be healed, it'll be by a priest of Shakri and all the remaining ones are *on* the battlefield. So what good's getting me off the field going to do, eh? By Wim's musical arse, lad, you do talk nonsense sometimes. Also, in case you hadn't noticed, there's no sitting this one out – mortalkind is about to be wiped out and needs every one of us to do what we can. If we can't win, then at least we can choose the manner of our passing and go out with some pride. I do not intend to spend my final moments malingering in some sick tent, so get me on a horse and put a weapon in my hand, or have you completely forgotten how to follow orders? No, don't answer that, I don't want to hear anymore of your yap.'

Strap sighed. 'A simple thank you would suffice, you know, but you always did get tetchy when you were embarrassed or in pain, eh? Given you can't even stand, I would have thought just putting you on a horse would be the death of you, Old Hound, yet you certainly don't seem to be lacking in energy when it comes to barking at everyone and everything.'

'Be silent, and that's an order!'

Strap laughed harshly. 'If this is our last battle, then you won't exactly be court-marshalling me afterwards, will you? And even if it's not our last, I can't really see you surviving very long, so I could choose to ignore your orders completely. I could just choose to leave you there sitting in the mud and a pool of your own blood. An ignominious end for the legendary Scourge, eh? Alternatively, you could just thank me and show some good grace for once in your life.'

The Scourge glared murderously up at the younger Guardian. 'If you think you can make demands on me just because you think you have me at a disadvantage, then you've got another thing coming. Insubordination is insubordination whether the realm is going to rack and ruin or not. You're also helping ensure the end of the realm, for every moment you waste here, the fewer enemy are being killed and the greater their chances of success. Should I thank you for that, Young Strap? Then, thank you. You're too kind. But don't go thinking you've heard the last of this!'

Strap smiled. 'See, that didn't hurt too much, now did it? Just because the realm's going to rack and ruin doesn't mean it's alright to forget our manners, now does it? You may wish to go out with pride, Scourge, but surely you also want to go out with dignity and displaying more noble behaviours, always assuming you possess such. If this is the moment of mortalkind's greatest test, then this is the moment when we need to be at our best, is it not?'

'Shakri be praised, the Jaffrans are almost here. Maybe they can save me from your banal yap. I'd all but welcome my death rather than listen to any more of this. At least Lacrimos won't whine and complain at me interminably!'

'If the pair of you have quite finished!' General Constantus shouted across at them. 'There's a battle going on and we could do with your help. Honestly, why must you Memnosians constantly bicker like an old married couple? Keep it up and you'll do this Demon-King's job for him. Vallus, get the Scourge on one of those mounts. Good man. See, Strap, we Accritanians don't have trouble following orders.'

'No, you just get yourselves possessed by demons because you're too idle to pay the gods their due until there's some crisis, when it's usually too late,' Strap replied.

The Scourge nodded. 'Well said, lad.'

Lord Ristus raised his blade threateningly. 'I will not stand idly by while you insult our kingdom!'

'Hold, Ristus,' General Constantus intervened. 'We will set our unruly Memnosian cousins an example in what it is to be civilized. It is their only hope. Now, at these demons! For the pantheon! Forward!'

The Memnosian and Accritanian infantry poured on to take the fight to the sphinkaes still remaining and the thousands of Jaffran troops coming to fight beside their demon-gods.

⚜ ⚜

All rat-boy's instincts and experience told him he should run if he wanted to survive, but he knew there was no hole deep and dark enough in which to hide from the Demon-King. He'd seen the dread lord in his dreams and never been so scared in all his life. To be sure, rat-boy had been scared of something his entire life – be it of hungry Outdwellers in the catacombs, King's Wardens intent on culling the numbers of scavengers living beyond the walls of Corinus, the child-eating man-spider, evil necromancer-kings, or pretty much anyone else these days, for they disapproved of him eating people even though it kept him alive, meaning they basically disapproved of him being alive – but nothing compared to the terror he felt at the thought of this Demon-King. The terror was increasing too, for now his waking thoughts were haunted by visions of the Demon-King, not just his dreams. His mind was a blasted and smoking landscape in which demons enacted all manner of cruel torture and depravity on mortals and in which the entire human race was enslaved and marched in chains towards the mouth of a giant, dark keep, a keep from which no one emerged.

Rat-boy had managed to survive longer than most other young Outdwellers – although he had no idea exactly how old he was – by ruthlessly putting his own needs first, constantly watching for an opportunity, moving faster than anyone else and always expecting some threat to appear and ruin everything. One time during Voltar's reign when he'd been so hungry he'd been tempted to eat stones, he'd been forced to kill and devour a boy he'd pretended was his friend. He'd hurriedly eaten his "friend's" flesh raw, for he knew the larger boys would soon smell the fresh meat and come to take it from him. His empty stomach had of course rebelled and he'd thrown it all back up, but he'd snatched up the larger pieces again and crammed them down as he'd run. After that, he'd played the friend trick on a number of occasions, and it had seen him through difficult times.

People were so weak and gullible. One minute they'd be trying to hunt him down and stick him with sharp things or tear his soft bits out with their teeth, and the next he'd use the word *friend* and they'd completely change, as if he were a magician that had them under his spell. How did they expect to stay alive for more than five seconds with such inconsistent behaviour?

It was thus that he'd learned the Great Secret that people were more than happy to risk their lives for an idea. At first, he'd hardly been able to believe it was true, but each time he'd successfully played the friend trick, the more he realised it was true. Ha! What fools! Still, it meant he now had a power of sorts and had an advantage over those with whom he competed for survival. He discovered that *friend* was just one idea for which others would kill themselves: there were also others like the promise of future gain; family; loyalty to the Outdwellers (of all things!); and most bizarre of them all, love. Even more stupid, people would then deify these ideas and obey without question what so-called priests told them to do. Unbelievable! But also an opportunity for rat-boy.

He'd convinced a number of younger Outdwellers that he was the priest of the god of the catacombs, Chorsus, and that if they did as he told them they would always have enough to eat. Whenever one of his new followers claimed they were hungry and didn't have enough to eat, rat-boy would explain that Chorsus would always provide enough to keep his followers alive. When one of his followers then died, he would tell the others that the individual had not done as rat-boy had told him and therefore been punished by Chorsus.

Rat-boy had come to dominate a large group of followers. In the early days, he'd simply eaten a few of them in secret to quieten his immediate appetite, but then he'd set them all to work bringing him a constant supply of meat. His gang of youngsters, who worked in a group and had a near fanatical devotion to their priest, soon became feared amongst the Outdwellers, for they had no trouble taking down and dismembering any of the adults who were ailing or aged. A few adults even came to rat-boy to join his congregation and pledge themselves to Chorsus.

And all because of an idea! Of course, just as he'd reached a point where he had enough to eat on a regular basis, he came to the attention of the bigger predators. They'd come for the followers of Chorsus in the darkest hour of the night and spirited them away. Rat-boy had been bound and gagged, and then dragged in front of Trajan himself.

They'd all heard of Trajan, of course, but rat-boy had never known anyone who claimed to have met him. Rat-boy had come to think of Trajan as being just like Chorsus – one of those ideas that were used to keep people sacrificing themselves. Rat-boy was therefore utterly horrified to discover Trajan actually existed. It would have been like turning the corner of one of the tunnels in the catacombs and coming face-to-face with the invented god Chorsus who was irate that rat-boy had been taking his name in vain for so long.

Trajan was old beyond counting. That an Outdweller could live so long told you he was crueller and more cunning than any other Outdweller who had ever lived. Rat-boy had effectively been incarcerated in Trajan's home with the old man and told that if he attacked Trajan or tried to escape, then he would be hunted down and eaten alive by Sotto and Dijin. No one wanted trouble with Sotto and Dijin, rat-boy included.

The old man had sucked on his gums, looked rat-boy up and down, as if deciding whether there was enough meat on him to go to the trouble of slaughtering him, and then cackled: 'Why, you're naught but a waif, eh?'

Rat-boy said nothing, his eyes darting around and his nose twitching. The old man smelt of stale sweat and urine – too infirm to look after himself, clearly, and potentially easy prey.

'Hmm. But quick and feral, eh? You may wonder why you're here, and then again you might not. Either way, I'm going to tell you, so pay attention. No, quit looking round the place and look at me. Right, now, the problem is you're too smart, see? You're disrupting the peace amongst the Outdwellers, causing the sorts of anarchy and problems that would see us destroy ourselves. And messing with the gods is not something you want to be doing, not something *I* want you to be doing! You'll end up robbing the people of their freedom and happiness entirely, which is all they have left to them. Is any of this getting through to you?'

Rat-boy watched the old man in silence, wondering what such old flesh would taste like. Perhaps it would be tough but with a strong flavour. He began to salivate.

Trajan sighed. 'Normally, I would have someone causing such trouble killed immediately. But the thing is… well, you're just so young. In some ways, it's not your fault you're like this. You've never known any different, have you? Look, someone who's so smart and clearly has such potential should be an asset to his people, not a constant threat, so starting today, I will be overseeing your education. You'll be staying here with me, so choose yourself somewhere to sleep and get used to the idea. I hope it works out, really I do, because otherwise Dijin will be having himself an extra meal, no matter that children are sacred to Shakri.'

Rat-boy was only half listening to the old man's ramble, and what he had heard hadn't made much sense. Someone had once told him that the old became mentally infirm in the same way as they broke down physically. In some ways, it would be a mercy to put the old man down. Temptation was just about to get the better of him when Trajan materialised a steak out of nowhere and threw it to rat-boy.

He'd sniffed at the meat, suspicious that anyone would freely offer up food. Yet he already knew the old man was insane, so that probably explained it. Rat-boy had snatched at the steak, in case Trajan intended to take it back suddenly, and then scampered to a dark corner to feast on it.

And so his education with Trajan had begun. He'd been confined to the single cell of Trajan's house for months on end. He'd not become bored, however, because he'd constantly watched for opportunity and because Trajan had visitors nearly everyday. Rat-boy listened to the long conversations about ideas, learning a few more tricks, and then at the end of the day shared the gifts of meat Trajan had received from his latest visitors. The boy still did not understand why the old man would want to share his meat with him, so finally spoke his first word to his captor.

'Why?'

Trajan had smiled by way of answer and then begun to ask rat-boy to complete certain tasks for him outside of his home, taking messages to other Outdwellers, carrying parcels, and so forth. Rat-boy did not understand why he should complete these tasks, but he did so anyway. It pleased the old man – not that that really mattered to rat-boy – and when the old man was pleased he would sing one of his scratchy old songs in the evening. Rat-boy liked the scratchy old songs, although he couldn't say why. He liked completing a task, coming home to his supper with Trajan and then listening to a scratchy old song. Some days there wasn't even any meat but rat-boy found he forgot about that once the old man began to sing.

The nature of the tasks Trajan had given him then began to change. Instead of dealing with messages and objects, he now had to deal with people, getting them to do things or agree to things to help Trajan. Sometimes, rat-boy had to help other people, because then they would be in a better position to help Trajan.

'Why?' rat-boy demanded more forcefully of the old man.

'Why what?'

'Why should people help you? What idea do you use to force them to do things?'

Trajan cackled. 'I don't force people to do things, do I?'

'Well, no, but people do things because you ask them. Why?'

'Why do you think?'

'I-I… I don't know. They must be scared of you!'

'Are *you* scared of me?'

Rat-boy almost laughed. 'No, you're just an old man. They must be scared of your idea… or of Sotto and Dijin.'

Trajan shook his head. 'But why then do Sotto and Dijin do things for me, eh? Why do *you* do things for me? Have I scared you with an idea, eh? I don't think so.'

Rat-boy frowned. Curse the old man. 'There's another Great Secret, isn't there! Tell me what it is!'

Trajan grinned toothlessly at him. 'I have never heard of these Great Secrets of which you speak. It causes me to imagine a conspiracy against us by great magicians or the gods themselves. You may have the right of it, but that I do not know. All I know is it's important to have purpose. What is your purpose, rat-boy?'

'I – ' he started. 'I live here and do the things you tell me…'

'Why?'

Curse the old man. He didn't want to admit it was something so ridiculous as wanting to make the old man happy so that he would sing a scratchy old song. It would also be dangerous to admit it. It would give the old man too much power over him. But then maybe the old man already had too much power over him because didn't rat-boy do everything he asked?

Trajan relented. 'It is not necessary that you tell me now or that you understand your purpose immediately. It takes most people a lifetime to discover theirs – if they ever discover it – and by then it's usually too late. Most would happily sacrifice all the years they've had just to have known it sooner. If you're lucky, you'll find yours before the end, and you can come and give me my answer. If you answer me well, this house and all I own will be yours, although you may never feel like thanking me for it.'

Rat-boy had therefore started to watch everything around him more keenly in order to discover his purpose, and there were few who were as watchful as rat-boy. He saw everything. He saw those who moved with most purpose and had the most effect on the lives of others, and he deliberately moved closer to them in order to learn the secret of their purpose. He'd guided Saltar and his companions through the catacombs to Voltar's throne room so many years before, able to navigate past the Chamberlain's wards because he'd watched so carefully. A few years later, he'd spied six men dressed in black robes smuggling a child out of Corinus and had carried news to the Green Witch. Recently, he'd spotted Orastes being led out of Corinus by the god Aa and pursued them. Throughout, he'd felt he'd been coming closer to knowing his purpose, but it had always remained tantalisingly just beyond his reach. Travelling with Orastes had been a wonderful adventure of sorts, where he'd seen and done things of which he'd never imagined. Orastes had become his blood brother, his friend... no! *Friend* was just an idea with which to trick people and make them kill themselves.

It was only now – just before the end, as Trajan had said it would be – that he began to see some purpose. It was only now – with his thoughts invaded by the Demon-King and the knowledge that there was no way to hide or survive – that he understood the events around him and his own actions in relation to them in ways that could not be selfish. He was no longer scared of not having enough to eat or dying, because that fear could not do anything to help him survive. Where once he would have stood by and watched or run when seeing a demon attack someone he knew, as that would have been the best way to save his own skin, now he felt free to intervene and affect the outcome based upon his own desire. Now, when he saw Dijin being menaced by three sphinkaes, he began to see a purpose rather than a trick in the idea of *friend*.

The Demon-King whispered seductively in his ear. 'I will need a priest, rat-boy, and you have the necessary understanding of such things. I will not trick you with ideas and talk of purpose. Can you not see that purpose is just another of these ideas and that Trajan has been tricking you with it all along, just so that you would continue to do as he told you? Do not let him continue making a fool of you. Become my priest.'

'Do you know any scratchy old songs?' rat-boy asked innocently.

The Demon-King hesitated, baffled. Before any new doubts could assail him, rat-boy leapt forward into the path of one of the sphinx's paws coming down on Dijin's blindside.

※ ※

Claws as hard as hard as steel cut downwards, severed one of Ristus's arms and cut him open from neck to navel.

'No!' Constantus cried and pushed soldiers aside to get to the lord's side.

'Back, General! Guard the General!' Colonel Vallus shouted and surged after the aging soldier.

The sphinx slashed down again, but Vallus planted the butt of the banner he carried firmly in the ground and ducked low, allowing the demon to impale its paw. The sphinx yelled in pain, brought its head down and snapped to each side. Vallus jumped back, dragging Constantus with him, but the men around them weren't so lucky. Three were killed instantly and one was horribly maimed.

Cursing himself, the gods and all demonkind, Constantus staggered upright and threw himself at the Jaffran monstrosity.

※ ※

Rat-boy threw his small flask of water at the sphinx and watched with satisfaction as its golden fur charred and then began to burn. Ever watchful and never one to miss an opportunity, he'd scooped up the blessed liquid from the river when the Outdwellers had faced the elves on their flight from Holter's Cross. The sphinx jumped back and then rolled on the ground to try and smother the holy flame, but only succeeded in spreading it to the second sphinx.

Dijin delivered a thunderous blow to the third sphinx, staggering it, and glanced down at rat-boy. 'Dijin thanks rat-boy. Rat-boy can share meat and blood, but not taste good.' Then the giant jumped and brought both fists down between the sphinx's eyes. It lost its footing and Dijin did not hesitate to move in and deliver a killing blow to its larynx.

Meanwhile, Sotto danced in behind the second sphinx, slashing tendons and hamstrings and then expertly opening up its guts. 'How about we hang the meat for a while, Dijin, so that it's properly drained of blood before we try it? Perhaps cooked with onions?'

Dijin frowned and stopped to think, momentarily distracted from the fight.

There were two more sphinkaes in their immediate vicinity, the others having moved to the flanks to face, and massacre, the mortal cavalry. These two slunk and wove around the others of their kind – giving the burning sphinkaes a particularly wide berth – and then fixed the Outdwellers with their gaze. Rat-boy froze, unable even to twitch his nose. He wanted to scream for help, but his lungs could no longer draw breath, let alone exhale to form speech. Death stalked closer. At least he had discovered a purpose for himself before dying. He would have liked to tell Trajan, because it would have pleased the old man and then he would have sung a scratchy old song.

'Fear not!' came a high-pitched voice. 'Their demon magicks cannot touch the priesthood of Shakri.'

Master Ninevus sauntered forward and the sphinkaes turned tail, their spell immediately broken. Distrus caught up to the priest's side and winked at rat-boy.

'See how the might of Shakri thwarts all our enemies. Come, my priests, and let us end this conflict!'

Master Ninevus ran forward with his priests towards the oncoming Jaffran troops.

'Wait, they are not demons!' the Scourge called raggedly from the top of a horse not far away.'

Master Ninevus either did not hear the commander or he had complete faith in his goddess's protection, for he deliberately placed himself in the middle of the short distance that now remained between Kate's army and the Jaffran troops. He raised his hands on high and said to all the mortals assembled on the field: 'Desist! For Shakri would not wish to see one more death this day. Feel the blessing of Her love, that which is the divine spark of every one of us.'

And a miracle occurred there in the churned mud of the field beneath Corinus, for every Memnosian, Accritanian and Jaffran stilled. Thoughts of bloody murder and righteous revenge vanished from their minds and they looked around themselves in wonder. They lowered their weapons, no longer any use for them.

Yet Ja'rahl had made the Jaffran people his own through millennia of blood-letting and ritual. Their will was his and it rolled irresistibly across the field now: 'Kill the demon priests, all of them!'

Dozens of javelins were hurled from the Jaffran ranks. At such close range, the priests of Shakri never had a chance. Ninevus was immolated so many times and at so many angles that he was actually pinned upright with arms still raised in an eternal supplication to mortalkind.

'Master!' Distrus cried, and it was a further miracle that the acolyte himself was not killed.

There was another moment of stillness on the field, of shock rather than wonder, as all stared at the mortification of Master Ninevus. Something had happened that was so fundamentally sacrilegious, so *broken*, that the world itself had stopped. The earth gently shook as if crying in grief and the sky cried tears of mourning. The trembling grew out of control and then the ground between the two armies cracked wide, flames almost instantly leaping up from below. Out of the fire rose figures who were majestic and terrible to behold.

'The pantheon is come!' Kate whispered in hope.

❈ ❈

Ja'rahl smiled as the bitch-mother of the false Memnosian gods began to speak. At last, the remaining demon lords of the cowardly pantheon dared show themselves. All had transpired as he'd hoped and planned. The throne of power and then absolute freedom would finally be his, after millennia of suffering as slave and servant. How he hated this blood-drenched, shambling corpse in which he'd been trapped for so long, even though it had once been his own flesh. It limited him and was no reflection of the true glory of his being.

At a nod, his blood priests rushed forward with their bowls. They were protected from the pitiful magic of the false gods by his blood and will. These priests were extensions of him – his limbs, his body, his mind. And soon the realms of mortal and demonkind would be mere extensions of his mind and will.

❈ ❈

With tragic eyes, Shakri looked round at her assembled children and broke their hearts. 'What has become of us? Is this death and destruction all we have aspired to as gods and mortals?'

'Nay, for the balance was created to allow us all more!' rumbled Lacrimos in his most terrible aspect, many lacking the courage to look upon him, just as few could bring themselves to turn their eyes from Shakri's perfect form.

Gart sighed. 'Until demonkind ultimately brought about the end of the balance. Always was I opposed to allowing their irreducible Princes a place in this realm. But you others shouted me down. Now see where it has brought us. The earth is all but devoid of growth and seed now.'

Incarnus nodded. 'And it seems that even vengeance will be lost to us. We will be naught but vainglorious taunts and posturing here at the end.'

Wim capered a little and then hunkered down. His eyes rolled around crazily and then He scratched His divine arse. 'Not that I ever did, for it was never my role, but who would fight it when it would only speed the end? Magic will ultimately have its way and unravel.'

Aa, who now joined the other gods, began to lose His smile. 'No new adventures then? No brave and risky enterprises?'

Shakri shook Her head in woe. 'Will you not all drop your weapons?'

The Memnosians and Accritanians did so, and a number of Jaffrans made to do the same but could not quite manage it.

⚰ ⚰

Lines and strings of blood were thrown through the air, forming a net and covering the gods of Dur Memnos. The will of Ja'rahl smothered the field. The magic of his blood, will, command and patterning bound them. They became an extension of his will and then he understood. He understood and was freed by that understanding!

Irreducible. More than the paltry, lesser beings of the realm. A Prince! The House of Hermes. Ha! They had trapped him in this form, robbed him of his knowledge of self! Istris had never been more than an itinerant demon of lesser rank. It had always been thus! They had cruelly stripped him of his birthright, preyed on his nature to stabilise the pathetic magic and balance of this trivial realm. The outrage to do such to one of his noble blood!

And the Demon-King was nothing more than one of his usurper brothers, one who presumed to rule without having been fully tested. Well, his brother would be found severely lacking, for he, Ja'rahl, Prince of the Hermes, had claimed the throne of the pantheon's power before the Demon-King had been able to arrive to make his claim.

Ja'rahl's rule was now absolute. His will, mind and being were the realm, and the realm was his. Any that entered in only did so at his forbearance, and he most certainly was not feeling in a forbearing mood. He forced the major gods of the pantheon to their knees before him and cracked their skulls with the pressure of his displeasure. The fluids of their brains began to leak and he sucked at the released energy that was so much richer and enriching than blood.

Parasite, they called him. *Leech! Vampire! Lyche!* He quietened them. They did not understand the deep thought and philosophy of the Hermes. He needed silence and isolation so that he could draw in the cosmos. The peace of the eternal descended on the realm.

The Demon-King and the millions of demonkind continued to crawl towards his throne. Let them come and prostrate themselves, for they were no threat and would add to his realm. Ah, the peace!

❋ ❊

Yet something was wrong. Cold mercury in his gut. A slice of the void interpolated into the balance and continuum of the realm. Fracture and disjuncture. Misalignment and dislocation. Wrongness.

He desperately searched the realm for the source but found nothing. Every god and mortal being remained a frozen statue, as per his will and command. He blinked, back in his corpse once more. Wh-?

A child with blue eyes and black curls looked up at him. Ja'rahl reached for the boy's mind, but was unable to get a grip on its surface. There was no childish innocence in his look either, only flawless determination and emotions set at absolute zero.

'Magic doesn't work on me because there's something broken inside me,' the child explained. 'This is Monster-cutter.'

Ja'rahl lowered his eyes and watched in horror as a blade sliced him in half through the waist. He fell in two and tried to prop his torso up with his two arms. But the blade relieved him of those limbs. He fell flat, twisting his head back and forth, gnashing his teeth. He was decapitated. He mouthed empty syllables attempting a final spell. Then his head was chopped in two. A blink, and his brain was stamped underfoot.

'Now, let my mother and my blood brothers go, you bad, bad monster!'

Ja'rahl wailed thinly and disappeared beyond the hearing range of every living thing.

❋ ❊

And now came the Demon-King on his gargantuan cerberus, progressing with pomp and the sound of clarion horns that banished all other sound. Archdemons formed his entourage and filled the skies. Creatures of unimaginable beauty and all too imaginable nightmare framed the great return of demonkind to the realms of cosmic power.

The Demon-King wore every face, was known and unknown to all. He was friend, foe, sibling, parent, lover and nemesis. Spiral horns crowned him and destruction and desire were the smoke of his breath. His eyes were the past, present and future. *He* was the past, present and future. There was only him.

The mortals before Corinus were surrounded and hemmed in by the millions of demonkind. There would be no escape. With the mortals thus contained, their gods were also bound. So began the rule of the Demon-King.

'Bring me the Builder! Bring me my brother Balthagar so that he may abase himself before his King!'

Chapter Thirteen: In wanting more

The corpse's eyelids flickered and then opened. It stared up at the stone ceiling above it. Everything was dim. It didn't know if that was down to the lack of illumination in this place or whether its senses had not yet come back to full life and perception.

I am Balthagar. No, I am Saltar.

Saltar turned his head. There was no sign of the Chamberlain except for an outline in the dust where his body had lain up until recently. Why hadn't the Chamberlain tried to wake him? Had some crisis connected with the Demon-King forced him to leave Saltar's body here to gather cobwebs? Or had the Prince of the Arachis scuttled off to effect some new scheme? The latter would certainly be more true to the Chamberlain's fundamental nature and philosophy.

Of more concern to Saltar, however, was where Kate and Orastes were. Given the dust that had been allowed to settle over his body, he'd clearly been away for some considerable stretch of time. Had they not noticed his absence and come to look for him? What force could keep them from his side? Did the Demon-King have them already? He couldn't think it. Perhaps they had thought him genuinely dead, but surely they would have buried him if that had been the case. And Mordius would have reassured them that he was merely displaced rather than entirely undone.

Filled with unease and urgency, Saltar tried to raise his head, but it felt nailed to the floor. Pain sizzled through him, and he welcomed and embraced it, for it was his body fully coming back to itself, capillaries dilating, blood beginning to flow once more, nerves conducting messages from his brain to the rest of his body, muscles spasming and starting to work again, life returning! It was a tortured ecstasy, a happy execration of the flesh.

He was racked for long, long minutes, during which time he laughed, cried, gasped and begged for mercy, but finally he could stand as a living, breathing man in Shakri's realm once more. The world tilted alarmingly. He was very weak. His body had used up nearly all of its reserves during its death and resurrection and he felt utterly wasted. If he didn't replenish himself quickly, then he would find himself lying back in the dust, perhaps never to rise again.

He extended his senses, desperately searching for a nearby source of life-energy, but found nothing. He shifted his vision and examined the vague scintillations that constituted the thin light in the tower room. He drew on it and was relieved to discover it would just about sustain him as long as he moved slowly. The room darkened instantly as he absorbed its light and an inky pool of darkness surrounded and clung to him. The void travelled with him and it was as if he saw everything from down a long, dark corridor.

He managed to get to the door just before he exhausted all the light in the room, and struggled out into the empty corridor and stairwell beyond. Still there was no major source of life-force within the extended range of his magical senses. There weren't even any burning torches along the walls, just a grey, diffuse gloom everywhere. Where were all the people? The palace was usually busy with guards on sentry duty or patrol, maids coming and going, pages hurrying along with messages, trade representatives and plaintiffs. Now, it felt abandoned and was eerie with echoes. Were these actually the empty corridors of his own mind? Perhaps he'd never woken up properly and was instead trapped within this ghostly plane, to wander lost forever.

He travelled down through the tower, leaving only a cold darkness in his wake, a darkness so complete that it would leech away the life-force of any who dared enter it. It *was* the void, and he was responsible for starting its spread! If he didn't find energy soon, then the entire palace would be consumed and lost forever.

Trying not to panic, he stumbled on, annihilating all as he went. This was not how it was meant to be. He wanted to be the Builder, not the Betrayer or Destroyer! Surely there was life left somewhere. What had become of the realm and its gods in his absence? With terrible foreboding, he entered the main part of the palace of Corinus.

'Kate!' he croaked. 'Mordius! Scourge! Anyone? Where are you? Chamberlain, answer me!'

There was no response. Finally, he passed a large window that overlooked an interior courtyard. On the sill was a vase of relatively fresh flowers and he wasted no time drawing all their life-force into him. As the orange blossoms withered and crumbled to dust, he managed to steady himself and ensure the darkness around him was no longer absolute, although the murk remained.

The flowers could not have been there more than a day or so, and that meant there must have been people here up until very recently. The thought calmed him and his fear that Corinus had become an eternal tomb that would be entirely engulfed by the void receded somewhat. Now, he just needed to know his family were safe.

Saltar broke free of the palace and crossed the precinct in which it stood. He saw no one but sensed a storm of strange energies ahead. The sky was stained with filth and damage and strange planes of bruised colour made the whole look fractured and broken.

As he moved into the city proper, he at last sensed and glimpsed living people. They sought to hide from him, and he realised that the thick shadow that surrounded him must be unnerving indeed. They cringed and cowered in alcoves or slunk away down dark alleys. He sensed many in their houses, behind barred doors and tight shutters, retreating under tables and beds or into strong-rooms. They were in fear for their lives, and apparently without hope, for they simply waited for their doom to come.

Tempted as he was to draw energy from any number of those nearby, he could not bring himself to do it. Stealing someone's life, even a fraction of it, was tantamount to murder, no matter how much one part of his mind whispered it would be justified if he took life from a few in order to save many, and that he could always return the life-force later. 'Stop it!' he ordered the dissenting voice and settled for taking sustenance from the moss that grew in gutters and in between the bricks of various walls. Even so, the energy came slowly, just as blood thickens and arteries begin to harden with the onset of rigor mortis. Was the realm dying then? Was he too late?

He came to a fountain and drank until his voice sounded human again and his stomach bulged uncomfortably. There was little life-energy to be had from the water, however, for it was somehow thin and depleted. It was like a ghost of what it had once been. Shakri's realm was faded and dull now. Its substance had dwindled. Was it his imagination or did things seem slightly transparent when he looked at them askance?

He ran as best he could, knowing that every passing second was precious and perhaps the last the realm had. At last, he stumbled down to the city walls and laboured up a set of exterior stairs. A deathly pale, young guard – surely too young to bear arms – recognised him and reached down the last few steps to help pull the Battle-leader up onto the ramparts.

Chest heaving and heart fluttering, Saltar raised his head to look out over the plains beneath Corinus. Much as he needed air, his breath caught in his throat and all the fears and dread he'd fought to keep at bay overran him. He desperately prayed that he was still asleep or dead, and that what he saw was just some bad dream or the overwrought vision of a failing mind. He didn't want to believe that all he'd worked so hard to build had been reduced to this hell on earth, where mortals and their gods were nothing more than the playthings of mayhem and perversion.

As far as the eye could see, the landscape was crowded with a chaos of devils and demons. Their cacophony prevented rational thought. Every building and boulder had been torn apart and left as rubble. Every tree and blade of grass had been reduced to black char and smoke. The ruination was complete. Lakes of urine and a thick layer of excrement over the ground sent up a miasma and stench that made the eyes water and the gorge rise.

His eyes frantically searched the heaving, roiling mass that surrounded the city. And there they were: a group of humans herded together in the shadows of impossibly large demons who stood as high in the air as Saltar was atop the walls and mount of Corinus. He spied the colour, the blessed colour green! He selfishly prayed it was her, no matter who else was already dead. The energy he sensed there was spiked and savage in the way he always associated with his wife. But of his beloved son he could feel nothing! Was that Strap and the Scourge? Surely then there must be hope for his young Orastes! They wouldn't let anything happen to Orastes, would they? They were always there to put things right, weren't they?

But this time there might not be any salvation, for were those energy signatures not a small number of the gods? Surely that was not all that remained of the pantheon, was it? Yet he knew it was. The realm had been brought to its knees and reduced to all but nothing. The gods were rendered empty and powerless by it. The pantheon had fallen and the balance had broken. All was lost and the magic that sustained this reality had unravelled. The Pattern had petered out, no future remaining to this realm, and even its past and present beginning to disappear.

The titanic, looming demons were a confusion of every known and unknowable form, and from them emanated a malice that could be physically felt. They slobbered, slavered and masturbated over the remaining humans in anticipation of the climax and final moment of destruction that was about to come. Although Saltar could see significant numbers of other humans intermingled with the demons, he sensed they were already possessed and lost to the realm. The Moment of Ending and the triumph of demonkind was here.

Over it all presided a hideous and magnificent beast astride a cerberus the size of a mountain. The Demon-King was crowned with twisting horns that rent and bent reality around them. They blazed with a cosmic energy as bright as the sun and could only be looked upon for the briefest of moments. The Demon-King laughed and leered as the philosophy and destiny of the Nihil was made manifest.

'Ah, Balthagar, there you are at last! Were you hiding in fear of me, brother? It is well that you fear me, is it not? Kings should be feared. Come, bow before me!' the Demon-King breathed across the field, carelessly poisoning, gassing and incinerating swathes of lesser demons as he did so.

'What have you done, Vidius?' Saltar asked in a voice forked by sadness and anger. All on the field heard him, for distance and perspective had started to collapse.

The Demon-King laughed with smug satisfaction. 'What have I done? Is it not apparent? It is only because you are so obviously simple that I excuse your presumption in questioning me. Brother, I have freed demonkind. I have claimed the Relic as my crown so that it may restore demonkind to its former glory. And now I come to take the throne of power of this realm, as is my right. Through me, demonkind will have its place in the cosmos fully restored. Then, our cause will be the further advancement of demonkind, as the entire cosmos is brought under our dominion. Truly, it is only I who have the scale of vision to rule over all. You will therefore bow to me now, brother!'

Saltar shook his head. 'You speak of demonkind's former glory? Surely you must know there was no glory in our past, for you have stolen some of my most ancient memories along with the Relic that was once my crown and upper mind. There was only aeon after aeon of war, Vidius. The suffering and loss was unparalleled and indescribable. You have freed demonkind, brother? Nay, I think not. Rather, you are dooming it. Do you not see that the way in which you are using the Relic – what you have done to this realm and will seek to do to the rest of the cosmos – will only see us repeat that war and ultimate failure? Far from advancing demonkind, you are ensuring it will be defeated once again, perhaps defeated once and for all, for the cosmic forces will not be inclined to show us mercy a second time.'

'You speak of things you no longer understand, Balthagar, for it is me who now wears the crown and holds the full wisdom and memory of our kind.'

'Vidius, hear me!' Saltar pushed on. 'You hold to the same philosophies that saw us undone all that time before. Mortalkind has shown us new things and new ways of being that we might embrace for our advancement. Give up this Relic of the past and let us build a realm for demon, god and mortal together. Otherwise, the power of the Relic will insist that its ways are repeated so that its magic can become self-propagating. It is probably affecting your mind even now, turning you towards its own way of thinking. Think for yourself, Vidius! Magic constantly asserts and reasserts itself. Just see how this realm repeats the same cycles of near-destruction and salvation, of death and rebirth, of Shakri and Lacrimos, in order to continue its own pattern within the cosmic Pattern. You know I speak the truth, for you and I have lived millennia in this realm and been through that repeating cycle. Break free of this Relic and its insistence, Vidius, for then we may become something new and advance! Otherwise, it can only end in our destruction!'

There was the briefest moment of hesitation and look of doubt on the Demon-King's face, and then it was gone. A knowing smile took its place. 'Ah, brother, always were you the most relentless of us. Always was your will imposed upon us. It is not the insistence of the Relic that is the threat, but the uncompromising insistence and magic of the Prince of the Spartis! Perhaps I should not have even let you speak, for that allowed you a moment to insist and exert yourself again, did it not? Lay aside the Relic, is it? Fear to cause destruction, should I? *I am Nihil!*' the Demon-King stormed, his voice a hurricane that cracked the walls of Corinus. '*Such destruction is our will and philosophy! You are no more than a pretender to my throne! A usurper! You spread dissent and treason against me. Well, it will not – must not – be tolerated, for the good of demonkind! Prepare for your punishment, brother, for it is long overdue. Resist, and all these friends of yours will have the flesh stripped from their bones!*'

'Do not do this, Vidius!' Saltar pleaded. 'Remember, I have fought you before and already defeated you. That cycle will also repeat. I beg you not to do this.'

'*The gods will be raped by every demon here, which will surely take the rest of eternity! Resist, and this thing will happen. And you are powerless to resist, for there is little life-force left in you, I sense. Bow down and submit to me for it is the last time I will command it.*'

Saltar knew the Demon-King was right. He was still terribly weak from his death and resurrection. He lacked the power to draw energy from any of demonkind, especially as they were ruled and controlled by the Demon-King's own magic. And there was nothing of Shakri's realm left to bolster Saltar either... nothing except for the few remaining mortals.

Saltar raised his powers and knew what he had to do. The Demon-King immediately shored up his own magicks, so that he would be ready to defend himself and retaliate. Rather than draw energy from the mortals that he could use to lash the Demon-King, however, Saltar instead pushed his own life-force out towards all those possessed Accritanians on the field. Motes of gold and blue sparks of energy hit each Accritanian and made the life-force in them burn stronger than ever before, driving Cholerax out of every one of them.

Utterly spent, having given far more than he had to spare, Saltar collapsed on the rampart, smacking his head on the stones. He could no longer defend himself, and lay as vulnerable as a newborn to the attack that the Demon-King now readied to launch.

Hundreds of thousands of Accritanians were suddenly returned to themselves and a revitalised Shakri surged up from Her knees. She had never been able to bring death to the mortals of Her realm, but there was nothing to prevent Her from bringing destruction to the demons who invaded from another realm. With Aa and Incarnus to either side of Her, She cut a violent and merciless path through to the Demon-King.

'For the pantheon!' Kate cried and led Memnosians, Jaffrans and Accritanians charging in behind their gods.

Lacrimos uttered terrible words and thousands of the newly dead rose at His command to add themselves to the ranks of the living. In addition, no small number of ancient skeletons clawed their way up out of the earth to beset the vast demon nation. Then the Divine Slayer hurled fearsome death magicks across the field to wither and tear apart His enemies. The laws of Shakri's realm still operated sufficiently to cause untold grief to any enemy who dared enter in and assume a form there.

'Annihilate them all!' the Demon-King bellowed, the agitated heads of his cerberus snapping up and vanquishing large numbers of the smaller demons around his feet.

Long spidering limbs wrapped themselves around the cerberus and the Demon-King. Arachnoid fangs rose up behind the Demon-King's head and sank into his neck. The archdemons of the Arachis were in revolt and fighting broke out amongst the demons.

'So, Chamberlain, you have played your hand!' the Demon-King laughed as he tore limbs off the Arachis archdemon seeking to bring him down. 'I had anticipated this. See how the Co-optis, Hermes and Nihil loyal to me quell your house even now. Come, show yourself Chamberlain, so that the Prince of the Arachis will at least suffer with his house. No matter, I will find you in your webbed lair later. As for the Spartis, they stand at a loss as to what to do – ah, I see you do not even have the strength to command them, Balthagar. Leaving only the Fortis. Scourge, or Janvil to give you your true name, you are demonkind! Will you not come stand with me?'

The Scourge clung grimly to his saddle, his wounds so grievous that he did not trust himself to do more than stay in his seat. Yet he did not flinch from meeting the Demon-King's awful gaze. 'That is not true! I have nothing to do with demonkind. Vidius, you always were as deluded as you were sadistic. You are about as likely to know the truth as you are to able to resist a lude offer from your whore-mother.'

The Demon-King's laughter only increased. 'You only need look at that vain and manipulative bitch who's been bedding you to know the truth, Janvil. She has seduced you with Her smiles and wiles, Her words and curves, has She not? You will see the truth in Her eyes, Janvil. Has She told you that She was the one to gift you with millennia of life? Has She told you that She was the one who made you undying and able to defeat Lacrimos? Has She told you that She is love, She loves you as absolutely as She does Her entire creation, and that you are Her true Guardian? Has She thus bought your loyalty so you will defend Her and Her realm and seek to expel any and every demon from it? Has She turned you against yourself and your own kind, Janvil, you who should be the most steadfast of us? Has She lied to you, manipulated you, made a fool of you and cuckolded you? Look Her in the eyes and tell me what the truth is if you will not hear it from me! I dare you to do so, Prince of the Fortis! Tell me that this love of yours is no delusion if I am the one deluded! Tell me!'

He could not help himself. The Scourge sought the eyes of his beloved, who stopped and turned back towards him, abject misery on Her face. Tears filled his eyes and everything blurred. 'No, it is not so,' he whispered.

She shook Her head, no words.

'Please!' he moaned.

'I *do* love you, Janvil!' She averred.

Was that enough for him? He knew it was. It had always been enough, no matter the suffering, difficulty or humiliation to come with it. He *was* steadfast, and not about to give up on his love just when the suffering, difficulty and humiliation were at their greatest, just when he felt that love more keenly than ever before, when it was greater than it ever had been before. He glared up at the Demon-King: 'I pity you, you aping jackanapes! This love is no delusion. You *are* deluded, Vidius, always were and always will be. I am nothing of demonkind!'

Shakri nodded Her head, tears spilling down Her cheeks, adoration for him in Her eyes.

The Chamberlain limped and crawled along the parapet to Saltar. He weakened with every step and soon his legs appeared broken or paralysed.

He dragged himself by hands and arms along the last dozen yards, tearing his nails, his fingers becoming a mess of black ichor. His voice was faint and flecks of ichor filled his breath as if he was suffering terrible internal damage. 'Brother, I am failing, hmm? There is nothing left I can do. The Pattern is no more and no sleight of hand I know of will save us. You must draw life-energy from me while you can, yes?'

'Then you utterly reject and renounce your demon heritage, Janvil?' the Demon-King asked, his laughter so hard and loud that it shook the firmament.

'Quickly, Saltar, before the words are spoken! My life-energy is freely given!'

'I do renounce it and all it stands for!' the Scourge railed at the Demon-King.

'Then the Prince of the Fortis is no more and the house is commanded directly by the crown!'

Giants as tall as the heavens strode out of the bloodied sky, hammers as big as the sun in hands that could eclipse the moon. Their faces were cruel with intent. They had come to unmake the mortal realm.

'Now you've done it! Nice one, *Janvil*.' Strap breathed.

The Scourge swore. 'Bastard tricked me.'

'Well, what do you expect of a demon, lover-boy?'

'Oh, quit your yap, you talk too much. Besides, shouldn't you be shooting arrows or something? The Divine Lunatic Wim is still on the loose, isn't He?'

'Unfortunately, I'm out of arrows. I used too many saving you from those sphinkaes, didn't I?'

The Demon-King and his archdemons contemptuously flicked Aa and Incarnus aside. Then they slapped Shakri and Lacrimos to the floor. 'There is no point in this resistance. The pantheon cannot stand against me, for I hold the Ungod here in my hand. She has been waiting a long time for this, I believe. Please feel free to educate them, my dear!'

A young girl with a malicious grin on her face came to stand on the edge of the Demon-King's hand. She glared down upon the remaining members of the pantheon and gestured for Mordius and Marr to come forward from behind her. 'Now your crimes will be revisited upon you. For the simple reason that I would not join you against the Creator, I was imprisoned for time beyond memory. The tyranny of your will was imposed upon me just as it was upon all the mortals of this realm. Yet you have helped forge this moment in doing so. Ultimately, you have perpetrated the crime against yourselves, for now you must either join the Demon-King with him as your Creator, or you will find yourself imprisoned by his will forever more. Yes, the cycle repeats.'

The witch giggled and continued: 'Life and death are no longer ruled by you in this realm, for here is my pet necromancer, Mordius, once known to you all. He is of course the last of the necromancers and therefore has the power to hold absolute sway over death, just as Harpedon did before him. Yes, Lacrimos, well you might quail, for through this mortal the death of the pantheon will also be realised. Just as life in this realm is now circumscribed by demonkind, so death will also be circumscribed, for Mordius will act by my will just as the Demon-King's will is achieved through me! So, come, little magician, and pass my sentence of death on your pantheon. Is it not glorious here at the end that you mortals finally get to throw off these divine tyrants? The coming of demonkind sets us all free! It is circumscribed, inscribed and prescribed by the glory of the Ungod and the Demon-King!'

Eyes glazed over, Mordius raised his hands above his head and began to drone words of power to focus and channel the witch's instruction. A thunderhead formed around him and he became the ultimate priest of corruption and destruction about to deliver his maleficent benediction to the world. His robes billowed out and the wind screamed the exquisite pitch of death. A cruel tempest battered every god and mortal to the ground. The pantheon wailed in fear and horror.

'Mordius, no!' Kate cried, curled up on the ground with eyes closed and hands clapped over her ears. 'For the love of Shakri, no!'

The witch cackled hysterically and clapped her hands in time to the lightning that began to strike around the gods' heads. Mordius lowered his hands and grabbed the witch by her upper arms. 'Now, Marr, now!'

The animee had drawn his blade and moved forward even as Mordius was still speaking. Colonel Marr slashed open the girl-witch's throat even as she tried to command the demon that she presumed still possessed the necromancer. But the demon Jack O'Nine Blades had been forced out of Mordius when Saltar had gifted himself to all the possessed mortals on the field; thus her ebbing spirit found no grip and finally slid into oblivion cursing.

The Demon-King roared in anger and took Marr in his other hand, instantly crushing and squeezing him out through his fingers. In panic, Mordius threw himself off on the hand on which he stood and hurtled headfirst towards the ground far below. He was glad that he had not betrayed himself or his friends before he died. He just regretted that he'd not been able to do more to save them. Still, it was better all round if no more necromancers existed. Then, in anguish, he remembered all the stories about Harpedon's failed attempts to end his own existence.

As it was, burly arms broke Mordius's impact right at the last second. He looked up into the pockmarked face of a gibbering loon. Wild hair grew from the nose and ears of the face, but there was nothing as wild as the rolling eyes there.

'That was lucky, eh?' Wim said, carrying Mordius in his arms like a babe.

'Enough of this!' boomed the Demon-King, his displeasure crushing every demon to the floor. 'Mordius, will you defy me if it costs you the boy?'

Mordius's face became ashen. He looked round and saw one mortal boy standing alone amongst all the fallen mortals and gods.

'Uncle Mordius, are you alright?' Orastes called.

The Demon-King smiled evilly and reached down for the child.

Kate, delirious as she was, got to her knees and raised a loaded crossbow. 'Don't you dare touch him, you sorry, jealous and pathetic loser!'

She released her bolt and it spiked the Demon-King's wrist, but then it passed through harmlessly and the hand continued to come down casting a shadow over Orastes.

Strap plucked an arrow from the mud and fired it at the Demon-King's heart. The Scourge hurled a dagger, although it cost him another pint of blood to do so and then collapsed flat on his face in the slurry of the ground to start drowning and asphyxiating. Sotto and Dijin, rat-boy and Distrus, and Constantus and Vallus all hauled themselves up and started locating weapons.

'Stupid mortals!' the Demon-King sneered. 'My magic and form cannot be thwarted by your tawdry toys and childish desires. You think yourselves heroic, do you not? You believe your never-say-die spirit might somehow see you through, do you not? You are less than children! Arrogant and trivial creatures not worthy to know even a moment's existence. To think such pitiful beings would even be allowed egos! Each of you selfishly thinks all will be well if just your individuality survives, no matter the large number of those already ended. Oh, you may shed a tear for those that are lost, but there's nothing heroic in that, nothing! Well, it's time you all had a lesson in futility. First you will watch the boy die, and then your leaders will die one by one. The Green Witch, Constantus, the Scourge. And as each of you dies, you will see your gods become weaker and decrepit, until they are nothing but detritus. You will see all hope disappear and then you will truly know yourselves for what you are – over-reaching and amoral vermin! And it will start with the death of the boy.'

Aa floundered to rise, His magnificent clothes ruined and His hair bedraggled. He used His sword as a crutch, but could never reach Orastes in time. Gart lay spread-eagled in the muck and was hardly recognisable as anything living. Incarnus lay battered, His armour so bent out of shape that it refused to articulate properly, leaving Him stranded on His back. Shakri and Lacrimos moved as if blind and deaf, confused and feeble. The gods were beaten and could not save a single child.

The Demon-King's hand slapped down on top of Orastes and Kate screamed in grief. Then the Demon-King flinched. He barked in irritation and quickly withdrew his hand, black ichor pouring from it. He tried to stem the flow, but it poured on.

'Magic doesn't work on me because there's something broken inside me,' Orastes shouted helpfully. He waved his sword. 'This is Monster-cutter, and you're a very, very bad monster!'

'Gah!' the Demon-King replied, tore off his offending hand at the wrist and grew himself a new one. But that had the same wound and he continued to lose vital substance. He became slightly smaller in size, although not by much. He grabbed the nearest archdemon, tore out its sinews and used them as a tourniquet for his wrist. Finally, the flow of ichor slowed to a dribble and the hand shrivelled up and died.

The Demon-King grinned. 'I might have known Balthagar's whelp would want to play as well. But no more of these games! We will do this the old-fashioned way then. Demons, you will start slaughtering these mortals at will. Form ranks, sound the drums of doom and wind the horns of destiny. Forward!'

As one, millions of demons rose and turned to face the few thousand mortals. They stepped forward, massively dwarfing Kate's army in both the size of being and number. The mortals and their fallen gods were cast into deep shadow. The giants of the Fortis filled the sky and prepared to bring the heavens crashing down on Shakri's realm, to finish it once and for all.

'Oh dear!' cried Wim, frighteningly sober and rational. 'No more dice, no more cards, no more spins of the wheel. Sorry, Mordius!'

'Hold, Vidius!' Saltar shouted from the parapet atop Corinus. 'I command it! If you end these mortals now – wanting though they are – before the rule of the Demon-King has been ratified by every house, you may lose everything. The Spartis still have not bent their knee to you. Finish these mortals too soon and demonkind may lose itself its only recourse should your rule not be entirely resolved.'

'Then let battle be joined, brother, for I intend to spear you on the horns of my crown. You will writhe there for the rest of eternity and you will gift the house of Spartis to me, or I will see it dismantled. I will *not* halt the slaughter of the remnants of mortalkind, for we have already had too many false starts, have we not? The destruction of this realm is required by the philosophy of the Nihil, and the destruction of this realm will further resolve my rule. I suspect the death of Kate and Orastes will undo you, will it not? I will enjoy finishing you brother. Here I come!'

The Demon-King flexed his massive thews and sprang high into the air towards the distant turrets of the city. Saltar expanded, timed his leap and rose to meet his enemy. The Battle-leader butted the Demon-King in the stomach, but it was as if his head met stone, and he was temporarily concussed. Enough air was driven out of the Demon-King nonetheless to see him bend double. Saltar had intended to meet his brother's chin with his fist as the head came down and forward, but in his daze he missed. The Battle-leader's wild swing twisted him in the air and the Demon-King was suddenly behind him. A thick arm wrapped itself around Saltar's neck, putting him in a headlock and beginning to squeeze.

Saltar expanded himself further, seeking to break the hold, but Vidius simply expanded his own size to match. The squeeze continued and became stronger as Saltar became weaker. As one Prince fell, so the other rose, as the sun falls and the moon rises in its turn. Saltar's vision began to become eclipsed with darkness and all he saw were stars. In desperation, he hurled himself backwards and the Demon-King's lower back smashed into a star. Vidius arched in pain with the impact and Saltar broke free.

Even as the Demon-King had been bent back, however, his tail had come up and circled Saltar's neck again. It began to crush his throat. Saltar raised his hands and tried to prise himself free, but with his lungs and brain starved co-ordination was becoming increasingly difficult and his fingers were thick and clumsy. His chest burned as if filled with fire and his mind saw only yellows and reds as his blood became a lava that ate away at his essential being.

'You see, dear brother,' Vidius whispered in his ear. 'I was always the greater. You only ruled because I indulged you for a while, indulged you as the younger brother, for the ways of the Nihil are more ancient and knowing than you will ever understand. But I fear I spoiled you by indulging you. And you are no longer so young, brother. Your demanding tantrums of aspiration cannot be excused in this more mature time. There is only the removal of all rights and privileges at such an age and moment – the removal of freedom and the removal of existence. Goodbye, brother!'

The stars were starting to wink out at the edges of his vision. In a final bid to save himself, Saltar bent his right leg and kicked the heel of his foot back up between the Demon-King's legs. The Demon-King squawked and his tail around Saltar's neck loosened. Saltar drew a mighty, shuddering breath from the cosmos and started to struggle free.

'Ooo! That smarts! Naughty, naughty!' Vidius admonished and retightened his tail.

Then Vidius used his tail to dangle Saltar away from him and lash him into a star. He whipped him into another, bashing him over and over. Saltar's bones were shattered time and again and he found it harder and harder to reknit or reconstitute them.

The Demon-King grabbed a meteor in each hand and hammered them into Saltar's temples. He used them to smash in the Battle-leader's nose and teeth. Then he thumbed out Saltar's eyes and put burning supernovas in their place.

Saltar's skull was an inferno that lit up the heavens, a cataclysm to rend the ether and this plane of reality. Then the Demon-King lowered his head and rammed his horns through Saltar's navel and solar plexus. He raised his crown back up and there Saltar writhed upon the twin points of meaning and nothingness, beginning and end, existence and the void.

'See your fallen Battle-leader, your saviour of nothing!' the Demon-King echoed through the heavens and cast Saltar down to the despairing and dying mortals below.

Insensible, Saltar fell as a comet of doom down through the atmosphere; his trail a red weal and burning scar and then a gaping wound in the fabric of creation. His huge body smashed into Corinus, instantly flattening half of the buildings and all but mercifully killing large numbers of its devastated mortal population.

The core of what had once been the mighty Builder punched down through the ground and into the catacombs beneath the city. Fire so intense it began to melt the rock engulfed the top half of the mound.

'No hiding now!' the Demon-King chortled as he descended from on high to end all time and the struggle of existence.

❇ ❇

Through the smoke-filled tunnels crawled a mangled and twisted creature. Madness burnt in its eyes and malice constantly worked its twitching features.

Its jaws worked up and down chewing and biting the air hungrily. Its sharp teeth clicked together and its tongue flicked saliva down its chin.

'I will take back whatever remains from you, hmm? Look what you have done to us, Balthagar! You have murdered us all with your insanity of mortal manners and mercy, hmm? It is only right I now take my due, for at least that way I may have enough to serve as vassal to the Demon-King.'

The Chamberlain crept closer to the charred corpse that was Saltar and sank his fangs into the burnt and crisped body. The Battle-leader's flesh had become charcoal and his blood a black oil, but power still remained within, if it could but be drawn forth. Ah! There was a perfect diamond at the centre, created from the titanic pressures and temperatures the Builder had borne and suffered throughout time. It was the matrix of iridescent and irreducible power at the heart of Saltar.

The Prince of the Arachis tapped greedily into it, intent on making it his own. After all, it was no longer of use to Saltar. Yet something was wrong. No! Rather than being drawn forth, the power was draining the Chamberlain into itself. It was excruciating, but his fangs had become temporarily fused with Saltar's flesh and bone, making it impossible for him to free himself of the vampiric corpse. The Chamberlain's mind became heated and stretched until it was as thin wire and then it was slowly pulled out through his fangs.

'Mercy!' he squeaked, tears of self-pity running freely down his face. 'I yield, hmm?'

The corpse opened its eyes, their newly grown whites shocking against its blackened flesh. The Chamberlain was released and he fell back, cradling and crooning to himself.

I apologise, brother, but I had no choice, Saltar projected to the Chamberlain. *And I must beg your further help, for I still cannot see well, have difficulty in moving and cannot navigate these catacombs the way you can. Quickly, Chamberlain! If you are prepared to help me, it has to be now, for our brother Vidius will be here momentarily. Make your choice, Chamberlain!*

A taunting voice drifted down from the top of the hole Saltar had punched through the earth. 'Come out, come out, wherever you are! I know you're down there, little Balthagar. I can sense that some last vestige of your power yet remains. I can feel you moving. You cannot hide from me. Your King has come to collect his due, to accept your contribution to the throne and his future rule. The price must be paid. You will hand over the last of yourself to me so that I may wear it as a jewel to augment my glory. If you willingly yield what is rightfully mine, I will make the end quick for you, perhaps even allow Kate and Orastes to become members of my court. But if I must come down there to make my point more forcefully still, then I will make sure the end is as unpleasant as possible before I finally snuff you out.'

Gart, hear me! I know you linger still, for these catacombs are still intact. I beg you to shore up the existence of these tunnels as long as you can, even if all else begins to fail and even if you yourself begin to fail. These walls must retain their integrity and stand against the Demon-King for as long as possible!

� ✜

The rock of the mount of Corinus remained stubborn, and Vidius realised it would take forever to get inside by simply battering at it with his giant fists. He didn't dare take too long, for fear that Balthagar would begin to regain some semblance of strength. So, loathe as he was, and cursing roundly, he reduced his size and dropped down through the hole into the darkness.

He landed lightly and looked all around – nothing could remain hidden from his eyes, even in the absence of light. Yet there was nothing here! Where was his wretched brother? Surely Balthagar would have been in no condition to move once Vidius had cast him down. So what went on here?

Vidius extended his senses and realised Balthagar was not far away down the tunnel ahead, at a junction from which extended three other tunnels. His brother moved with agonising slowness. Vidius smiled, for it would be a simple matter to over take him and... But wait, was that another life-force at Balthagar's side? Ah, that would explain things. Then the life-forces disappeared from his senses completely!

The Demon-King roared his anger, which caused the tunnels to start crumbling, and then began to power forwards. His bulky muscle caught and tore on protrusions in the rock, but he instantly repaired any harm to his body and increased his speed further. None could outpace or escape him. He suddenly collided with an invisible wall and found himself suspended in midair, all forward momentum lost. It was as if he was caught in some sort of invisible web...

'Chamberlain!' the Demon-King howled. 'I will see every demon in your house executed for this! Do you really think these tedious wards will do anything but delay the inevitable by a hand of seconds? Your worst offence is to bore me like this, do you know that?'

Vidius shredded the ward and bounded down the tunnel he was sure contained his quarry. But their life-forces ghosted a constant distance ahead of him, no matter how much he exerted himself, and then began to fade! He realised he'd been tricked again – this time with some sort of illusion.

Grinding his teeth down to their gums and then jawbones, he raced back down the tunnel and took the one branch down which he sensed life. He stopped a minute later, sure that his prey were unable to move at the speed he sensed they were travelling. Another damned illusion!

He now knew Balthagar and the Chamberlain must have actually taken the third branch at the junction and hidden themselves behind yet another ward, so that he would not be able to sense them and so that he would end up pursuing illusions instead. He repeatedly smashed his fists in fury against the walls on either side of him, not caring that the roof cracked and slabs of rock fell in on him. He reformed and recreated himself over and over, pulverising everything around him until he reached the junction again, passed through the new ward and finally sensed their real life-signatures ahead.

'Now I have you!' he shouted and laughed with manic mirth. 'Here is where it ends, my little Princes! It's too late to beg for mercy, too late for rehearsed apologies and regrets. Too late for negotiation and bargains. Too late for prayers and curses! Too late for reprieves and reprisals. Too late even for wishes and what ifs. It is all for naught. It is all for the Nihil, as it always was, was always meant to be and always will be. There is nothing more you can say; there is nothing more that you can do; there is just *nothing more!*'

The Chamberlain half stood and half crouched in his way. Saltar was some distance beyond, in front of a strange and foetid pool that turned the air thick with noxious fumes. The stench was so overwhelming that it all but rendered a body senseless – it crawled into eyes, ears, nose and mouth and blocked, stuffed and choked. The pool swirled with sickly browns and greens, and then every so often the surface would bulge and a bloated bubble would release more putrid gas into the air.

Vidius sensed a confusion of both life and death in the turgid slop. It was a bog of complete corruption, he realised, something which should not really exist, but something existence was also unable to combat or hold back. With the decline of the realm, it was not surprising a substance like this would become more potent and irresistible.

The air was utterly toxic and caused the skin of all three of them to blister and peel. The Demon-King's body convulsed as his lungs and internal organs were damaged by the poison, but he recreated himself anew and drew in more air so that he could speak.

'What is this place, brothers? The condensing of all the ills and evils of this realm? It is fitting that you should find your end in this mire of filth and this bath of bile, for it demonstrates all that this realm, pantheon and mortalkind were ever worth. The excrement and effluvia of millennia, no?'

The Chamberlain straightened slightly and tilted his head. 'It is known as the Soup of Plenty, hmm? It is not for you, brother. You may not pass.'

The Demon-King snorted, strode forward and smashed a heavy fist into the side of the Chamberlain's head, caving in half of his face and throwing him into the wall of the tunnel. A ragged mess now, the Chamberlain slid down to the floor and hiccupped a wet laugh or two.

The Demon-King smiled. 'I am glad you find your end as amusing as I do, brother, for there is joy in it for all demonkind.'

The man-spider spat black ichor and managed to clear his throat enough to gurgle: 'You were always too obsessed with the violence and destructive power of physical action, brother, hmm? Never did you contemplate the beauty and implications of the Pattern's web in the way the Arachis did. In that, the Arachis were always greater than the Nihil. And your weakness and obsession have found you out, brother, for in striking me you have poisoned yourself with basilisk venom.' The Chamberlain coughed and black ichor gouted from his mouth. In a dying whisper, he said: 'Do you feel it seeping into your core, brother? Is it harder to move your limbs now? Hmm? It is time we slept, brother, yes? The sleep of eternity at last. Goodbye, brother.'

'Fool!' the Demon-King sneered down at the now departed Chamberlain. 'What need I fear basilisk venom when both yourself and our brother Balthagar found ways to survive it? You helped Balthagar through these tunnels, did you not, so he must have some sort of resistance to it!'

Ignoring the creeping stiffness in his neck, Vidius looked up towards Saltar, who stood frail and swaying at the edge of the infernal Soup. 'As for you, I should never have let you off the points of my crown! There is still the matter of your contribution towards the throne. I will take your resistance from you. The tithe must be paid!'

With that, the Demon-King lowered his head, squared his massive shoulders, bellowed and charged. Saltar turned his back on him, having neither the strength nor inclination to prevent or avoid him. The horns punched through Saltar's back and spine and hoisted him aloft, where he arched in silent agony for a moment. Then Saltar raised his hands and feet as quickly as he could and grabbed onto the roof just above him. He pushed and pulled with all his might, adding to the Demon-King's forward momentum enough to tip his balance and propel them towards the waiting Soup of Plenty.

'No!' the Demon-King hollered as they toppled forwards. He flailed and scrabbled at the wall along the left side of the pool, the only thing that might still save them. But the dead and shrivelled left hand of the Demon-King could find no purchase and they plunged beneath the surface of the awful ooze.

Saltar felt himself slipping off the horns, but clung on grimly. Then they reared back up and Saltar was thrust back above the surface by the Demon-King's rising head and torso. With his flesh already beginning to dissolve off his bones, the Demon-King desperately tried to form and reform himself, but the basilisk venom that had now worked its way into his vital essence paralysed him and prevented him from creating the long limbs and levers he needed to pull himself free. He started to thrash about as he was eaten away by the harrowing, hungry sludge.

Saltar was jerked off the horns and thrown onto the ground at the edge of the pool. He felt the last of his flesh withering away and his bones being gnawed by a pack of Grim.

'Balthagar!' the Demon-King squealed. 'Brother, help me! I see I was wrong! I see it now! It is not too late, brother! Take the crown and save us both!'

His hand a rigid claw, Saltar gripped one of the Demon-King's horns as Vidius's horrifying face began to run like hot wax. The crown came free and Saltar pushed it onto his own broken brow.

'It is too late for reprieves and reprisals, brother,' he rasped. 'Too late for wishes and what ifs. It is all for naught, just as the Nihil always wanted.'

Almost tenderly, Saltar picked up the Chamberlain's body and cradled it. He was so light – little more than a collection of brittle bones. Saltar coaxed them into some sort of shape; and then they stirred and became animated. The Chamberlain opened wary eyes and flinched. He'd seen the horns and knew himself to be in the clutches of the Demon-King.

'Peace, Chamberlain,' Saltar rumbled, and helped the man-spider to stand.

'A strange request, hmm?' the Chamberlain responded guardedly.

'I am Saltar still, not the Demon-King you knew.'

The Chamberlain eyed him suspiciously but chose not to say anything.

Saltar sighed. 'Come, then, and let us see if any still remain. I pray it will not be just you and me left in the middle of a barren wasteland. I can restore nothing if there is nothing with which to build. I will *be* nothing if my wife and son have been taken from me.'

Chapter Fourteen: When it is not theirs to have

altar and the Chamberlain emerged from the smoke and fire engulfing Corinus and looked out over the plain in wonder. For the first time in a long, long time, Saltar felt a smile touch his lips. It felt strange, but good. It transformed him, and transformed the world around him in turn. Where he had been expecting to see hills and valleys formed of the piled bodies of the dead, with cascades and rivers of blood all around, where he had feared to discover marauding tribes of demons, cannibals and ghouls; instead, all was peaceful and sweet music played.

The Spartis had surrounded the mortal host, presumably to protect them from the other houses, but apparently no fighting had then taken place. It appeared that a lone musician had begun to play and caused every god, mortal and demon to forget their anger or cause. Millions were held rapt as they listened to the symphonious spell played by the one small figure. The notes of the melody were somehow amplified by the surrounding landscape, such that it was no longer clear whether the earth and listener resonated because of the music or whether the resonance of earth and listener actually helped create the music. The harmony was not just interwoven with the realm's fabric; it was a unifying part of that fabric. It was a universal voice and expression of being, one that encompassed even demonkind in its conception.

Truly moved, Saltar rediscovered his hope for the realm and mortalkind once more. 'I did not think it was possible. Come, Chamberlain, for I see Kate and Orastes there. I see Mordius too. And the Scourge and Strap, Constantus and Vallus. Can it be, or is it some cruel illusion?'

'To think the royal musician was capable of this, hmm? I nearly killed him on more than one occasion, you know?'

They passed down to the plain and approached Lucius. There were dark rings of exhaustion and suffering around his eyes and he quivered as if with a palsy.

'Lucius, my friend, all is well. Rest now,' Saltar smiled at him.

351

The musician nodded gratefully and let his shoulders slump. He plucked the final chord and phrase and let it slowly fade until it was so quiet none could know if it actually ended or rang on forever more.

No one moved, all bound by the spell for a few moments more. Had any of them present ever known such tranquillity before?

'You have humbled us, Lucius,' Saltar said.

The musician frowned and shook his head. 'Nay, lord, for much of this suffering was brought about by my playing in the first place. While on the road, my music seduced far too many away from the protection of the gods. And I do not forget that I have always owed you a debt that can never be repaid.'

'Be that as it may, as Demon-King, I tell you that demonkind would have found a way even had you not been out on the road seducing so many an unwary but eager ear. Indeed, Lucius, you were merely one of those unwary but eager ears for Jack's seduction, were you not?' Saltar nodded. 'Yes, you were, and it was here at the end that your true test took place. You were not found lacking, you should know that.'

Lucius managed a wan smile and nodded.

Saltar turned next to the Chamberlain, who instantly became tense. 'Brother, you were not found lacking either, but I must seal this realm once and for all so that its magic will not be so constantly corrupted and prone to unravelling. I am not sure if you should remain here.'

The Chamberlain hissed. 'But you vouchsafed me a place in this realm when I helped you against Voltar, hmm? That was our binding agreement, yes?'

'Indeed it was, brother, indeed it was. You have tainted yourself with basilisk venom, however, which makes you a greater threat than you have ever been to this realm. If you insist on remaining, then it will be in the sort of prison the Ungod suffered for millennia. Is that what you wish?'

The Chamberlain looked distressed. 'But what alternative is there, brother?'

'You return with demonkind to their realm, and you return as their sole Prince.'

The beady eyes of the Prince of the Arachis narrowed and twitched. 'Return to that prison, brother? Do not say so! I may end up the sole Prince of demonkind, but I will be just one more prisoner all the same, hmm?'

Saltar shook his head disappointedly. 'Come, brother, enough talk of prisons, for it limits you. You have always seen this realm as a prison as well, have you not, a place where the dislike of others is your constant punishment?

Do not forget that should you escape this realm or the other, there is always the Prison of All Eternity waiting for you. Your ambition for omnipotence and your mind are your only prison. But enough, brother, for you choice does not change: an eternity of isolation in a swamp, or an entire realm of your own where you can scheme to your heart's content and perhaps learn of a new and greater way of existence for demonkind. For you have learnt much during your time amongst these mortals, have you not? If you had not, then I do not think we would even be standing here now with you given a choice of destinies. And so you will choose.'

The Chamberlain grimaced. 'Then open the gateway, brother, and I will lead demonkind... home. What power though will sustain the demon realm if you now wear the Relic, hmm?'

'The crown has two horns, does it not? You will have one, if you agree never to use it to challenge the cosmos or any other realm. In particular, none of demonkind will ever again seek to enter the realm of mortalkind.'

'I agree to bind myself and demonkind by these terms, hmm? But what of you Baltha... *Saltar*? Will you not come with us, for none of demonkind will challenge your rule? If you remain here, your own nature will only disrupt the magic that sustains mortalkind, will it not?'

Saltar adopted an expression that was impossible to read. 'How could I leave my son and wife, who gave me meaning when nothing else remained? Chamberlain, I will sacrifice my irreducibility to remain with them. I will become mortal. After all, mortality is a higher plane of existence, I have come to believe, and I think you have sensed something of that too.'

The Chamberlain inclined his head. 'So be it. I do not know what else to say, so it must be time. Here, the Pattern of demonkind separates from that of mortalkind, hmm? There is a greater, unifying Pattern, of course, so I suspect we will meet again one day, brother, yes?'

Saltar frowned. 'You'll forgive me if I say I hope not, Chamberlain, or that at least it will not be until Eternity reaches its end. Here is the horn and there the gate. Goodbye, brother!'

❈ ❈

'And good riddance too, I say,' the Scourge bit savagely as the last of demonkind disappeared into the haze beneath the fractured sky.

'Janvil,' Saltar said in warning, 'you too will need to leave.'

'What!' growled the Guardian, and others made to protest too, including the gods.

Saltar raised his hands. 'Hear me! Scourge, you only survive now because you are still more than mortal. Look at your wounds, by the pity of both Shakri and Lacrimos! Is that not your heart I see glistening and beating through the tear in your chest? You must leave with the gods, dear friend.'

'And I will happily have you returned to me, beloved!' Shakri said with divine allure. 'Casting you out of the pantheon was the hardest thing I've ever had to do, believe me! But it had to be done so that you could save us all from both blood-mages and demonkind. I was forbidden from telling you why it had to be so, as otherwise you may have discovered your origins before the time was right. My love for you has only ever grown as long as I have known you, and can only increase. Will you not return to me, beloved Janvil?' She pouted irresistibly.

The Scourge attempted his usual gruffness, but was unconvincing. 'So you *were* manipulating me throughout. I knew it!'

Tears that were devastating to behold and in turn prompted tears in any who saw them pricked Her perfect eyes. 'It was all for love, sweet Janvil. Will you not forgive me?'

The thousands on the field held their breath as they waited upon the answer of the Divine Consort. 'Oh, very well! Someone needs to keep you gods in line!'

There were shouts of celebration, but Saltar's face remained serious. 'That is true, Scourge, for if this realm is to survive, then the gods will need to be kept in check and far more removed than ever before.'

'I will not hear such blasphemy, whether you are demon or mortal!' Lacrimos uttered darkly.

Incarnus rose to His full height in His awesome armour and hefted an infinitely sharp two-headed axe. 'None will dictate to us!'

'And none can dictate to chance!' giggled holy Wim.

'Mortals cannot survive without our blessing and intercession,' Gart added more reasonably.

Saltar refused to be deterred. 'You only speak thus based on your nature. You must understand now that it is the constant playing out of your wills and conflicts through mortalkind that has so destabilised the balance. Mortalkind has only been capable of necromancy because of the constant warring between Shakri and Lacrimos, the constant erosion of the boundary between life and death, the tearing of the veil between the realm of Shakri and the realm of Lacrimos. The threat of the blood-mages only came about because you have been in the habit of allowing mortalkind, priests and otherwise, access to the sorts of powers that should normally only be the preserve of gods. You have brought much of this on yourselves. It is not me who dictates to you, but the repeated and near-apocalyptic events suffered by the realm. Shakri, if you truly love mortalkind, you and your pantheon will withdraw and pledge not to interfere with the lives of mortals again.'

The Scourge gave a satisfied laugh, drawing glares from a number of the gods. 'It's for your own good, you know. And let's face it, you've needed some dictating to for a long time. It's a shame it didn't happen sooner, before so many lives were lost. If you properly withdraw, then there will be less rogue magic about to cause trouble amongst mortalkind. In fact, it will not be mortalkind that requires Guardians to police them anymore, it will be the pantheon instead. In the past, I have played Guardian to the pantheon to defend it, but now I see there is another duty there for me – making sure none of you transgresses the balance. It is a duty that I will take on with relish, believe me!'

'I will not submit to – ' Lacrimos began to growl.

'Oh, but you will, my fine fellow!' the Scourge shot back. 'For I have taught you that lesson several times before, have I not? I will be happy to repeat it for you now, if you like.'

'Not here, not now!' Saltar snapped. 'Things are fragile enough as it is. Shakri, are we agreed? Will you be so bound? If not, then I am not sure what of this realm I can restore. There is already so much that has been lost and can never be restored. Would you further limit that by disrupting the new magic of existence from the start? If the realm of mortalkind is not properly sealed even from the interference of the gods, then I am positive there will be no saving it the next time it begins to unravel. And if you do not agree, then the realm will surely begin to unravel again almost instantly, for it is in such a debilitated state.'

With a tinge of sadness, the Mother of All Creation looked round at all Her gathered children, lingering on each face and meeting every eye. 'My beautiful children,' She smiled with more tears in Her eyes, 'I see I must let you go now, let you stand on your own two feet and let you find your own way in the world. Not to do so would be cruel, I now see. You must be allowed the chance to fail and suffer for your mistakes, painful though it will be for me to watch, or how else will you learn and grow? In some ways, it is like the moment when I had to cast my beloved Janvil out. Very well, we will set mortalkind free until such time as they are ready to exist side by side with the pantheon.'

Saltar nodded.

'There is just one favour we would ask of you,' Shakri added, 'and that is to set free those members of the pantheon that I now know are imprisoned in a godhouse on Jaffra.'

'Allow me to lead the expedition, dear Shakri!' Aa piped up, appearing as if from nowhere. He had apparently regained the bounce in His step, the curl in His moustache and the shine on His buttons. 'It will be my last adventure here in the mortal realm. I will be accompanied by the Harbour Mistress of King's Landing and the people I led here to safety. We will see the Jaffrans ferried back to their home so far away.'

Kate pushed her way forward, and soldiers hurried to get out of her path. 'You're not going anywhere until we sort a few things out. How dare you!'

Aa began to back away. 'Now, Kate, you have to understand I couldn't tell you because you wouldn't have let me take him!'

'Too bloody right, I wouldn't!' she snarled, drawing a knife and stalking towards Him. 'Do you know I nailed a man to a table in front of his family because of you! I attacked Holter's Cross because I was convinced the Guild had taken him. People died, damn you!'

Aa moved quickly to put Incarnus between Himself and Kate. The god of vengeance tried to step out of Kate's way and an almost comical dance began.

'Mother, does that mean I can't go with Aa to free the other gods?' Orastes asked innocently. 'Rat-boy, Distrus and me are blood-brothers with Aa. We killed lots of monsters together.'

'You're not going anywhere!' Kate yelled.

Saltar waved his son over to him with a smile, picked him up and kissed him. 'Your mother's just explaining a few things to Aa is all. Everything will be fine, you'll see. Look, here's your Uncle Mordius.'

'Uncle Mordius!' Orastes exclaimed in delight. 'I've got some stories *I* can tell *you* if you like. Mother made me a general, you know!'

Mordius tried to salute, making a mess of it, and the boy giggled.

'Kate, be reasonable!' Aa pleaded.

The Scourge shook his head and observed to Strap: 'Definitely not the right thing to say.'

Strap nodded. 'Red rag to a bull.'

Constantus offered them his flask. 'He's effectively just told her she's behaving unreasonably. Hardly wise. Insult to injury really.'

The Scourge didn't hesitate to take the flask and a shot of brandy. 'Ah, that's good! The pantheon has some weird stuff called ambrosia that they drink. It's all well and good, but I'm not sure anything can ever beat the old Stangeld, you know. Oops, she nearly got Him there!'

'Surely Kate can't really hurt Him, can she? He is a god after all,' Constantus frowned.

'I wouldn't be too sure, what with all that's gone on. If there's any mortal who can give one of the gods a good hiding, it would be Kate,' the Scourge speculated.

'Constantus, what will you do with all these people? How many are there? Did Cholerax bring the entire population of Accritania here then?' Strap asked.

The General gave him an exhausted look. 'Oh, don't! It's going to be a logistical nightmare all too soon. Most of them are half-starved and separated from all those they know and love. There is very little food and shelter round here for them. Cognis only knows how many injured there are. We need to get them back on the road home as soon as possible, but most are too exhausted to put one foot in front of the other... and that's always assuming home still exists! I need to check with Saltar. I just don't want to think about it all right now. I wish Lord Ristus had survived, as then all this would be his problem. By the pity of Malastra, give me that flask back, Scourge, for my need is far greater than yours!'

Colonel Vallus cleared his throat. 'General, I think I may have the answer. If my eyes do not deceive me, that is Adjutant Spindar over there, is it not? Aren't logistics his area? And he does need to make up for how he behaved when possessed by Cholerax, does he not? He will be eager to get back in your good books, I imagine.'

'Oh, excellent, Vallus! I think you have just done more for me now than you have ever done before. I'll see you promoted for this! I'll be back in a minute, Scourge, so that we can have a proper drink and opportunity to reminisce before you take yourself off with the pantheon. In some ways, these will be your last moments of mortal freedom, will they not, so better make the most of them, eh?' Then the old General began to stride purposefully towards his adjutant. 'Spindar, at attention!' he bellowed in his best parade-ground voice. The Adjutant jumped and looked suitably terrified.

'And I think you can finally join us for a drink, Strap, now that you're all but old enough.'

'Too kind, Divine Consort, too kind. I can make myself available but you probably need to check with Shakri first. She might not give you permission, and I wouldn't want you upsetting Her so soon in your new relationship.'

The Scourge clenched his jaw and then forced himself to smile. 'But I insist, Young Strap, for I need to dispense all my wisdom to you if I am not going to be around to keep you in line from now on. You are so immature and foolhardy that I fear for your future safety. You have so little constancy and resolve that I can only fear for the future safety of the entire kingdom if I am not there to command you.'

'As it happens, Scourge, you will soon leave this realm, just as the other demons have left. The realm will then be a far safer place, methinks. If I understand Saltar correctly, there will be far less magic around too. I'm thinking the kingdom will not even need Guardians for a good long while. I might just take a break and go on the road for a while with Lucius. What do you say, musician, eh? Shall we bring cheer and fresh hope to every inn throughout the kingdom?'

Lucius, who'd sat himself down on the one patch of grass that had miraculously avoided being churned to mud during the battle, looked up wearily but managed an encouraging nod. 'If you sing well enough to hold a tune, then I'd welcome you. And if you can caper a bit, that's always popular with the patrons.'

Strap cleared his throat and began:
There was a young lady of Tumblydown
Who went with her ass all over the town
It brayed as she danced and offered a ride
To any young man with love on his mind!
'That will do! There's a child present!' Saltar warned.

Wim and many of the people nearby looked disappointed, for they'd been cheered by the sound of the singing and begun to clap their hands and nod their heads in time to the rhythm. And the humorous words to the tune reminded them of the simple joys of life and love, something they yearned for after all the realm had been through.

Saltar sensed he'd upset the mood. 'Oh, sorry. But you have a good voice, Strap! You have my blessing if you wish to be guard and travel companion to the royal musician. Indeed, once we have begun to restore Corinus, we must have you perform a series of royal concerts for the people. You might consider learning a few ballads that aren't quite so... earthy?'

Strap grinned and bowed low. 'It will be my pleasure, Battle-leader!'

The Scourge sighed and clapped Strap on the back. 'Well, I suppose you've earned the break, lad. I would warn you against the temptations posed by inns – the beer and barmaids – but I suppose the kingdom is in want of more children, eh?'

Shakri, in a sheer tunic that hid nothing and only accentuated Her curves, came to stand next to the Scourge, Her body touching him in several places. 'Yes, a bit of wantonness can be healthy sometimes, eh, Janvil?'

The Scourge shifted awkwardly, trying to put some distance between them, but the Mother of All Creation pursued him. 'Damn it, woman, not here! Do you have no sense of decorum or decency?'

'Beloved, love knows no bounds or limit and, as you have often shown me, can be quite indecent,' She said huskily in his ear.

'The gods be cursed, Mother, where's He gone!' Kate shouted, dragging Shakri's attention away from the suddenly relieved-looking Scourge.

'Daughter, we can hardly afford to lose another of the pantheon, now can we, so I allowed Aa to return to the gods' own realm? We must all soon take our leave as it is.'

'But I didn't get to say goodbye to Aa!' Orastes wailed from Saltar's arms.

Shakri came close to the boy and laid a calming hand on his brow. 'There now, you see, He will always be with you whenever you wish to start a new adventure. He is proud to have fought by your side and says you were the best monster-hunter He ever met. And your parents are also proud of you, Orastes.'

Saltar nodded. 'I am the proudest father there ever was. If you hadn't been brave enough to stab the Demon-King's hand, I would never have been able to beat him, you know.'

'Really?' asked Orastes with wide eyes and an uncertain smile.

Huge Incarnus came forward, His steps shaking the ground. He bowed low before Orastes and said in a booming voice for all to hear: 'Never have I known such a fearless mortal. You humble all of us and I would have you as my high priest one day.'

Kate came to join Saltar and Orastes. The severe lines of her face softened as she looked upon her son. She gently kissed his forehead and murmured: 'And I am more than proud, Orastes. I love you and just hope I have not been too hard on you. I all but tore the realm apart looking for you, I was so worried. I am the happiest mother alive!'

Orastes beamed proudly, put a small arm around Kate's neck, a small arm around Saltar's neck and squeezed them both. His head came back up and his face fell a bit. He turned his eyes to look off towards where Distrus cut a forlorn figure knelt at the feet of the impaled and still-standing Master Ninevus.

'Is that Distrus, your blood-brother?' Saltar asked gently. 'And you mentioned rat-boy too.'

Orastes nodded sadly.

'Well,' Kate said. 'The son of a Battle-leader needs to train with his companions everyday. Perhaps it would be easier all round if they were to move into the palace with us.'

Orastes's face lit up. 'Really? Can they come live with us, mother?'

'Of course. And do not worry about Master Ninevus. See, both Shakri and Lacrimos go to speak to Distrus and let him know all is well for his master's spirit.'

Saltar's eyes found Mordius. 'Three students for you then, old friend? Three times the trouble, eh?'

Mordius rolled his eyes in mock horror and waggled his hands in distress. 'Bring back the demons!' he cried.

❄ ❄

'Is the fighting finished now then, Sotto?' Dijin asked as the two of them stood watching the gods and the Scourge waving and walking away into the distance.

'I certainly hope so, my friend, I certainly hope so.'

'Good,' the giant Outdweller sniffed. 'Can we get something to eat now then? None of that demon flesh was any good. I need something else to settle my stomach. Do you think anyone would miss a few of these Jaffran bodies? I've never tried Jaffran before and...'

'Enough, Dijin, enough! I hear you – you're hungry. We'd best not take any of these bodies here, though. You know how people get these days. Let's see what we can find up in Corinus. I'm sure Trajan will have used this chaos to help secure himself some extra supplies. And if rat-boy is now to have access to the royal kitchens, who knows what may be in store?'

Dijin hummed happily. 'Just so long as you don't try and make me eat those veg-vegebubble things again. They're watery and make me feel weak.'

'Whatever you say, Dijin, whatever you say. I suspect you can have as much of whatever you want to eat.'

'Really?' Dijin asked with a thoughtful frown. 'That would be an awful lot, I think. I wouldn't want to be greedy, Sotto.'

Sotto smiled. 'Well, it's not like you'll be eating any of the vegebubbles, Dijin. So there'll be plenty for everyone else, won't there?'

'Oh, yes!' Dijin exclaimed. 'You're a good friend, Sotto, you really are.'

'And so are you, Dijin. Do you know how I know that?'

'Yes!' Dijin shouted happily. 'You know that because I didn't eat you! Friends don't eat each other, do they, Sotto?'

'No, Dijin, they don't!' the Outdweller laughed and led his big friend up towards the city to see what could be saved, salvaged or stolen.

⚹ ⚸

He sat in the throne and waited, fearing she would not come. Afternoon became evening, became night. And then, in the dark moment before the new day began, the door to the throne room briefly opened and a shadow moved inside. She avoided the pools of light cast by the candles along the walls, but he could tell from the way she moved, from the faint scent on the air and the *feel* of her presence that it was her.

She came to the edge of the darkness and stopped. He could feel her watching him. At last, she spoke: 'I knew you weren't dead.'

Saltar shrugged slightly. 'To be honest, there were moments when I wasn't so sure.'

A pause. 'Have you really given up your irreducibility?'

He nodded. 'I had to if the realm was to be properly sealed so that we could all be safe and live normal lives.'

Kate almost came into the light then, but pulled back at the last moment. 'I'm not sure what normal is anymore. You are mortal then?'

He smiled crookedly. 'I think so. I wouldn't want to put it to the test, that's for sure. It means we can grow old together, Kate. We will see our son grow, perhaps have grandchildren.'

She hesitated. 'It took Orastes an age to get to sleep tonight. That's partly why I was late coming here. He is full of tales of the demons he fought with Aa. It terrifies me to hear them. Orastes is also excited rat-boy and Distrus are now here in the palace, because he wants to go hunting monsters with them everyday. Saltar, promise me the realm is sealed and that there are no more monsters.'

He did not hesitate with his answer. 'Kate, the realm is properly sealed. No more monsters will be able to find us or threaten our son.'

She stepped into the light in front of the throne. She looked exhausted, almost desperate. 'So I will not need this armour anymore?'

He shook his head. Kate slowly began to unbuckle her breastplate and backplate. It took her an age, because the buckles were encrusted with blood.

Then came the greaves and thigh pieces. She finally stood before him naked, her flesh pinched and pale.

He opened his arms and she curled into his lap. He held her for a long time.

'I'm scared,' she whispered. 'Does that make me a coward?'

'No,' he murmured. 'I'm scared sometimes too. The gods were scared of the Demon-King at the end. When we love other people, we're always scared for them. If we were never scared, the world would be a loveless place and hardly worth the saving.'

'I'm glad you did save us though.'

'Me too. I couldn't have done it on my own though. I heard something about a demon host at Holter's Cross, you killing a dragon and your army defeating the sphinkaes and Ja'rahl.'

She shrugged. 'I did it for you and Orastes.'

'Well, when we're loved like that, Orastes and I need never be scared, eh? We have faced the worst the cosmos could throw at us and still survived. I think the cosmos will think twice before trying anything else, don't you? We have given the big bully a bloody nose and sent him crying back to his mother. Even the gods know better than to mess with mortalkind now. I swear, I thought Aa was going to pee His pants when you were after Him!'

Kate giggled and snuggled into him. Her big, infinite eyes slowly closed, her breathing gentled, and she found untroubled dreams at last.

❈ ❈

Mordius shook his head to get rid of the strange echoes from which he'd been suffering since he'd taken back full possession of his own body. The ghostly voices had fortunately been becoming more indistinct with each passing day, and only really troubled him when he was particularly tired after a long day of teaching.

He put the rare and precious copy of *The Meaningful Meanderings of Memnosian History* – produced by the temple of Cognis just before its destruction five years before – back on its shelf next to the five other slim tomes that constituted his entire library and probably represented every book in the entire palace of Corinus. He shrugged out of the constricting shirt, tunic and hose, which now constituted his usual daytime garb, and donned instead his old but far more comfortable magician's robes. These days, such robes were generally regarded with suspicion and prompted all sorts of whispering, so he only tended to wear them when alone in his apartments. Today, however, he

362

would wear them beyond his rooms because of the audience he would have. It just felt right.

He massaged his temples, shrugged his shoulders and slowed his breathing until he was more relaxed. He sighed as the nagging in his head finally receded and allowed him to start thinking more clearly. Feeling much better, he left for the meeting he'd been meaning to have for a good month or so but hadn't quite got round to in all the chaos.

He passed through the palace, and was let into the throne room by the guards. Saltar's head came up from a report he'd been studying and smiled in welcome, gesturing for Mordius to join him at the two armchairs and small table set discretely by a window behind the throne. Two goblets of red wine were set ready and waiting on the table, and Saltar passed one to Mordius as they sat. They drank and enjoyed a few long moments of companionable silence.

'So how is my old friend and master? A few more white hairs than on the last occasion we managed to find the time to raise a toast together, eh, Mordius?'

'It is amazing to me that all I have ultimately suffered is a few white hairs. The wider kingdom has not fared so well, Saltar. I am one of the lucky ones, I think.'

A nod. 'Luck had more to do with it in the early days, I suspect. At the end, though, Wim was laid low and we witnessed the final playing out of things put in train millennia ago, did we not?'

Mordius demurred. 'Perhaps, perhaps not. Let's not forget it was Wim who caught me when I fell. So the playing out was not entirely inevitable, nor entirely predestined, now was it?'

Saltar pondered for a moment. 'I'm not sure, to be honest. There seemed to be some sort of Pattern and organising logic to it all, but I could be wrong. It might have something to do with the greater, unifying Pattern of the cosmos that the Chamberlain mentioned when he departed, Mordius.'

The small magician, shrugged. 'It might be. What I do know, however, is that I'm glad for all our sakes that I stole your body from a battlefield and raised you from the dead all those years ago.'

'As am I, believe me!' Saltar laughed. 'Come, tell me. How are your new students treating you? Keeping you on your toes, I hope.'

'Keeping me on the back foot, more like it. There's no end to their questions. I quickly realised I was going to need help in certain areas, so drafted in Vasha and Larc to assist me. Even then, we do not have all the answers. We've realised that we need to talk to you and Kate to capture the

363

details of all that has happened. Otherwise, we might lose all that knowledge. If we can have it written down and copied, then the lessons and insights can be shared with larger numbers of people for the good of all. Knowledge will be one of our best safeguards in the times ahead. We might even start being able to read the Pattern again, in the way that a High Priest of Cognis like Philasteres – Lacrimos rest his soul! – and the Chamberlain once did. Then we will be able to foresee future threats to the realm. If we don't document everything while we can still remember it, it will be lost forever, and we may be left unable to pre-empt and deal with future dangers. With the gods now removed from the mortal realm, just imagine what will happen to the temples and the faith of their congregations if we start to forget and lose our understanding of the gods! Just think, Saltar. The balance would fail again and the realm would be lost. So I must task the remaining priests of every temple with the creation of religious narratives and tracts. Oh, and then I must send delegations to Accritania and Jaffra to ensure that similar work happens there. There are also Strap and Lucius of course. And I must send to Lebrus too. He has a son, you know, whom he may want to come study here for a while, and it might be good if rat-boy, Orastes and Distrus go to learn with Lebrus some time. I think we need to establish a seat of learning here in Corinus as soon as we can. It's certainly something that excites Vasha and Larc and means they are in no hurry to return to the Needle Mountains. But what of the Brethren? Do any remain or is that knowledge already gone? Oo, there's just so much to do, and so little time!'

Saltar chuckled. 'And here I was worried that you wouldn't have enough to do once magic was no longer significant in this realm. Don't worry, Mordius, there's always enough time. The realm will remain safe from all dangers for a long, long time.'

'No!' Mordius said with a passionate urgency. 'People can only remember things for so long. We must get to them while it's all still fresh in their minds. Otherwise, we may miss out on crucial details. And another thing! I'm not convinced the realm *is* entirely sealed. You may have others fooled, including the gods, whom we both know wouldn't behave themselves properly if they suspected, but there's no way the realm can be sealed, is there?'

All trace of humour immediately disappeared from Saltar's face. His eyes bored into Mordius. In a guarded voice, he replied: 'You make no sense, old friend. You heard the gods agree to end all interference in mortal affairs. The Scourge is now the Divine Guardian accordingly. I am now mortal and you saw the last of demonkind depart this realm forever.'

Mordius's eyes narrowed. 'Saltar, I deal with rat-boy on a daily basis, and he is far more sly and capable of changing truth than you will ever be. You and I both know that there are still inconsistencies within the mortal realm and that the paradoxical nature of the magic that sustains it must ultimately see it begin to unravel once more. I do not know where you have hidden this Relic of yours, but I suspect its power should not be allowed to exist in this realm. And then the magical potential within Orastes is *broken*, is it not? You cannot pretend differently to me, Saltar. You forget that I have been within the boy's mind. Do you know what I found there? A gargoyle, Saltar. A demon, no less! The divine spark of Shakri's magic is meant to be the basis of his existence, so how can it be broken?... unless it is not just Shakri's magic at the heart of his being. Saltar, you were irreducible and still of demonkind when Orastes was born. Clearly, he inherited...'

'Alright, enough!' Saltar shouted, banging his fists on the arms of his chair and causing the wood to crack. His chest heaved and it was a good while before he got his anger and breathing back under control. He sighed harshly, and finally more gently. 'Yes, Mordius, yes, it's true! But you must never speak of this to anyone else, old friend, can you promise me that? *No one* can know. You should not even raise it with me again, in case we are ever overheard. Promise me! I must have your word.'

'I will take it with me to the grave. And even beyond that – I will not even reveal it once I am in Lacrimos's realm. But shame on you for even requiring my promise!'

Saltar scrubbed his face with his hands and groaned. 'I'm sorry. You have proven your trust time and again and never wavered. I am truly sorry for having made the demand. But there is nothing as important as this. You see – not all knowledge should be captured and shared. I will tell you a great truth now, Mordius. A rule of existence is that there must be at least one Great Secret. Should it ever be betrayed and discovered, then surely all magic will unravel and that existence will ensure its own undoing. You yourself have just described how the gods would start to behave and how they would end up damaging the balance if they ever realised the truth. Do you understand how terrible and dangerous knowledge of the Great Secret is? Do you?'

Mordius nodded in mute horror and began to feel sick. 'It is a curse, is it not? I feel it in my very soul. Ah, woe is me. And there is no way in which I may erase my existence, to destroy my knowledge, is there? I will merely end up in Lacrimos's realm. Perhaps He might then...'

'Do not even think it, Mordius! He would be damaging the balance if He sought to erase your existence entirely. You must keep the Great Secret with you, then, till the end of this realm.'

Then Mordius brightened. 'If I die, though, then to be reborn, surely I will have no memory of my previous life, self and knowledge. I will be free of the Secret once more.'

Saltar smiled sadly. 'For a while, at least. There will be some moments of reprieve. But your being and essence will never fundamentally change, though it will grow and develop. You will always have an enquiring mind and a certain genius. You will rediscover the Great Secret more quickly with each lifetime. Believe me, I know, for I have been through it myself. You will study the books of previous generations, many of which you are about to create, and infer the Great Secret more easily each time as the knowledge of mortalkind grows. You see, then, that the damage is already done and that one day this realm must end.'

Mordius became paler than Saltar had ever been when dead. In hardly a whisper, he said, 'Then perhaps you're right – I should not be too quick to document what knowledge exists. I should gather just enough to ensure the people do not lose their understanding of and faith in the gods, and nothing more. Others will take on further work, of course, but I will be very slow to encourage them. Perhaps some ignorance will be enough to allow us moments of bliss.' His breath shuddered in him. 'The end will not come soon, will it?' he begged of Saltar, Battle-leader of Dur Memnos, Demon-King, and once the irreducible Balthagar.

Saltar eased himself in his chair as best he could, his elbows wobbling slightly on its broken arms. He gave Mordius a reassuring look. 'I'm sure we'll have a good while yet, whole lifetimes in fact. We will see our children grow, generations come and go. Perhaps an entire millennia or more. Much can happen to change things between now and then, Mordius, so let's try and stay positive, shall we, as it makes existence a far more enjoyable experience all round? Who knows? We may come to glimpse something of the greater, unifying Pattern, and find a way to forestall the end. Or perhaps we will discover we have friends elsewhere in the cosmos, and the Chamberlain will return the favour he owes us by coming to save us at the last moment. We can't know everything now, and indeed we don't want to, because that's when things will all start to get difficult. In the meantime, however, what I can safely say, old friend, is that we'll definitely need to call for more wine. I think we're running out.'

Here ends Book Three of the Flesh & Bone Trilogy.

I would like to thank all those readers who have shared this journey and come this far. I hope I have proven an entertaining travel companion.

A J Dalton is now working on two new projects:
The Book of St George
The Chronicles of a Cosmic Warlord.

About the Author

A J Dalton is one of the UK's leading authors of metaphysical fantasy. He has worked as a teacher of the English language in Thailand, Egypt, Poland, the Czech Republic and Slovakia. The influence of these diverse cultures lends a rich and vivid quality to his prose.

Necromancer's Fall is his third novel. He has also written a number of articles and short stories. He currently lives and works in both Manchester and London.

To find out more about metaphysical fantasy, the writing of A J Dalton and getting published, go to http://metaphysicalfantasy.wordpress.com.

Printed in Great Britain
by Amazon